Totally Bound Publishing books by Nikki McCoy:

Drakon's Treasure
Forsaken Hunger

I0646145

Drakon's Treasure

FORSAKEN HUNGER

NIKKI MCCOY

Forsaken Hunger
ISBN # 978-1-78430-964-0
©Copyright Nikki McCoy 2016
Cover Art by Posh Gosh ©Copyright January 2016
Interior text design by Claire Siemaszkiewicz
Totally Bound Publishing

Published in 2016 by Totally Bound Publishing, Newland House, The Point, Weaver Road, Lincoln, LN6 3QN, United Kingdom.

Totally Bound Publishing is a subsidiary of Totally Entwined Group Limited.

FORSAKEN
HUNGER

Dedication

To the many authors who inspired me to become a
writer with their beautiful words and alluring stories
that made me dream higher than I ever thought I
could. To my loving husband and the tireless efforts of
my editor and publishing house. Thank you so much!

Chapter One

It was a good hour for sin—prime for hunters on the prowl. The air was charged with the promise of dark deeds for the willing and the unwilling. Then again, innocence was relative in this part of the city. There was a thin line between the criminals and their victims, and an even thinner one between them and the real demons who preyed upon their weaknesses.

It made his job so much easier. No one would come running for the death of one more drug trafficker. It would be a simple strike and kill, then on to the next target.

Saden unfurled from his crouched stance atop an empty factory building and strode across the gravel roof to the far end for a better vantage point. He bent low at the corner and took in the scents and muted vision of Lady Night. In the near distance, people lined the entrances to the seedier clubs in the district. Those that catered to the worst Los Angeles had to offer.

Humans with more money than morals and the demons who walked undetected among them.

None of them knew how good they had it. Their lives, however thinly glorious or fucked up, held the promise of a future. Even the fate of death was theirs to embrace if they chose it. They would never know the reality of existence beyond redemption. Never be forced to endure what they couldn't even imagine. There were some laws and consequences no amount of praying to any religious sect could redeem you from. And he knew that more than most.

A sharp gust of wind from behind blew his black, shoulder-length hair into his eyes. He whirled around and grasped the knife at his belt. The air above him shimmered, swiftly displaced by a large shadow barely discernable against the backdrop of the star-filled sky. Its outline became clearer as it swooped down to land on the roof.

A heartbeat before it touched the gravel, its form changed to take on substance. Great, shadowed wings drew in to become arms and the pointed tail split into two legs. The shape of the dragon was gone and in its place stood a man dressed in black.

Saden took in the man's blond, spiked hair and familiar features, and cursed. Not a threat. Merely a temporary inconvenience.

"I'm not in the mood, Blade," Saden ground out. "Go back and tell Serrakus he can damn well wait for me to get this job done. He should know by now I don't take out my targets until I can prove their guilt." He turned back to scan the distant crowds still filtering in and out of the nightclubs.

It wasn't unlike Serrakus to check up on his Drakons if they took too long on assignments. The Drakonem held zero tolerance for failure or delay, but Saden refused to be the angel of death for some poor sap who happened to be in the wrong place at the wrong time.

Too often, he'd seen the justice of the Drakonem imparted without real truth behind it. And equally often, the Drakons under their control would carry out their sentencing with no questions asked, only to avoid punishment.

He, however, would gladly take his Drakonem's wrath if it meant keeping an innocent from death. He — a Drakon. The worst of all condemned criminals among the demon world. Saden suppressed a smirk at the irony of his morals.

Blade scowled as he moved to stand beside Saden. "Hello to you, too, asshole. Serrakus didn't send me."

"Then why are you here?"

"My assignment's done," Blade said with a shrug. "Had to deliver some young phantom to Serrakus. Apparently the kid ran away from home and tried to make it big using his power to convince humans to give him their wealth."

Saden frowned. "A phantom? What was his tribe doing this close to the city?" He was vaguely familiar with the elusive Dresidiens. Aptly called phantoms by other demonic races for their mind-walking abilities, they could discern and control the thoughts and desires of others. The lure of their power was said to be as strong as any deadly sin if used for the wrong reasons. It was why Dresidiens tended to dwell in the forests and deserts, away from civilization.

From what he understood, that choice was as much for their protection as it was out of preference for solitude.

"They were migrating south to Mexico for the winter. The kid's family stayed behind on the outskirts long enough for the mother to give birth. Apparently, he took that as an opportunity to prey on the masses. He didn't kill anyone but he might as well have. The exposure he caused reached the local police and the press. It could take his tribe weeks to erase what he's done."

Blade was right. The careless exposure of demonkind was as damning as a murder charge. In severe cases like this one, the punishment of being made a Drakon was inevitable. "How long was he sentenced for?"

"Don't know yet. Probably a year. Officially." Blade cast him a doubtful glance from dark blue eyes. They both knew it would be a lot longer than that before the phantom was finally granted death. One year roughly equated to ten, no matter how well a Drakon served its Drakonem. "Serrackus hasn't given me any new jobs yet so I thought I'd keep you company."

From the strain in his friend's voice, Saden knew there was more to Blade's presence than simple boredom. Blade seemed to be almost vibrating. His lean body was coiled with tension rather than the easy confidence it usually held. It wasn't hard to realize what was going on.

Every Drakon had a limit. When the stress of their condemned lives and the brutal authority of the Drakonem came to be too much, only one of two outcomes ensued. Most were beaten into submission, the pain somehow snapping them back to reality. Others lost their minds completely and became a liability the Drakonem weren't willing to risk. Those were forced to serve the rest of their sentences as warders—jailors of other Drakons and permanently bound to the realm of their masters.

Saden had been on the brink of insanity once himself. If not for an old friend, his mind would likely have shattered then—his soul lost to a fate worse than the one he was already living. Now, it was another person who kept his sanity in check, though she would never know.

For Blade, it was sex. The only vice they were permitted. The man would drown in it if he could, and had more than his share of willing females to choose from with his blond, pretty-boy looks and athletic build. The fact that he wasn't in the arms of a woman right now told Saden just how bad his friend's situation was.

"You doin' all right, man?"

Blade rolled his broad shoulders and gave a thin smile. "Yeah, I'm cool. It's your ass you should be worried about. Heard your mark was trained by the best of your kind before leaving their ranks. Isn't he one of the top players in this district now?"

"They're not my kind," Saden growled. He may have been born a Vampyre, but he was no longer one of them. "And he's nothing more than an exiled Vampyre who traffics in human drugs. Hardly worth my time. It's no wonder that race is going extinct when they have to ask the Drakonem to send a Drakon after their own trash."

He ignored Blade's raised eyebrow and tapped into the sliver of Drakonem soul that was tethered to his own. It warmed to his call, singing along his nerves and centering in his chest until he was able to fling a part of it out like an invisible net. It immediately connected with the live beings nearest him and used their core energy as synapses to carry its pulse from person to person, searching for its target. A few blocks away, it found its mark and relayed the information instantly to Saden.

Two human bodyguards flanked the exiled Vampyre he'd been ordered to kill. They were steadily making their way toward the target's limo parked at the side of the building Saden and Blade stood on, as was Messing's MO. This stop was just the first of many he made every night to regulate his drug enterprise. With the clubs swinging in full action, it would be an easy, unseen execution — all according to plan.

The only difficulty would be separating the two humans long enough to take out their boss. For as much as they deserved the same fate, they were governed by their own laws and therefore considered innocents in the eyes of the Drakonem.

"Think you can distract the human bodyguards while I deal with my target? They'll be coming up on our right in two minutes."

Blade smirked and extracted two black shurikens from his shoulder harness. "I can do you one better and put them out of their misery. A little provocation and Serrackus will never know the difference."

"Distraction," Saden reiterated, shaking his head. "Unless you're willing to take the punishment when our Drakonem finds out."

Which would be inevitable. The piece of Drakonem soul that lived inside him, making him a Drakon, was loyal only to its true master, Serrackus. It would report any unsanctioned kills carried out by its Drakon vessel no matter the reason for the deaths. Even if Blade took out the humans himself, Saden would be held responsible as the humans were associated with his target.

The Drakonem justice system was supposed to allow for the deaths of innocents if those innocents posed a serious threat during the capture of a target. But the Drakonem rarely observed their own rules. They were demi-gods in their own right with unquestionable authority over the criminals they controlled.

No. Killing the humans for any reason would only give Serrackus an excuse to exercise his sadistic tendencies.

"It'd almost be worth it," Blade said with a grin. "Postpone his upcoming vacation for a few weeks." When Saden just glared, he lifted his hands in surrender. "Fine, we'll do this your way." After sheathing the shurikens, he started for the other end of the roof, mumbling under his breath, "You were a hell of a lot more fun before you took responsibility for your girlfriend."

Saden grit his teeth, saying nothing. Besides, Blade was right. Before Daneya, he'd taken as much pleasure in pissing Serrackus off as Blade still did. Despite the multiple punishments and extensions to his sentence that defiance had gained him. That didn't make Daneya his girlfriend, however. Far from it.

She was merely the object of his promise to an old friend. Nothing more, nothing less. Certainly not the object of his desires, or at least not as far as he was willing to admit. Even to himself.

He turned his gaze back to the empty street below and saw Messing and his bodyguards rounding the corner of the block ahead. The trio was dressed in similar Italian pinstriped suits with Messing half a head taller than the others. Typical for most Vampyres. His aristocratic looks and relaxed gait gave him an air of smug confidence Saden couldn't wait to crush.

It was moments like this, taking down the true criminals in the demonic world, that made his existence tolerable.

"Shit. We've got company," Blade said from his position at the opposite corner of the building.

Saden grunted. "Quit jerkin' off to the obvious and get down there."

"I don't mean leech boy and his goons over there. Your girlfriend came out to play and she's brought three of her friends to make it interesting."

"What?" Saden ran over to Blade and peered over the edge.

Climbing out of an unmarked van were four dark figures clothed in black combat fatigues. It was obvious what they were from the organization of their movements to the weapons they were geared with. Vigilantes. Members of a secret society who called themselves Defensores Contra Malum. Protectors from evil.

The DCM was an organization made up of several units that had been around almost since the dawn of mankind. While their original goal was a noble one, to protect their race from rogue demons who walked the earth, their ambitions had somewhat changed over the centuries.

Many had taken it upon themselves to eradicate all demons who posed a threat to their way of life. Some had reason enough for their hatred. Most, however, were simply fanatics who would stop at nothing to 'purify' their world.

Daneya's tall physique was unmistakable among the others. He would recognize her anywhere—the red tint to her burgundy locks, tawny skin and the confident way she carried herself. The fatigues she wore hugged her lean body, accentuating her curves as she adjusted her weapons. She was the picture of a proud warrior, even if her cause was misguided.

"What do you want to do now?" Blade asked.

Saden cursed under his breath, momentarily caught in indecision. It wasn't unheard of for vigilantes to unknowingly track the same targets as Drakons. Daneya had been a member of her DCM unit for nine years. He supposed it was inevitable that he would run into her at some point. Yet, he couldn't let her interfere. Messing was crude but dangerous, and he was Saden's mark.

If anyone else took him out, Serrackus would know and hold him responsible. The punishment for failing could last months. He couldn't risk being absent for that long. It was his job to protect her, as he'd been doing for years.

Damn it! How the hell could he have missed her energy when he'd scanned for his target?

"Lead them away from here. I'll take care of Messing and his guards."

"Sure you don't want to let them create the distraction for us? Messing's men might actually pick a few of them off while you take him out."

Saden growled softly. "I can't risk Daneya getting hurt. Keep her safe or I swear—"

"You'll use my balls for target practice," Blade finished. "I know, I know. Can't blame a guy for trying, though. Your girlfriend needs to wake up and smell the shit she's hangin' around with."

Saden shook his head and strode back to his position. Messing was nearing the corner of the building now. Saden looked back in time to see Blade jump off the edge on his side. A chorus of startled shouts rang out followed by pounding boots on pavement. He gave Blade the few precious seconds necessary to draw Daneya and her group away then leaped down to the ground, his trench coat billowing out behind him. The trio spun around, no longer interested in the sounds of pursuit on the other side of the building, and drew their weapons.

The man on Messing's left was stacked like a linebacker with a massive chest almost freakishly disproportionate to the rest of his body. The one on the right made up for his average build with a barely concealed arsenal strapped to his midsection.

Linebacker stepped in front of Messing and pulled a hunting blade from his belt. "Leave."

Saden flashed his teeth. "So soon? And here I thought we could be friends."

Disbelief sparked briefly in Linebacker's eyes before he charged. Saden braced himself and pivoted at the last second, using the man's momentum to grab onto his wrist and twist the blade from his hand. Another half turn and Saden ducked a wide punch then hooked an uppercut into the man's gut. He grasped the back of Linebacker's neck and slammed him face first into the side of the building.

One down, two to go.

At the sound of gunshots behind him, Saden ran crouched over for the cover of an alcove a few yards away. He hunched down on the balls of his feet and waited. The limo was at the far end of the street with him in between them and it. They would have no choice but to come his way.

"Get to the car!" Arsenal yelled, his voice dangerously close.

Just as Saden caught Messing making a run for the limo from the corner of his eye, Arsenal did exactly as expected and came high around the corner of the alcove. Saden yanked hard at Arsenal's ankle and sent him toppling backwards to the ground. He was on him in the next instant, shoving the man's gun to the pavement then pounding a fist into his face.

Arsenal lost consciousness at the same time the limo purred to life. Saden threw one of the daggers from his back harness and was up and running before it punctured one of the limo's front tires. Messing came back out to meet him, but not in time. Saden easily knocked the revolver out of his hand and dragged him fully from the driver's side.

Messing sneered his contempt. "I haven't violated my exile. The house of Avram has no right to send a leisonguarde after me."

Saden laughed darkly. It was almost galling that Messing thought he could flaunt his crimes without being noticed. Wealth and power always came with the price of attention. "Oh, but you warrant much more than a Vampyre warrior. The Drakonem don't look kindly on demon rogues that kill humans with their pretty little drugs."

Messing's eyes widened as realization set in. He recovered quickly, though, and went at Saden with newfound fervency. They traded blows evenly, Saden reluctant to use his power just yet. Messing was indeed a seasoned fighter as Saden had discovered during his research. It had been too long since he'd had an equal match with a target and it felt good to stretch his skills.

It came to an end quickly, however, when a single shot rang out somewhere in the near distance. Simultaneously, the car window next to them shattered. They spun around to find Daneya standing next to Arsenal's limp body. She looked like a wild, avenging angel in combat fatigues with a gun pointed straight at them.

"Shit," Saden cursed, then hit the pavement rolling as Messing dove in the opposite direction.

Daneya advanced without hesitation and fired several more rounds. When Saden came to a stop, she was already poised above him, peering down the barrel aimed at his head. A glance to the side showed Messing's tall frame sprawled in a pool of his own blood in front of the limo.

Saden was going to have to act fast. Ordinary bullets merely slowed a Vampyre down, and pissed them off in the process.

"Who are you?" Daneya asked in a low voice. The backlight of the dim lamppost a block away kept her expression hidden.

Saden could only stare, partly stunned by her very proximity. For so long, he'd watched her from afar. Protected her and even grown to admire her. Now she was standing only a few feet away with a question he was completely unprepared to answer.

Who was he? Her guardian? A stalker? *Yeah, that'll ease her suspicions*. And what the hell had happened to Blade? He should've distracted her!

"Who are you?" she repeated, taking a half-step forward.

A deep growl startled them both. Messing was conscious again and pulling something from his suit jacket. Saden kicked the gun from Daneya's hand then jumped up. A bullet ricocheted off the street by their feet just as he pushed her back against the building wall. Using his body as a shield, he twisted around and summoned the Drakonem power within him. It flared to his call and shot out in an invisible arc toward Messing. Blue-white flames sprung up around Messing in a blinding rush, coating him and smothering his screams until all that was left was a pile of smoking ash.

Saden turned back to scan Daneya's body for injuries. She appeared to be unscathed, but her amber eyes were bulging and her slender frame shaking. She was taller up close than he'd expected. Only a handspan shorter than his six foot five inches. The heat of her quickened breaths raised chills across his neck. It sent a rush of emotions he hadn't felt in too long curling through his chest and down to his groin. Even the scents of leather and something sweet wafting from her sparked a reaction in him.

Without thought, he brought a hand to her cheek and feathered his fingers over it, then trailed them gently beneath the curve of her jaw. Her skin was incredibly soft and warm, her pulse thrumming against his thumb. There was something about her… Something fierce, yet inviting…

Slowly, her gaze shifted from Messing's remains to Saden's face. At her sharp intake, he realized his mistake and tamped down the power of the Drakonem. But it was too late. He knew what she'd seen. The soulless, ice-violet eyes reflecting the power of a Drakon instead of his normal green irises.

Shock turned to fear-fueled anger and her body went rigid inches from his. "Drakon," she murmured.

Saden's chest tightened as all the hate and terror that one word held seemed to roll over him. He drew his hand back down to his side. Had he really expected her to see him differently?

Somewhere in the back of his mind, his conscience shouted a resounding, *Yes!* She had always been a source of pure light for him. The way she controlled her life with morals built on justice and the convictions in her heart. Despite being involved with the DCM, her courage had always helped him get from one tortured day to the next.

Idiot, he berated himself. He should've known. To her, he was nothing more than a Drakon. The filth of demonic societies who garnered more hatred than Saden's dead target could ever aspire to. Damned beyond redemption or forgiveness.

A sharp pain sliced through his abdomen and he caught the glint of steel in Daneya's hand as he reared back. She took that opportunity to bolt, backing away swiftly then turning on her heel to race down the street. Saden stood, unmoving, and watched her disappear around the corner. What felt like a leaden weight pushed down on his lungs until it was hard to breathe.

Blade's symptoms of coming too close to the edge of madness crossed his thoughts again. He recalled being there so keenly. The desperation to find a reason, any reason, to go on fighting.

Somehow, this moment was so much worse.

A sound drew him from his reverie.

He turned to see Blade standing behind him with a knowing expression. Saden ignored the tearing ache at his side and strode stiffly to retrieve his knife from the limo tire, seeking his other form as soon as it was sheathed. The change that had once been so alien to him came now like second nature. He felt his corporeal body fade, molecules blending in with the power of the Drakonem spirit that infested his. Gravity became a natural law governed only by his thoughts, allowing him to escape into the night air.

On the outside, he appeared only as a shadow vaguely resembling the outline of a dragon.

He sped through the skies undetected. The concrete civilization below changed to valleys and forests bathed in the glow of the moon. Finally, he reached his destination and took back his form on the second-story balcony of his house. It rested on more than twenty acres of untamed land and was the only place where he came close to privacy.

He shut the open balcony doors behind him then made his way through the dark interior of his bedroom. After throwing his trench coat and weapons harness to the floor, he went to the bathroom in the outer hallway and flipped on the light. He stripped out of his torn shirt to inspect the cut Daneya had parted him with. It was only a flesh wound but still deep enough to require stitches.

With a sigh, he pulled a first aid kit from beneath the sink then began cleaning the wound with soap and warm water. Halfway into it, the hairs on the back of his neck rose and he glanced at the door. "Damn it, Blade. What do you want now?"

Blade remained silent from his position in the doorway. Saden ignored him as he threaded a needle and pinched the swelling edges of his sliced skin to sow them together. Or tried to. The silence of Blade's unspoken words was deafening.

Saden gave up on concentration and snarled at his friend. "What happened to you out there?" When Blade still said nothing, he added, "I thought I told you to take care of Daneya."

Blade shook his head and picked up the wet washcloth from the sink. "Sit down." He pushed Saden onto the toilet seat, knelt down in front of him and started wiping at the blood that had spilled through Saden's fingers. "I had them on my tail but your girlfriend's one sneaky little fox. She broke away from the group and doubled back before I noticed she was gone. By then, I couldn't risk letting the others find you as well."

Saden clenched his jaw in anger, straining to keep from striking out. Tonight had gone all wrong. Daneya shouldn't have seen him. Should never have known about his existence. Thanks to his fuck-up, she was likely packing her things now and moving herself and her daughter into the DCM compound.

"Don't go there." Blade's tone held warning as he took up the needle and began stitching. "You were probably the first Drakon she's ever seen. Better you than some other who might not have let her go so easily. She doesn't know who you really are."

The look of utter horror that'd filled Daneya's eyes earlier flashed before his vision. His gut clenched as the same leaden weight squeezed his lungs once again. "I think she already knows who I am," he said bitterly. A nameless Drakon. Not worthy of any decent person's regard. When Blade frowned, he flicked a dismissive hand. "Never mind. I need to go back out. She'll be moving again after this."

He'd come to learn over the years that Daneya had a flighty spirit. Every year she changed locations without fail. Never too far from the DCM compound but always in a different town, and sometimes under a different name. Whether it was out of fear for her daughter's safety or an old habit she'd picked up from her family, he couldn't quite figure out.

"It's past midnight," Blade commented. "She won't be going anywhere till morning. You look like you could use some rest."

"I'm good." He raked a hand through his hair impatiently. "We'll need to keep an eye on the DCM compound as well. Once Daneya reports her run in with me, they'll increase their security. It could pose a problem for the other Drakons in this area."

Blade nodded his agreement.

Drakons were, by necessity, reclusive beings. If not already destroyed, trust was one of the first things beaten out of them at the beginning of their term. Yet, there still lay a measure of shared duty among most of them, and that included watching each other's backs whenever possible. An increase of guards in the DCM meant more vigilantes out in the field. Which equated to more interference between them and the Drakons. If any of the vigilantes were killed during the process of taking down a target, for whatever reason, it would be the Drakon responsible for that target who suffered for it.

Saden watched his friend tie the last stitch then stood to inspect his handiwork in the mirror. "Good work."

"It should be. I get enough practice with you around."

Saden snorted and cleaned up the mess. Although they were two of the best in their line of work, constant injuries were part of the job, no matter how careful one was.

He went back to his bedroom, keeping an eye on Blade as he threw on another pair of black jeans and a matching T-shirt. His friend appeared calmer than he had on the roof, though that didn't mean things might not get worse later. "Go take advantage of the downtime before Serrakus finds another job for you. Get some sleep." *Get laid*, he thought inwardly. "I'll catch up with you tomo—"

The rest of his sentence was cut off by a wave of intense, searing pain. It raced through his system like wildfire, boiling his blood until his senses blurred. He doubled over and clutched his burning stomach.

Speak of the devil. Serrakus never failed to summon him at the most inconvenient times. In the next moment, the blaze dampened to a low flicker, ready to flare up again if Saden didn't obey the call soon. As he felt the sliver of Drakonem soul within him recede from its master's touch, dread filled his thoughts.

Had Serrakus somehow found out about Daneya? It wouldn't be the first time the Drakonem had sent another Drakon to spy on him. If that was the case, there would be no bounds to the punishments Saden would endure for daring to care for someone. Serrakus took particular pleasure in making sure none of his Drakons found comfort in what was left of their lives.

Saden would probably be sent to another part of the country, or possibly to another continent.

He couldn't lose Daneya…

Saden shook his head. Jumping to conclusions was useless. He had to find out what Serrakus wanted first.

"You okay, man?"

He looked over at his friend's worried face. "It's Serrakus."

"Already?" Blade burst out. "This is ridiculous. He's been working you solid for the past five months. You can't keep going on like this."

Serrakus had been sending him out on jobs without so much as a few hours' relief in between, though Saden knew as well as Blade there was nothing to be done about it. "Watch over Daneya for me, will you? Track her if she moves again."

"I know you refuse eat, but when's the last time you slept? Or shaved for that matter? You look like shit."

"Blade…"

"All I'm saying is that you should take a breather before jumping into this next job. Your target will still be there and so will Daneya. She's a big girl and doesn't need you looking over her shoulder every—"

"Just watch her!" Saden snapped.

They glared at each other in heavy silence. Saden knew his friend was right. The strain of running on fumes was starting to affect his focus. He'd be damned if he was going to admit it, however. Not even when Blade pulled the 'I told you so' card on him later when he finally crashed, as would undoubtedly happen.

Blade let out a long-suffering sigh. "Fine, but I'm raiding your fridge first." On his way out, he mumbled, "If there's even food in there."

Saden donned his harness and trench coat then faded to his dragon form on the balcony and took flight.

Chapter Two

The Drakonem realm was in a parallel plane that existed on the same physical space as the human realm. As a Drakon, Saden could access it at any given time. Where he arrived in it depended on the location of his departure from the human realm. The center of Serrakus' domain was only eight miles north of Saden's land.

He landed in a small grove of birch trees hidden at the corner of a large horse ranch. The heat of the summons was growing again, spreading like acid through his blood. He quickly invoked the power of the Drakonem spirit and cast it outwards. It weakened the field of space in front of him to create a temporal rift. A tear in the atmosphere that acted as a gateway big enough for him to enter. The rift closed as soon as he stepped through, enveloping him in a different kind of darkness.

The burning sensation quickly died altogether. Ahead of him lay the passageway that led to Serrakus' office. Behind was one of the many entrances which opened up to the maze of catacombs that made up

Serrakus' territory. If one were to take in the view from outside, they would see a labyrinth of stone and mortar hallways interspersed with large buildings that held the prison cells.

The dungeons were all underground as well as the training areas. The gaseous atmosphere outside painted the sky a dull maroon that never changed with the rotation of the earth. Here, time was irrelevant for the most part. Nature and the turning of the seasons were non-existent. As stale and insufferable as the air was inside, the outside held little improvement.

It was one of the punishments the gods had decreed in their wrath over the Drakonem's betrayal of them. To be trapped forever in a realm that could harbor none of the beauty of the human realm.

In Saden's opinion, the gods had been far too easy on their first-born race. Then again, maybe the gods had deserved their betrayal. They certainly didn't deserve the worship of the demonic races they had created after the Drakonem.

For more than a millennium, they'd been absent from the world. Any communication was held strictly with the Drakonem, and only to reward them yearly for the work their Drakons carried out.

Serrakus was due for his reward soon. A week's vacation from this realm to spend anywhere he liked on earth, so long as he abided by the rules the gods had set for all Drakonem. No interaction with demons of any kind. No lasting ties. And no detrimental interference into the lives of humans.

Maybe then Saden could get his much needed rest.

He turned right at the end of the passageway and came to a long corridor. The change in scenery was abrupt and significant. Thick obsidian took the place of rough stone walls and creamy, gold-veined marble lined the floor instead of hard-packed dirt. Since this realm lacked natural energy resources to create electricity, fire was the only source of heat and light. Every other sconce affixed to the walls held a lit torch that flickered as he passed by.

A single, bald warder stood guard outside of the only door at the corridor's end. Laurs hadn't gone mad like most waders. He was one of the Drakons who truly relished murder and mutilation, which he'd proven his first and last day out on the field. It made him one of Serrakus' favorites.

"Saden," Laurs drawled. "It's been a while since our last session, but don't worry. Serrakus promised you to me the next time you screw up."

Saden tensed at the memory of Laurs' whip tearing the skin from his back. Six months wasn't all that long ago when you were on the receiving end. "Just open the door."

Laurs chuckled softly and stepped aside to let him into Serrakus' office.

The opulence was almost overwhelming in the massive room. Furniture from several different eras created the look of a warehouse showroom. Art ranging from simple trinkets to Egyptian and Greek statues of the male and female anatomy littered the floor and walls.

There was no rhyme or reason to their placement. They were all merely a reflection of Serrakus' gaudy tastes. Tapestries and paintings brightened the obsidian walls while multiple, hand-woven rugs softened the marble flooring underneath.

All of it was an accumulation of the things Serrakus had acquired from the human realm during his vacations. There was more, much more in the Drakonem's bedchambers, but Saden forced that thought from his mind. The past had no place in this time.

To the left in front of a large, red brick fireplace were two warders. From the chainmail on their outfits and weapons strapped to their sides, Saden assumed them to be trainers. Those in charge of teaching new Drakons how to fight and kill. A woman knelt slouched between them dressed only in rags. A trainee who had fallen behind, no doubt.

Serrakus didn't acknowledge Saden's presence in the slightest. Instead, he took a long swig of Scotch from a glass on a nearby end table. He towered above everyone in the room at over seven feet tall, as was typical for his kind. In the nearly six decades since Saden had met him, he hadn't changed at all. His wardrobe still consisted of only the finest silk suits, currently Armani, and his short brown hair was trimmed to precision. No matter the circumstance, he carried himself with the kind of regal authority that shot past narcissism and went straight to egocentric psychopath.

The Drakonem set down his glass then walked back to the trainee with arrogant contempt shining from his pale, silver eyes. "Perhaps I haven't made myself clear. What made you think you could defy my trainers and enter the human realm on your own?"

The woman raised her dirt-smudged face to glare at the men flanking her. "I've been training for three months now. I'm ready for an assignment. I told them to tell you but they refused." She shrugged a dismissive shoulder. "I had to take matters into my own hands."

Ahead of her game, then. Saden understood her impatience. A Drakon's official sentence didn't start until their Drakonem deemed them worthy to go out into the field on assignment. Time spent for punishments, recovering from wounds or further training didn't count toward their term either. It was why one year could so easily turn into five, ten or more. Little facts the historians of each race kept to themselves.

"Eager," Serrakus commented.

The woman took that as a compliment and smiled up at him.

Rookie mistake.

Serrakus laid a hand on her head almost compassionately. "Unfortunately, eagerness does not win my favor."

There was no warning to his intent. The trainee jerked spasmodically at the electric current Serrakus delivered from his palm. Her muscles bulged beneath dirty skin and face contorted in a rictus of pain. When the voltage increased, her hands constricted into claws and eyelids peeled back.

Saden looked away, sickened by the low hum emanating from Serrakus. He'd felt the touch of the Drakonem's power on countless occasions and had no desire to watch another endure it.

When Serrakus lifted his hand, the woman slumped forward, barely catching herself from falling face first on the floor. "I'm sorry," she rasped. "I'm sorry. I won't—"

"Do it again?" the Drakonem finished for her. "Oh, I know." He jolted her again with what sounded like a stronger current. This one lasted longer as well. When it was finally done, the trainee collapsed in an awkward heap. "Take her to the bowels and leave her there for a few months."

The trainers picked her up by the arms and dragged her out of the room. She would spend the next two months locked in a windowless cell the size of a large dog cage. A fairly light punishment considering her offense. Serrakus must be in a good mood.

He refilled his glass from a crystal decanter then moved to lean back on a mahogany inlaid desk at the far end of the room. "I felt the death of your last target earlier. I trust it was a clean kill?"

Saden kept his expression neutral as he walked closer. He didn't want to volunteer any information Serrakus wasn't already aware of. "Nothing out of the ordinary."

When Serrakus only nodded and took a sip of his liquor, Saden relaxed his shoulders. This meeting was about another job and not Daneya after all. His sense of relief was short-lived, however.

Crouched against the right wall was the slim figure of a young man. Shackles chained his wrists and ankles together and long, dark hair hid his face like a curtain. He had the caramel tinted skin of a Dresidien, bare except for a thin pair of tan pants.

The target Blade had spoken of. Saden was sure of it.

Serrakus' eyes lit up as he followed Saden's gaze to the phantom. "You haven't seen my latest toy, have you?" He strode over and bent to slide his fingers through the phantom's blue-black locks.

When the phantom shied away, Serrakus wrenched at his hair, forcing his head back. Alarm and hatred warred on the phantom's angular face. The tribal tattoos that bloomed on the skin's surface of every Dresidien with the passing of age were made visible. Saden counted four speared rings across the base of the neck. The bottom most ring was very faint, meaning he hadn't quite reached his four decade mark.

Dresidiens didn't fully mature until their fortieth year. That put this one barely on the cusp of becoming a man. Still a mere teenager.

Serrakus regarded Saden with a gleeful expression. "Remarkable, isn't he? Almost as pretty as you were when you came to me."

Bile threatened to rise in Saden's throat. He knew exactly what kind of 'toy' Serrakus intended to make the phantom. All the Drakonem took advantage of their prisoners. Three hundred and fifty-seven days out of the year was a long time to wait for only one week of sexual debauchery in the human realm. A shortage of willing partners was never a problem either. Many Drakons would jump at the chance to please their masters if it bought them a release from punishment or a shorter sentence.

Serrakus, however, didn't care if his victims were willing or unwilling, male or female. He took without mercy and threw the leftovers to his warders.

It took all that Saden had to keep from attacking Serrakus right there. Not that he could've hoped to inflict damage. A Drakonem's skin was leathery and nearly impossible to penetrate.

The phantom lurched to the side in an attempt to break free. That brought a snarl from Serrakus who smacked him hard with the back of his other hand. "He'll learn his position soon enough. Just like you did." Serrakus went back to his desk and shuffled through some of the files there. "I have a new assignment for you. It was reported to me that a Vampyre was seen disposing of a dead female body. A human female. You might recognize the alleged perpetrator. Gabriel Aikins."

Saden snapped his attention back to Serrakus. "What?"

Serrakus grinned thinly. "So you do remember. It's good to see the love of family still holds, even though you've lost your soul."

Again, the urge to strike the Drakonem was nearly overwhelming. Serrakus knew exactly who Gabriel was to Saden. A liar. A traitor. And the reason Saden had become a Drakon. Saden clenched his fists as fury drummed through him.

Serrakus opened one of the files and glanced at it briefly. "One of my Drakons saw him placing the body in a dumpster for the police to find. So far, the police have no leads on the crime."

"How long have you known about this?" Saden growled.

The Drakonem continued without pause. "I've recently contacted the Rei'jin of the house of Avram. The Lady Ilsa has denied the accusations presented against Gabriel. They claim he has an alibi for the night in question. Apparently, he was in his lab doing research until the following morning. I'm inclined to have it checked out for myself, though." He licked his lips and narrowed his eyes. "I thought you might want first dibs on this, seeing as how you and your uncle are so close."

Saden bit back the urge to disclaim Gabriel as family. There was something else going on. It wasn't like Serrakus to tip off the authorities of any race the accused belonged to before sending out a Drakon to investigate. As the ruling superior of her Vampyre house, the Rei'jin would have notified the accused if she thought him innocent, giving Gabriel the chance to hide any evidence that might incriminate him.

Serrakus also didn't make a habit of letting his Drakons choose their assignments.

Whatever Serrakus was hiding couldn't be good. For Saden, at least.

"Where is Gabriel now?"

"He hasn't gone anywhere since the issue was brought to me. I'm sure you remember where he's located in the human realm. I want him brought to me *alive* in no more than two weeks along with enough evidence to sentence him for murder." He dropped the file and approached Saden until only a few feet separated them. "Can you handle this, or would you prefer to cower here while I send someone else?"

Saden ignored the taunting derision in Serrakus' tone.

Was that his hook? Bait the Drakon with a target too tempting to resist? If Saden killed Gabriel—and nothing on earth would give him greater pleasure—Serrakus could postpone his death indefinitely. Worst case scenario, he could be made a warder and serve the rest of his sentence trapped in this realm.

No. He couldn't risk that. But damned if he was going to pass up the opportunity to bring Gabriel down.

"I'll take care of it." He fought the impulse to recoil as Serrakus laid an open palm on his chest. Heat flared over his skin as the transfer was made. With the additional infusion of the Drakonem's power, Saden would be able to track Gabriel as a target and sense him no matter where he was.

Saden cast one last glance at the phantom staring at them. The kid's black eyes seemed to beg him for help.

He wanted to. *Gods*, how he wanted to rip the kid from Serrakus' control and return him to his tribe. There was nothing he could do, though. Any attempt to help might make his situation worse.

With a grim set, he turned and left, anxious to get out of this realm.

* * * *

"Are you sure you're okay? We can stay the night if you want."

Daneya sucked in a breath for patience. Erin meant well, she knew this, and honestly couldn't blame her friend for worrying. She must have looked like a train wreck when she'd met back with the rest of her team. Adrenaline was still pumping through her veins and her hands wouldn't stop trembling. All she wanted to do was lock herself inside her home and find out as much as she could on Drakons.

For the fifth time, Daneya tried to muster all the confidence she could bear. "I'm fine, really. I'll call you in the morning."

Erin didn't even pretend to be fooled. "Uh-uh," she said, shaking her head. "We're staying here until you tell us what happened to you tonight. Floyd, get our stuff."

Daneya slapped a staying hand on Floyd's arm when he reached for their backpacks. "What if I promise to call Vincent?"

Floyd looked to his wife questioningly. Erin pursed her lips then nodded once. "Okay, but you're spilling all in the morning."

After hugging her friend, Daneya grabbed her own backpack and climbed out of the van. She watched her team leave then ran into her house and locked the door behind her. One minute later, a stream of whiskey splashed into her stomach, bypassing mouth completely. She took another shot for extra measure then filled a tall glass.

It was going to be a long night.

The thought of carrying through with her promise to call Vincent came and went just as quickly. He was the director of their DCM unit and deserved to know more than anyone what had happened. She should call him.

She *would* call him. Just not tonight. There were too many questions that needed answers and Vincent's presence always seemed to…complicate things.

Quietly, she took the stairs to the second floor and crept into the first bedroom on the right. The hallway light left on for her created deep shadows inside. As she came to the bed on the other side, a sense of peace calmed her nerves.

Curled up under the down comforter was four feet of slumbering innocence. Her daughter looked so much younger than her nine years in her sleep. Auburn tresses spilled across her pillow and framed her sweet face.

This, right here, was always the best part of Daneya's day. Coming home to the one person who made up her entire world. The one she had sacrificed everything for. Looking back, she knew she would do it all over again if given a choice. It didn't matter where Mckenzie came from or how she came to be. They were family. Blood. More than that, Mckenzie was her happiness.

The very reason she fought so hard for their safety.

And the reason she would probably have to move them…again. Daneya let out a breath as cold reality crept back in. She had no idea what a Drakon was capable of and didn't want to stick around to find out.

She kissed her daughter's forehead then went to her own room farther down the hall. After showering and changing into sweats and a white tank top, she headed downstairs to the study. Cherri's light snores rumbled from the bedroom next door. Normally, her best friend stayed up to greet her when she got home late. Like her, Cherri also worked for the DCM organization. Her job as a filing clerk allowed her to work from home and take care of Mckenzie when Daneya couldn't.

On nights when Daneya went out on operations, Cherri made sure to lock up the house early.

In the study, she searched the bookshelves for anything that might give her information on the creature she'd encountered earlier. The collection of historical texts and volumes she'd accumulated over the years was extensive and rivaled the archives at the DCM compound. There had to be something here that referenced Drakons. She knew they could originate from any of the multiple species of demons, so looking into one particular race likely wouldn't help.

Ah, there.

She pulled down a leather-bound book from one of the top shelves labeled, *Demon Gods: Traditions and Practices*. In the living room, she made herself comfortable on the couch. After another long swallow from her glass, she set it down on the coffee table then pulled the large book onto her lap.

Most of the writing was dry and long-winded. It detailed the discovery of a pantheon of pagan gods and how it had impacted human societies and cultures. She thumbed through these sections until she came across an accounting of the gods themselves. It was disappointingly short, giving only the names of the few who held the highest ranking. The word 'Drakonem' caught her eye and she delved into the relating section.

The creation of the Drakonem, also known as dragon spirits, was the first trial of the primordial demon gods. Through their combined efforts, this ancient race was given immortal form and sent to flourish on earth. They were imbued with spirits that held great powers, one of which was the ability to transform into the shape of a dragon. Several sightings have been recorded in art and later scriptures that have accounted for many of the dragon tales surviving today.

Daneya glossed over the following stories of human and Drakonem interaction. Most of it she already knew from previous research. She came to another passage that appeared to hold relevance and continued reading.

The Drakonem were highly cherished by their makers and gifted with a treasure. That treasure was the blinding love and service to their gods. However, the gods' children soon fell from grace, much as many of the angels had fallen from heaven. They became enamored of the worldly treasures they saw embraced by humans, such as greed and lust. Over time, they eventually forsook the gift of their makers and began to worship only themselves.

Anger overtook the gods at the betrayal of their firstborn and they lashed out in terrible vengeance. Most of the Drakonem were destroyed in the ensuing years. Their ability to procreate was stripped from their beings. Some believe it was by mercy of a handful of the gods that the rest were cast into an alternate realm. There they were imprisoned to spend all of eternity in a world devoid of the treasures that had been their demise.

Afterwards, the pantheon of gods fell into chaos. They separated ways and decided to create their own individual races. These races were born into the world with only two rules in common. The first forbade them from annihilating each other. The second banned them from ever bringing harm to humans as humans are a main source of sustenance for some of the demonic races.

A chill sped down Daneya's spine at the mention of sustenance. It was a fact she was all too familiar with. She skipped ahead again, impatient for the information she was seeking. It had to be in here somewhere. A corner of her mouth twitched up in a grin when she finally found what she was looking for.

The Drakonem are known primarily as the keepers of the most violent criminals of the demonic races. When a demon commits an unforgivable crime, usually involving murder, it is given by its own kind to the Drakonem for punishment. It is believed that the Drakonem infuses each of these criminals with a piece of its soul, binding the two irrevocably together. This ritual transforms the demon into a Drakon, stripping it of its previous demonic nature. In essence, the demon loses its power and heritage to become a vessel of the Drakonem it is bound to.

Drakons have no will of their own. Ironically, by the command of their masters, they police the criminal activities of all demonic races. While they live in the realm of the Drakonem, they are able to come and go from our world in order to carry out their duties. While sightings of these creatures are very rare, they are not to be taken lightly. Drakons are trained killers without conscience or morals. Weapons may slow them down but only a Drakonem has the ability to kill them. They can be easily identified by their pale, glowing eyes, said to be the power of the Drakonem soul shining through them.

Without conscience or morals. She drew up the memory of the Drakon she'd seen. There was no contesting the fact that he was a skilled fighter. Messing had been reputed to be trained by the best of his kind, yet he'd been no match. The grace and fluidity of the Drakon's movements had clearly shown who the superior fighter was. And the way he'd so casually summoned blue fire to incinerate Messing… That kind of power was beyond frightening.

But for some reason, Daneya couldn't relate that man to the mindless evil she'd dealt with in her life. His energy…his touch… Heat rose to her cheeks and her skin tingled where his fingertips had been. She trailed her own fingers over her jaw, remembering the gentleness of his caress. If she didn't know better, she might've thought she was the first of her kind he'd come across instead of the other way around.

His eyes had been daunting at first. A shocking, ice-violet that had been as cold as the depths of a glacier. Then they had changed, warmed, taking on a vibrant emerald hue. For the briefest moment, she could swear she'd caught a glimpse of true emotion in them. A mixture of longing and...pain? Was it possible for Drakons to experience turmoil or happiness, or anything?

Daneya shook herself and took another drink of whiskey. What she'd seen and the information she had didn't quite add up. Why had the Drakon spared the lives of Messing's guards? Then there was the matter of the demon that had distracted her team at the same time the Drakon attacked their target. It seemed too coordinated to be a coincidence.

She skimmed through the rest of the book but there were no more references to Drakons or Drakonem. Loud knocking at the front door made her jump and curse. Noiselessly, she slid open the under drawer of the coffee table and took out a 9mm from the hidden bottom compartment. At the door, all she could make out through the peephole was a man with his back turned toward her.

A shot of adrenaline raced through her bloodstream, causing her muscles to tense. It could be the Drakon. Maybe he had followed her home to eliminate her as a witness.

And rang the doorbell as a polite formality?

Perhaps her co-workers were right and she was getting too paranoid for her own good. Although it *was* paranoia that had kept her alive over the past nine years. In her line of work, there was no such thing as being too cautious.

She swung the door open and immediately aimed the gun at the man's head.

"Whoa!"

Shit! "Vincent!" she exclaimed. "What are you doing here?"

"Apparently about to get one hell of a lobotomy." The director of her DCM unit cocked his head to the side with a lopsided grin. "Erin said you needed to talk to me. Said you might forget to call me yourself."

Daneya suppressed a growl as she lowered her weapon. God save her from the good intentions of others. "I didn't forget to call you. I was going to do it in the morning."

"So what's wrong?"

"Nothing. Nothing bad. We can talk about it later."

"Well, something's got you all jumpy."

"It's not that important. Honestly."

"Then why don't you tell me now?"

"I'm fine!" They stared each other down, she in exasperation and he with an insufferable, smug look on his face. This time she did growl, realizing her efforts were futile. She stood to the side and waved him in. "Whiskey?"

"Sure," he said a little too brightly.

After getting him a glass, she took her seat again and closed the book.

"Doing a bit of light reading?" Vincent sat on the other end of the couch. From the state of his rumpled clothes, he looked as if he'd only taken the time to throw on a jacket before coming over. His usually short, styled hair was tousled and broad shoulders hunched forward.

Daneya felt guilty for adding to the obvious exhaustion that aged him beyond his thirty-six years. The man was meticulous at his duties and cared as much about those under his command as he would family. She hesitated, not quite sure how to break it to him that a Drakon was stalking his territory. Their territory.

Vincent took a sip from his glass then placed it next to hers. "Erin was really worried about you. She told me you broke ranks by leaving the team to go off on your own. By the time they'd met up with you, Messing had escaped. Is this true?"

Daneya knew the censure in his tone was more concern for her safety than the failed mission. "Not entirely. Messing didn't escape. A Drakon killed him."

The building explosion was slow in coming. First puzzlement, disbelief then finally anger flashed over Vincent's face. Blood flushed through his square features, coloring his sandy roots. "A Drakon?" he shouted, jumping to his feet. "Why the hell wasn't I notified of this before now? And what the fuck were you thinking, going in there without backup?" Alarm etched his gray eyes and he clutched her shoulders with both hands. "Are you hurt?"

"No!" She grasped his hands and gently pushed them away. "I'm all right. Keep your voice down. I don't want to wake—"

"What's going on?"

Daneya grimaced as Cherri stepped into the room from the back hallway. Her strawberry blonde curls were mussed and a pink robe over flannel pajamas sat haphazardly on her petite figure. Daneya thought about sending her friend back to bed then discarded it. Cherri could be as stubborn as she was at times, and had a right to know if they were in danger.

"I think we'd both like the answer to that question," Vincent said. He resumed his seat with Cherri taking that as her cue to follow suit. She sat down in an armchair across from them and tugged on the lapels of her robe.

Daneya took a deep breath. "When I got to the scene, Messing's human guards were already down. I saw Messing fighting with another man. I thought maybe it was a civilian in the wrong place at the wrong time. After I broke them up, I put enough bullets in Messing to keep him out of commission for a while, or thought I had. When I went to question the other man, Messing started firing on us. The next thing I knew, I was up against the wall of a building and Messing was on fire. I've never seen anything like it. The Drakon just looked at him and suddenly Messing was a tower of blue flames. He disintegrated to ash in seconds."

"What's a Drakon?" Cherri asked.

"A stone cold killer," Vincent grumbled. "A creature without a soul that feeds on death and carnage. The grim reaper of demons."

Cherri's blue eyes seemed to pop out of her skull. "You went after *that*?"

"No," Daneya assured her quickly. "We were only after Messing." She recalled the information she'd gained from the book. "Maybe that's why the Drakon was there as well. He could've been after the same target."

Vincent grunted. "Why did you separate from the others? That's against regulation."

"I know. I just… A demon came at us right as we were about to make our move. We gave chase, but it was almost as if he was just distracting us. It felt off. That's when I doubled back to find Messing."

"Well, you're lucky that Drakon didn't kill you along with the human lackeys."

"That's just it. He didn't. Kill the guards, I mean. They were only knocked unconscious." She remembered now what had happened in that split second of confusion. How the Drakon had shielded her body with his against Messing's flying bullets. "He protected me," she said with wonder. Whether it had been on accident or purpose, it was the truth.

"I think we should get you examined by the doc. You might have a concussion."

"My memory's fine. The Drakon didn't even come after me when I ran." She couldn't believe she was saying this. Her fear was no less than theirs regarding this new threat. However, she couldn't ignore the facts.

"What did he look like?" Cherri asked.

Daneya shrugged. "Like a normal guy, I suppose." Handsome. Rugged. Full of hard muscles with a face that was dark and mysterious. Everything about him had been dangerous. Enticing. She shook those errant thoughts from her head. "Uh…he had dark hair and was wearing a black trench coat. And his eyes… They were green, but I think they glow white when he uses his power."

Silence spanned over them for several seconds until Vincent shifted. "Even if he did let you go for now, I think you should err on the side of caution and move from here."

Daneya sighed. "I think you're right. I don't want to take any chances."

Cherri glanced at their glasses of whiskey and stood. "I'll go put on a pot of coffee. I think we could all use some."

As soon as she left the room, Vincent moved closer to Daneya. He brushed away a lock of her hair then cupped her cheek intimately. "Move in with me."

Daneya could only stare in shock. It wasn't the first time he had made an advance on her, but it was the boldest. And she was completely taken by surprise.

Vincent chuckled softly and feathered a thumb across her lips. "If you want to, that is. I can take care of you and Mckenzie. And Cherri if she wants to come, too." His eyes studied her face with no small amount of desire. "I know you're not ready for a full relationship. Whatever lies in your past has made you the woman you are, and I respect that. I want you to give me a chance, though. I think we both deserve it."

He was right about one thing. The secrets of her past did still have a strong hold on her. She wanted to let him in. Vincent was a good man, attractive in a gruff sort of way and tough when he needed to be. He had been there for her from the beginning. Helped her find the resources to go to college and become a weapons specialist. He was especially fond of Mckenzie as well.

But she couldn't bring herself to commit that solidly to another person.

Not yet. Perhaps not ever.

"I don't—"

"Temporarily," he cut in. "You'll need time to find another place and you can't risk staying here." He lowered his voice and whispered, "Don't make me beg."

Daneya laughed. "Okay. For one week."

Vincent leaned in close enough for their breath to mingle. Just as she was about to duck her head to avoid his kiss, he instead pressed his lips to her forehead. "It's settled then."

Chapter Three

Cherri Murkoff put the last of her clothes into the dresser then pushed her suitcase underneath the bed of the guest bedroom. Another twin bed had been set up temporarily next to hers for Mckenzie. They would be bunking together on the second floor of Vincent's house until a more permanent residence was found. Daneya would've taken the room with her daughter but she frequently kept odd hours and didn't want to wake her.

The trouble of moving yet again didn't bother her nearly as much as she knew Daneya feared. She was grateful to her friend for everything she had in her life. The companionship and security of knowing their past could never be repeated. Not with the protection the DCM offered. It wasn't a perfect life, but it was better than anything she might find on her own.

Daneya was like a sister to her, and Mckenzie the daughter she'd never had. They were her family. The only one she'd ever known.

Still, it could be hard to live with the woman at times. They were opposites in so many ways. Where she longed for a houseful of children and a husband that could give them to her, Daneya was happy with her solidarity. It was almost impossible to fathom. How a woman who could have so much denied herself almost everything.

Cherri stared out of the open window and felt the cool breeze on her face. The setting sun painted the picturesque neighborhood in muted shades of tan and peach. The entire private community located on the outskirts of North Valley was owned by their DCM unit. The organization was almost totally self-sufficient. The only trade they conducted was in the patenting and selling of breakthrough technology invented by their own people. Mostly, this consisted of software, security systems and weapons tech.

Daneya had contributed in her own way with a few unique designs, such as bullets that could lodge into the dense cortex of a Vampyre's bones and splinter them.

On the driveway below, Daneya and Vincent were bringing in groceries from his jeep. Cherri could hear snippets of the same argument Vincent had been pressing since that morning. He was trying to convince Daneya to take his bedroom for the week while he slept on the couch in the living room. As chivalrous as that might seem to an outsider, Cherri knew the real reason for his insistence.

Getting Daneya to move into his bedroom brought him one step closer to integrating her into his personal life. Even if it was only for a short while.

Daneya was having none of it, however. Her rebuffs were subtle to spare Vincent's feelings. The way she demurred with a smile and slipped away from his touches. It was hard to tell whether Vincent was even aware of the nuances of her body language.

A shard of jealousy speared Cherri's chest, familiar and deep. How dare her friend spurn the advances of a good man? Throw away the chance to make her family complete. She had no right! Not when so many other women spent their whole lives without. Alone. It wasn't fair that opportunity should come to those who didn't appreciate or accept it.

Cherri felt the resentment within her grow. She hated and took comfort in it at the same time. It was like poison and the only thing strong enough to smother the more painful feelings. Her loss and despair of ever having a child or family of her own.

She clutched her stomach and forced her thoughts away from that dark abyss. She loved Daneya, no matter how hard it was to watch her friend screw up her life.

With effort, she tamped down the echoes of her chaotic emotions and joined the others in the kitchen. Mckenzie was standing over the counter stuffing her face with a slice of pizza straight out of the box. Her mother had taken over the kitchen table with her guns spread out before her. It was a habit of Daneya's to clean them when she got home from work, although she kept them unloaded around McKenzie. Cherri was only surprised Daneya had limited herself bringing just three from their house. Her private collection consisted of more than twenty.

Vincent looked up from where he was packing groceries into the refrigerator. "Hi. Daneya told me you like to cook but I thought you might want a break tonight. Help yourself to some pizza."

Mckenzie handed her a paper plate and napkin while biting into a second slice.

"I gave you and Daneya the next few weeks off to take care of things," he continued. After watching Daneya disassemble and clean her weapons for a minute, he said, "I hope at least one of you takes advantage of the vacation. Does she always do this?"

Cherri smirked and loaded her plate with food. "Every night. We've learned to love her despite her many…quirks."

Vincent grunted. "You really should eat something, Daneya." He could've been talking to the walls for all his commanding tone had an effect on her. "Hey, pipsqueak. Tell your mom to stop working and eat."

Mckenzie skipped over to the table where she dropped the pizza box onto the gun parts. "Eat, woman."

Daneya looked up in irritation. "What are you doing?"

"Taking his side."

"Since when did that happen?"

"Since he bought me with pretty words like 'PS3' and 'games'."

Daneya narrowed her gaze on her daughter. "You bug me."

"You love me," Mckenzie countered enthusiastically. She let out a peal of laughter when Daneya snatched her and began tickling her sides.

Cherri smiled through the dull ache in her heart, blinking away tears before anyone could notice. The bond she had with Mckenzie was nothing compared to what the girl shared with her mother. They were so alike and so happy. Mckenzie was the spitting image of Daneya, down to her blooming beauty and sarcastic quips.

That could've been her once, holding her child. Before her dreams had been stolen away by demons.

Speaking of which… "Did you remember to grab my laptop from the house?"

Daneya squeezed Mckenzie in a hug then pushed her away playfully. "It's in your briefcase in the living room."

Cherri resisted the urge to fetch it and return to the guest bedroom for privacy. That would have to wait until later.

The rest of the night passed by amiably enough, though the hours seemed to creep by. She itched to get on her laptop for reasons she hadn't told Daneya about yet. It was too soon, and too personal.

Vincent eventually gave up on his argument and helped Daneya inflate an airbed for her in his exercise room downstairs. The house grew quiet as everyone settled in for the night. Twenty minutes after Mckenzie fell asleep, Daneya knocked on the door softly and peeked her head in. Cherri, anticipating this, waved her in. The bags under Daneya's eyes and lines of concern on her face as she sat beside her daughter were plain to see.

"Don't worry so much," Cherri placated. "You're doing the right thing."

"Am I?" Daneya sighed and scrubbed her eyes. "I shouldn't keep moving her around so much. I'm a terrible mother."

"You're a great mother," she countered. "Our life isn't exactly normal. Besides, you offered her a choice a few years ago, remember? You were ready to give it all up for her. Quit the DCM and start a new life. Kennie chose to stay in this life because she knows how important it is. You're the most unselfish person I know." Most of the time, but she kept that to herself.

Daneya smiled sadly. "I couldn't do any of this without you."

"Yeah, you could. Now go to sleep. The zombie look on you is not becoming."

Daneya chuckled, kissed her daughter then left. Cherri lay impatiently in bed, counting the minutes on the wall clock until an hour had passed. Silently, she slipped out of the room with her laptop in hand and locked herself in the bathroom at the end of the hall. Her heartbeat quickened as she pulled up her instant messenger. It was thirty minutes past her nightly scheduled time to chat with her mystery man and she feared he'd already gone to bed.

Relief flooded her at the sight of his user name, RKM1246, on her friend's list. She didn't know his real name or what he looked like. Only that he claimed to hold the answer to her prayers. They'd met a month ago in a local singles chat room. He'd been so different than the other men online. Patient and charming. Somehow, in mere days, she had found herself divulging her innermost secret and shame to him.

That she desired more than anything to have a child, and that she was unable to. The doctors had declared her barren after the miscarriage of her first and only pregnancy.

This man, whoever he was, said there was a remedy for that. He was a healer who specialized in alternative medicine. She knew it could be a hoax. A cruel scheme to play on the wishes of a desperate woman. But what if it wasn't?

She typed in 'Hi' and held her breath.

The response was immediate.

RKM1246: Hi. I was starting to worry about you. Is everything all right?

Cherri2000: Good now. Sorry I'm late.

RKM1246: Don't be. You're worth the wait.

The warmth that seeped into her cheeks spread to the rest of her body at his next words.

RKM1246: Have you thought about what I asked last night?

Had she thought about accepting his request to meet with him? Only about every five minutes or so. Adrenaline hit her veins at the idea of going through with it. Could she meet with a virtual stranger in the middle of the night? Then again, could she really afford not to? Her life so far was a book full of regrets, and not going would just be one more to add to the list.

RKM1246: Or did you forget?
Cherri2000: No. I haven't forgotten.

She bit her lip, fingers poised over the keys. There was still the threat of the Drakon, but it couldn't know about her. Could it? She typed in her acceptance and held her breath.

RKM1246: Great! Meet me at the Sunsprings Café.

She recognized the address he entered. The twenty-four hour diner was twenty minutes away from the house she shared with Daneya. Hurriedly, she got dressed and snuck out of the house. While guilt tread on her excitement for keeping this from her friend, it was no greater than the jealousy that often wracked her. If this panned out to be a mistake, then no one except her would be the wiser. If not…

She reined in her nerves as she pulled into the parking lot of the café. Once inside, she searched anxiously, only just realizing she'd forgotten to trade names with her online beau. Motion caught her eye from a booth toward the back. Her jaw dropped slightly when the man who was waving stood up.

He was huge! And gorgeous enough to be intimidating. He had the muscular build of a boxer with a chestnut-colored mustache that matched his hair cut in a military style. She strained her neck to look up at him as she stepped closer. Compared to her, the man was a giant.

"Cherri2000?" the man asked in a deep voice.

Cherri blushed at her user name. Not original, but catchy. "Yes. How did you know it was me?"

The man flashed pearly whites and enveloped one of her hands in both of his. "I knew you had to be the most beautiful woman who walked through that door, and I was right."

Heat coursed through her as he brought her hand up for a kiss. The line was cheesy and absolutely effective.

"Can I order you something?"

"Coffee, please."

He signaled for a waitress after they sat down. A steaming mug was filled for her though she only wrapped her hands around it, too nervous to take a drink.

"My name is Rhys, by the way."

"Cherri." She stumbled through the first few minutes of pleasantries, far too out of practice with flirting to offer sophistication, but Rhys didn't seem to mind. He exuded confidence and his light brown eyes never strayed from hers.

After a while, she grew relaxed in his company. They talked about their dreams and wishes, which seemed to coincide on every issue they raised. Somewhere along the way, she came to realize she could love this man. Was already falling in love with him.

Her euphoria faded a small measure when the subject changed to children.

Rhys lifted her chin with a crooked finger when she fell silent. "Don't look so sad, beautiful. I promised you I can help, didn't I?"

Curiosity overrode her depression. "You only said you're a healer. You didn't tell me exactly how you can fix…" *My problem.* Her mouth went dry and her throat constricted around the words. She had only spoken to Daneya about it years ago and time hadn't distanced her wounds. The squeeze of his hand gave her the courage to continue. "I was seven months along when I lost it. There was some internal damage… The doctors told me I would never be able to carry again."

Rhys didn't ask how she'd come to lose the baby and she didn't volunteer that information, too thankful for his discretion.

He clasped her hands tightly and focused his gaze on hers. "Those doctors were wrong. I've helped a lot of women overcome obstacles in regards to childbirth. The damage *can* be reversed with the right procedure. I'd like to be the one to perform it, if you'll let me."

This was said with such conviction that it left little doubt to his abilities. "How do you know it'll work?"

"Miracles happen every day, and they're not beyond our reach. Do you trust me?"

She was vibrating with the hope he promised. It all sounded too good to be true, yet why would he lie? What possible advantage could he have to gain by deceiving her? She had no fortune to give, only herself and her faults. "Yes," she whispered.

Rhys' expression was triumphant. "You honor me. I'd like to talk with you more about it, but not here. We should go somewhere more private and comfortable. How about your place?"

Cherri drew back her hands in uncertainty. "I don't know. I'm in the middle of looking for a new house and staying with a friend until I find one." She thought she caught a glimpse of irritation in his eyes that was gone in the next instant.

"What happened to your roommate? What was her name—Daneya?"

"Oh, yeah. I still live with her. A friend of hers is putting us up for the time being."

"I see," he said with a smirk. "You're scared to introduce me to her. Afraid she won't approve?"

"No! That's not it at all." After a pause, she admitted, "Okay, maybe just a little. I haven't told her about you yet."

Rhys nodded contemplatively. "I would invite you to my place, but I live over two hours away. I'm here visiting a friend for the week. Unfortunately, I don't think I'll be able to take time off work again for a while."

When he hesitated with disappointment written across his features, Cherri became anxious again. Worried she might lose her chance with this man. "I can talk to her tomorrow, my roommate. I'm sure she'd love to meet you." *Once she gets over the shock of the surprise.*

Rhys' face brightened significantly. "That's great! Write down your number and address and give me a call when you're ready. I can come out this weekend."

She wrote the information on a napkin with the pen he provided. Afterwards, he helped her with her jacket then cupped her face gently.

"You won't regret this."

Butterflies swirled in her belly as he took her mouth with his, delving inside with heated passion. She felt lightheaded and alive for the first time in years. This was it. She'd finally hit the jackpot after a lifetime of misery.

He slowly pulled away and murmured, "I'll see you soon."

Cherri drove back to Vincent's with a perpetual smile on her lips. The troubles of tomorrow were a shadow in her mind. They couldn't touch her. Nothing could ruin this moment.

* * * *

On the other side of the clear Plexiglas wall, specimen 4-7 glared at Gabriel with undisguised malice. She was a true beauty among the other specimens, with long cornsilk hair and a delicate bone structure. She was also one of the few who still retained muscle tone this long into her captivity. Most lost their trim figures after the second year due to listlessness and depression.

When it had become apparent that lack of exercise and apathy affected the health of their fetuses, he'd installed several items into his facilities.

Each cell was now outfitted with many of the comforts one might find in a real bedroom. Complete with a vanity table, a bookcase full of sanctioned reading and viewing materials, and a television mounted to the wall. Each of his facilities was also equipped with an underground fitness gym accessible to all of the specimens in rotations.

Despite all of this, it became increasingly difficult to motivate the human females to care for themselves after a certain length of time had passed.

Not his 4-7, though. She was just as high-spirited now as she'd been her first day at the facility over three years ago. Her fiery temper reminded him so much of another specimen he'd had under his charge. A wildcat that had brought forth something raw and primal within him.

Daneya Perodee.

He clenched his jaw at the memory of her. So young and temperamental. She had challenged every aspect of his being. It was that quality above all that he had admired and fallen in love with. Even when she was a child, he had known she belonged to him. A traitor may have stolen her away from him some time ago but he would get her back, and soon. No matter what it cost.

Gabriel forced his attention back to the cell. 4-7's wrists and ankles were bound by padded leather cuffs to the edges of her bed, as was customary during a routine check-up. The small lump in her lower abdomen was barely visible beneath the cotton hospital gown she wore. She was four months into her third pregnancy and coming along nicely. When the male nurse finished drawing her blood, Gabriel noticed the now vacant look in her eyes as she turned her head to stare at the wall.

She was running out of energy again.

The nurse carried his supplies out of the room along with the portable ultrasound machine he'd used on her earlier. He wrote a quick note in the specimen's chart then handed it to Gabriel. "The baby's doing fine, sir. Growth and heartbeat are good. I'll inform the dietician to increase 4-7's caloric intake. She's not gaining as much weight as she should. Other than that, she's healthy. Oh, and she'll need to be serviced soon."

Gabriel nodded. "I'll take care of her myself." His skin tingled in anticipation of that particular duty. It wasn't just about the sex for him, although that was definitely a perk. It was about power, a concept that 4-7 needed to be reminded of constantly.

"Of course, sir. 4-2 and 4-11 also need to be serviced. Do you want me to assign men to them?"

"4-11… Isn't that the one you've taken an interest in?"

The nurse bowed his head in humility, as was proper for a poignot. A Vampyre with a lesser power more suited to serving others in their society's hierarchy. Even here, *especially* here in the bowels of Gabriel's covert operation, the protocols of their kind were adhered to.

As a servant, it was not within the nurse's authority to assume the responsibilities of a superior. Only the leisonguardes, the warriors Gabriel had recruited into his fold, had the right to service the human females in their custody.

"Sir, I meant no disrespect. I-I only," the nurse stuttered, then took a deep breath. "I've managed to lower her stress levels to an acceptable rate. She responds well to me."

"Indeed she does," Gabriel agreed wryly. He'd witnessed their interaction the other day and noticed the affection they so obviously held for each other despite their discretion. 4-11, if he recalled correctly, was a seeker. A human who desired to join their race by mating with one of their kind. The bond would extend her lifespan to that of the Vampyre she mated with. Although she had come to them of her own volition, Gabriel was sure she hadn't anticipated the pregnancies taking such a toll on her.

He waved his hand dismissively at the nurse's alarmed expression. "You have my permission to service her until she gives birth. After all, what is best for the specimen is best for us all. They do bear our next generation."

The nurse bowed deeply in gratitude then hurried back into the room to release 4-7 from her straps.

Gabriel smiled as he continued down the corridor of cells. Perhaps if 4-11 kept up her record of excellent conduct and childbearing, he would let them mate. He was not an unreasonable man, and it was possible her body could stand to bear a few more babies before her womb became infertile.

He was amazed once again at the success of his plan formulated almost sixty-five years ago. Not his entirely, he admitted grudgingly. The idea had originated from a member of his kind's mortal enemy, the Djinn. Spirits created by the god Ekros from smoke and black fire who needed living, willing hosts to contain their energy. This Djinn, who called himself Forrest, had stumbled upon a secret his race had kept hidden for nearly a millennium. In his inspiration to use it to his kind's advantage, he had approached Gabriel with a proposition for an alliance. One Gabriel had accepted on mutual terms for the benefit of his own kind.

The secret was simple, really. And such an obvious answer to the dilemma of his people that he couldn't believe he hadn't thought of it himself.

He was a korvaute — a leader among Vampyres who had devoted his entire life to science and the procreation of his kind. During the centuries of war waged against the Djinn, their numbers had dwindled at a drastic rate. The leisonguardes were dying faster than their race could reproduce. If their course wasn't swayed, annihilation could be a certainty.

Vampyre females were born with a finite number of eggs in their ovaries, much like human females. However, a Vampyre female had, on average, only three to four eggs. To make matters worse, those eggs became fertile only after the female had bonded her aethra, her soul, with that of a male Vampyre. Once bonded, the female could only become pregnant by her mate.

While it was possible for a male Vampyre to bond with and impregnate a human female, there was no biological advantage other than the fact that the Vampyre genes were dominant. Each child was thus born a full-blooded Vampyre. The possible risks of exposure by accepting so many humans into their race were too great.

When a Vampyre and a human bonded, the female's body underwent changes with the commingling of her soul to the Vampyre's aethra. Most of her eggs become infertile, rendering her chances of pregnancy to the same as those of a female Vampyre. None of their scientists had been able to explain or prevent this. Not even him with his rare ability to alter living tissue in the body.

The secret Forrest had divulged to him had turned out not only to be a means to cease most of the fighting between their races, but also to increase the reproduction of Vampyres.

If a male Vampyre were to allow a Djinn to enter his body for the duration of intercourse with a human female, he could successfully impregnate her without the permanency of bonding his aethra to the human's soul. The Djinn could infuse his dark energy into the female to influence her body and enable conception.

Periodically, more transfers of the Djinn's energy were needed. Although sex wasn't required for the act, it was often enjoyed by his men. This 'servicing', as they called it, kept the female alive throughout the pregnancy. Otherwise, the growth of the fetus's aethra would drain her of energy, resulting in not only the fetus's death, but possibly the mother's as well. The healing arts of a Djinn's energy were as powerful and effective on a pregnant female as they were on the host the Djinn inhabited.

When the experiments started working, Gabriel had informed a handful of his trusted superiors, cousins to the Rei'jin of the house of Avram who dealt directly with the leisonguardes. They decided to keep it a secret from the majority of their race. The offspring Gabriel kept were then doled out to their families and those of the leisonguardes in league with them to be raised as their own.

They did this quietly so as not to alert others to their scheme. It went against every law Vampyres had regarding their interaction policies with humans.

But Gabriel didn't care. This was saving his race. And as far as the royal houses were concerned, their numbers were multiplying and it was all due to his breakthrough advances in research.

As per his agreement with Forrest, half of the infants went to those Djinn who were also aware of their forbidden treaty. The infants were brought up to accept the Djinn as family and eventually become their willing hosts. With the joining of the Djinn's energy and the Vampyre's aethra, the Djinn could live eternally in the Vampyres' bodies. The Vampyre's aethra, a source of elemental or psychic power unique to each one, also acted as a conduit for the Djinn's spirit. Combined, the Vampyre's power was more than doubled. This made Vampyre hosts more desirable than any other species.

Because the majority of Djinn would never condone the support of their enemy in any fashion, Forrest kept his involvement with Gabriel under wraps as well. Instead, as a general among his kind, he claimed to have orchestrated a truce between them and Vampyres. A ceasefire that the superiors in league with Gabriel upheld.

It was the ultimate solution for both sides.

As Gabriel stepped out of the elevator to ground level, one of his assistants flagged him down. "Dr. Aikins, Lady Ilsa and korvaute Weiss have requested a conference call with you. I've patched it through to your office."

Gabriel ground his teeth in irritation. What the hell did the Rei'jin and korvaute Weiss want now? The business with the Drakonem should be done. He still had no idea who had made the accusation a week ago, or more importantly, who had witnessed him disposing of one of his specimens. Most likely it was a member of a different race. If it had been one of his own, Commander Weiss, head of all leisonguardes, would have sent a team to investigate before involving the Drakonem.

Fortunately, thanks to one critical mistake of the past, Gabriel had long since prepared himself for this possibility. When Commander Weiss had demanded to check out his workplace, Gabriel hadn't hesitated to take him straight to the building constructed specifically to act as a front for his real operation.

A state of the art laboratory built directly on his property behind his small mansion. It was fully equipped with an active security system, trained poignots with medical degrees, and all the technology necessary for his supposed research into the fertility of Vampyre females. Even the electronic records in his database there had been thorough enough to fool the high council of the house of Avram. Gabriel had also provided fabricated paperwork from the private office in his mansion for good measure.

The entire investigation had been dropped in three days. What possible reason could they have for this further interference?

He strode past the nursery to the cluster of offices at the back of the facility and entered his. It was designed to appear exactly like the one at his laboratory, where the call had been routed from. After donning a white lab coat, he clicked the alert on his desktop computer then faced the widescreen mounted to the far wall.

Lady Ilsa's regal image appeared in front of a background of colorful paintings unique to their culture. She was seated in a high-back chair wearing a blood-red satin dress that hugged her sleek form provocatively. Long black hair framed her pale face, accentuating her thick lashes and full red lips. She was the accumulation of centuries of pure-bred royal lines and mates chosen solely for their beauty and grace. The effect was mesmerizing until it came time to conduct business. As far as he knew, only one of the five Vampyre houses across the world had royalty who did not rely completely on their council and commanding officers to handle their governing affairs. And that one resided in Siberia.

One of Lady Ilsa's many mistresses stood behind her, brushing her hair sensuously. It was no secret that the lady enjoyed an alternative lifestyle. She flaunted her female lovers as freely as she did her riches. No one minded this, so long as she abided by the same breeding law that ruled all Vampyres. That every male and female do their part in the procreation of their race unless physically unable.

So far, the lady and her consort had two sons to boast of.

The mistress rushed out of sight when korvaute Weiss moved to Lady Ilsa's side. His peppered hair and granite countenance matched his demeanor, cold and intimidating. He spoke first in a deep voice. "Korvaute Aikins. Sorry to interrupt your studies. We wanted to check in to make sure you haven't been disturbed by any…outside parties."

Gabriel sat down behind his desk with a frown. "I don't quite follow you, Commander."

"The Drakonem who contacted us a week ago seemed a little too suspicious for me. I think he may not be done with you yet."

"Just what are you trying to say?"

The lady huffed exaggeratedly. "He thinks a Drakon may have been sent after you. Personally, I don't see any cause for alarm. You have nothing to hide. If there is a puppet out there, he will only return to his master empty-handed."

Weiss' lips thinned in disapproval. The Lady wasn't exactly known for her patience, or her knowledge of history. But one didn't chastise royalty outright, no matter high your rank.

When Gabriel saw his head leisonguarde, Rhys, enter his office, he lowered a hand to signal the man to stay out of sight.

"While this may be true," Weiss went on, "I would like to assign you additional guards. I can post half a dozen at your house and a dozen at your lab. I also think you would do well to keep a personal bodyguard to accompany you at all times. While Drakons are essentially mindless killers, they shouldn't be underestimated. If one is after you, as I suspect there is, I wouldn't put it past the creature to fabricate evidence against you."

Gabriel would've laughed at the irony of that statement if the situation weren't so dire. Commander Weiss had a well-earned reputation for excellent instincts, and Gabriel wasn't about to question them now. Neither could he accept the man's offer of additional guards, though. Anything they saw could equally jeopardize his operation.

An idea came to him and he kept his face troubled. "I see, and I greatly appreciate your concern." He tipped his head toward the Lady. "I wonder, Commander, if you would allow me to choose the leisonguardes to protect me. Many of them are my friends. I could have a list to you by this evening."

Weiss seemed taken aback by his personal request but didn't argue. "Very well. Take care, Doctor."

When the screen went blank, Gabriel threw his coat off and stalked to his liquor cabinet. A Drakon! His little slip up was quickly turning into a fiasco.

"A Drakon?" Rhys asked, mirroring his thoughts.

Gabriel downed a shot of vodka then poured himself another before turning to his most trusted leisonguarde and advisor. "Korvaute Weiss is under the impression that the Drakonem may have sent one after me."

Rhys took a seat opposite the desk and planted his booted feet on the chair beside him. "I've never known the commander to be wrong about a hunch. You should heed his warning."

"Of course I should!" Gabriel shouted. When Rhys merely lifted a brow, he sighed and rifled a hand through his dark brown hair. "I'm sorry, my friend. You're right, which is why I agreed to the additional guards. Choose men that you trust to keep up appearances at my home and laboratory. I'll have to stay away from the facilities for the next week or two until this situation blows over."

Gabriel wasn't too worried about a Drakon discovering his facilities. Each one was registered as a business under the ownership of humans. And those humans were hosts for the Djinn he was working with.

If anything suspicious were to happen, they would report to him immediately.

He took a sip of his liquor then sat down again. "All this for a dead little human whose name no one even cared to get."

Rhys snorted. "I've already talked to Forrest about having his men commandeer a funeral home in this area. That'll take care of any future complications with the disposal of specimens."

Gabriel sighed again, suddenly tired. "Give me some good news, Rhys. How did your meeting with that woman go?"

Rhys grinned widely. "I found her."

A bolt of elation slammed into Gabriel's chest. He sat forward with narrowed eyes. "You found my Daneya?"

"I have her address right here." He handed a napkin to Gabriel, who took it greedily. "It's about an hour away. She and her daughter are staying temporarily with a friend. Cherri told me they'll be there for a short while at least."

Gabriel stood and began to pace, feeling his excitement build by the second. "Good. This is good. We can leave with a team as soon as the sun sets."

"It's not going to be that easy, sir. I checked out the friend she's staying with this morning. He's the director of the DCM unit in this area and his house is located in the middle of their residential community."

"They're still just humans. They pose no threat to us."

"Maybe not, but a Drakon does."

Gabriel scoffed darkly. "We aren't even sure if there truly is one sent to investigate me."

"All the more reason to be careful," Rhys countered. "Cherri is expecting a visit from me this weekend. Let me convince her to meet me somewhere with Daneya and the girl. I can take them with only a few men and bring them back here."

"That's three days away," Gabriel said, shaking his head. "I can't wait that long."

Rhys jumped to his feet and jerked Gabriel to a stop. "You have to. If a Drakon has been assigned to you, it can sense where you are at any time. It could track you right to Daneya."

"I said no!" Gabriel shouted. "I've waited too long to sit on the sidelines now. I have to go."

Rhys fumed silently, his hand flexing on Gabriel's arm before he finally let it drop. Gabriel couldn't fault his friend's anger. He knew going after Daneya himself would place his entire operation in danger, but he couldn't sit idly by while others went to fetch his wayward possession. Daneya was his, and he would be the one to bring her home.

"I'll take a team with me under cover of night. We'll be in and out before any of the surrounding vigilantes ever know we're there."

"What do you mean 'I'?" Rhys asked warily. "I'm going with you, too."

"I need you to stay here and station those additional guards at my house and laboratory. Besides, if anything does go wrong, and I'm not saying it will, I don't want Cherri to recognize you. We might have to use her later." Gabriel waited for acknowledgment of his orders. By the look of turmoil on his friend's face, he knew the conversation wasn't quite over.

"I'll stay on one condition. I want the woman, Cherri."

He cocked his head in surprise. "For yourself?"

Rhys' voice softened and his lips twitched. "She is submissive and trusting. I think she'll make a good specimen."

Gabriel had the distinct feeling that wasn't all Rhys wanted to make of her, though he kept his thoughts to himself. If the little human made his friend happy, he was all for it. He nodded once. "You have my word."

After Rhys left, he downed the rest of his vodka then took out his cell phone with a smile on his face. He had a kidnapping to prepare for — and not a lot of time to do it in.

Chapter Four

Saden stood cloaked in shadows by a line of trees at the start of the quarter-mile driveway. At the other end lay Gabriel Aikins' mansion. A testament to modern architecture with sleek angles and glass surfaces. He barely recognized it from his childhood years. Back then, it had still retained the authentic charm of its Dutch Colonial style.

He shook his head at the downward progression of the race he'd been born into. For all the majesty of the Vampyres' heritage, their greed and lust for power were beginning to rival those of humans. It made him glad he could no longer claim ties to them, or their dying culture.

Unfortunately, his memories weren't so easily erased.

He recalled the day his parents had died in the ongoing war against the Djinn. Both had been leisonguardes of great skill. He'd been seven years old at the time, and his sister two. They had been moved into his uncle's house that night. There had been some dispute about whether his sister should go to a couple who lacked children since his uncle was unmated, but his parents' instructions on their welfare had been explicit. They had trusted Gabriel to care for their children.

Saden was only thankful they had died before they could find out just how misguided their trust had been.

For a moment, just a moment, he was tempted to abandon his mission. Walk away from the house he'd sworn never to visit again. gods, how he wanted to! That had been the one good thing that'd come out of being made a Drakon. The promise that his past life was no longer his right to embrace. Yet here he was, charged with immersing himself in it once again. Of all the sick degradation Serrakus had subjected him to over the years, this definitely topped the list.

Saden summoned the piece of Serrakus' soul that lived inside him and flung it out in search of his target. Unexpectedly, Gabriel's energy flared to his senses not ahead of him, but behind by about thirty miles. What the man was doing and where was not his concern at the moment, however. Right now, the distance gave him time to sneak into the mansion and find what he could.

He faded to his dragon form and took flight. Movement around the perimeter of the mansion caught his attention. He circled twice, counting six armed men and women pacing along the perimeter.

Damn Serrakus!

His enquiry about Gabriel to the Rei'jin of the house of Avram had destroyed any tactical advantages Saden might've had. Without the element of surprise, he was screwed in more ways than he could count. It left him vulnerable and his mission exposed, but not impossible. He still had a few secrets of his own.

He took back his corporeal form on top of the mansion near a sunroof. After attaching a suction cup to the glass, he concentrated his Drakonem power into a single point and used it to slice a large circle out of the glass. It came away easily and he laid it aside before dropping down into the room below. He was in Gabriel's extensive library on the second floor. Two doors down the outer hallway, he came to his target's study. Unlike the exterior of the house, the interior hadn't changed much. The dark wood furniture and low-key decorative style was the same as he remembered.

Saden was betting the man's habits hadn't changed either. Gabriel had always been a paranoid sort, even in the privacy of his own home. Everything of a personal nature, including family heirlooms and photos, were likely still in the attic where Saden had discovered them long ago. Those weren't all Gabriel chose to keep hidden. Upon moving in as a boy, Saden had uncovered many of the secret hiding places his uncle had installed in the house. Including the one in his study.

Saden went to a corner of the room and pushed aside the credenza there. He knelt down and felt along the bottom of the wall until his fingers found a small pressure panel. It triggered a spring mechanism that released the lock of the hidden door. Judging by the silent ease with which he was able to push the door inward, it was apparent Gabriel still kept this secret alcove in use. It was the hind end of a utility closet in the outer hallway and designed to be completely unnoticeable.

An overhead bulb lit the small area, showing two tall filing cabinets and several stacked tubs. Saden rifled through one of the tubs first. Papers were organized within by color-coded files, and all of them dated back to at least four decades ago. No matter how incriminating they might be, Saden needed current evidence. If Gabriel was still experimenting on humans as he suspected, nothing short of up-to-date, irrefutable proof would be enough to detain the man.

He used a picklock on one of the cabinets and searched through the files on the top shelf. Each one seemed to be the profile of a human female. They included pictures, life histories and medical records. The dates on these were more recent, going back only over the past ten years. When he pulled out the first file to read further in depth, his blood ran cold.

Daneya's headshot stared back at him from a corner of the file, her amber eyes wild with fear. He scanned over the information on the following page, his gut clenching in dread.

Name: Daneya Perodee
Age: 17
Known relatives: Mother, Trina Perodee. Father, Scott Perodee – Died in a car accident in 1995. Sister, Emily Perodee – Deceased.
Address: 4455 Tunnel Ln. Riverside, CA.

Saden stopped reading. His hands shook and vision clouded over with rage. Seventeen. She'd been *seventeen* when this information had been gathered on her!

He stared at the photo again. There was no doubt in his mind it had been taken by Gabriel or one of his cohorts. No one showed that much fear without good reason.

How had Gabriel managed to capture her? During that time, Marco had been watching over her. The same man who'd asked Saden to protect her when his punishment had forced him out of the country. Yet

Marco had mentioned nothing of Daneya's involvement with Gabriel. His thoughts whirled at the implications of this. The knot of dread building in his gut became a foreboding weight he couldn't ignore.

He had to check in on her.

After replacing the file, he pulled out his cell phone and called Blade. Heavy panting met him on the other line, then his friend's voice.

"Yeah?"

"Blade, did you track Daneya like I asked you to?"

"Sure, of course," Blade said breathlessly. "She took her daughter and roommate and moved in with some guy. Name's Vincent Condretti. He's the head of the DCM unit here."

"Where does he live?"

"In a gated community on the outskirts of North Valley, about twenty miles northeast of her house. Why?"

Saden cast the Drakonem's power out again. Gabriel was on the move, headed in the same direction Blade had given. Fuck if this night just didn't get better and better. He put a lock on the alarm hammering in his chest and said, "Get to Vincent's house. Now! I'll meet you there."

"Saden, what's going on?"

Saden heard a whiny moan in the background on Blade's end and frowned. "I'd ask you the same thing but I really don't want to know. Just get your ass over there. I think Gabriel might be making a move on Daneya."

"*Your* Gabriel? Shit, okay. I'm on my way. Hey, uh, where do you keep your towels?"

"My...what?" He paused for a second as Blade's question sank in. "Are you in my house?" he yelled as quietly as possible.

Blade hesitated then answered, "I hung a tie on the front door."

Saden growled. "Just get dressed and get the woman out of there before you leave." He hung up, swearing as he put everything back in order.

Outside, he replaced the glass on the sunroof, zeroed in on Gabriel and sped toward him in his dragon form. The Vampyre was going faster now, probably traveling in his vehicle on the highway. Saden rose higher in the sky to gain more speed. Fifteen minutes later, Gabriel's spark of energy came to a halt.

Frantically, Saden searched for the community Blade had spoken of. The cluster of houses was set slightly apart from the rest of the rural neighborhood, with Gabriel at its center. He swooped closer to what had to be Vincent's house, though it was cloaked in some sort of guise. A shroud of shadows to conceal it from outside view. He'd seen the like before from Vampyres who could use their aethra to manipulate light and dark.

Two cars were parked in the driveway and two more by the curb. Saden resumed his true form by the SUV and touched the hood. The engine was still warm. Gabriel's car. He sent a bolt of Drakonem energy through the engine to fry the wiring.

A high-pitched scream came from inside the house then was cut off abruptly. Saden ran forward almost blindly, the guise thickening to completely obscure the structure of the house, and felt his way along the exterior. When the cold, smooth surface of glass met his touch, he shattered it and jumped through. The guise didn't extend to the interior, but none of the lights were on. He called forth a huge ball of blue fire that lit the entire room before petering out. That split second gave him enough time to make out two Vampyres crowding in on a human male and another wrestling with a female farther away.

Saden kept the Drakonem power buzzing just beneath the surface within him so that his eyes glowed with it. It gave away his position but also allowed him to see the outlines of everyone in the room. He snatched one of the Vampyres wrestling with the human male and hurled him across the room. In the next moment, the human caught him on the jaw before he could react and aimed a gun at him. Saden knocked the gun out of his hand at the same time the second Vampyre hurled himself at the human. They went down hard in a tangle of arms and legs.

Saden grunted as the first Vampyre slammed into him from behind. He twisted on the floor, drew a knife from his belt then flipped them over. The Vampyre cried out when Saden pinned his hand to the floor with the blade, then fell silent when Saden punched him unconscious.

A body was thrown somewhere to his right, marked by the crashing of a piece of furniture. Saden recognized the bulky frame of the human as it slumped awkwardly over broken planks of wood. He spun in a low kick that tripped the second Vampyre then took him out as well.

Light spilled down from the hallway upstairs where Gabriel held Mckenzie trapped in a firm hold. In front of them at the top of the stairwell stood another Vampyre with Cherri's limp body hanging from one of his shoulders.

Mckenzie struggled in Gabriel's grip until she caught sight of her mother. "Mom!"

Saden looked over to find Daneya fighting with the third Vampyre over control of a knife between them. At Mckenzie's shout, she lost focus and turned around. It happened before Saden could move. The Vampyre's hands jerked at the sudden release of tension and the blade was plunged into Daneya's side.

Saden saw red, his only instinct to kill the man that threatened her. As Daneya hit her knees, he charged only to crash into Blade's solid form as his friend appeared suddenly in front of him. Blade tossed him to the side then took out the Vampyre in one blow. When Saden tried to charge again, Blade grabbed his trench coat and shook him violently.

"Get Daneya," Blade yelled. "Get her out of here! I've got the others."

Saden watched in a haze of anger as Blade ran to the stairs. His hands trembled as he gathered Daneya in his arms and carried her out of the house. He laid her gently in the back seat of the compact Volvo parked behind Gabriel's SUV. She was fading in and out of consciousness from loss of blood. After stripping out of his coat, he ripped off his shirt and pressed it to her side. It appeared as if the blade had missed any vital organs, though he couldn't be sure. He had to examine the wound more closely.

As he glanced back at the house, he saw Blade running out to meet him with Cherri thrown over one shoulder and Mckenzie at his side. Saden took Cherri and sat her in the passenger seat while his friend urged the girl into the back with her mother.

"Where are you taking them?" Blade asked.

Saden thought quickly as he jumped into the driver's side. He couldn't risk taking Daneya to a human hospital. Gabriel wouldn't give up that easily. "My house."

Blade nodded then cursed when a shot rang out. He clutched his arm then looked back to see Vincent standing in the doorway of the house with a gun trained on him. "Get going. This won't take long."

Saden heard a few more shots go off as he directed a sliver of Drakonem power into the ignition. The car rumbled to life and he hit the gas. He sent another burst of power at the hinges on the metal gate bordering the community and rammed the car through it. When Mckenzie screamed from the back seat, he flicked his gaze to the rearview mirror and saw her staring back at him with wide eyes.

Forcing calm into his voice, he said, "It's okay, Kennie. I'm not going to hurt you. Your mom calls you Kennie, doesn't she?" When no response came, he switched tactics. "My name's Saden. I came to protect you and your mom but I need your help. She was badly hurt. Do you see the wound on her side?"

This time, Mckenzie looked down and nodded.

"I need you to press the shirt into it. You have to stop the bleeding. Don't worry about hurting her. She can't feel it right now." He kept one eye on her and one on the road as she followed his instructions. "Good girl."

After a while, Mckenzie looked back at him. "Who are you?"

Saden hesitated, not quite sure what to say. "I'm someone you can trust. I know that's probably hard to believe given the circumstances, but you'll just have to take my word for it."

Surprisingly, the girl didn't argue. He pulled onto the highway and gained more speed.

"I think we're being followed," Mckenzie said.

Saden saw two cars coming up fast behind them in both lanes. Before he could think of a strategy, a column of blue fire blazed across the road between them and the encroaching vehicles. Tires squealed on the pavement and he watched first one, then the other car swerve wildly off the road. He sent a silent thanks to Blade who was apparently flying above them.

"That was your friend, wasn't it?"

Saden frowned. "It was. How did you know?"

"His eyes glowed when he created fire. Yours were glowing too but they aren't anymore."

A corner of his mouth lifted at the girl's deductive reasoning. "His name's Blade. You can trust him, too."

Nothing more was said for the remainder of the trip. Blade was waiting for them outside when they reached the manor. He took Cherri while Saden got Daneya. Saden carried her to the master suite on the second floor and laid her down on the bed. In the adjoining bathroom, he soaked several washcloths in warm water then grabbed a first aid kit from below the sink. He set everything on the comforter beside Daneya and began cleaning her wound. Although the knife hadn't punctured her organs, the cut was deep and her blood loss critical. She would die if he didn't do something soon.

Healing her with his power was the only option.

As with the fire, the power came directly from the piece of Serrakus' soul within him. Use of its healing qualities was strictly forbidden, in the field or otherwise. Drakons were only permitted healing through their masters. It was how the Drakonem could torture their Drakons for days or weeks at a time then send them directly on an assignment afterwards. Serrakus would sense it the moment Saden tapped into the power to heal Daneya. Fortunately, the Drakonem wouldn't be able to determine who was being healed. If asked, Saden would simply tell him he'd used the power on himself.

Saden pushed aside the material of Daneya's tank top and flannel bottoms then gestured for Mckenzie to come closer. "Get on the bed, little one. I need to heal your mom and it's going to sting a bit. Hold her arms to the bed." He placed Daneya's wrists above her head then guided Mckenzie's hands over them. "She's going to fight for just a minute then it'll be over. Can you handle that?"

Mckenzie's face was pale, her face streaked with smears of her mother's blood. Tears shimmered on her long lashes but didn't fall. She firmed her lips and nodded once bravely.

Saden called the healing power forth and directed it at Daneya's injury. A white glow bathed the area and slowly seeped into the open flesh. He cupped his hands over it and concentrated on willing the power to mend the torn muscles. When Daneya started to writhe, he pushed down lightly, grateful that Mckenzie was able to keep her cool and hold her mother.

It was done quickly.

Saden sat back and inspected the pink, puckered scar that resided where the gaping wound had been. It was the best he could do. Only Drakonem were able to regenerate the skin fully before it could harden to scarred tissue. Which was the reason why Saden's body wasn't a disfigured mass of scars by now.

"Is she going to be all right?" Mckenzie whispered.

His answer turned to a sharp gasp. He lurched forward and caught himself before toppling onto Daneya. Scorching pain ripped through his being, consuming him whole in the blink of an eye. It felt as if claws of flames were tearing him apart from the inside. His thoughts scattered, breath evaporated until there was nothing except living agony.

Then it was over.

Saden came back to himself slowly, his senses returning from behind a fog. Serrakus was not pleased.

Saden had no doubt that was a mere taste of what was coming to him for daring to use his power to heal. That was another day, however.

"Are you okay?"

He stared blankly at first at the true concern written on Mckenzie's youthful features. It had been so long since someone had expressed that emotion toward him that it took a second to gather his thoughts. "Yeah," he rasped. "It's nothing."

"It didn't look like nothing," Blade commented from the doorway.

Saden scowled and turned back to Mckenzie. "Your mom's going to be fine. She's just tired. In that closet over there, you'll find some clothes." The belongings of his mother he hadn't had the heart to throw away. "Why don't you pick out something for you and your mom to sleep in. I'll be right back." When the girl nodded, he took the supplies back to the bathroom with Blade on his heels.

"You healed her, didn't you?"

Saden readied strips of gauze and a needle and thread. "Sit down. I'll take a look at your wound."

"Saden—"

"She was going to bleed out," he snapped. "I had no other choice."

Blade glared at him then shook his head. After taking off his trench coat, he sat on the toilet lid and rolled up his shirt sleeve. "I'm surprised Serrakus didn't demand you go back immediately."

Saden wiped the bullet wound in Blade's upper bicep with one of the washcloths. His friend was lucky. It'd gone clean through without hitting the bone. "He's probably too busy playing with his newest toy." He wasn't going to mention the phantom but from the look of fury that sparked in Blade's eyes, he didn't have to.

"Son of a bitch!"

"We'll help him soon, I swear. Right now, I need you with me."

Blade grumbled a few more choice words for their Drakonem then inclined his head. "I know. I'll do what I can for you. Whoa, whoa, whoa. Don't use that shit."

Saden paused in pouring alcohol onto a cotton swab. "Again? You do this every time. It's only antiseptic."

"It hurts."

"Quit being a baby."

"I got your baby right here, asshole. You better not touch me with that, Saden. I'm warning you... Aaah!" He flinched exaggeratedly when Saden daubed the swab over his wound.

They both turned at a giggle from the other room. Mckenzie was watching them, holding a white gown in her arms. The trepidation she'd held earlier seemed to be gone. She clucked her tongue while shaking her head.

Blade gaped then furrowed his brow. "Hey, no comments from the peanut gallery."

Without skipping a beat, she shot back, "Want me to kiss it and make it better?"

Saden covered his laugh with a cough. The girl definitely had her mother's spirit.

"Are you hearing this?" Blade asked him in mock offense.

"I'd take the offer."

"Thank but no thanks. She's as mean as you are."

Mckenzie shook her head, mumbling, "Sadness," as she walked away.

When the girl was out of earshot, Blade's lips curved in a smile. "I kinda like her. She's got spunk."

Saden grunted and finished cleaning the injury, then started on the stitching. "How was Cherri?"

"She's fine. Got a nasty bump on her head, though. I put her in one of the guest bedrooms downstairs."

"And Vincent Condretti?"

Blade grinned. "He won't be straight shootin' any time soon. Other than that, he'll be all right. How did you know Gabriel was going after Daneya, by the way?"

Saden told him about his new assignment and the files he'd found in Gabriel's house.

Blade let out a low whistle. "I don't like it. Serrakus has to be up to something. It's against the rules to send us out after people from our pasts." There were too many complications. Too much liability in personal vendettas. Drakons had to be objective on their missions. Otherwise, they could lose sight of their only purpose — to serve their masters.

"Whatever it is, I'll handle it. I can't back out now. Not with Daneya and Mckenzie involved."

"And what do you plan on doing with them?"

He sighed heavily. Honestly, he hadn't thought that far. All that had mattered was getting them to safety. "I'll have to keep them here until I've dealt with Gabriel. They're not safe with the DCM unit." Saden ignored his friend's eloquent expression. Convincing Daneya that he was her best bet would be next to impossible. And with good reason.

If Serrakus found out he was harboring her, the Drakonem would recall his mission in an instant. Cherri, Daneya and her daughter would be on their own and Gabriel would find them again. However, the alternative was out of the question.

He thought back to how close he'd come to losing everything earlier. If he'd killed the Vampyre who had stabbed Daneya, it would've been game over. Serrakus would have sensed the death at his hands immediately and sent warders to take him back. "Thanks, by the way," he said in a low tone. "For stopping me."

His friend needed no further explanation. He simply dipped his head in acknowledgment.

Saden dressed Blade's injury then put away the supplies. There was still one unfinished detail to take care of. "The car I used—"

"I'm on it," Blade said as he picked up his coat and strode out of the room.

Saden followed him out and strode to the other end of the hallway where he grabbed a few toiletries from his bathroom then towels, sheets and an extra comforter from the linen closet. When he returned to the room, he put everything on the foot of the bed. "Why don't you go into the bathroom and clean up," he said to Mckenzie. "I'll make the bed."

Mckenzie hesitated briefly then took what she needed to the bathroom.

Saden gently placed Daneya in the armchair next to the bed before replacing the stale sheets with a fresh set. Nothing in the room had been changed or used in sixty years, much like most of the house. It had never even occurred to him that it might see company again. To him, it was a tomb of memories he foolishly clung to. The only happiness he'd ever known. It felt strange yet good to bring life back to its empty walls, even if it was only temporary.

Running water from the shower came on as he was changing out the comforter. After laying Daneya between the sheets, he checked her forehead. She was running a slight fever and her ashen face contrasted sharply with her burgundy hair. It would take her at least a few days to regain her health.

Carefully, he peeled off her blood-stained shirt and tossed it to the floor. Her skin underneath held more color, tawny and smooth in the glow of the overhead light. He found himself mesmerized by the subtle curves of her body. Without thought, he ran his fingers down the column of her neck and over the shallows of her clavicles. She was incredibly soft, her warmth inviting. Unlike any female he had ever experienced.

Not that he'd had many of those. Experiences, that is. His first had been decades ago at Blade's insistence, and had turned into nothing short of a disaster. He still recalled every detail of that night. The prostitute had called herself Candy, cheap and false like the rest of her. She'd been patient, though, and more than willing to be his first. He'd known the motions of his role. Known what to place where and how to position his body. Yet when the time had come, he'd been too nervous to take control.

He hadn't wanted to hurt her.

She had eventually taken over but that'd only made things worse. Saden had felt humiliated at his failure. Trapped in the role of submissive, as he had been so many times in the past. He'd ended up running away, ashamed of himself, his past and the bleakness of his future.

Saden knew Blade's intentions had been pure. To show him that sex didn't have to be painful or a power struggle for dominance. Yet, that concept had been too new for Saden to grasp. Several years later, he had tried again with better results. Had even found perfunctory satisfaction in his release. That was far from the pleasure he knew should be there, however.

Far from the beauty he saw before him in Daneya's body.

He traced her defined ribs, the palm of his hand brushing the swell of her right breast. Gooseflesh rippled over her skin in response to his touch. Her nipple was rosy and puckered in the cool air. He slid a lock of her hair to uncover the other breast. It was ample and firm and would probably fit in the palm of his hand. The bend of her tapered waist was enticing, pronouncing her small rounded belly. He slowly drew down her flannel bottoms. The patch of hair covering her most private part was almost black and, for a moment, he was tempted to run his fingers through it to see if it felt as soft as her skin.

When he trailed his hand down the side of her thigh, something happened that hadn't occurred in longer than he cared to remember. He grew hard in the confines of his jeans and a yearning began to coil deep in his groin.

Saden snatched his hand back and jumped off the bed, horrified by his actions. *What the fuck am I doing?* Bile churned in his stomach and rose like acid in his throat. He more than anyone knew what it felt like to be molested. Yet, here he was taking liberties with the only person who kept his insanity at bay.

He looked away in disgust, yanking at his hair with both hands and relishing the pain it brought. Maybe he was a soulless monster after all. To turn what had started out to be an attempt to make her more comfortable into some sick and twisted desire. He was no better than Gabriel. No better than...

Saden tore his thoughts from that path. The water in the bathroom shut off, bringing him back to reality. He looked back to Daneya's mostly naked form and swore. No matter what he'd done, Mckenzie would think worse of him if she saw her mother like this.

He hastily stripped the bottoms from Daneya then dressed her in the gown Mckenzie had retrieved for her. He'd just pulled up the covers when the girl came out of the bathroom. She'd chosen a T-shirt for herself that fell down to her shins. The comical appearance she gave helped to soothe Saden's frayed nerves.

He cleared his throat and jerked his chin toward the bed. "I thought you might want to sleep in here tonight. Your mom might be out of it for a while so come down for breakfast in the morning when you're ready."

"How long will we have to stay here?" Mckenzie inquired as she climbed onto the bed.

Saden didn't want to lie to her. Serrakus had given him two weeks for his assignment, and Daneya's involvement with Gabriel only made things more complicated. "Until I can be sure you and your mom are safe. Probably a week or so. Is that okay with you?" He didn't know why he asked. It was inevitable. But her opinion mattered to him.

Mckenzie seemed to mull over this then tilted her head. "I guess I don't mind."

That triggered another question he had. "You're awfully calm about all of this. How are you doing?"

She shrugged and slanted her gaze away. "I'm kinda used to this. Mom's been hurt before and we move around a lot. Hazards of her job. I know she feels bad for not giving me a normal life but...she does what she does for a good reason, right? She's like a warrior. Are you one, too?"

Saden smiled sadly at her innocence and candor. It would be gone tomorrow when her mother told her what kind of creature he really was. For now, though, he cherished it. "Something like that. Go to sleep. I'll see you in the morning."

He shut the light off on his way out, half dreading what tomorrow would bring.

Chapter Five

A warm breeze wafted over her face, bringing with it the scents of evergreens and clean earth. Daneya blinked open heavy lids and looked around in confusion.

She was in an expansive room made of smooth, stone walls and hardwood flooring. Sunlight streamed in from an open pair of French doors leading to a balcony on her right. White lace drapes billowed in the breeze, seeming to dance to the song of birds outside. The tapestries covering the walls to provide warmth held beautiful scenes of nature, lending the feel of freedom to the room.

The overall effect would have been captivating if not for the strangeness of it. Daneya shot up in alarm then fell back on a wave of dizziness. Her head swam and nausea threatened her stomach. When the disorientation passed, the events of the night before came flooding back. The attack at Vincent's house. Mckenzie's terrified scream and…

Gabriel.

He'd been holding her daughter when... Daneya struggled to remember what had happened. There had been a piercing burn at her side then...nothing. She shoved a light blue comforter from atop her then scrambled to inspect her midriff.

What the hell am I wearing?

It appeared to be some kind of white gown fashioned from the early fifties. She yanked it up from around her ankles and found a thin, puckered scar on her side where before there had been smooth skin. That was impossible. Gabriel didn't have the kind of power to advance healing.

She climbed out of the bed and fought against the feeling of weakness in her limbs. Whatever he'd done to heal her wound apparently hadn't extended to her health. The injury had taken more out of her than she was wanted to admit, but she couldn't focus on that now. She had to find Mckenzie. If that bastard hurt her daughter, she would skin him alive. Balls first.

At the other side of the room she found a spacious bathroom full of gleaming porcelain and gold-veined marble. She was about to dismiss it until she saw the toiletries lined up on the sink counter. They were all hers, down to the exact floral scented shampoo she used. Even Mckenzie's personal effects were there next to hers.

Just what was Gabriel trying to do—bribe her with kindness while holding her hostage in his house? Did he think she would be grateful?

It wasn't his MO, yet she couldn't deny those were her belongings. The very idea sent a sickening chill through her. That's when she turned to find a set of her clothes laid out on the foot of the bed. Her mind whirled at the disturbing implications but she pushed them aside. She'd take whatever advantages she could get.

She threw on her black jeans and V-neck sweater then crossed the room to a walk-in closet. It was packed with men's and women's clothing hanging from both sides, none of which were hers. After searching the top shelves for anything she could use as a weapon and coming up empty, she pulled down one of the metal rods holding the clothes. It was solid and roughly the length of her arm. Heavy enough to do serious damage despite her weakened state.

The outer hallway extended some distance to the right, and the left side opened to a wide stairwell that went down as well as up to a third floor. The steps were carpeted in red velvet and the banister intricately carved from thick mahogany. It was appalling to see such beauty wasted on a madman like Gabriel. And even more so that it was paid for by the success of his experiments on humans.

As far as she was concerned, the entire ruling house of Vampyres in this area deserved to die for supporting his cruelty. Whether they were aware of his operations or not.

The faint sounds of a television drifted through the air as she made her way down the curving staircase. They were coming from a room to the right of the massive foyer she came to. A different sound drew her to the left down an arched corridor. Through glass walls on the right she could see a large dining room with white sheets draped over what appeared to be a long table and chairs. The furniture against the walls was also covered as if the room were being renovated.

Another sound snapped her attention to the open door on the left that led to a kitchen. It was big enough to accommodate the entire living room at her house twice over. Daneya's heart beat faster at the sight of a man washing dishes over the sink. His back was turned to her, offering an easy target. Noiselessly, she crept on bare feet past the island in the middle of the room and swung the rod at his head. At the last second, the man spun around and caught it in one hand.

It was the Drakon!

Daneya's mouth fell open in shock. She couldn't believe she hadn't recognized him sooner. The broadness of his tall frame, the black hair that fell in waves to his shoulders. And his eyes as they stared at her now. Such a vibrant green they seemed unreal. The strong angles of his features were striking and set in a calm expression. Almost as if he'd been expecting her.

A flare of disappointment struck her unawares and she drove the ridiculous emotion away. It didn't matter if this creature was in league with Gabriel. He was a threat in and of himself.

"Take it easy," the Drakon said in a cool tone.

Daneya stepped in and kneed him as hard as she could between the legs. He went down with a loud grunt, the plate in his other hand shattering on the tile floor. She struck him with the rod on his exposed ribcage with enough force to crack ribs then aimed for his skull again.

"Mom!"

She whirled around and nearly dropped her weapon in relief. Mckenzie stood just inside the doorway with Cherri at her side. Behind them was a man with spiked blond hair dressed in loose shorts and a T-shirt. Unlike the others, he didn't look surprised. In fact, he crossed his arms over his muscled chest and leaned casually against the doorjamb.

Daneya backed away from the Drakon then motioned her daughter over. "Come here, baby. Cherri, are you all right? Where's Gabriel?"

Mckenzie walked to her with hands raised. "Mom, it's okay. They're not going to hurt us. They saved us."

"It's true," Cherri chimed in. "They stopped Gabriel from taking us. Just let them explain."

As soon as Mckenzie was within reach, Daneya pulled her close then focused on the Drakon. He was on his feet again, holding his ribs with one arm and watching her warily. "They're lying. This is the Drakon, Cherri. The one I told you about. He can't be trusted."

Her friend glanced uncertainly at both men then cast a look of guilt to Daneya. "I know. They told me."

"What? Then how can you stand there defending them?"

Cherri took a step forward with one hand raised pleadingly. "They might be criminals, but they're on our side. They protected us against Gabriel's attack. Think about it for a minute, sweetie. If they'd wanted to hurt us, they would've done it by now. They are…" She let out a sigh. "They are the lesser of two evils, I know, but right now they might be our only choice."

Daneya couldn't believe what she was hearing. There was no compromising with demons. It was one of the first rules they learned in the DCM. While Cherri might not be a vigilante, she was still a member of their unit. "And Vincent?" she asked. "How do you know they didn't kill him?"

"They said they didn't, and I think I believe them," Cherri said hesitantly.

The blond man straightened with a sneer. "He would've deserved it, though. Bastard shot me in the—"

"Blade," the Drakon cut in. "Not helping."

"Mom, look."

Daneya turned when her daughter tugged on her arm. Mckenzie was holding the .22 short pistol Daneya had given her on her last birthday. It had marked her transition from self-defense training to offensive.

"Saden gave it to me this morning. He said he wanted me to feel safe. And Blade bought me a brand new X-box to play on. An X-box!"

"How did he...?" She turned on the Drakon. "You were in my house?"

"I kinda told him where we live," her daughter admitted sheepishly.

"Mckenzie!"

"He saved your life!" Tears were brimming Mckenzie's lashes now. She swiped at them hastily then said, "You were dying and he healed you. I saw it."

Daneya couldn't speak as she hugged her daughter with her free arm. The raw pain in Mckenzie's voice felt like daggers to the heart. She wanted so much more for her baby. Not a past that wouldn't let them go.

"Let me show you something, Daneya, and I'll answer every question you have." Saden's words were soft and low.

Daneya considered herself a great judge of character, but for the life of her, she couldn't detect any deception in his demeanor.

"No Drakon in the human realm would kill an innocent," he continued. "The consequences far outweigh any gains."

So that was why he'd spared the human guards who had been with Messing. She pointed the rod at the blond. "And what is he? An accomplice?"

"I'm the worst kind of Drakon there is," Blade said in a threatening tone. "The kind that'll terrorize you in your dreams. You haven't known true fear until—"

"Blade," Saden snapped.

"Oh, for fuck's sake!" Blade threw his hands in the air then turned to leave, mumbling, "A guy can't even get his rocks off in this house." From farther away, he yelled, "Don't come running to me when she puts a bullet in your head in the middle of the night and warders come to drag your ass back to hell."

Saden didn't seem phased by this. He merely shook his head then pulled a bottle of orange juice from the fridge. When he handed it to Daneya, she took it reluctantly. "Come with me."

Daneya looked to Cherri who waved her hand. "Go on, hon. Kennie and I will clean up here. And don't worry. I won't let her out of my sight."

She gave a tight smile then kissed her daughter. Cherri's judgment might be skewed by the circumstances, but Daneya knew she would guard Mckenzie with her life. With new determination, she followed Saden up the staircase, trying not to stare at the way he moved with fluid grace. Not even a limp faltered his steps. If he was in any pain from her assault, he didn't show it.

He took her to the bedroom where she'd woken up and stopped in front of an intricately carved, inlaid oak dresser. It was gorgeous, like the rest of the furniture she hadn't noticed until now. What intrigued her most, however, was the fact that everything was covered in a thick layer of dust. As if the room hadn't been used in years.

"So this is your house. You do pretty well for a criminal."

Saden didn't acknowledge the comment. Instead, he pulled a cell phone from his back pocket, punched in a number then handed it to her. "You have one minute to inquire about your boss. The phone is untraceable so don't try to extend your time."

Daneya set down the bottle of orange juice then took the phone and saw her friend Erin's number on the screen. How the hell had he gotten that? She bit back the question and pressed the send button, afraid he might change his mind. Erin picked up the line immediately.

"Hi, Erin. It's Daneya."

"Daneya? Oh my God! Are you okay? We thought you were dead." Erin's voice fairly shook with relief.

"I'm fine," she answered, keeping her eyes on Saden. "Is Vincent with you?"

"No. He went back to his place after they released him from the hospital. Where are you?"

"What was he admitted for?"

"Just a broken arm and a concussion. He was banged up pretty badly, though." After a significant pause, she said, "Daneya, you're starting to scare me. What happened to you? And Cherri and Kennie? Vincent is going crazy trying to find you guys."

She pursed her lips, tempted to take her chances unarmed with Saden and at the same time knowing it was futile. "I can't tell you right now. Just let Vincent know we're all right and I'll see him soon." She hung up and handed the phone back to Saden before Erin could start in on another round of questions.

He tucked it back into his pocket then opened the top drawer and pulled out a black finish Rhino revolver 60DS with a custom etched emblem on the handle. A design she had crafted herself for her favorite weapon. The same one she'd kept locked in a three hundred pound gun safe in the closet of her own bedroom. He opened the cylinder to display the loaded chambers then closed it and held out the gun.

When she reached to snatch it away, though, he refused to let go. Instead, he slowly brought his other hand to her elbow and slid it down to her grip on the rod.

Daneya sucked in a breath, frozen by his closeness. She was not intimidated by him. Not by his cool composure, his masculine scent or the heat of his hand on hers. She was in complete control.

When Saden arched an eyebrow and squeezed her fingers, she flushed and quickly made the trade.

Control. Right.

"He's right, you know," she said flippantly, trying to cover her reaction. "I may not be able to kill you, but I will put a bullet in your head if I find out you're lying to me."

A corner of his mouth quirked up in a cocky half-grin. "I won't lie to you, and you wouldn't come close."

While he went to the closet to replace the rod and fallen clothes, Daneya ground her teeth at his infuriating confidence and tucked the gun into her jeans at the small of her back. "I came pretty close in the kitchen, didn't I?" Granted, the knee to the balls was a cheap shot, but she hadn't been in the mood to play fair.

The look Saden slanted her could've reflected her thoughts exactly. The top drawer of the dresser was full of the rest of her weapons, including knives and holsters. All of which had been hidden in several different compartments at her house.

The urge to feel appreciative conflicted strongly with the anger over her privacy being violated. Not even Vincent had made it past her living room, though it wasn't for lack of trying. For a killer to waltz into her house and go through her things was…

A chilling thought came to her and she checked the next drawer down. It too contained her things. Her very *private* bras and underwear along with more clothes. She straightened with a growl on her lips. "You plan to keep us here."

It wasn't a question, and he didn't try to deny it. Instead, he finished in the closet then moved closer to her near the open balcony doors. The backlight darkened his face and the five o'clock shadow on his jaw. "Only until I take care of Gabriel. You'll be safe here."

"I can take care of myself."

"Drink your orange juice. You lost a lot of blood last night." His voice was soft and held an indefinable emotion.

Heat coursed through her at the subtle reminder of what had happened. Her hand went to her side and traced the small scar there. "He saved your life," Mckenzie had said. It left her feeling humble and confused. What sort of criminal assassin, and a demon at that, went out of his way to save the life of a human? And how had he done it? When she asked him the last question, he shrugged casually.

"It's a power of the Drakonem, therefore accessible to Drakons. We cannot heal completely like them, though. You'll always have the scar."

"How did you find me?"

"I tracked my target to you. Gabriel was recently accused of disposing of a dead human body. I've been assigned to investigate him to find out if he was involved with the human's death."

"It was a female, wasn't it? The human." She swallowed hard when Saden nodded with a frown. It had found her again. The past she'd spent so many years running from. The DCM was a part of it, the result of it, but separate somehow. With them, she was the hunter. A purveyor of justice who sought out the monsters in the dark so normal people could live their lives in ignorant bliss.

In Gabriel's world, she was just one more victim without a face.

"I thought…" She cleared her throat and tried again. "I thought Drakons only killed their targets. Will you kill Gabriel when you find your evidence?"

"You sound very sure of his guilt."

It was a bald lead-in to the question she knew he wanted to ask. She hadn't told anyone about her association with Gabriel, and she wasn't about to start with a stranger. At least not until she could figure out his angle.

He studied her for a minute then gazed outside. "We deliver justice when the authorities of any demon race can't or won't. The ruling house of Vampyres that Gabriel serves has denied the accusation made against him. They claim he is innocent. My Drakonem master feels differently. If I find evidence, I am to take it and Gabriel to my master for sentencing."

"To become a Drakon?" Daneya spat out incredulously. "He deserves to die for his crime!"

"Death is not always a punishment, leisontee. Sometimes, it can be a blessing." His voice was far away, haunted.

From anyone else, she would have ridiculed those words. From him, they sounded as if spoken from experience. For the second time, she wondered what manner of killer he was.

He waved for her to join him on the balcony. It wrapped around the back side of the manor and led to an open, rooftop veranda. The outdoor furniture there lay in abandonment similar to the pieces in the dining room. The table was weather-beaten and the chairs stacked haphazardly against the wooden railing.

Beyond that, miles of beauty surrounded them. It was apparent that the land in the immediate area had been nurtured once. Where the ground was rough with overgrown weeds and bramble, she could imagine smooth, fresh grasses and small ponds by the copses of bushes. About a quarter-mile out was a line of unbroken vegetation. It extended as far as she could see, a thick mixture of evergreens and other coniferous trees.

The manor itself was of shingle-style architecture, from what she could make of the tilted roofs. Ivies crawled freely along its stone walls, burrowing in cracks without hindrance.

"Does this all belong to you?"

The wind teased Saden's hair, catching it in the stubble on his jaw until he stripped it back. He looked more real in the sunlight and not the creature of darkness he'd appeared to be the night they met. "The property is mine. You're welcome to explore it if you like. As well as the manor."

"And if I tried to leave?"

"I can sense you at a close distance. I would find you and bring you back before you could make it off my land." His words were steady and held more of a promise than a warning. He closed the gap between them and lifted a hand as if to touch her face, then let it drop. "You don't have to tell me how you know Gabriel. I'll find enough evidence to incriminate him. Until then, you have my word that I won't let him near you. You and your daughter and Cherri are safe here."

The intensity of his gaze shook her. For the first time since finding him in the kitchen, she wanted to believe him. To trust in him. She felt as though she were sinking in quicksand with him holding the only branch to pull her out.

Many times over the years, she'd imagined what she would do if she met Gabriel again. And in all of those scenarios, he'd been on her turf. Vulnerable and defenseless. Yet when he had found her at Vincent's house, he had proven himself to be the superior. Again. She had almost lost her daughter and her life.

Now, her only protection was her enemy. A demon that confused her with promises of safety. What could he possibly hope to gain from sheltering her and her family?

"Why did you save me?" she asked.

Saden blinked then furrowed his brow. "You are an innocent."

"You must run into innocents all the time in your line of work. Do you take them all home and heal them, too?" From his hesitation, she knew he was hiding a secret of his own. So he did have something to gain, and it had to be more than the information she could offer him. She readied another question, but he surprised her by flashing a smile.

"Only the obstinate ones." He turned and strode to the end of the veranda, leaped onto the railing and stepped off.

She ran to the edge in time to see his body dissolve into dark particles that expanded into the faint form of a dragon. In the blink of an eye, it transformed from a shadow to shimmering light then disappeared altogether in a blur of speed.

After convincing herself that the adrenaline racing through her system was from shock and not concern, she narrowed her eyes at the sky and muttered a quiet, "Show off."

A mental review of all she'd learned didn't tell her much. One thing she did know... Drakons weren't the immoral, mindless creatures her book had warned about. Otherwise, Saden would've used her as bait to incriminate his target instead of giving her the means to protect herself. Even against him.

Still, he was cloaked in mystery and she more curious than ever. She would eventually discover what he was hiding from her. It was only a matter of time.

The rest of the day passed without event. Cherri cooked dinner for the three of them which they ate on the island in the kitchen. It was clear something was bothering her. She was quiet and distanced. When Daneya asked if something was wrong, her friend simply smiled and shook her head. While cleaning up afterwards, Cherri made an offhand comment about wanting her laptop and being frustrated over the lack of an Internet connection. Daneya tried to distract her with conversation then gave up when Cherri became unresponsive.

It was probably just nerves over the situation. All of them were on edge.

Well…the two of them were.

Mckenzie was merely excited to have a break from school, despite the reason for it. Blade kept her busy with video games and idle chatter, for which Daneya was grudgingly thankful. She was too tense to keep up with her daughter's typical frenetic energy. As she checked and cleaned all of her weapons on a covered coffee table in the living room, she watched their interaction. A constant battle of skills amidst challenges and laughter on the only pieces of modern equipment in the room.

Blade broke every preconception she'd had about Drakons. He was wary around her yet acted like an overgrown child in Mckenzie's presence. The two of them were in their own little world most of the time, and for the life of her, Daneya couldn't find a reason to personally hate him. He was just too damned immature.

After giving Cherri a gun to keep with her in her room, Daneya took Mckenzie upstairs and put her to bed. A few hours later, Daneya was still awake. Her thoughts kept wandering to Saden and what he was doing. He hadn't shown up after their talk earlier and she was eager to know if he'd found anything on Gabriel. She also wanted more information on him, which was hard to get when he wasn't around. But he had said she was free to explore the manor.

Mind made up, she got dressed and crept out of the room. What she'd seen of the downstairs had consisted mostly of ghost rooms with white sheets and layers of dust. As if Saden had acquired the house fully furnished from a long deceased family and hadn't bothered to refurbish it. A disturbingly odd choice of residence for a creature whose real home was akin to a hell realm.

She decided to check out the third floor first. It was only half the length of the second and contained two rooms to the right of the hallway. After flipping on the light of the closest one, she stepped inside and stared in wonder.

Three of the walls were made entirely of mirror panels that reflected the bare wooden floor. The fourth running along the outer perimeter of the manor was made of the same seamless stone as the walls in her bedroom. A full array of weapons was mounted to its surface. From katanas and staves to swords and rattans, all had been hung with obvious care by their owner.

It was a weapons practice room.

She gingerly took down one of the samurai katanas and ran her fingers over the recently conditioned sheath. The curved blade inside had also been treated not too long ago. It gleamed brightly in the overhead light and its edge was razor sharp. She was betting the other weapons were just as cared for, though it was difficult to believe they belonged to Saden. All of them were of antique design, some dating back to the eighteenth century. Whoever had owned them previously hadn't purchased them simply for display.

She replaced the katana then went to the next room over. It took some effort to open the door. The hinges creaked loudly from disuse when it finally budged. The air inside was musty and the bulb in the light fixture above was blown. She fumbled along the wall and found a tall lamp plugged in. The light it provided was minimal at best, forcing her to extend its cord as far as it would reach. The room appeared to be used for storage. Stacked atop boxes and large chests were more boxes. The small window on the other side had been boarded over and veils of cobwebs adorned the deep shadows farther in.

After clearing a spot on the floor, she sat down and poked into the nearest box. It held a child's things—dolls, a wooden train set and books that dated back decades ago. The box beneath it carried what she assumed were mementos. Small trinkets and decorations that likely held intrinsic value to whomever they had belonged to. It made her wonder about the previous tenants of the house.

In an unlocked chest to her left, she found blankets and embroidered pillows. On top of them was an old photo album which she took out and opened. The pictures inside were all black and white and themed a boy and a girl separately. They aged with their families as the pages went on until they became an attractive couple. The woman was gorgeous and refined, yet clearly well-built. She wore form-fitting leathers in most of the pictures that pronounced her lean muscles. And the man with her…

Daneya looked closer. He had above average height, wavy black hair, broad shoulders and a face with an edge of mystery. A lot like the current owner of the house. They had the same high cheekbones, firm jaw and similar styles of clothes. The only difference was the maturity lines that creased the face of the man in the photos.

"What are you doing?"

Daneya jumped, her hand flying to the knife she'd brought with her. When she saw it was Saden, she let out a breath but kept her hand where it was. His tone carried all the anger that clouded his expression and darkened his eyes.

"I couldn't sleep."

He remained still for several seconds before relaxing his posture and leaning on the doorframe. She could smell sweat and nature on him through the scent of his leather coat.

"You don't have to be afraid of me."

When his eyes flicked to the knife at her waist, she slowly put her hand down. "Not afraid. Just cautious." His low chuckle seemed to resonate through his entire frame. She compared his face again to the man in the photo. "These are your parents, aren't they?"

There was another significant pause. "They were leisonguardes. Two of the best in the house of Avram."

Leisonguardes. Vampyre warriors. Protectors of their kind against other demon races. A measure of relief swept through her at the knowledge that Saden had been born a Vampyre. Of all the demon races, she was most familiar with that one, and not solely due to Gabriel. She knew they, as a whole, respected the value of human life and followed the law of their gods — that no human shall be harmed by demonkind. That conviction was second only to the value they placed on family.

The fact that Saden's parents were warriors explained the weapons practice room next door. "This was their house."

Saden put his back to the wall and slid down to his haunches, resting his arms on his knees. "My father built it himself for my mother. He had the gift of working with minerals. He could manipulate them with his aethra to alter the shape and texture of the natural elements they're found in, like wood and stone. He crafted this manor and everything in it. The walls, the furniture and floors. They'd planned on retiring here."

She recalled what she knew of a Vampyre's aethra, its soul and source of power unique to each individual. A Vampyre's very essence, containing all the talents and intuition of the Vampyre itself. The aethra could be manifested into a form of pure energy and used to perform tasks dependent upon the Vampyre's proclivities. It resembled a human's natural inclination toward fields such as art, machinery, insight into others and so on.

The aethra was also the reason Vampyres needed to feed. Unlike a human's spirit, the aethra was not self-sustaining. It required a constant replenishment of the energy that was expended through its power.

For the most part, Vampyres chose to feed from their own kind. Their bodies naturally produced excess energy during heightened states of intense emotions, such as joy and pleasure, which they could then share with each other. Pairings with other demon races, even humans, were rare but not impossible. She knew that when stimulated, a human could generate sufficient amounts of energy for a Vampyre to absorb.

Intense fear had been Gabriel's favorite emotion to induce in order to feed.

She forced that thought away and flipped through more pages until she saw a small boy with the couple. He was laughing in many of the pictures with dark unruly curls and expressive eyes. Later, a baby joined them. "You had a brother."

"She was my sister."

Daneya nodded. "And what happened to them?" She already knew the answer. The entire manor was shrouded in absence and loss. Yet, she needed to hear it. How such a loving family could end with only emptiness.

"My parents were killed in our war… Their war with the Djinn," he corrected himself.

His voice held a depth of suffering that made her shiver, but when she looked up, his face was set in a hard mask.

"My sister and I were taken in by a relative after that. This house lay untouched for years before I was able to purchase it."

Daneya studied him for long seconds, a part of her heart breaking over the tragedy of his past. She didn't have to imagine what it felt like to have parents who were ripped away. To be torn from a loving home and placed under the care of strangers. She'd lived that life twice over and still remembered the pain of it keenly. Her sister had been there to pull her through most of it, but then she'd died as well. Leaving Daneya with nothing. Not even a house full of forgotten memories.

The thought triggered another question she had. "How did you buy this place? I thought Drakons lived in the Drakonem realm."

"Many of my targets are wealthy. I take only what they no longer need. It took me three years to save up enough to buy the land."

She couldn't hold back a sneer of disgust. "You scavenge from your victims?" In the back of her mind, she chastised herself for being surprised. The man had committed a crime worthy of making him a Drakon. It was probably in his nature to take what he wanted. Yet, she'd expected more from him.

His laugh was rough and cynical. "Yes, and I kill without remorse. I steal for greed and live like a king in this mansion of riches. Is that what you want to hear?" Strands of hair fell over his eyes as he shook his head. "The bank my parents took a loan from had foreclosed on the property. The manor and everything in it was about to be auctioned off to the highest bidders. I couldn't stand by and let that happen."

A sliver of guilt pierced her for ignoring her instincts and making the wrong assumption about him. Nothing she'd learned of him so far had warranted her animosity. If the roles had been reversed, she'd have done the same to save her family's possessions. And if the food and shelter he provided for her and her loved ones now was paid for by lowlifes like Messing, who was she to argue?

But his sarcasm had stabbed her pride, and before she could think better of it, she asked, "Would your parents appreciate you staying here if they knew what you've become?"

As soon as the words were out, she wished she could take them back. Her rebuke was petty, whether he deserved it or not.

A range of emotions played across his handsome features. That she'd wounded him was most apparent, and it magnified the guilt that clenched her chest. By the time she opened her mouth to apologize, he was calm again. And more distant than ever.

"Go back to sleep, leisontee. You need your strength." He stood up and left as silently as he'd come.

Daneya sat for a while longer, immersed in the tangle of her emotions. Saden was far more dangerous than she'd first suspected, and not because of what he was. He confused her and contradicted the very sense of moral justice she'd built her life upon. The line between good and evil was clear, the two sides as opposite as black and white. Yet he was introducing a gray area she couldn't deny.

How could someone with such good intentions like his have fallen so far from grace? And if she could no longer label him a monster, did that mean she could trust him?

She put the photo album away then went back to her room. Sleep eluded her for several more hours after that. The hurt on Saden's face plagued her thoughts and was still fresh in her mind when she awoke the next morning.

Chapter Six

Phoenix relaxed on his perch in the rafters of the vast opera hall. Below him, the singers had just started their performance of *Les Misérables*, capturing the attention of their audience. He closed his eyes and listened to the harmonic quality of their voices. They rose and echoed off the cavernous walls, joined by the fluidic melodies of the band.

Inside him, he could feel Sasha stirring, emerging from her cocoon of self-isolation. The opera was the only thing she truly responded to anymore. She loved the freedom it inspired through expression. The way the music told of beautiful and tragic stories with the emotions it invoked.

While she never took control of his body to watch the performances, she could feel the experience through him. Phoenix came here as often as he could just to feel her joy flow through him. He would do anything for his little Djinn.

Theirs was a symbiotic relationship, though it differed considerably from the kind a Djinn normally shared with its host.

Originally, the Djinn were created by the god Ekros to be compatible only with Vampyres, the creation of his twin brother, Tallos. A Djinn could live forever in the body of a single Vampyre, sharing control over the body as well as the power supplied by the Vampyre's aethra. The Vampyre in turn fed off the life force of the Djinn's soul, using it to regenerate its aethra.

The ever regenerating healing properties of the Djinn's essence also allowed Vampyres to live eternally and walk in daylight. Due to the toxic reaction of the sun's UV rays to the chemicals the aethra produced beneath the skin, the Vampyre's flesh would otherwise burn like acid under direct sunlight.

Nearly a thousand years ago, a great portion of the Djinn began demanding more and more control over their hosts, eventually locking the Vampyres into their own bodies. No one knew how they'd managed to accomplish that. The natural laws set by Ekros and Tallos that governed their creations should have made it impossible. Those of the Vampyre race still in control quickly rebelled. They refused to allow the Djinn to continue using their bodies as hosts.

The twin gods were forced to amend their laws, giving Djinn the ability to enter any willing host and Vampyres to feed from the energy of other life forms. Though the Djinn remained immortal, the Vampyres lifespans were reduced to approximately six hundred years.

The two races had been battling ever since.

Despite Sasha's almost total reclusion within Phoenix's body, her spirit still made him immortal. He could die if he wanted to. Accept the gift of death that each Drakon was promised at the end of their sentence. But that would mean evicting Sasha from his body, something he would never do. She'd been his salvation once, and now he was hers. If she chose to remain hidden inside him forever, he would go through countless more centuries of torment as a Drakon just to keep her safe.

Phoenix smiled when Sasha began singing along to her favorite song in the musical. Her voice was like whispered silk and bells chiming in his mind. He was about to lean back on the ceiling beam behind him when a burning sensation slammed into his gut. It rippled over his flesh, scorching every nerve before fading to a barely perceptible irritation.

Serrakus was calling.

With a sigh, he got up and climbed over to the suspended walkway hovering behind the stage. Sasha was already retreating into her shell, leaving him with the distinct impression of a pout.

"Don't worry, sweet," he told her mentally. *"I promise you another performance before I start on this next job."*

She responded with a happy trilling noise.

Outside on the rooftop of the building, a gust of night wind blew his long, dark blond hair. He stripped it from his eyes then took flight in his dragon form. Ten minutes later, he came to the area he usually used to create a temporal rift in this part of the city. It led to a sort of back door to Serrakus' part of the Drakonem realm. Another blaze of pain bowled through him just as he took back his corporeal form in the alley behind a biker bar. He staggered and cursed, reaching out to a dumpster for support.

Impatient bastard.

A single burst of Drakonem power from him created an undulating fissure that closed as soon as he was through. The darkness of the corridor he entered was broken by occasional torches mounted to the walls.

He was in the western branch of the dormitory area. It housed those Drakons under Serrakus' control who hadn't yet learned how to scavenge their kills and create a false identity to blend into the human realm. Sometimes it could take years, regardless of whether they knew what they were doing or not.

Here, it was too easy to get in trouble. Warders watched your every move, just waiting for you to fuck up so they could report it to Serrakus. And if you chose to annoy them by being a model Drakon, they'd help you out by setting you up for failure. Serrakus didn't care about truth. He pampered his sadistic warders. If they wanted to entertain themselves with a little extra torture, he was more than glad to oblige.

As a result, most of the residents here spent more time in punishment than out in the field.

Phoenix turned down two more dank corridors, ignoring the few Drakons he passed on the way. If there was one thing he'd learned in his three and a half centuries as a Drakon, it was that friends and criminals didn't mix. He'd seen too many betrayed by their so-called friends for the fleeting favor of Serrakus.

It was better to remain alone. Detached. Easy for him, being the host of a Djinn. It was no secret, and had earned him the hatred of everyone he knew, even fear from many. But they didn't know Sasha, didn't care about her peaceful nature, and he preferred it that way. She was far too fragile to deal with the shit he put up with on a daily basis.

At the end of the hall leading to Serrakus' office, Laurs stood with his arms folded across his massive chest. The warder sneered as Phoenix approached. "How's your little companion doing? Is she going to come out to play the next time I get you alone?"

Phoenix stared at the man's dead eyes, refusing to give in to his taunts. Laurs was one of the few aware of the fact that Sasha would occasionally take control of Phoenix's body when the agony and desolation of his punishments became too much to bear. At those times, he was merely the observer and she the one to experience everything through him.

With Laurs, she had done so only once during a particularly brutal session. Phoenix had been weak from weeks of nonstop torture, the flesh stripped from numerous parts of his body. His mind had been teetering on the brink of insanity. His will so defeated from degradation that he would have given up if not for Sasha's intervention.

He hadn't wanted her to come out around Laurs but she had forced her dominance to protect him. Unfortunately, Laurs had noticed. Phoenix had come to the next day when Serrakus came to heal him. Whatever Laurs had done to him while Sasha had been in control had sent her deep within her shell for months. She'd closed off all communication with him and to this day, wouldn't tell him what had happened.

Laurs chuckled at his silence and opened the door to Serrakus' office. When Phoenix strode past, he leaned in and whispered, "Tell her I miss hearing her screams."

Phoenix stilled, muscles straining with the effort to keep from flooring the guy. It wasn't worth it. Serrakus would have him in chains for the next month. But *damn* it would feel good!

He crossed to the other side of the room where Serrakus sat at his desk. Another Drakonem lounged in the reclining chair of a three piece sectional to the side. Lucius was somewhat of a drifter among his kind. He bored easily and often paid visits to his brethren to break the monotony of his master routine, leaving the charge of his Drakons to his trusted warders. His long, silver hair contrasted sharply with his youthful features. In human years, one might guess his age to be no more than twenty-five.

His new flavor of the year knelt at his feet dressed in a skimpy red and gold belly dancing outfit. Beads and feathers adorned her braided hair and her coffee colored skin glistened with a coating of scented oil. Her back was straight, head held high with the pride of her position as his concubine. She was a newly made Drakon then. Not yet trained in the grueling demands of her role.

Phoenix couldn't blame Lucius, really. It was hardly frowned upon in this reality to take advantage of the willing before their hearts were spoiled by bitterness. Serrakus, on the other hand…

Lucius watched Phoenix through pale, silver eyes, his long legs stretched out and a snifter of liquor resting in one hand. Serrakus was prattling on about the feats of his Drakons, oblivious to the fact that his guest was no longer paying attention. Lucius' gaze was avidly focused on Phoenix.

At the beginning of Phoenix's term, the Drakonem had tried to buy him from Serrakus for the price of three of his own Drakons. Back then, his interests had lain in making Phoenix his sexual slave. When Phoenix had made it clear he'd wanted nothing to do with Lucius' advances, Lucius had respectfully rescinded his offer. It hadn't taken long, however, for either Drakonem to see the real value in him.

The endless skills of a ruthless killer.

Like Phoenix, Sasha was also wanted for crimes against her own kind. Since she was a Djinn and therefore couldn't be trusted to abide by the rules of a

Drakon, her sentence was death without the requirement of paying the dues for her crimes first. However, the only way to kill her was to destroy her essence while she was outside of her host, and Phoenix was not about to ask her to leave. Serrakus could kill him, which would force her out, but that would mean losing an experienced Drakon that he could, essentially, use for the rest of eternity.

So long as Sasha was inside him, Phoenix was under Serrakus' control.

Lucius now wanted him for that same reason. Last Phoenix had heard, the Drakonem's trade offer had gone up to eight Drakons.

"I'll give you ten for him," Lucius said, interrupting Serrakus.

It took a moment for Serrakus to catch on to his proposal. When he did, he scowled and shook his head. "Give it up, my friend. This one has earned me far too much favor with the gods to give up. He does five times the amount of work as most of my other Drakons."

Phoenix breathed an inward sigh of relief. While there was no doubt he would fare better under Lucius' control, Lucius would probably make him a warder in charge of other Drakons. Phoenix had no desire to be a leader of any kind, no matter the benefits.

"There was even mention of extending my vacation this year because of him," Serrakus continued. "With Saden's future contribution, I might be looking at two weeks this round instead of one."

Lucius looked sharply at Serrakus. "I thought you told me Saden's term will be up after he completes his current assignment."

"Ahh, but I haven't told you what his assignment is." Serrakus sat forward in his chair, silver eyes gleaming with mischief. "I sent him after the Vampyre responsible for him becoming a Drakon with the stipulation that he bring his target in alive. Saden never could let go of his grudge against the man. When he gives in to his resentment and kills his target, I'll be able to renew his sentence for another ten or fifteen years, not including time for punishment. The gods will congratulate me for enforcing the laws and Saden will be mine to use for a while longer."

"He doesn't know this is his last assignment?"

"Of course not," Serrakus scoffed. "I can't risk him doing this one by the book. He's one of my best Drakons. I need him to fail."

"How can you be so sure he'll kill his target? I've met Saden and he doesn't seem the type to give in to his emotions so easily."

Serrakus shrugged a shoulder with an utterly guiltless grin on his face. "I may have contacted the target's Rei'jin and informed her of the matter. By now, her council has already told the Vampyre that I'm likely having him investigated. With the Vampyre aware, Saden will most certainly expose himself. That alone would allow me to extend his sentence for another ten years at least."

"That's quite the underhanded scheme you have going there," Lucius said in a tone filled with disdain.

Serrakus either didn't notice or didn't care. He laughed gleefully and downed the rest of the scotch in his glass. "Thank you."

Phoenix kept his expression neutral, though inside he was seething with rage. To intentionally keep a Drakon alive past his or her time to die was beyond cruel. Death was a privilege for them. A right earned through years of abject service. Phoenix freely gave up his right by protecting Sasha. He accepted the consequences. Saden, however, wasn't being given a choice. It went against everything they were promised at the start of their term.

Although he didn't know Saden personally, he knew some of what the Drakon had endured over the course of his sentence. Saden, more than most, deserved an end to his suffering. Unfortunately, the only ones with the power to intervene were the gods, and all they cared about was the order of peace among the demon races enforced by their precious Drakonem.

Serrakus shuffled through a stack of papers on his desk then pushed his chair back. He kicked something on the floor out of his way and stood up. A young-looking Dresidien toppled out from behind the desk before scrambling to get his knees under him. He pushed his legs together in an attempt to hide his nakedness, though it did little good with his ankles in fetters and wrists bound to them behind his back.

Hatred blazed in the depths of his black eyes, an emotion that would see him through the worst of his trials if he could manage to hold onto it.

"Your target is a Vampyre who's been found guilty of murdering two humans for financial gain," Serrakus said to Phoenix as he rounded the desk. "Kill him and return to me when you're done." He placed his hand on Phoenix's chest and transferred the power to track the target.

Phoenix left the room quickly. He didn't stop until he was back in the human realm surrounded by fresh, night air. He inhaled it deeply to clear his thoughts. Saden's predicament still weighed heavily on his mind, yet he could do nothing about it. *Shouldn't* do anything. No good had ever come from helping others.

"You want to," Sasha whispered softly.

He smiled grimly and gazed up at the dark sky. Sasha rarely spoke, and only to get a point across. *"You were listening. It means nothing. Even if I offered my help, he would reject it."* After a minute of silence, he raked his hands through his hair. *"You think I should do it anyway."*

She answered with a rush of approval in her usual wordless manner.

With a quiet chuckle, he took his dragon form and swiftly left the city behind, already regretting his decision to aid the other Drakon.

* * * *

Lucius stared after Phoenix's rushed departure. He pondered absently over the Drakon's ability to intrigue him even after all these years. Phoenix had proven himself a walking contradiction more times than Lucius could remember.

There was the fact that he housed a Djinn despite his horrific past with them. That he seemed to care for her above all else. His will to survive, even though Lucius knew he longed for death. Not to mention his respect for a world that had turned its back on him numerous times.

And now, Lucius got the feeling that Phoenix was about to contradict himself again. The subject of Serrakus' betrayal of this other individual, Saden, had certainly seemed to rile him. Lucius had marked the subtle tension in his frame and narrowing of his eyes while the topic had been discussed.

This from a man who was known for being utterly withdrawn from emotion.

It aroused Lucius' curiosity more than anything had in too long. The stirrings of an idea came to him as he glanced down at his lovely phantom. She just might be of more use to him than he'd first given her credit for.

"Lucius?"

"Hmm?" Lucius looked up, still half lost in thought.

"Don't tell me you're too far gone in your cups already," Serrakus teased. "I asked if you wanted to join me in a little entertainment tonight."

Lucius hid his revulsion with a wide smile, trying not to dwell on what Serrakus' idea of entertainment was. While he detested everything about Serrakus, the man was good for an occasional bit of information. He finished his liquor then stood, pulling his slave up with him. "Sorry, my brother, but I must be going. Thank you for the...interesting company. I hope the gods look kindly on you for your upcoming vacation."

He hurried to the door before Serrakus could form a protest. The warder in the outer corridor pulled a lever that opened a nearby wall panel. Lucius took the hidden stairwell beyond to the rooftop one floor up, his slave following close behind. When they were alone, he turned to Allorha and clasped the flare of her hip. The maroon sky softened her dark Dresidien skin, painting her a deep copper.

Originally, he'd spared her the initiation process of becoming a Drakon one month ago with the intent of using her to spy on his fellow Drakonem. Without a fragment of his soul inside her, she still retained her powers to travel into the minds of others to gauge their thoughts and feelings. It had also saved him the period of adjustment it would've taken for her body to acclimate itself to the rigors of what it meant to be a Drakon. The intense withdrawals of power and spirit that Serrakus' current slave had obviously been struggling with.

Among other things.

It seemed his little plan had finally snagged something worth pursuing. "Tell me, my lush, what you gathered from the Drakon in there."

Allorha leaned into his touch seductively. "The one who calls himself Phoenix, master?" When Lucius nodded, she trailed a finger down the middle of his beige, silk shirt. "He grew upset when Serrakus mentioned his business with the other Drakon, Saden. It was as if he were being betrayed as well. This Phoenix feels strongly for the treatment of Saden, though I cannot understand why. He has no love for anyone except the creature living inside him."

"The Djinn," Lucius supplied.

Her eyes widened and she reared back until he caught her. A normal reaction given the history of the Djinn. They were not known for their synergy with any of the demon races.

"Easy. He is harmless enough unless provoked. Did you learn anything else from him?"

She dipped her lashes in thought. "I think he intends to do something about Saden's situation. I can't be sure. His emotions were conflicted when he left."

Lucius' idea quickly formulated in his mind as excitement spread through him. He was anxious to see what Phoenix planned to do about a situation that was, quite literally, out of his control. While leaving the realm was not an option at the moment, that didn't mean he couldn't send another in his place. By giving Allorha only the power to take dragon form, she could spy for him while still retaining access to her natural gifts as a phantom.

She could be his eyes and ears in the human realm and report her findings to him. Which shouldn't be too difficult a task for her. After all, espionage for material gain was what had landed her in her current predicament. That and the extreme exposure of her kind that had resulted in the death of a human senator.

It would be a risk trusting her to do his bidding unsupervised, but she was a quintessential gold digger at heart, and he the only one to reward her.

"Come, my black-eyed beauty. I have a job for you." He strode some distance away then transformed into his dragon self. Unlike the shadowed imitation of the Drakon, it was a true form bequeathed to his kind by the gods. Muscles stretched and bones split and reknit themselves as his skin changed from pores to scales.

The process took only a matter of seconds. When it was complete, he cradled Allorha in one of his claws and flew back to his territory. There were preparations to make and locations to seek out.

This was going to be fun. He could feel it.

* * * *

Warm sunlight spilled into the room from the open balcony doors. Daneya rolled over in bed and stretched out an arm. She reached farther in her half-sleep, seeking a warm body that wasn't there.

Mckenzie.

She shot up and looked around the room frantically. After searching the bathroom and hallway, she heard a distant peal of laughter and ran outside to the balcony. Down in the yard below stood Mckenzie, Blade and Saden. They were standing in a loose circle speaking in tones too low for her to catch. Once she coaxed her heart out of her throat, she made a mental note to strangle her daughter for leaving the room without letting her know. And to have another talk about unlocking their doors in the morning.

She watched Saden kneel beside Mckenzie and hand her something she couldn't quite make out. Blade ran through the tall grass about ten yards away then waved to them. It wasn't until Saden moved his arm in a pitching motion that Daneya realized they were trying to teach her daughter something. When Saden stood and backed up, Mckenzie stretched her arm in the same motion toward Blade.

Daneya barely caught the glint of steel in her daughter's hand before it was hurled through the air. A heartbeat later, Blade dissolved into shadow then reappeared in another spot at roughly the same distance. Mckenzie adjusted her aim and threw again with Blade doing his disappearing/reappearing act a second time.

They repeated this process twice more in rapid succession. When Blade finally stopped bouncing from place to place, he held up a hand with all four knives in it and whooped loudly. Mckenzie jumped up and down and laughed brightly while Saden clapped behind her.

It dawned on Daneya that they were teaching her daughter to throw knives. Using Blade as target practice. Not exactly an activity she approved of, but the happiness on Mckenzie's face was unmistakable.

A shroud of guilt settled over her. She couldn't remember the last time she'd played with her Kennie or scheduled time for just the two of them. She was always so busy with her job or worrying about keeping them safe.

A part of her wanted to run out and join them. To forget about her trepidations and enjoy the freedom of the moment. It was more tempting than anything had been to her in a long time.

She looked over to Saden and sucked in a breath when she saw him staring straight at her. Even from so far away, she could feel the intensity of his gaze. It made her hyperaware of her body in a way she was unfamiliar with. She touched a hand to her clenching stomach and felt her bare midriff. A quick glance down showed she was still dressed in her night wear. Thin shorts and a tight tank top.

Shit!

When she looked back at Saden, she could swear a smile flitted across his face before he faded to his dragon form and disappeared. Ignoring the heat scalding her cheeks, she went inside and took a cool shower.

It had been two days since she'd last seen Saden and their conversation was still fresh in her mind. The way he'd pulled away from her after she had ridiculed him. She couldn't understand why her opinion had mattered to him. She was just an innocent in the way of his target, wasn't she?

Regardless of what had passed between them, she had to find out more, *do* more than sit around and go stir crazy. She was a fighter only second to being a mom, and she wanted in on bringing Gabriel down.

Now she just had to convince Saden of that.

Downstairs on her way to retrieve her errant daughter, she heard banging noises coming from the laundry room farther down from Cherri's bedroom. She followed the sounds and found Cherri standing in front of the washing machine with both hands covering her face and shoulders hunched in.

"Cherri?" She stepped closer and reached out to comfort her friend.

Cherri swiped an arm across her face then whirled around, flashing white teeth in a smile that almost looked like it hurt. "Daneya! You scared me. I-I was just finishing up here. Did you need something?"

Daneya frowned, taken aback by Cherri's false mood. "Are you feeling okay?"

"Of course," Cherri answered lightly. She hastily brushed her red-rimmed eyes then starting folding clothes from a basket atop the dryer with hands that trembled.

No. Her friend was definitely troubled. "Did Blade say something to you, do anything? If he laid a hand on you —"

"It's not that!" Cherri burst out. She sniffled once then turned around, eyes cast downwards. "I just... I had plans this weekend. I met this really great guy..." Her voice faltered and she shook her head. "It doesn't matter. Maybe it wasn't meant to be. Our lives are too complicated anyway, right? I mean, how do you explain to your date that your best friend's a paranoid weapons specialist and you were held hostage by criminals trying to protect you from a Vampyre maniac?" She let out a slightly hysterical laugh and threw her hands in the air.

Daneya was silent, stunned. Cherri had every right to her frustration, yet her words stung deeply. More than that, Daneya couldn't believe she'd missed such a vital event in Cherri's life. Trust with men didn't come easily for either of them, and for the same reason. How could she have missed the fact that her friend had apparently given hers to a man she didn't even know about?

She cleared her throat and tried again. "I know this is hard, but it'll be over soon. I'll talk to Saden and find out —"

"I know, I know," Cherri cut in, wiping a fallen tear from her cheek. "Things could be worse. I get that. It's just... What if this guy was the one? I really thought..." She waved a dismissive hand and grabbed the basket. "Do what you have to. I'll be in my room."

Daneya watched her go with a mixture of helplessness and resolve. She had to do something, and soon. Saden could try to avoid her all he wanted, but she would track him down if necessary. This was her fight as well.

Chapter Seven

It wasn't until after lunch that Daneya was able to get Blade alone. Mckenzie was taking a nap due to having snuck out of their bedroom at five o'clock in the morning, and Cherri had gone right back to her room after eating.

She found Blade in the living room playing one of the video games he'd brought over for Mckenzie. With a frown, she sat down in an armchair to the side. While the thought of escaping had crossed her mind more than a few times, she was betting if Saden had the power to sense her location, Blade did as well. Besides, the man was always there. Always playing some game or joking around with her daughter.

Blade pounded at buttons on the game controller and let out a snarl. "Argh! Fuckin' like a humming bee!"

"I'd have thought, being a Drakon, you would be a little more…mature," she ventured.

Blade sent her a sideways glance then went back to his gaming. "Maturity is a myth. It's just an illusion we put on for women to get them into bed."

Daneya opened her mouth then closed it. There was no arguing with that statement. She shifted in her seat, suddenly unsure of where to start with the questions she desperately wanted answers to. "Saden told me he was a Vampyre before he became a Drakon. Were you one, too?"

He slanted her a bored, sideways glance. "No. I was a Rakshasa."

A shapeshifter, then. Interesting. "Are you much younger than Saden?" By his Hollywood looks and juvenile behavior, she guessed him to be several decades younger, if not centuries.

The man let out a condescending laugh. "I'll be a hundred and sixty-two this year. That puts me in the lead by almost a century. Look, I ain't exactly into small talk so why don't you get to the point?"

Fair enough, she thought. "I want to ask you a few questions about Saden."

He snorted loudly. "So you can add more fodder to the cannon? Have something else to criticize him for? I don't think so."

"He told you about that?"

"Didn't have to. The fact that he's asked me to stay here while he works nonstop says it all."

She paused, shaken by the animosity in his tone. "Why do you hate me so much?"

This time he set his controller down and gave her his full attention. "You serve an organization that's corrupted by its own insularity. Defensores Contra Malum," he spat out. "Protectors, my ass. The only thing you protect is your freedom to murder demons without restraint. You have no respect for the laws we have to abide by just to keep you humans safe. When was the last time you stopped to investigate the so called 'evil' you eradicate? To find out if they truly deserve to die or not?"

"We always check our targets before taking them down," Daneya said, feeling her own anger rise in defense. "That Vampyre Saden took out the night I met him was responsible for the deaths of at least six humans. He was killing them with the drugs he trafficked. Do you expect us to simply stand by and wait for you Drakons to step in and take care of those situations? I've known at least a hundred more demons like Messing that *we* took down for the protection of mankind."

"Can you honestly tell me they were all like Messing? That every single one of the demons killed by the DCM were guilty of crimes against humanity?"

The response clawing its way out got stuck on the tip of her tongue. She couldn't refute his insinuation. Not completely. There were stories of innocent lives being taken by mistake. She'd even witnessed it once first hand. Her team had been after a rogue Rakshasa, a shapeshifter, and found what they'd thought was his hideout. They'd gone in full bear, only to find out later that the Rakshasa they had killed wasn't their target. It had been logged as an unfortunate accident in the line of duty. A tragedy utterly forgotten by the next day.

"That's what I thought," Blade said with contempt.

A surge of indignation swept through her. "You have no right to pass judgment on me. Yes, there have been mistakes, but they weren't made by me. And at least ours were unintentional. You don't know the hell I've been through because of your kind. Or the family and friends I've lost. Gabriel took everything—" She choked on the last sentence, realizing what she'd been about to say.

Blade's expression softened. "We all have our monsters. You should take more care with whom you choose to face yours."

"Does Saden hate me as well for being a member?"

He chuckled at that. "No. He has a disease. It started in his heart and spread to his groin area."

She shook her head in confusion, but he didn't elaborate. They stared at each other for long seconds, at an impasse on the subject. Finally, she decided it wasn't worth it and gave a small grin. "Siding with criminals would be bad for my reputation."

"Yeah, but we look damn good. That's gotta count for something."

She laughed at that, her thoughts inevitably turning back to Saden. "Tell me what it's like. To be a Drakon."

He sighed heavily and narrowed his gaze. "Do you really want to know?" When she gave a nod, he stared out of the nearby window and said quietly, "It's like nothing you can conceive of. When a Drakonem places a piece of his soul inside you, it takes over and suffocates your body from the inside. Whatever powers a demon inherits from his parents are extinguished. In Saden's case, it was his aethra, his very soul. When he lost it, he didn't only lose his power and need to feed. He lost the ability to embrace life.

"Imagine an existence without the capability to experience true joy, or love, or even a simple moment of happiness. We can remember them, though. Occasionally, the loss can be enough to drive a Drakon insane. The physical deprivation can be just as painful. Sleep never brings rest. Food and drink contain no sustenance. We live in a perpetual state of hunger and thirst."

"I've seen you eat," Daneya interjected softly, trying to wrap her head around what he was telling her. It didn't seem possible to live such a life without losing one's sanity. Let alone to keep one's morals in place. The cruelty of the Drakonem justice system seemed beyond excessive, even for murderers.

She felt beneath her shirt for the scar on her abdomen. He could've left her to die. Or let Gabriel take her, giving him more evidence to the Vampyre's violation of their laws. Instead, he had healed her and offered safety to strangers. She honestly couldn't say if she would be that compassionate without a soul.

Blade cocked his head to the side. "Like I said, we can remember what it felt like. Sometimes it helps. After the soul 'gift', we're stripped of everything that once made us the person we were. Our names and heritage. Our very wills are broken down by anything the Drakonem thinks will do the job. Beatings, isolation, playing on our fears. It doesn't matter how strong you are. I've seen men hold out for years only to break harder than the rest. All a Drakonem has is time, and they use it to their advantage. Their task is to remake us into puppet killers. Train us to do their bidding without question or hesitation with the promise of death at the end of our sentences.

"Some of us manage to hold on to respect for ourselves and life in general. Try to help each other out if that's the goal. Although in Saden's case, I don't know how he survived his first five years as a Drakon with his dignity intact."

"What do you mean?"

He chewed on his lip while studying her, as if trying to decide whether he wanted to answer. "Saden was nine years old when he was made a Drakon."

Daneya felt the blood rush from her face. "That's impossible."

He lifted a single eyebrow. "I guarantee you it's very much possible. Normally, a Drakon is ready for his first assignment within a year of his initiation. Saden was held back for five. Because of his age, it went unquestioned by the gods."

"He was too young to kill." The incongruity of her assumption hit her as soon as the words were out. Killing was probably what had caused him to become a Drakon in the first place.

"Oh, he was ready. You learn fast when your only choices are to follow orders or endure endless torture. It was our Drakonem that found another use for him. Five years, that kid went through a hell that would've shattered grown men." He paused and stared out of the window again. The anger and disgust in his voice sent shivers down Daneya's spine.

Eventually, a small grin curved his lips. "He didn't let that defeat him, though. One day, he got up the courage to sneak through a rift with me into the human realm. By the time I had found out he'd followed me, I couldn't take him back. Our Drakonem would've punished us both. So I let him tag along. The little shit actually ended up saving my hide when I got jumped by a group of criminals associated with my target. Serrakus found out afterwards and we were punished, but Saden had already gotten in his first kill. Serrakus couldn't keep him as a slave anymore."

"A slave?"

Blade jerked his gaze back to her, as if he'd forgotten she was there. Time stretched on until he jumped to his feet and strode out of the room.

"Wait!" Daneya followed him to the kitchen where he grabbed a beer from the fridge. "One more question and I swear I'll leave you alone."

He waved a hand then downed half of the bottle in one swig. "I've already told you too much."

"Please. If I am to trust him, I need to know this." She took his tense silence as consent and plowed on, partially afraid of the answer she might get. "Did Saden commit murder? Is that why he became a Drakon?"

Again, there was an interminable pause. "What did he tell you about Gabriel?"

The change of subject caught her by surprise. "Only that Gabriel is his target, and that he's searching for incriminating evidence of a crime Gabriel committed. Why?"

Blade switched subjects again. "Demon laws don't conform to varying circumstances like your human laws do. Our authorities don't care whether an act of murder was carried out through self-defense or revenge, or whether it was intentional or by accident. It's only the repercussions of the act that are judged. How many people and how greatly they're affected by the crime. If the severity is too high, the authorities will call upon the Drakonem to deal with the offender."

He stopped on his way out of the kitchen to meet her gaze squarely. "Whatever you take from this, make sure you know your true enemy. Saden didn't deserve what happened to him and he doesn't deserve censure from you."

She watched him go as her mind rapidly assessed the last parts of their conversation. That Blade believed Saden's crime was born of forced circumstance was clear, and she was inclined to trust him. She'd conducted enough interrogations to know when she was being lied to.

It was the reference to Gabriel that threw her off. Blade had mentioned him only after she'd asked about

Saden's crime. The two had to be connected somehow, which meant Gabriel was more than a mere target.

Could he have been partly responsible for the conviction of a nine year old? Could Gabriel do that to a child knowing the consequences? She nearly laughed out loud at that. The Gabriel she knew was capable of that and so much more. It twisted her insides to think of the happy little boy in the photo album being stripped of his innocence for a crime that may not have been his fault.

'Five years, that kid went through a hell that would've shattered grown men.'

Blade's words swirled through her mind. She knew what it was to lose everything. To have life turned upside down by events she couldn't control. When her parents had died in a car accident, she'd been only four and her sister thirteen. They'd been split up and thrown into the system. Daneya had spent the next five years dealing with her loss on her own. Being moved around to three different foster homes before Emily had turned eighteen and was able to take custody of her.

Although those had been some of the darkest years of her life, she'd had reason to hope. Emily had never given up on her. What must it have been like for Saden, with no future except that of a trained killer? To be disowned by his entire race and made a Drakon.

A slave.

The term was one she was intimately familiar with. A brand from her past that still haunted her dreams.

She had to talk to Saden. Had to know what happened to him and how Gabriel fit into the picture. The only problem was finding him.

That night, Daneya tucked her daughter into bed but instead of joining her, decided to make use of the weapons room upstairs. It'd been a while since she had practiced weapons combat and she needed to release her pent up energy. Just as she stepped out of the room, she heard a door close at the opposite end of the hallway. Blade never came to the second floor and Cherri's bedroom was downstairs. It could only be Saden.

She rushed down the hallway on bare feet and swung open the door, not wanting to give him the chance to disappear again. When Saden turned at the sound of her entrance, she stopped abruptly and felt heat course through her. He was wearing only a towel that hung low on his hips. Beads of water glistened on his tan skin, and the light from a single lamp marked the contours of his muscles. She couldn't keep her eyes from roaming over the ridges of his abs up to his broad chest covered with a light dusting of black hairs. He was clean-shaven and the lines of his face arrested her as they had before. His green eyes gleamed dully, then narrowed in concern.

"Is everything all right?"

Daneya swallowed past the dryness in her throat. Everything was so far from all right she didn't know where to begin. She'd forgotten the way her body reacted around him, as if it had a mind of its own. He was just a man. A dangerous one at that. Yet, he provoked something inside her that she couldn't control.

"No," she said, at the same time realizing what he'd meant. "Yes. I mean, everything's fine. I just wanted to speak with you."

He frowned slightly then turned to go to a walk-in closet. Daneya's gaze was drawn to several pale lines spanning his broad back in a crisscross pattern. She'd seen the like before once on a kid in one of her previous foster homes. They were whip marks. He came back out a minute later in a pair of black jeans, tugging on a T-shirt. His hair was mussed and fell in wet tendrils down to his jawline.

"What do you want to talk about?"

"I want to know what Gabriel has to do with you becoming a Drakon."

His mouth dropped open in surprise. "I see you've been talking with Blade."

"I have a right to know if he's more to you than just a target," she pressed on. "He was after me, remember? Besides, trust works both ways. You know where I live and who I work for. It's only fair that I learn more about you."

She held her breath, waiting for his answer. While her logic sounded good, she held no real advantage over him. If he wanted to, he could keep her in the dark until he finished his business. Especially since information on Gabriel was tied to his past. But she was determined to piece together his puzzle.

Amusement conflicted with the knot of dread churning in Saden's gut. He'd known Daneya would eventually find out about his involvement with Gabriel. She was too smart and inquisitive to be satisfied with anything less than full knowledge.

He hadn't been prepared to face her, however. Her last line of questioning had affected him more than he'd expected. In all the years he'd protected and admired her from afar, never once had he thought one day he might be judged by her. Or that it would have such an impact on him.

It was ridiculous that her opinion mattered at all. Looking at her, though, he knew he'd be a fool to deny it. She'd captured his heart and interest from the day

Marco had asked him to watch over her, and his feelings since then had only grown.

He sighed inwardly and opened the large oak chest at the foot of his bed. She was right about deserving to know what he did about Gabriel, even if it meant revealing his past. Inside the chest underneath a stack of documents, he pulled out a picture frame bundled in a silk scarf and handed it to her.

She unwrapped it and stared at the photo for long moments. Her dark, honey eyes flicked up to him then down again in disbelief. "This is you and your family…with Gabriel."

"He was my uncle," he said hesitantly, trying to gauge her reaction. Whatever her past was with Gabriel, it couldn't help to know he was related to the bastard.

Absently, she walked to his bed and sat down hard. After reading the caption on the back of the frame, she met his gaze again. "Your name isn't on here."

"I was called Jeremy Aikins at that time."

"That's right. Blade told me your names were taken away. What does Saden mean?"

"'Forsaken' in the Vampyre language. It was given to me by my Drakonem." At her frown, he added, "When I told him the truth about what had happened, he found it amusing. He gave me the name to always remind me of my past."

"And what did happen?"

Her voice was soft, free of disdain, and he wanted more than anything to keep it that way. It seemed fate had other plans. If he didn't tell her, her distrust would eventually turn to resentment and hatred. After this assignment was done, he would no longer spend countless nights wondering what it might be like to have her look upon him as a decent man. He would know it could never happen.

And if he did tell her…

Well, he was a criminal with blood on his hands. She, a vigilante whose job it was to rid the world of filth like him. How could she *not* condemn him for his past? His only gift, only future, was death. There was no sense in fighting what he couldn't change.

He scrubbed his face then leaned back against the dresser behind him. "Gabriel's preyuna and unborn child died during childbirth years before I was born."

"Preyuna?" Daneya cut in.

"His mate, or wife in your language. After that, he became a korvaute, a leader in the field of biology, and devoted his entire life to the propagation of the Vampyre species. He tried everything, even using the power of his aethra to manipulate the genetic code of female Vampyres in hopes of increasing the amount of eggs they're born with. Nothing worked. When my parents died, he accepted responsibility for me and my sister. I took care of her and went into training to become a leisonguarde like my parents.

"One day, he came home and told me the Djinn were about to attack his facility. That they wanted to destroy his research and kill anyone associated with it. He feared with the information in his files, they would be able to track down everyone involved, including me and my sister. Since my power was the ability to read and alter the functions and operations of electronic devices, he wanted me to destroy his computers after he'd saved as much information as he could. I didn't know…"

He remembered that day clearly. The urgency and sense of duty that had compelled him to do whatever it took to save his remaining family from the Djinn. He'd have done anything Gabriel had asked.

"He took me to the control room at his facility then left to get the rest of his assistants out. I sent my aethra into the mainframe, but when I started the process of destroying his files, I discovered the information they really held. Gabriel wasn't running from the Djinn. He was in league with them. He'd been using their power to circumvent the need for bonding, allowing him and his men to successfully impregnate human females. He had lied to me. By the time I'd pulled out of the mainframe to question him, it was too late. He had rigged his security system to blow just minutes after it detected my interference.

"The explosion should've killed me. When Gabriel and his men came back and found me alive in the rubble, they tried to finish the job before their authorities got there. They failed."

His skin tingled in memory of the steel cable Gabriel had used on his back. A group of Gabriel's men had joined in after that, breaking most of his bones with their boots and fists. How he had survived the next day of his trial and sentencing was anybody's guess. He would've welcomed death, especially after being told the lies Gabriel had stacked against him to the Vampyre council.

"Next thing I knew, I woke up, healed, in my Drakonem's office. Serrakus told me Gabriel had claimed that I blamed him for the death of my parents. That I sabotaged his research out of revenge and blew his facility. Three humans were found dead in the wreckage. When I told Serrakus the truth about Gabriel's dealings with the Djinn, he was pissed off but for a different reason.

"Apparently, one of his Drakons had witnessed a Djinn kidnapping a human female and taking her to Gabriel's facility. Gabriel must have found out that he was being investigated and used me to destroy the evidence of his crimes. A few days later, Serrakus discovered that the humans who'd died in the explosion had been hosts to three of the Djinn working with Gabriel."

Saden let the familiar blanket of his cold rage keep his other emotions in check. He couldn't look at Daneya. Couldn't face the scorn that was probably burning in her eyes. It was because of him that Gabriel had been able to continue his experiments on humans. If he had stopped to think for just one second—put his reason above his pride and seen through his uncle's lies, maybe…

"Why didn't you tell this to your council?" she asked in a hushed tone. "They could've acquitted you of the charges."

He laughed sarcastically. "And pitted the word of a renowned korvaute responsible for increasing their numbers and ending their war with the Djinn against that of an orphaned nine year old? They would never have believed me. Besides, it couldn't change the fact that three humans were dead because of me. And Serrakus wouldn't have given me up regardless."

Deafening silence filled the room. He slid his gaze to the door, waiting for Daneya's back to fill it as she left. He waited for the fury of her shouts and insults. For her to fly at him in a rage. When none of that happened, he risked looking back to her and frowned at the expression on her face. It was calm. Contemplative.

"It wasn't your fault," she said finally.

Saden could only stare in disbelief. "It was because of me that Gabriel got away with what he was doing. I still have no idea how many females he's used and thrown away since then. If I had let the Drakon investigating him finish the job, Gabriel could've been stopped years ago."

Her next words punched the breath out of him. "Blade told me you were Serrakus' slave for five years. What did he mean?"

He was going to kill Blade next time he saw him. "It's irrelevant," he said, shaking his head.

"Saden—"

"Don't!" He moved to his desk beside the balcony doors and took a knife from his harness to check the blade. The air in the room was filled with tension so thick it sang along his nerves. That period of his life had no bearing on their current discussion. It was a dead memory, buried in the grave he had erected for it in his mind. There was no need for her to know.

The picture of Daneya's fear-stricken face in Gabriel's file flashed before his vision. The image he hadn't stopped thinking about since he'd seen it in the Vampyre's house. For all he knew, she had been Gabriel's slave at the time the picture was taken. Before Saden had become her guardian. If that was the case, could his past really be so different from hers? The thought sent chills down his spine.

He wrapped his hand around the blade and squeezed, pressing harder when the edge bit into his palm. "The Drakonem get bored from being trapped in their realm for most of each year. It's not unusual for them to give certain Drakons the opportunity to take a break from their duties in exchange for sexual favors. Serrakus just doesn't care whether his slaves are consenting or not." A drop of blood fell from his palm and splashed onto the desktop. He stared at it unseeingly until a hand reached out and covered his own around the blade.

He lifted his gaze to find Daneya watching him. Her eyes were so steady and clear, he wanted to escape into them. Leave the brutality of his life behind and lose himself in her strength. For it was nothing less that kept her with him now.

She slowly opened his fingers, set the blade aside then wrapped his palm in the silk scarf. "It wasn't your fault," she reiterated. "Sometimes things happen that are beyond our control."

Her faith struck him deeply. She had every right to curse him for his mistake in trusting Gabriel, yet here she was offering solace. Standing so close he could barely breathe. "How do you know?"

Her brow creased as a tear fell past her thick lashes. "I have to. Otherwise my life doesn't make any sense."

That tear crushed all of his reservations. Never had he thought to be in the position to comfort the one who'd unwittingly kept his sanity all these years, but he wasn't about to fail her.

Not when she needed him.

He cupped her face in both hands and tilted it back. Her beauty was mesmerizing, in spite of the inner turmoil that strained her features. When he slanted his mouth across hers, he could feel her rigidness. Taste the salt of her tear on his lips. Then she opened to him and made his head spin with a rush of pleasure.

He delved into the cavern of her mouth. It was so much sweeter than anything he could've imagined. Her courage and vulnerability. The way her tongue danced with his in a slow caress. More than that was her willingness to trust him, even if only for the moment.

He breathed in her soft sigh and whispered, "You are braver than anyone I've ever known, leisontee."

"You keep calling me that. What does it mean?"

"Little warrior."

She splayed her hands over his chest, a small smile lifting a corner of her mouth. "You think I'm brave?"

Conviction filled his voice when he answered, "I know you are."

After a brief pause, she stepped into him, bringing their bodies flush to one another. Warmth seeped into him and he wrapped his arms around her. Wanting more, needing more. This time when their lips came together, she held nothing back. He could feel her urgency in every sweep of her tongue. It was intoxicating and sent a wave of sensation coiling through his gut.

"Stay with me tonight," she murmured softly.

The hushed plea was more than he could resist. He clasped her slender waist and lifted, moaning when her legs wrapped tightly around him. Her pelvis pressed against his burgeoning thickness and shot a spike of adrenaline through his system. They stayed locked in their embrace until he lowered her onto the bed. His hands seemed to have a mind of their own as they traveled down her narrow ribcage to the hem of her tank top. Her skin beneath was incredibly smooth, tempting him to explore further.

Everything about her body contrasted sharply to his. She was small to his large frame, soft to his hard flesh. Still, he could feel her firm muscles rippling beneath his hands. He kissed his way down the column of her neck to the shallow of her throat. It wasn't until she pulled off her top to reveal her bare breasts that he came back to himself.

This night wasn't going at all how he'd expected. It was better, by far, but still dangerously out of control. He didn't want this to be a mistake. To see the regret on Daneya's face when she woke up in the morning.

"Are you sure about this?"

"Not a bit," she said breathlessly.

When she reached to pull him down for another kiss, he resisted hesitantly. Part of him wanted to slap himself for being cautious even as he knew it was necessary. "Daneya—"

She huffed exaggeratedly then looked at him with such yearning, it scattered his thoughts. "I can't say that I know what I'm doing. I've never done this before. But I do know I'm tired of being safe. My whole life has been a series of calculated risks and missed opportunities. I'm afraid all the time of what *might* happen. Just once, I want to know what it's like to be free." She brushed her fingers lightly across his lips. "Please, Saden. Give me this."

He took possession of her mouth again and closed the distance between their bodies. Her words circled his thoughts like a desert storm, hot and furious. She had no idea what they meant to him. For so long, she had been his savior, reminding him what it was to be free with her perseverance. Now, she was asking him to return the favor. The irony of it left him feeling lightheaded.

He spanned her tapered waist and moved lower to take each of her rosy nipples into his mouth, sucking on them until they were firm and hard. She arched up with a low moan and threaded her fingers through his hair. Moving farther down, he trailed kisses over her small, round belly and slowly tugged off her cotton pants.

Long, slim legs parted for him and he suppressed a shiver at the sight of her glistening entrance. He knelt between her thighs on the edge of the bed then leaned down to nibble on her neck while bringing one hand to the nest of her curls. They were soft and slick with her desire. When he pushed in first one finger then another, the feel of her muscles clenching him made him swell to the point of pain.

Without warning, she flipped him over and straddled him. Her hair fell like a curtain around them, closing them off to the rest of the world. She hurriedly took off his shirt then skimmed her lips over his buds, flicking them with her tongue. The sensation of her nails gently raking his abs to his waistline had him near panting with anticipation.

She sat up then and smiled, a lock of her hair covering half her face in coy mystery. But when she began unfastening his jeans, he saw her hands tremble slightly. It reminded him with sudden clarity that she was no more experienced than him at making love. Perhaps even less so. Not once had he seen her take home a lover or even spend casual time with a guy. For a while, he'd had his suspicions about Vincent, though they'd never been confirmed.

He helped her pull down his pants then kicked them to the floor. The rush of cool air on his aching erection was replaced by the warmth of her hand. A groan was torn from his throat as she stroked him tightly. Pressure rapidly built within until he thought he might burst.

Her hesitancy returned when she leaned in close and bit her lip. "Should we use protection?"

"Drakons can't carry disease or impregnate women. Part of the package." With a deep kiss, he rolled her over and cradled her body beneath his, wanting as much as he could get. If this was the only intimacy they shared, it would have to last him through the dark expanse of his future.

He lay between her thighs then stilled when his tip rubbed against her damp threshold. Memories of his past experiences crowded his mind. This wasn't like the occasions where he'd sought temporary, physical release. For as strong as Daneya portrayed herself on the outside, he knew she could be just as fragile, and not only in spirit.

"I don't want to hurt you."

She framed his face with her hands and whispered, "I think I know that now."

When he slid past her cleft and lodged himself in her heat, they both let out gasps. The feel of her silken core gripping him sent tendrils of fire racing through his bloodstream. He forced his eyes open and stared down at her, watching for signs of distress. Her breaths came faster as he rocked his hips, burying his shaft deeper inside her with each thrust.

"Are you doing okay?"

She nodded and curled her legs around him. The change of angle urged him farther into her. He drank in her soft sighs with long kisses, quickening his pace as her sheath pulsed around him.

Happiness spread throughout his entire being, or at least the closest he could come to the memory of it. In her arms, his past melted away like so much unwanted tension. He wasn't a killer with a damned soul. He was merely a man loving a woman who needed him.

For this one moment in time, they were free.

He sat up and pulled her into his lap, lifting her hips in time to his fast pace. She took control and rode him with a passion of her own.

Head thrown back, she clutched at his shoulders and moaned, "Saden."

"I'm right here, beautiful."

And he was. The pressure mounting in his groin reached a searing peak. At the last second, he dragged her mouth to his and swallowed her scream. His own orgasm bowled through him with fierce intensity. It raced along his nerves and took his breath away.

They remained in each other's arms until the fever gradually passed. She buried her face in his neck and tickled his skin with a soft laugh. "Thank you."

He was about to respond when a distant call stopped him.

"Mom?"

Daneya lurched back and stared at him with wide eyes. "Kennie." She scrambled off of him and threw on her clothes in a rush.

Saden raked a hand through his hair, torn between trying to keep her and letting her go. "Daneya—"

"Mom," Mckenzie called again.

Daneya straightened her shirt then paused with her hand on the door. "Will I see you tomorrow?"

"Yes, but—"

She was gone in the next instant.

He growled quietly and pinched the bridge of his nose. Dead air filled the room in her absence. Her parting words floated through his mind. While he hoped they meant she wanted to see him again, tomorrow wasn't exactly something he was looking forward to. The time had come to gather more information on Gabriel, and the Vampyre's recent increase in security wasn't going to make it easy.

Since resting was out of the question, he got dressed and prepared for another round of scouting. It was going to be a long night if he couldn't find a way to get Daneya off his mind.

Chapter Eight

The air was crisp with an overcast of gray clouds in the sky. Fortunately, with the strong gusts of wind, it should clear up shortly. He needed as much sunlight as he could get for his plan to go through without a hitch. Saden took back his true form on the porch steps in front of the manor. Blade was waiting for him by the door with a beer in one hand.

"Don't you ever get tired of drinking that?"

"You'd drink it too if you could remember what it does," Blade shot back.

He shook his head and strode inside. "Have you seen Daneya this morning?"

"Why? Missing her already?" The teasing humor in his voice made Saden eye him warily. He held up both hands with a wide grin. "Hey, the vents in these walls carry sounds like a lonely siren."

Saden sneered in disgust. "You're a sick man."

"I try. Haven't seen Daneya yet. Kennie and Cherri bomb are in the kitchen."

He headed that way with Blade following behind. Cherri didn't bother to acknowledge their entrance from where she was washing dishes at the sink. Her melancholy mood of late was getting worse by the day. Though Blade had informed him that she stayed mostly to her room, it worried Saden. In his experience, the old adage of having to watch out for the quiet ones was no misnomer. Especially when it wasn't their natural state. Something was troubling the woman and it put him on edge.

What sounded like an argument faded when Mckenzie saw Blade step into the room. She jumped up from her seat at the island and ran to him with a sandwich in her hands. "Taste this and tell me it isn't made with pure awesomeness."

Saden peered over at the banana and pickle slices drooping from the peanut butter filling and snorted. "Go ahead, Blade. Tell her."

Blade shot him a dark look then ruffled the kid's hair. "I don't need to taste it. It was made by you so it has to be awesome."

Mckenzie beamed a full set of pearly whites then went back to her chair. Cherri pursed her lips in disapproval, but didn't say anything. Instead, she dried her hands then kissed Mckenzie on her temple. "I'll be back for lunch, brat. Don't get into too much trouble while I'm gone."

After the woman left, Mckenzie swallowed her mouthful and got up again. "Why do you guys always wear trench coats whenever you go outside?"

Blade and Saden glanced at each other then walked to the island. One by one, they pulled out their weapons from sleeves, pockets, harnesses, belts and boots. By the time they were done, half the island was covered in an assortment of blades, garrotes and other toys they'd acquired over the years.

Mckenzie's eyes were round and her mouth a perfect saucer. "Wow! Can I play with some of them?"

"No," they answered in unison.

Her little face pulled down in a pout. "But you taught me how to use throwing knives yesterday."

"Those can be used in self-defense," Saden replied. "I don't want to undermine your mom's rule about limiting what weapons you use until you're sixteen."

"She told you about that?"

He realized his mistake too late. Like everything else he knew about Daneya and her daughter, he'd learned from spying on them. Hovering close by in his dragon form or sitting outside their windows at night while not on assignment. Not exactly a truth he wanted to make them aware of yet, if ever. A single, lifted brow from Blade told him he was on his own on this one. "I mean, I would guess that was her rule. It's what I'd do if I had a daughter."

Mckenzie seemed to accept this with a gloomy slump of her shoulders.

When they were done loading their weapons back up, Blade tossed his empty bottle into the trash and pulled another from the fridge. "Cheer up, half-pint. I'll show you how to use a grappling hook later to—" He grunted and nearly doubled over as blood rushed out of his face.

"Blade?" Mckenzie said in alarm.

Saden grabbed her arm before she could run over. "He's fine, little one. Just needs to take a quick breather."

Blade recovered with a grim smile. "No worries." To Saden he said, "I'll be back soon."

Saden nodded, figuring it should only take his friend an hour to get his next assignment from Serrakus. Which gave him plenty of time to make the window for his plans on Gabriel. "Why don't you make a list of the music you like and I'll pick it up while I'm out later," he said to Mckenzie in an attempt to distract her. He went to the counter and poured a cup of coffee.

"Anything I want?"

"Anything your mom won't try to kill me for."

"Well, that cuts the list in half," she muttered. "You won some points last night, you know."

He sputtered and coughed around the coffee in his mouth. "Excuse me?"

"With Mom. She was smiling for the first time in days when she came out of your room. I don't know what you said but whatever it was, it worked."

He tried to ignore the stirring in his chest without success. He'd made her smile. Definitely an improvement. With effort, he reined in the urge to ask Mckenzie what else her mom might've said or done after leaving his room last night.

"Mom told me you were a Vampyre before you were…changed. Is that true?"

Saden paused in his inventory of the groceries they had left and gave her his full attention. "It is."

"So that means you had a power, right?"

"Yeah. Basically I could manipulate electronics."

"Oh." She studied her sandwich as if it somehow contained the mystery of life. "Is it true that Vampyres can bond with humans to have babies?"

Apprehension set his instincts into overdrive. These weren't normal questions for a nine year old. Even one who belonged to a member of the DCM. "It's rare but it happens. Why the sudden history lesson, Kennie?"

"If a half Vampyre, half human kid had a power as well, when would it start showing?"

"Kennie—"

She held up both hands and adapted a perfect expression of innocence. "Just curious. Really."

That explanation didn't fly with him for a second. He made a mental note to ask Daneya how much she wanted her daughter to know about Vampyres. "Normally, Vampyres can access their powers through their aethras at three or four years old. While a hybrid is biologically born a full-blooded Vampyre, it wouldn't come into its power until around the mid-teen years."

As she nodded in contemplation, he noticed faint shadows under her eyes that hadn't been there before. Her skin wasn't showing its usual healthy glow either. He felt her forehead with the back of his hand. "Are you feeling okay?"

"I'm fine."

Daneya walked in at that moment, worry creasing her brow. "What's wrong? Are you sick?"

"Nothing's wrong!" Mckenzie said in exasperation. She flashed Saden a look he could swear begged him not to speak of their conversation then carried her plate to the sink. "Can I play video games until Blade gets back, Mom? He said he wouldn't be long."

"Sure, sweetie." When Mckenzie passed by on her way out, Daneya squeezed her daughter in a fierce hug and kissed her temple. "Love you."

"Love you, too."

Saden watched Daneya with no small amount of trepidation. Half of him expected to be accused of taking advantage of her last night. The other half was caught up in the memories that still permeated his thoughts. Her tenderness beneath her warrior exterior. It was that contrast in her nature which appealed to him most.

She marched over to him until only a yard separated them. "I'm going with you."

"What?" It was then he noticed the black, long-sleeved shirt, cargo pants and combat boots she was wearing. A gun was holstered at her waist and her hair was pulled back in a tight braid.

"You're going to infiltrate Gabriel's house while the sun is high, right? It gives you the advantage since UV rays don't affect you anymore."

"How did you know?"

She cocked her head to the side. "I've been on enough missions to know when one's about to go down."

He almost grinned at her brazen confidence. Almost. There was no way in this realm or any other he was going to let her go. Too many variables existed that could put them both at risk. One little mistake and she could end up in Gabriel's custody. He would be recalled by Serrakus for working with and endangering a human while conducting his assignment. Not to mention the complications of getting her in and out of a mansion patrolled by leisonguardes undetected.

No. It was not going to happen.

"I think it's best if you stay here."

"And I think you could benefit from a partner in this," she countered. "Gabriel knows you're on to him and he'll be ready. You need someone to watch your back."

"This is a simple recon job. I'm just getting information on him. I'll be in and out."

She narrowed her eyes in scrutiny. "You're afraid I'll get hurt."

I'm always afraid of that. He touched her cheek gently, more than relieved when she didn't pull away. "There is that."

"Well, I'm not a naïve little girl anymore," she said in a hard tone. "I can take care of myself. And you."

Those last two words stunned him for a brief second. While he knew she longed to go for her own reasons, the knowledge that a part of her could conceive of wanting to protect him made him want to forget about his mission, take her upstairs and pick up where they'd left off. Fortunately, his irritation at her persistence was enough to keep his head clear.

"And what will you do about Mckenzie if anything goes wrong?"

"I trust Blade to return her and Cherri to Vincent if I don't come back. Besides, we won't fail. This is just like every other job I've done since joining the DCM."

"Is it? Because it looks to me like this is some kind of personal vendetta to get back at Gabriel for trying to kidnap you." Or revenge for kidnapping her the first time. It made him think again about the peculiar questions McKenzie had asked. Her cheeks flared a bright crimson and her hands curled into fists. "Even if it were, could you deny the same? You can't tell me that when your Drakonem gave you this assignment, you didn't feel some urge to exact justice for what Gabriel did to you."

He growled softly, unable to argue with that. At this point, she and Mckenzie were the only things keeping him from giving in to the temptation of killing Gabriel. Consequences be damned. "I can't let you go, Daneya."

"Why not?" she cried, flinging her hands up in the air.

Because you're mortal and I'm not! he wanted to shout.

They glared at each other in tense silence until she seemed to drop her anger and stepped closer. So close, he could feel her breath on his neck. "I don't regret what we did last night. But I'm not above putting that bullet in your head if you try to keep me here." Her threat was undermined only by the yearning in her eyes. "Please, Saden. I need to do this."

He was fucked. He knew he was, even as he cursed himself for his weakness when it came to her. With a low groan, he jerked his chin toward the door. "If you're coming, you'll need better weapons than that gun."

Saden ignored her triumphant grin and led her to the weapons room on the third floor. A quick revision of his plan formed in his mind as he looked over the instruments hanging on the far wall. He chose several compact items she could carry on her person without sacrificing her speed or range of motion.

"I'm best with a gun, though," she said, looking askance at the set of shurikens he gave her.

He bit back the fact that he was already aware of that at the last moment. "A Vampyre's power lies in the manipulation of whichever element they are most in tune with. Natural or fabricated, physical or mental, the element can be comprised of any one of those things. The sound of a gunshot will give you away. Once your position is made, the Vampyre can turn your weapon against you. I've seen a man shredded alive from the blast of a round being magnified by a thousand and sent back at him in calculated currents. That was done by a Vampyre with the ability to manipulate wind."

She gaped inelegantly then handed him her gun, replacing it with the shurikens. "Good to know."

"Keep in mind, we're there to get information. Nothing more. Kill only if you have to and get out when I say so."

"In and out. Got it."

"I have a few things to check on before we leave. I'll meet you downstairs."

She opened her mouth as if to say something but instead, pulled him down by the nape of his neck for a searing kiss. His arms folded around her of their own accord, crushing her to him. Everything else disappeared as it had last night. There were only the two of them and the acceptance she made him feel.

A sliver of reality pierced his conscience at the danger he was falling into. His emotions around her were beginning to spin precariously out of control. The line between innocent and protector becoming blurred each time she touched him. He had to keep a level head. Had to be able to walk away when the time came to let her go.

She bit his lip teasingly before breaking apart and leaving the room. Saden took a minute to readjust himself and collect his thoughts. Something told him he was in a lot more trouble than he'd bargained for.

After a shower and change of clothes, he went to the garage. The sedan he'd purchased the morning after taking in Daneya and her family would stay in case Blade needed to get Mckenzie and Cherri out of the manor. While he thought the motorcycle would better suit Daneya's style, it was too loud with zero protection. Which left his pride and joy—a two door Maserati Gran Turismo MC, built for speed with an engine that purred like a kitten.

He stripped out of his trench coat and popped the hood to check the fluids.

At a whisper of sound to his left, he spun around with a knife already in hand. A man emerged from the shadows wearing black leathers that set off his dusky blond hair. He was as tall as Saden with a familiar goatee and relaxed posture. "Phoenix?"

The man greeted him with a dip of his head. "Saden. How are you?"

Saden gripped the knife harder, a sneer curling his upper lip. While he didn't know Phoenix personally, he was well acquainted with the guy's history. A traitor among his own kind. The worst kind of criminal there was. It was said he had led a group of Djinn to his clan of Rakshasas. Every man, woman and child had been slaughtered mercilessly except for him. By the time the Drakonem had captured him for his crime, he'd already become a host to one of the Djinn involved, making him immortal.

That had been over three centuries ago.

Saden understood Serrakus' greed in keeping Phoenix alive for so long. However, if given the chance, Saden would kill the murderous betrayer and the Djinn that hid like a coward inside his body. Their union was an affront to everything the Vampyres and Rakshasas valued. The peaceful way of life both races strived for. Phoenix's reputation for being an utterly cold, ruthless Drakon only cemented Saden's view of him.

And the asshole was trying to pass off pleasantries in his garage as if they were old acquaintances.

"What the fuck are you doing in my home? Serrakus gave me two weeks to complete my assignment."

"I didn't come here on behalf of Serrakus. I came because of him."

"What do you mean?"

Phoenix trailed his fingers over the vinyl covering the motorcycle. "You should be careful who you choose to keep close. In this life, relationships can only bring complications. Especially with humans involved."

Son of a bitch! Saden's heart punched into overdrive. Serrakus couldn't know about Daneya and Mckenzie, otherwise he'd have sent warders after him. Not a lone Drakon. Which meant Phoenix had been spying on him and decided to play a little game of blackmail. There could be no other reason for his presence. "Are you threatening them?"

"I'm warning you. Forming attachments may not be in your best interest right now."

He flipped the knife from hilt to tip and flung it at Phoenix, done with the man's cryptic bullshit. Phoenix dodged the blade a second before Saden slammed him hard into the wall. "If you lay a hand on them or tell Serrakus, I will make sure you spend the next century locked away with only the warders to keep you company."

Phoenix's gray eyes flashed in the dull light. "I'm not here to harm them," he ground out. In the next breath, he had Saden's back to the wall. "You're on your last assignment. Serrakus is setting you up to take a fall so he can keep you longer. I heard him bragging about it to Lucius a few days ago."

Saden frowned, too stunned to speak. Gabriel was his last job? If that was true, it explained why Serrakus had tipped off Gabriel to the investigation by alerting the Rei'jin of the house of Avram. He swallowed heavily as the implications of Phoenix's news hit him.

He could be free.

No more degradation or pain. Days of endless suffering and nights filled with bloodshed. He could be at peace in the oblivion of death. For him, there would be no afterlife or ritual ceremony of his passing. It would be as if he'd never existed in the hearts and minds of his people. The gift of an end to erase his shame.

Pure elation filled him, arrested immediately by the thought of Daneya and Mckenzie. Even if he were to take care of the threat Gabriel posed to them, it might not be enough. He was convinced now that the Vampyre had continued his operations after setting Saden up fifty-six years ago. There was no telling how much his enterprise had grown since then. If Daneya was a loose end because of her knowledge, another Vampyre—or Djinn—would merely take over in Gabriel's absence and come after her.

While Blade had sworn to protect her and her daughter if anything happened to him, it wasn't the same. Daneya was fearless in the field, and sometimes brash. Saden had saved her countless times when she'd gotten in over her head. He wasn't sure if Blade was ready to handle her from the sidelines.

And what would happen when Blade inevitably made some mistake to warrant a prolonged punishment? No one would be there to watch over Daneya and Mckenzie.

"Why are you telling me this?"

Phoenix backed away, his face expressionless. "I have my reasons."

Whatever they were, Saden didn't trust him. But neither did he have a choice. It was too dangerous to move Daneya and her family to a different location. He couldn't risk them trying to escape while he was doing his job. And Phoenix would simply follow them if he wanted to. If Saden tried to put him out of commission, Serrakus would find out and punish them both.

He strode back to the entrance and hit the panel to open the garage door. "Get out. Show your face around here again and I'll stay alive just to make you suffer."

Tension permeated the air between them. The door leading to the manor swung open and Daneya peered in curiously. Saden jerked his gaze back to Phoenix where now there was only empty space.

"I heard voices," Daneya said. "Is Blade back?"

He scraped a hand through his hair and shook his head. "I was just talking to myself. I'll be in soon."

She glanced around once more then went inside.

When Blade returned half an hour later, Saden and Daneya left with Mckenzie and Cherri looking on solemnly from the front porch. He wondered how much Daneya had told them of what was going on. Probably as much as he knew she always did. Minimal truth with colorful assurances that she would come back safe and unharmed.

It was what his parents had done with him when they were alive. Only they hadn't been able to follow through with their last promises to return.

He vowed silently to do everything within his power to make sure Daneya kept hers.

Chapter Nine

About ten miles from Gabriel's mansion, he turned onto an abandoned dirt road that came to a T some distance from the highway. The intersecting road had once connected Gabriel's land to his neighbors' and was now overgrown with weeds and brush. Still accessible, however. It came to an end at the bottom of the slope the mansion rested on where they both got out. A brief scan with his Drakonem's power told him all was as expected.

After putting on his trench coat, he pointed to the sliding glass doors leading into the mansion from the back. "Wait here until I signal you from those doors. Gabriel is asleep in his bedroom in the right wing on the first floor. I'll take care of the four leisonguardes patrolling the left. We're going up in the middle to his office on the second floor. Stay close to me and as quiet as possible. Got it?"

She looked off to their left where the roof of another building was visible above the surrounding trees. "What about that? Is it owned by Gabriel as well?"

"His laboratory, which I'm pretty sure is a front for his operations. It runs on a skeleton crew with a joke of a security system. We won't find any information there."

As he started to dissolve to his dragon form, she called out to him. "Be careful."

He smiled then took flight. The glass on the sunroof he'd accessed previously was still cut, allowing him to lift it with a suction cup and enter undetected. Gabriel hadn't installed any security measures in his own home. Likely too cocky to think a Drakon would dare break into it with leisonguardes there.

The outer hallway opened up on the left to a banister overlooking a parlor room. A man and woman lounged on a sofa below watching television with their backs turned to him. Though the room was expansive, it was still too confined to accommodate his dragon form, leaving him with little opportunity for surprise. After taking the staircase down, he crept up noiselessly behind the two.

The man sat up abruptly and turned the TV off. "Wait. I think I felt a vibration."

Saden clapped a hand over the man's mouth as the woman scrambled to her feet. She managed to pull out a gun just before he hit her with a low bolt of power, rendering her unconscious. In the next moment, he was yanked forward over the couch and fell flat on his back. The man grinned above him with one hand held palm out.

Bad move.

In the time it took the Vampyre to channel his power, Saden rolled over and kicked him square in the gut. Another kick sent him sprawling to the floor.

Seconds later, a voice carried from an open doorway leading to a dining room. "I know I heard something."

Saden ran to the wall and stood with his back to the side of the doorway. He struck when the third guard stepped through and took him down with a fist across the temple. On the other side of the dining room, he waited by the swinging door and listened for sounds of the last leisonguarde. When footsteps drew near, he slammed the door inwards, catching the man in the nose. The man reeled back then swung blindly and finally toppled to the ground after Saden delivered three rapid blows to his head.

Back through the parlor to a corridor behind the foyer, he came to a sunroom and waved at Daneya from the sliding glass doors.

She jogged up and slipped inside. "That was fast."

"You were expecting it to take longer?"

A playful smirk lit her eyes. "I don't know. I haven't really seen you in action yet."

"You saw me take down Messing."

"Doesn't count. I shot him full of lead first."

He shook his head, grinning. "We've got to hurry. The guards won't be out for long."

They took the staircase to the second floor. In Gabriel's study, Saden found the pressure panel in the corner and opened the wall to the hidden alcove. Inside, there was a large ceiling panel above that led to a section of the attic walled off from the main space. He was betting that was where Gabriel kept his recent records.

When he moved one of the crates to stand on it, he caught Daneya's questioning stare and shrugged a shoulder. "I liked to explore when I was a kid. Gabriel hasn't changed much since then."

The aged wood splintered around the lock on the panel and gave way at his force. He raised it then pulled down a collapsible ladder. Daneya went first and flipped the switch for an overhead light. The small area was cramped with several filing cabinets, a glass-front casement holding journals and folders, two full CD racks and a computer atop a plain wooden desk.

Saden scanned the CDs first. All were labeled with a year and the name of a state, totaling four different states in all from what he could see. It was the dates that immediately threw him off.

The earliest one started at the year 1939 and went in reverse chronological order from there. Odd, considering the fact that Gabriel's research hadn't earned him the position of Korvaute until after Saden had been born in 1948. His laboratory had been erected only a few years prior to that. 1939 was eighteen years before Gabriel had betrayed Saden. There was something significant about that year, he just couldn't figure out what.

"Look at this!" Daneya exclaimed. She flipped through a stack of manila folders. Each one contained the medical and family history documents of human females with their respective pictures attached. All ranged in age from eighteen to twenty-two and were reported with excellent health.

Daneya paused at one and yanked it from the pile. "I knew this girl. She was…a friend." A page of hand-written notes was stapled to the back of the last document in the file. She skimmed a finger along the words as she read aloud.

"'Specimen 4-6 gave birth to a healthy male on Aril 19, 1883. The child was taken into the home of one of my trusted assistants and his preyuna where I will continue to chart its growth until such time as it has reached its full maturity. Afterwards, as with most the other specimens, 4-6 expressed interest in staying on at my facility in the hopes of eventually bonding with one of my men.

"I explained to her that while her contribution to our race was greatly appreciated, we had no more need of her services as a child-bearing donor and encouraged her to return to her previous life. Her memory was then erased by one of my leisonguardes and she was compensated anonymously for her time and effort."

Unshed moisture gleamed in Daneya's eyes as she looked up in horror. "This is wrong—the year, the *facts*. She never volunteered for what Gabriel put her through. He used her for years then threw her away like garbage. Every single one of the babies they forced her to carry was taken away before she could even hold them. The only compensation she got was a bullet to the head when they were done with her, I'm sure of it. I tried everything to find her when I could, but she was gone. He killed her. I know it."

Saden didn't think she was aware of the pieces of her own past she was divulging to him. The naked pain in her trembling voice shook him as nothing else had. He took her into his arms and held her fiercely. "I promise you he'll pay for everything."

She tilted her head back to meet his gaze searchingly. "How could he destroy so many lives for the sake of creating more?"

Her words triggered a connection to the false dates Gabriel was using. "Because his own had been destroyed for the same goal."

"What?"

He looked over the CDs again. "1939. I remember that was the year Gabriel's preyuna and baby died in childbirth. He's using that year to mark the beginning of his experiments and recording them on a reverse timeline." At her stare of confusion, he explained, "I think Gabriel started his work with the Djinn in 1947. Replace that year with 1939 and count down from there for each subsequent year of his experiments. So this year, his research would be labeled with the date of 1873, exactly sixty six years from 1947, only in reverse from 1939."

"Why would he do that?"

"For the same reason none of those files contain any personal identification on the females. If anyone were to try to use the files against Gabriel, it would be almost impossible to prove he had anything to do with the females' captivity."

"So you're telling me we're screwed?"

He quirked his lips in a half grin. "You really got to learn to stop doubting me. Look for files that are dated within five years of 1873. We'll find the most recent information in those." While she did that, he did the same for the CDs, taking one of each state and putting them in an inside pocket of his trench coat.

"Aren't you going to check them on that computer?"

"Their data could be encrypted. And Gabriel might've installed a program into the computer to alert him if anyone tampers with it. We can check them at my place. Right now we need to get out of here."

As she gripped a small stack of folders and climbed down, he glanced around to make sure they hadn't missed anything. Then froze when he heard her gasp. "Daneya?" When he saw her rifling through the top drawer of the filing cabinet below, a thorn of dread pierced him. "Don't look in there!"

The words were out of his mouth before he could think twice. By the time he dropped down, she was holding up the profile with her picture on it and frowning at him. "You knew this was here?"

A number of excuses came to mind but none would come out.

"You lied to me. That night when you stopped Gabriel from kidnapping me, you didn't just happen to track him at the same time he was endangering an *innocent*." Anger seeped into her tone as her fingers slowly crushed the paper in her hands. "You'd already done recon on him."

"Daneya, I can explain—"

"My first instincts were true, weren't they? You somehow found out he was coming after me and wanted to use me as the evidence you needed to incriminate him. What happened? Did you suddenly grow a conscience when you saw him abducting my daughter?"

Shit! This was not going well. He had to get her out before the leisonguardes woke up. "That wasn't my plan."

"Then tell me!" she cried. "Tell me the truth because you sure as hell better not expect me to believe your knowing about this"—she waved the crumpled paper in the air—"is just a coincidence."

A shadow of movement was all the warning he had. He tackled Daneya just as a spray of bullets flew over their heads. In the next instant, he sent a bolt of Drakonem power at the ceiling of the study then shielded Daneya from the blast of debris that crashed around them. As soon as the dust settled, he found the female guard he'd taken out first lying half covered in debris on the floor. There was no chance of getting Daneya out from downstairs without running into the others.

He grabbed a standing lamp and used it to shatter the window in the study, then took out leather gloves and an Eddy belay device from his coat. When Daneya came near, he handed her the gloves. "Put those on."

"What are you doing?"

After fastening the grappling hook to the window sill, he attached the carabiner to the other end of the wire to her belt. "The rest of the guards will be here soon. Rappel down to the ground and get to the car. Whatever happens, don't stop until you reach my place."

She tucked the folders under one arm then balanced precariously on the edge of the sill. "Where are you going?"

"To buy you some time."

"Saden—" she started. Her eyes left his and widened as they focused on some point behind him. "Look out!"

The man from the parlor couch was standing in the doorway with a gun in hand.

"Move!" Saden shouted. He ducked a few rounds then rolled to the side of Gabriel's desk for cover. Strong vibrations began to shake the immediate area he was in and before he could gain his feet, the wood floor splintered and fell out from beneath him. The air was knocked from his lungs when he landed and his skull banged hard against the linoleum floor below.

The man jumped down and straddled Saden's chest, using one hand to crush his throat and the other to punch him repeatedly. Saden blocked the fourth punch then slammed a fist into the underside of the man's jaw, snapping his head back. He managed to shove him off then gulped in precious air. Past the ringing in his ears, he heard someone talking off to his left.

"Go get the one that escaped. We'll take care of this guy."

The sound of running boots faded from what appeared to be the kitchen. Saden pushed himself up and kicked the vibrations man in the temple. A heartbeat later, a second guard flung out his hand and released an arc of lightning that hit Saden in the chest. The force of it picked him up off his feet and slammed him back into the edge of a counter. He took a fist to the gut then went vertigo for a few seconds as he was thrown across the room. Through blurred vision, he saw the second guard advancing on him with an ugly sneer.

Saden waited until tiny sparks lit the man's upturned hand then pulled out a knife and buried it hilt deep in the man's calf. He yanked it out when the guard went down screaming and cracked the butt of it over the man's skull. After forcing his legs under him, he ran across the left wing of the mansion to the sunroom and caught sight of Daneya through the sliding glass doors. She had just arrived at the car with the third guard sprinting toward her at alarming speed. He was fully covered with a ski mask and gloves to protect him from the sun for a short while.

Saden summoned a burst of power but before he could send it, the third man stumbled and dropped to the ground. *What the hell?* Daneya couldn't have taken him down. She was already in the car and fishtailing out on the dirt road. In the next moment, searing pain tore through his midsection. He turned to find the female guard standing on the other side of the room with her gun trained on him. She shot another round that hit him in the shoulder.

The ground met his back hard and his vision spun sickeningly. The woman yanked him out of reach of the sun's rays, knelt down then swung a wickedly curved blade at his neck. He managed to deflect it enough so that it sliced across his collarbone. When she tried a second time, however, the knife never even got close.

Her eyes glazed and body stiffened before collapsing on top of him. He shoved her off and found a tranquilizer dart protruding from one of her arms.

Someone was helping him, he realized. Only problem was, no one else except Blade knew about this mission and he was busy protecting Mckenzie and Cherri. Who, then? His thoughts scattered when he heard Gabriel shout for his leisonguardes.

Time to go.

He lurched to his feet and stumbled outside to take his dragon form, teetering dangerously to one side when he flapped his wings to gain altitude. His right shoulder and side blazed from the strain of movement and made it nearly impossible to concentrate. With determination, he pushed himself on and ignored the mounting sensation of weakness from blood loss. This wasn't the worst he'd been through, and he'd be damned if he let Serrakus win this way.

* * * *

From his hidden perch in one of the distant trees, Phoenix lowered his tranq gun and watched Gabriel Aikins turn away from the window at the mansion. He shook his head grimly and sighed. Whatever had possessed Saden to take along his human companion on this mission was beyond him. And a female at that! She had likely been the cause of their delay in getting out in time. They were emotional creatures that never made sense in the best of situations.

Sasha let out a small surge of indignation at his thoughts. He smiled and sent an apology. Although any Djinn could assume either a male or female role, she had always identified herself as female.

"He won't succeed at this rate. He's too close to the target and his relation to the human woman is only complicating matters."

Phoenix felt her bristle inside him. Since deciding to help Saden against his better judgment, Sasha had remained aware the entire time he'd been observing the other Drakon. She was especially interested in the human called Daneya and her daughter, Mckenzie. Something about the pair and their intimate connection to Saden brought out a yearning in her. Phoenix suspected it was, in part, due to her own cravings for a family. Though she wouldn't admit to it.

For her, it had been an agonizing struggle to give up all hope of regaining the peaceful life she'd once lived. To face a future devoid of the happiness she had enjoyed until her fellow Djinn had destroyed everything and everyone important to her. It was still hard on her at times. Her memories the only things he couldn't protect her from.

If her reason for wanting to see this through with Saden stemmed from an echo of her previous life, he wanted to give her that happy ending through the Drakon. But wishes and reality hardly ever coincided. Saden had refused his help and any further interference by him would alert Serrakus.

"There's nothing more I can do," he told her gently.

"You can go to him."

It didn't take clarification to know just who she was referring to. *"No. Out of the question."*

"He's the only one."

"Not that. Ask me for anything else, sweet, and I'll do it."

She sent a tendril of longing through him that pushed at his opposition.

"No," he repeated.

Her persistence grew until it was near suffocating.

"I won't do it. If Saden wants to be a stubborn asshole, he can fight this battle on his own. You're not going to convince me. I said no. No means... Damn it, all right!" He growled and jumped down from the tree branch. *"You owe me for this. The next opera is mine to choose and you're singing every song in it."*

She preened excitedly as he changed forms and took to the skies. This was not going to end well, he was sure of it. How was he going to ask a brother he hadn't seen in over three centuries for help? Let alone try to persuade the chief of a Rakshasas clan to assist a former Vampyre turned Drakon.

Phoenix laughed inwardly, cursing himself as he flew toward his new destination.

* * * *

Daneya brought the car to a screeching halt and jumped out. She burst through the manor's front door and called out Saden's name. He had to be here. The last she'd seen of him, he'd disappeared from her rearview mirror amidst rounds of gunshots. It had taken all of her willpower to keep from slamming the car in reverse and going back for him.

"Mom!"

Mckenzie ran to her and she caught her daughter in her arms, but her attention was centered on Blade.

He strode into the foyer with Cherri following at a more sedate pace. "Is everything okay?"

"Tell me Saden's here." When he shook his head, the apprehension clogging her chest increased. The fact that Saden couldn't die was little consolation. It had been her mistake, her emotions that'd put them in danger. Sure, she wanted to make him feel the pain for lying, but on her terms, not Gabriel's.

Blade's dark blue eyes glossed over then snapped back to her. "He's close…and hurt. His energy is fading fast." He hurried outside with Daneya on his heels.

They all waited anxiously on the porch as long seconds stretched into minutes. Finally, the air in front of them shimmered, darkened and took on the form of a man. Saden hit the ground rolling and came to a stop on his back. Daneya dropped the stack of folders in her hand and raced to him, hiking one of his arms over her shoulders while Blade got his other side. Cherri and Mckenzie rushed out of the way as they half-carried him in. Blade navigated them to the guest bedroom beside Cherri's and pushed Saden onto the bed.

Or tried to.

Saden sat down on the edge and wouldn't budge until he had Daneya standing in front of him. "Are you all right?"

Daneya wanted to laugh at him. His face was deathly ashen and bruised, lips pale and shirt soaked through with blood, and still he was worried about her. It made her heart ache with an emotion she didn't want to contemplate at that moment. "I'm fine. I thought I'd lost you out there."

He chuckled as she helped him strip off his coat and throw it to the floor. "It would take more than that to bring me down."

She pursed her lips, cut his shirt from him with one of her blades then pushed him onto his back to inspect his injuries. There were two relatively small bullet wounds with no exit holes, which meant the bullets were still lodged inside.

"Saden." She shook him slightly to keep him from losing consciousness. "Stay with me. I need to take the bullets out before you can heal yourself."

"That's not how it works, sweetheart."

She turned to see Blade re-entering the room carrying first aid supplies, only then realizing he'd left. "What do you mean?"

"The bullets have to come out, but he can't heal himself," Blade said. "It's against the rules. Only our Drakonem can use the power they gave us to do that."

"He healed me, though," she protested.

Blade moved between her and the bed to put the supplies on the nightstand. "And he'll pay for it when he's done with this assignment. Serrakus takes personal offense when we use our power without permission. Hold him down on his other side. This is going to hurt."

Daneya swallowed heavily and climbed onto the bed beside Saden, her thoughts in turmoil. It didn't make sense for him to risk so much for her. Let alone commit an act that guaranteed consequences. There were still more pieces to the puzzle she hadn't found yet. Her instincts told her they were connected to the fact that he'd lied to her about seeing her profile.

"So what happened out there?" Blade asked while he cleaned the wounds. "I thought you two were going for information only."

"We were. We did. Things just got out of control." She hesitated then took a deep breath. It wasn't often she made a mistake to own up to. "I got angry and raised my voice which drew the leisonguardes to us."

He chuckled sarcastically. "Do this for a living, do you? Next time you might want to check your emotions at the door before playing with the bad demons."

"I didn't mean for this to happen."

"We're temporarily immortal, not indestructible," he continued angrily. "Maybe you should keep that in mind if you're going to tag along—" He was cut off abruptly by Saden's hand around his throat.

"Say one more word to her and see what I do to you," Saden growled. The menacing threat in his tone sent a chill down Daneya's spine.

It was Blade's turn to swallow heavily. His expression when he looked at her was completely out of character for him. Apologetic and contrite. To Saden, he said, "I'm sorry. That was uncalled for. I hope Daneya knows I was only talking out of my ass. And that I like my balls where they are."

Daneya coughed to hide her grin. When Saden lowered his hand, Blade started on his arm with a pair of long tweezers. There wasn't much need to hold him still. Other than the tightening of his lids and rigid muscles, he didn't even appear to be aware of what was going on.

She got the impression that this happened often in their line of work. It made her wonder again about the degree of loyalty and compassion they held. In a life that would drive most people insane, they seemed the exception.

For the first time, it dawned on her how lucky she was to have them watching over her and her family. To have Saden willing to let her stand at his side in this. Whatever the reason for his lie, she was grateful he was here.

Blade quickly removed the second bullet then wiped the wounds clean. Gradually, Saden's breathing leveled out and his body relaxed in rest. After applying the stitches and bandages, Blade got up and poked Saden to make sure he was sleeping. "Saden cares for you more than he should, and in the field, that's a distraction. I hope you keep that in mind if you insist on going out with him again." His tone was firm yet gentle.

She recalled the night she and Saden had spent together. Her desire to comfort him and her need to feel his strength surrounding her. With him, it hadn't been about power or control. They had been equals in everything. Even the horrors of their pasts. He had trusted her when she hadn't fully trusted herself. The patience he'd shown her was unlike anything she'd ever experienced.

For so long she'd kept her heart caged for fear of it being bruised. Yet, here Blade was telling her she was the one who could so easily deliver the pain. For some reason, she believed him.

"I have no intention of hurting him."

Blade dipped his chin then gathered the supplies and left. Daneya found another blanket in the closet of the room and laid it over Saden. Afterwards, she pulled up a sitting chair to the side of the bed and got comfortable. She owed him for the mess of his injuries, though she knew that wasn't why she was staying. He wasn't the only one who cared more than he should.

Sometime later, she looked over at a sound from the doorway. Mckenzie was hovering there, ringing her hands nervously. Daneya held out a hand and smiled. "Hi, baby. I forgot about you in all the fuss, didn't I? Sorry if I worried you."

Mckenzie took her hand. "I don't mind. Is Saden going to be okay?"

"I think so. He's tough." She glanced at her daughter who stood so bravely beside her. "You like him, don't you?"

Mckenzie's lips curved up. "He's nice. Don't you like him?"

"Yes, I do," she answered honestly.

Her daughter nudged the chair and canted her head to the side. "You know, I wouldn't mind if you *really* like him. He'd be good for you. Better than Vincent, I think."

"Kennie!"

"What? It's true. And I can tell he has a thing for you. He asks about you a lot."

Despite her efforts to remain indifferent, she could feel heat rising in her cheeks. When curiosity got the best of her, she asked, "Better than Vincent, huh?"

Mckenzie nodded vigorously. "And cuter."

They watched Saden quietly until Mckenzie stirred and edged toward the bed. "Mom?"

"Hmm?"

"I can help him."

Daneya sighed and scrubbed her eyes. "I know you want to, baby, but I think we've done all we can for him."

"No. I mean, I can heal him. With my power."

She snapped her head up and searched her daughter's timid expression. Everything in her froze and her mouth went dry. She'd known this day would come. When the other side of Kennie's heritage would make itself known. Yet, she was unprepared for it.

Cherri had argued with her in the beginning about telling Mckenzie the truth of her parentage. That she was part Vampyre and would eventually grow into the power of her aethra. They had both been afraid it might cause Mckenzie to feel alienated among her peers. But Daneya had feared the consequences of ignorance more. Being as integrated as they were into the DCM, she hadn't wanted to take the chance of Mckenzie accidently displaying her power in public.

Or, worse, hating her for withholding the truth. Mckenzie's unconditional love and friendship were the only things she truly cherished in this world.

"How do you know you can heal?"

Mckenzie shrugged and spoke quietly. "I've tried it on a couple of animals. You remember the stray dog you let me take in last year?"

Baxter. Named by Mckenzie after one of her favorite children's shows. The mangy thing had been run over and left to die. Daneya had wanted to take it to a vet at first but after a few days, it had made a full recovery. That had been Kennie?

"Do you hate me?"

Tears pricked her eyes at the slight tremble in her daughter's voice. She wrapped Mckenzie in her arms and squeezed tightly. "I could never hate you. There's nothing wrong with what you are, I've told you that. I hunt only the bad Vampyres who deserve to die. Okay?" When Mckenzie nodded, she added, "I'm so proud of you, but I think Saden will live without your help."

Mckenzie squirmed and stepped back, her eyes pleading. "I can do this. Please, Mom. I'm not afraid."

The maturity her daughter exuded awed her. When had her Kennie grown up so fast? She looked to Saden who was still sleeping in the bed. "It doesn't hurt you?"

"Nope. Just makes me a little tired. Can I do it?"

Indecision warred within her. This was new territory for both of them. However, if she said no, Mckenzie might perceive it as a lack of faith in her abilities. "All right. Just this once, and promise me you won't do it again on your own."

Mckenzie beamed excitedly. "I promise. Where was he hurt?"

She pulled down the blanket to reveal Saden's wounds underneath. She watched closely as Mckenzie placed her hands on Saden's abdomen and shut her eyes, wrinkling her forehead in concentration. Nothing happened for several tense minutes. Then, without warning, Saden's breath stuttered and his chest rose on a deep inhale. Upon letting it out, he relaxed farther into the mattress and his head lolled to the side.

Mckenzie looked up, her face worn but satisfied. "Better. See?"

Daneya gently lifted one of the bandages. The skin held together by stitches was healthy, pink and no longer seeping blood. As was the same for the wound on his shoulder. She filled her tone with as much confidence as she could muster. "That's amazing. How are you feeling?"

"Fine. I'm gonna go take a nap. Love you."

Daneya kissed her daughter then leaned back wearily in the chair. It wasn't hard to admit she was scared. Of the future and what Mckenzie's burgeoning power meant to their way of living. Staying on with the DCM seemed too risky and, at the same time, it was the only life she knew.

For a crazy moment, she wished Saden would wake up and give her the answers she desperately needed. Would he lend his strength, or ridicule her for keeping Mckenzie's heritage a secret?

Somehow, she didn't think it would be the latter.

After a while, her jumbled thoughts became a blur and she fell into a fitful sleep with Saden not far from her mind.

Chapter Ten

The great hall trembled with the roar of over two hundred men and women. Their cheers echoed along the walls, adding to the fervor of energy that rippled through the air. Roshon raised his glass with the others in a toast to the new alliance between his Thorien clan and that of the Mirkshaw.

It was a double victory for them. The Mirkshaw clan had political ties which had enabled them to put a halt to the deforestation of the land Roshon's clan had been about to lose. In turn, the Thorien clan had an abundance of warriors willing to offer their protection in exchange for potential mates. This hard-won alliance would combine their lands as well as increase their numbers.

Roshon only hoped his leader, Brice, would uphold his agreement to share power with the leader of the Mirkshaw clan for at least the next few centuries. Often, the pride and strength required to maintain leadership of a clan allowed for only one Rakshasa to preside over his people. Two territorial alphas living and working so closely together clashed with the natural order of their kind. Which made their relationship tentative at best.

It was necessary, though, if they were to stay on top of the threat their enemies posed.

More and more Rakshasas were turning Vanaras. Shifters who forsake the afterlife upon their deaths and become the nightmares of legend. Trapped in their bodies without souls, Vanaras quickly go mad as the hatred that drove them to make such a decision eventually consumes them. Unfortunately, their inevitable mindlessness makes them easily influenced and controlled by those who know what they're doing.

Due to the low number of Vanaras, this hadn't been a problem until the past fifty years or so. Warriors with unquestionable honor and integrity were falling to their enemies only to rise again as Vanaras. Men and women who Roshon had personally known to be avid followers of their faith. It didn't make any sense for these warriors to renounce the afterlife.

Even more peculiar was the fact that none of them were carrying out vendettas, the only reason to become a Vanara. They were simply attacking their former kind, and Roshon was convinced it was by command of the Djinn.

While he knew in his gut the Djinn had everything to do with this phenomenon, he could neither prove nor prevent it. It was infuriating to be so helpless against the assault of their enemy, and the reason why the festivities held little joy for him.

"Roshon!" Brice clapped him on the back, a wide grin parting his red beard. "I had my doubts about this alliance but your efforts were a success. Our clan will flourish with the Mirkshaws at our side."

Roshon tipped his head in acknowledgment. "I'm glad you're pleased. If you'll excuse me, sir, it's been a long day and I have other business to attend to."

The leader screwed his red, bushy eyebrows down in a frown. "And forgo the feast and dancing? Where is your woman? She should be here to liven your spirits."

"She's upstairs putting the little ones to bed and I promised to help. Enjoy the night, sir. We'll have plenty to do in the morning."

He left before Brice could get in another word. Through the throngs of people, he caught sight of Kent's tall figure and steered toward him. His second-in-command was easy to spot with straight ebony hair that fell to his waist and pale skin where most Rakshasas boasted a golden tan. He stood out among the other fair-haired members of their clan like a dark, avenging warrior with his unusual looks and constant, somber attitude.

Kent had elected to stay on duty for the night and was watching the celebrants for any signs of disorder. At Roshon's approach, he gave a cursory nod. "Chief."

"I'll be in my office if you need me. Make sure Brice finds his way to his bedroom alone. I don't want the other leader claiming ours was taking advantage of his Mirkshaw women without formal permission."

A smirk twisted Kent's lips. "You might as well ask me to stop the sun from rising."

"If I did, I'm sure you'd find a way to pull it off." He smiled at his friend's grunt then turned to go down a hallway leading to a back staircase.

Trax ran swiftly ahead of him, a streak of tawny fur blending into the shadows. The panther was more than just a companion or birthright. He was Roshon's geis. The other half of his spirit in the physical manifestation of an intelligent animal. All Rakshasas received their geis around the early age of three when their spirits divided into two separate forms. The human half retained logic and rational while the animal half became an entity of itself, containing all of the Rakshasa's baser instincts. Together, they were two parts of one whole. Connected in all respects yet independent of each other.

He felt Trax's relief mirror his own when they reached the second floor. Neither of them could stand the cacophony of large crowds, instead preferring the cool forests and company of his close-knit group of friends. Warriors all whom he trusted with his life.

He resisted the urge to go to the guest bedroom he shared with his mate and twin boys. They'd come for the night's celebrations and would return home with him in the morning. Brice had asked him on many occasions to move in but life in the leader's sprawling house was not one he would choose for his family.

At the door to the office reserved for his work, Trax sniffed then let out a low rumble, ears pinned flat to his head.

"What is it?" Roshon sent through their telepathic link.

Trax hesitated. *"I don't know. Something…"*

Roshon palmed the small dagger in his boot then unlocked the door. Everything was as he'd left it except for the open window letting in streams of moonlight. Not a guest, then. "Whoever you are, state your business."

Trax moved first, gliding into the deepest shadows on the other side and emitting a loud purr. His joyous contentment sang through their link. Puzzled by his geis' odd behavior, Roshon flipped on the light then sucked in a sharp breath. A ghost from the past stared back at him. An almost spitting image of himself with long, ash-blond hair, a trim goatee and sinuous build. It couldn't be.

"Cai?"

The man stroked Trax's sleek pelt then rose to his full height. "I go by Phoenix now. It's good to see you, Roshon."

Roshon couldn't believe it. Didn't want to believe it. Yet, there was no mistaking who stood before him. With only five years difference between them, his little brother appeared every ounce the warrior he'd always envisioned Cai would have become.

There was just one flaw that marked them worlds apart. The emptiness that shone from the depths of Cai's gray eyes and spoke of unfathomable loss. To anyone else, it might look akin to madness. To a Rakshasa, though, the desolation of existence without a geis was plain to see.

For a fleeting moment, Roshon wanted to welcome his brother back with open arms. As children, they'd been inseparable. Even after Cai had been condemned for the deaths of their entire clan, including their parents, Roshon hadn't wanted to give up on him. He'd loved his brother dearly.

That was the past, however. The man before him was no more than a stranger who housed one of his enemies.

He closed the door behind him and tightened his grip on the dagger. "If you have Drakon business with anyone here, you'll have to deal with me first."

"I'm not here at the bidding of my Drakonem."

The choice of words made the hairs on the back of his neck stand on end. "Don't tell me you're here because of that thing inside you. I know about the Djinn you keep."

Phoenix's face remained expressionless. "Not all Djinn are evil. You know that as well as I do. Besides, if Sasha were a threat, your geis would've sensed it."

He ground his teeth, unable to argue with that. While Trax was essentially a projection of himself, the cat was also the embodiment of his intuition with a personality of his own. When Roshon tried to detect any sign of caution in his geis, Trax merely yawned and padded over to the throw rug in front of the desk, saying, *"He's got a point."*

Reluctantly, Roshon let his nerves settle and slid the dagger back into his boot. "I can't be too sure anymore. The Djinn have found new ways to combat us." After pouring himself a tumbler of liquor from a nearby cabinet, he leaned on the edge of his desk. "Why are you here, then?"

For the first time, emotion flickered in Phoenix's eyes. Unease. "I came to ask for your help."

"My help?" Roshon repeated in utter shock. "*You're* asking for *my* help?"

"I am. A Drakon I know, Saden, is assigned to find proof of a Vampyre's crimes against humans. I have good reason to believe this Vampyre is also involved with the Djinn."

"That doesn't concern me. I have my hands full fighting for my own kind against the Djinn."

"The Vampyre, Gabriel Aikins, and the Djinn are working together to impregnate human females without the need for bonding. Gabriel is systematically kidnapping females and holding them against their will in order to procreate more of his kind. He gives half of the offspring birthed to the Djinn who raise them to become hosts."

Ice spread like tentacles through Roshon's veins. "It can't be. The Djinn don't possess that kind of power."

"I wouldn't have believed it either if I hadn't looked into Gabriel's experiments myself. Somehow, he's found a way to harvest his own kind and is disposing of the females he uses. As far as I can tell, this has been going on for several decades." Phoenix lowered his voice. "I don't think I need to tell you what this could mean for the other demon races."

Roshon was already ahead of him, his thoughts whirling at the implications of what he was hearing. With countless Vampyres on their side as willing hosts, the Djinn would gain advantage over everyone who stood in the way of their quest for power. Add to that the Rakshasas they were somehow manipulating into abandoning the afterlife and all of demonkind could be facing the rise of an army.

And what if the Djinn didn't stop with the Vampyres? He couldn't rule out the possibility that they might also be able to impregnate the females of his kind for the same results.

The idea of Rakshasas fighting for the Djinn might've been ludicrous if not for the inexplicable rash of Vanaras attacking his warriors of late.

Roshon cleared his throat. "Why should I trust you?"

"You shouldn't. But I'm not doing this for me."

"This is a lot to ask on behalf of a friend."

Phoenix's gaze shifted to the window, his body stiffening minutely. "Saden is no friend of mine, though he is a good man. He still needs to find irrefutable proof of Gabriel's experiments and, as it is, he won't be able to do that alone. The ruling Vampyre authorities in this area are under the impression that Gabriel is doing his work legally. They're providing him with leisonguardes for protection. If Saden fails, the entire case against Gabriel will be thrown out."

Roshon studied Phoenix for several tense seconds. Though it all seemed too unbelievable to be true, he couldn't find any deceit in his brother's demeanor. "What would you have me do?"

"I think Saden plans to infiltrate one of the facilities where Gabriel is holding the humans. It's the only way he'll get the proof he needs. Gabriel will be prepared for this. Saden won't be able to do it on his own. That's where you come in."

"So let me get this straight. You want me to pit my clan against a horde of leisonguardes and who knows how many Djinn to help a Drakon." He gave a cynical laugh and shook his head. "It's insane."

"Not your whole clan. Just you and a small group of your men. If Saden's Drakonem finds out he's working with you, his assignment will be compromised and Gabriel will be acquitted of the charges against him."

Well, that makes it a fuck of a lot easier, he thought sarcastically.

Phoenix withdrew a folded piece of paper from his back pocket and set it on the bookshelf behind him. "That's Saden's address. If you do this, you should also know he's working with a member of the DCM. As far as I can tell, she's on his side." He went to the window and climbed onto the sill.

"Cai," Roshon called, purposefully using his brother's birth name. He wanted to ask for clarification. What really happened the day their clan was slaughtered and why Cai had betrayed them. Why he still hosted one of their enemies. The questions he'd wondered for so long sat like acid on the tip of his tongue. Yet none of them came out. "It was good to see you again."

For the span of a few heartbeats, the mask of his brother's stone countenance fell away. His face reflected the same churning turmoil Roshon felt inside.

Then it was gone, and they were once more merely strangers with the same blood. "And you, Roshon."

He leaped from the window, leaving Roshon to stare into the empty space left behind. Countless minutes passed as Roshon reviewed their conversation over and over again in his mind. He didn't know how long he'd been standing there when his mate walked in and disturbed his thoughts by taking the tumbler from his hand.

"What bothers my handsome mate at this hour?" she asked demurely.

Roshon sighed and let the nuances of her British accent distract him from his reverie. The classic beauty of her soft angles, hazel eyes and chestnut hair captured his focus. Her warm breath mingled with his as he pulled her close for a lingering kiss then pressed his face to the curve of her neck. "You are my sun," he whispered.

"Always and forever," she replied softly.

He heaved another breath and drew back. "My brother was here."

Emma frowned in confusion. "Cai? I thought he was dead."

"So did I. Apparently he hasn't finished his service as a Drakon yet."

She turned in a circle then put a hand to her breast. "Is he here to—?"

"No. He, uh..." Roshon chuckled lightly. "He came to ask for my help."

"And what did Trax think of this?"

A smile nearly broke through his grim cast. She had a way of cutting to the truth that still amazed him after their two hundred years together. As a geis, Trax was as close to a living lie detector as he could get. If Phoenix had harbored any ill will toward him, Trax would've known it. The panther's golden eyes met his with all the conviction they'd held before.

"Trax greeted him as a lost brother."

Emma nodded and squared her shoulders. "Then I think you should help him."

Her faith and courage humbled him. She was so much more than he deserved in a mate.

"It won't be so easy." He explained to her the situation and danger if he were to get involved. While their kind wasn't in current opposition with Vampyres, neither were they allies. In helping Saden, he ran the risk of drawing the attention of the house of Avram to his clan. Not to mention the Djinn in league with Gabriel.

There was more at stake than just the potential for further threat from their enemy.

His mate mulled over his words when he was done. Finally, she canted her head to the side. "What do you want to do about it?"

Roshon scraped a hand through his hair. "I honestly don't know."

Emma stepped into his arms and kissed him lightly. "Decide nothing tonight. In the morning, we'll talk again. Okay?"

Her clean scent permeated his being and calmed his nerves. "You're right. Why dwell on that when I have more important things to occupy my time with?" He lifted her until her legs wrapped around his waist then buried his face in the mounds of her breasts.

Emma's bright laughter rang out above him. "At least you've got your priorities straight."

He growled in answer and took possession of her mouth again, grateful for this woman that tempered his soul.

* * * *

Sweat trickled down Daneya's temples and between her shoulder blades. Her muscles screamed in protest and arms ached from tension but she ignored all of it. The weight of the sword in her hands felt good. It had been too long since she'd practiced with weapons other than her guns. Going through the motions she'd mastered years ago brought her thoughts into focus like nothing else could.

She forgot about her stress and concentrated only on the blade moving as an extension of herself. It dipped and soared with her body's twists and turns.

"Nice moves."

She gasped and swung the sword down in a wide arc. Saden caught the flat of the blade between his palms only inches from his throat. If he was alarmed in any way at her slip, it didn't show. Instead, amusement sparked in his eyes as she panted an apology and lowered the blade. His hair hung in wet locks around his face and the scents of musk and aftershave told her he'd taken a shower before coming to find her.

"We need to talk."

Daneya reined in her swell of relief over seeing him up and about. She hadn't left his temporary bedside until an hour ago, just after midnight, to work out her stress in the weapons room. Although some color had returned to his skin and his reflexes were obviously good, she couldn't get the image of his deathly pallor out of her mind. It had shaken her more than she'd thought possible. She hadn't cared about the fact that he couldn't die or the information they'd managed to steal from Gabriel.

All that had mattered was keeping him alive and with her.

Sometime during the long hours of watching over him, that realization had hit her with daunting clarity. Instantly, she'd admonished herself for being ridiculous. It was Vincent she should've wanted at her side, or Erin or Floyd. Any of her friends in the DCM. But after a while, she'd stopped trying to convince herself of that. None of them had ever made her feel as safe as Saden did just by being near. Or as accepted.

She walked over to the weapons wall and slid the sword into its hanging sheath. "How are you feeling?"

"Better. Your daughter is a good healer."

Everything in her stilled. "I... I don't know what you're talking about."

"Don't you?" His green eyes glinted with steely determination to get to the truth. As he slowly advanced on her, the softness of his tone made his words all the more compelling. "It should've taken me days to recover from my wounds. When I called Blade, he swore he knew nothing about a healing. I know you and Cherri are fully human. That leaves only Kennie. Who was her father, Daneya?"

He stopped at arm's length, exuding quiet confidence that sent her heart pounding against her ribcage. The anger fighting its way to the surface was hard to hold onto in his presence. She backed away, needing more distance between them. "You have no right to ask me that."

Saden's jaw flexed in irritation. He seemed torn in conflict for a few moments then pinched the bridge of his nose. "I was locked in the Drakonem realm for a two year punishment at the time Kennie was born. I had a friend who was helping me through it when he could. His real name was Marco."

Daneya let out a startled breath. The name brought with it a rush of memories—some good, some bad. The

Marco she'd known had been her friend, her family and her savior. It couldn't be the same one Saden was referring to. That would've meant he had become a Drakon before Mckenzie's birth, an idea she refused to entertain.

"I knew Marco was protecting a human in his off-time," Saden continued. "A girl he considered a daughter to him. My punishment ended at the same time his began. He wouldn't tell me what he'd done, but whatever it was, it warranted the highest punishment we have as Drakons. Marco was sent to a Drakonem in South Africa and made a warder. A guard who remains trapped in the Drakonem realm for the duration of his sentence and oversees the order and punishments of other Drakons. Before he left, he asked me to watch over you and your new daughter."

"That's how you knew my file was at Gabriel's house," she breathed. "You saw it and came after me, not him. Didn't you?" When he nodded, a slightly hysterical laugh escaped her lips. This was insane. All of it. The connection she felt with him had just reached a whole new level of crazy she couldn't deal with right then.

Saden took another step closer. "I need to know the truth, leisontee. What happened to Marco while I was gone?"

She raised both hands in a futile attempt to ward off his questions. "How do I know you're even speaking of the same Marco I knew?"

"He was a leisonguarde once with a family. Preyune to your sister, Emily. He said he lost his freedom trying to protect both of you."

The memories thrummed inside her now, clamoring for precedence. She'd thought Marco had died with her sister the night they were attacked. Only to find him alive when he had come to rescue her from her worst nightmare. Then he'd disappeared again and she hadn't heard from him since. Saden's claim made sense of everything she'd wondered about in the past.

And it scared the hell out of her. Marco couldn't have become a Drakon. He was a good man who deserved a fate worthy of a hero. Not a criminal.

"I can't do this."

"At least tell me who Kennie's father is," Saden pushed.

She squeezed her eyes shut and shook her head. "No."

"Daneya, she could be in more danger than you realize. Tell me. Tell me the truth so I can help."

"It's Gabriel!" she yelled, body vibrating with emotion. Her next words came out shaky and raw. "Her father is Gabriel. He impregnated me when he held me prisoner."

Saden was quiet at first, then let out a string of invectives that echoed along the walls of the room. His expression was furious as he strode away and swung a fist at the weapons wall. The staff he hit snapped in half and clattered to the floor, knocking loose a few other weapons near it. His outburst somehow helped to soothe her frayed nerves.

"Tell me everything," he growled.

She should've walked away immediately. Demanded he let her go and never reveal what only Cherri knew. Would have if not for the honest compassion behind his rage that made her feel safer than she had in too long. Not since Marco had been a part of her life.

After a deep breath, she said, "When Marco married my sister, they took me out of the foster home and raised me together. A year later, he told me what he was and I remember I didn't care because he loved me and Emily so much. He gave us everything we had lost when our parents died. They tried for years to have a baby but there were complications. Emily couldn't get pregnant. One night, Gabriel came to the house and said he knew of a way to get around Emily's barrenness. Marco got angry and threw him out."

She shivered as that night came back to her. At fourteen years old, she hadn't understood much of their conversation. Emily had sent her to her room when Gabriel and Marco had started to argue. She recalled all too clearly, however, the way Gabriel had watched her every move. The way his eyes had seemed hungry, like those of a predator.

"As soon as Gabriel left, Marco packed our stuff and said we were going to a safe place where he would join us later. It was too late, though. Gabriel came back with a group of men and attacked us. My sister…" She cleared her throat around the painful lump that had formed. "Emily was killed trying to get me out. Marco got me to the car and told me to drive and never look back. I thought he'd died with my sister.

"I was found and returned to foster care after that. When I turned seventeen, Gabriel came back for me. I was his prize, he said, for having to put up with Marco's ignorance." Acid burned on her tongue as the memories spilled out. They wouldn't stop coming now that she'd opened the floodgates.

"The other women there had multiple partners to ensure they became pregnant but Gabriel kept me for himself. He was obsessed with me. I met Cherri there and we supported each other through the worst of it. A few days after Mckenzie was born, Marco broke into the facility to rescue me. I made him take Cherri and my daughter as well. I don't know how he got us out of there. Cherri was seven months pregnant and I was still weak. He did, though, and provided us with a house and enough money to start new lives. I never heard from him again."

"Cherri lost her baby, didn't she?" Saden asked in a low voice.

Daneya bit her lip and crossed her arms around herself, trying to stop the trembling inside. "The loss of Djinn energy was too much. Her baby died a week after we escaped. The doctors said there was no chance she would be able to carry again."

This time when Saden approached, she stood her ground. His face held none of the censure she was expecting, and when he wrapped her in a solid embrace, she melted into his warmth and strength. Tears she hadn't known were there dampened the front of his shirt. As the humility and shame of her past threatened to drown her, he held her tighter and whispered comforting words. More tears fell past her wavering control, competing with the silent sobs that wracked her.

They stayed like that for countless minutes until she finally came back to herself. "You must think I'm a hypocrite," she mumbled against his chest, "for joining the DCM knowing what my daughter is."

"No. You were only doing what was best for her. They taught you the skills you needed to keep her safe. I've watched you both grow over the years."

"Yeah, that's still creepy."

His deep laughter rumbled through her. "It makes sense now. Why you kept moving from place to place and why Marco never told me what really happened." When she looked up at him with a frown, he added, "I would've killed Gabriel if I had known what he did to you."

The cold conviction in his tone made her feel treasured, and she couldn't hold back the smile that curved her lips. It was little wonder why Marco, who'd loved her sister so much, had chosen this man to watch over her and Mckenzie.

"Come on." Saden kissed her forehead then pulled her to the door. "There's something you need to do." He took her to her bedroom where Mckenzie was fast asleep in the bed. "Vampyre children develop the power of their aethra at around three years old. It's up to their parents to replenish the energy they expend while using their power. Mckenzie is early for a human hybrid, who usually don't gain their powers until the teenage years. She needs you to restore what was spent when she healed me."

Daneya shook her head. "I can't do that. I don't want to hurt her." She recalled how Gabriel had forced what he'd called 'servicing'. Infusing her with the energy of the Djinn inside him while feeding off her fear and hatred. Each time had left her battered in the wake of his sexual lust.

"The exchange of life force between Vampyres is natural," Saden explained. "The fact that you're human doesn't change that. The love parents have for their children is the strongest energy there is. It'll sustain her until she's ready to absorb energy on her own. All you need to do is touch her and let your love flow through to her."

She stared down at her daughter, the perfect replica of herself, from the burgundy tresses to the strong will. Except Mckenzie was so much braver and free-spirited than she'd been at that age. It had never mattered who had sired Kennie or what she really was. Simply that she had been born innocent and deserved the kind of life that'd been stolen from Daneya.

Dark bags ringed her eyes now and her skin lacked the healthy glow of youth. Daneya lay down and gathered her daughter close, touching as much of her as possible. She concentrated on the joy Mckenzie had always given her, the pride of having such a miracle in her life.

Time passed without awareness. Eventually, Daneya opened her eyes and saw high color staining her daughter's cheeks a rosy pink. Mckenzie was warmer as well and a small smile played on her lips. Daneya looked over her shoulder to Saden but he was nowhere in sight. She slipped from the bed and out of the room, intent on finding him to thank him somehow. He had given her this moment and she wanted to share it with him.

After checking his bedroom, she went back upstairs on a hunch. He was in the weapons room as she'd suspected. The blades that had fallen earlier had been returned to their mounts. Except for the broken staff, which lay near a pile of Saden's clothes. He stood in the center of the room with only black jeans covering his lean body. His tanned skin glistened with a fine sheen of sweat as he wielded a pair of katanas with expert finesse.

She watched silently, mesmerized by the art of his skills. Each of his moves was perfectly calculated and the katanas merely an extension of his long limbs. Every inch of his naked torso rippled with fine-cut muscles that spanned out across his backside.

It was hard to believe that a man so handsome had come from such a brutal past. What must it have been like to crawl out from years of abuse at the hand of his Drakonem only to immerse himself in bloodshed in order to survive?

She couldn't imagine her Kennie, or even herself, going through the same and retaining the kindness Saden had shown them. A part of her wanted to shelter him from his life. To stop time until she could alter the finality of his future. She wasn't ready for this, whatever it was between them, to end. She wasn't sure she would want it to even after his business with Gabriel was complete.

Saden seemed to glide over the floor in a lethal dance of combat then stilled abruptly. His gaze found hers unerringly and Daneya felt her breath catch in her throat. Her body responded in a way she hadn't thought possible before the intimacy they'd shared the other night. As a woman did to a man she trusted with her heart.

With Saden, there was no struggle for control or fear of consequences. He was her equal, and right then, that was all that mattered.

She crossed over to him and leaned up to press her mouth to his. For a brief second, he didn't move. Then the weapons clattered to the floor, his lips parted and arms circled around her, crushing her to him. His passion was like a living source of fire that raced through her blood and set her head whirling. It was one of the things she admired most about him. No games or pretensions. Just the desire he wasn't afraid to show.

She tangled her fingers in his hair and pulled him closer, needing to feel as much of him as she could. When the hard evidence of his arousal pressed against her belly, it shot her own desires to new heights. Without warning, he withdrew sharply and put her at arms-length. She clung to his hands, spinning in confusion.

A shadow of pain etched Saden's eyes as he panted for air. "We can't do this again. I'm sorry. I don't want to be the regret you take away from this when you leave."

Then don't make me leave. The thought lingered in her mind, absurd yet more clear than any she'd had in the past week. It wasn't fair that she should find what she had always longed for in a man she could never have. Her entire life was about rules and sacrifices. How could she be asked to give up one more thing that made her happy?

She wouldn't. At least not for now. Life owed her that much.

"I won't regret you." When his face still reflected doubt, she removed his hands and closed the space between them. "I don't know how long we have, or what will happen when we finish your job. But I do know I'll regret it if I don't take advantage of you right now." She cocked her brow with a playful hint. "And I don't lie."

A half-grin lifted a corner of his mouth. "I've discovered that about you."

This time when their lips met, the kiss was slow and sensual. It stoked the embers of the flame still burning inside her. His tongue slid along hers in a lazy caress, sweeping into the cavern of her mouth and drinking in her every breath. The rest of the world melted away as he embraced her once again.

"What else have you discovered about me?" she whispered against his lips.

He trailed his mouth down the curve of her neck, licking and sucking her earlobe then moving on to her collarbone. His hands slid inside her shirt and grasped her narrow waist tightly. At his urge, she raised her arms and let him strip the thin fabric from her. In the next heartbeat, his hands and mouth were on her again, touching everywhere he could reach.

"I know that you love your friends like family."

The clasp at the front of her bra came apart under his nimble fingers. He swallowed her gasp with a scorching kiss and delved deeper into the recesses of her mouth. She leaned into the heat of his hands as they kneaded her breasts, sighing when he rolled and teased her nipples. Her own hands found the waistband of his jeans and unclasped the button. Another draft of cool air rushed over her as he pulled down her pants and yanked them off, leaving her utterly exposed. He quickly joined her by tossing aside his jeans.

"You always stand up for what's right, even if no one else agrees with you." His breath tickled her throat and sent shivers rippling over her skin. He kicked aside the katanas then laid her down gently on the cold floor, covering her front with the warmth of his body.

Daneya let the drugging sensations of his hunger wash over her. He was everywhere all at once, filling her with mounting pleasure so enveloping, she thought she might drown in it. When he flicked his tongue across one of her nipples then dragged it into his mouth, she arched up with a moan. The column of his shaft rubbed along her cleft and brought a fresh wave of arousal.

"And you're fearless when you fight. Not always a good thing when you're going up against a den of Vanaras by yourself."

A frown creased her forehead as she tried to recall his reference. She'd only made that mistake once and had gotten lucky when a fortunate rockslide at the entrance to their cave had cut off their pursuit of her. Wait… Daneya tugged on his hair until he was staring up at her. "That was you?"

The shade of his half-lidded eyes took on a different hue. Protective and fierce. "I would never allow harm to come to you."

Her own eyes pricked with moisture. She'd seen the truth of his statement earlier at Gabriel's mansion. Heard it when he'd threatened Blade for speaking rudely to her. It made her feel all the more cherished and wanted despite the circumstances surrounding the situations.

Saden skimmed down her belly to the triangle of dark curls covering her center. He bent her legs then buried his face in the crevice between them, igniting sparks beneath Daneya's skin. She gasped when his tongue slid seductively over her most tender area then dove into her heat. Ripples of intense sensations vibrated through her. A coil of pressure took root in her gut and wound itself around her insides.

He breached her entrance farther with first one finger, then a second. They slipped in and out, searching for and finding the spot that made her cry out in ecstasy. She grabbed onto his shoulders as her hips surged of their own accord, desperate to match the rhythm of his driving fingers. Over and over again his tongue flicked across her clit, teasing until she thought she couldn't take anymore. The pressure increased to a maddening point and she dug her nails into his skin, holding on as the floor seemed to fall away.

"Saden," she breathed.

He hooked his fingers inside her and rubbed mercilessly on her core. Her world shattered in an explosion of searing heat. Wave after wave of pleasure rolled through her, spinning her so far out of control she couldn't think straight. The tremor of his groan sent another tide of electric shocks pulsating through her.

Before she could react, he pulled her to her feet then lifted her. Instinctively, she hugged his waist with her legs and wrapped her arms around his neck. He walked her to the nearest wall, capturing her mouth with his. The taste of her on his tongue was intoxicating. Nothing had felt so intimate. Not even in her dreams had she imagined making love could feel this good.

When her back met the wall, he hiked her farther up then guided his tip to her threshold. In one sensual move, he brought her down and filled her completely. They moaned in unison, caught in the scorching connection of their bodies. Saden set up a slow pace. The length of his hard erection swelled within her, rubbing against her sensitive walls.

As he lowered his mouth to her neck, she stared out at the mirrors around them, watching the way his muscles flexed with each deep thrust. It was captivating. The contrast of his large build to her smaller frame. The stretch of his sinews to her softer skin. It was almost impossible to believe someone like him had been hiding just beyond her sight to keep her safe.

He quickened the force of his strokes, driving into her with increasing need. The coiling tension inside her returned. She swiveled her hips to meet his, reeling in the feel of his hardness buried deep within. His tip grazed repeatedly against her spot and sent ribbons of fire streaming through her. When her name left his lips on a growl, it tipped her over the edge. She arched back and shouted out her climax, shuddering in the strong circle of his arms. He found his own release seconds later and groaned into her mouth.

After finally catching her breath, she smiled and chuckled softly.

"What is it?" he asked.

She shook her head. "I don't know. I just feel…"

He leaned back to look at her and gave a lopsided grin. "Yeah. Me too. Can you stand?"

A sarcastic grunt slipped out before she could stop it. Standing was debatable at the moment. As her feet reached the floor, she tested the strength of her legs and found it passing. Barely. When they were both dressed, he guided her downstairs to her room but she refused to go in.

"I want to stay with you tonight."

He opened his mouth as if to say something then closed it. Once in his room, she tossed her clothes to the floor and climbed into his bed. Not quite sure what she was doing, yet knowing she needed to feel him beside her. After he shirked his own clothes and slipped between the sheets, she rested her head on his chest.

A question came to her as sleep began pulling her under. Something she'd wondered earlier during their conversation. "What will you take away from this after I leave?"

Time passed until she thought he might not answer, then quietly, he said, "My sanity. You've held it since the day I met you."

The words echoed in her mind, haunting her long after she drifted off to sleep.

Chapter Eleven

Daneya woke to the feel of fingers combing through her hair. She opened her eyes to find Saden lying beside her, watching her intently with his head propped up on one hand. His mussed locks and five o'clock shadow gave him a rugged appearance in the dim light of the bedside lamp. She recalled the events of the previous night but focused only on the last part. The reason she was in bed with him now.

No regrets, she remembered. And it was true. If anything, she felt more calm and content than she had in a long time, and it was because of him.

He was waiting for something, she realized. When she gave a lazy smile, he relaxed visibly and offered one of his own.

"I have to go," Saden said. "Blade has been keeping an eye on Gabriel and I told him I'd take over in the morning."

Daneya suppressed a groan. Not a topic she wanted to think about right after waking up. Though a necessary one. "What time is it?"

"Six in the morning."

"Take a shower with me?"

"Of course."

The answer was so easily given, she couldn't contain the wide grin that spread across her face. Truth was, she loved spending time with him. As hard as it had been to reveal her past, she felt better for it. Saden hadn't judged or critiqued her in her choices. All he'd offered was support, and she honestly didn't know how she would've handled the emergence of Mckenzie's power without his help.

That Marco had chosen him to watch over her only fortified her growing feelings for him.

They used the hallway bathroom next to Saden's room and stepped into the shower once the water was warm. Saden lathered a washcloth with soap then turned to her and began washing her backside and arms. She was startled at first. No one had ever tried to take care of her like this. It was slightly embarrassing, childish and…

Daneya let out a deep moan as he massaged the tension from her shoulders. His hands moved sensuously to her lower back then up again, kneading and rubbing in a way that was so far from childish, a delicious ache took root between her legs. He pressed his front to her back then started on her breasts, lathering with one hand and massaging with the other. It was extremely erotic and somehow chaste. There was no urgency to his actions. Just soothing comfort that had her melting into his touch.

He kissed her long and leisurely while stroking the washcloth along her sex, then knelt to reach her legs and feet. By the time he was done, she was ready to crawl back into bed and sleep until noon.

She rinsed off then took the cloth from him to lather it with more soap. Returning the favor proved to be more stimulating than she'd expected. He was full of hard planes and flexing sinews. When she came to his flaccid shaft, he eased her hesitancy by capturing her mouth again. And though he grew in her hand, he stayed at only half-mast.

Afterwards, she ran her fingers over the silvery lash marks on his back. "Why do you still have these scars? I thought you said the Drakonem could heal completely."

He stiffened then moved under the spray of water to rinse. "Those weren't from my Drakonem."

"Then who gave them to you?" She almost wanted to take the question back as soon as it was out. His agitation was palpable and expression closed to her. However, her curiosity wouldn't let it rest.

"They're from Gabriel, when he and his men tried to finish me off after the explosion of his first facility. My Drakonem thought I should keep them to always remind me of my past."

Daneya shivered at the gruesome scene her mind conjured. That of a nine year old boy barely alive in the wreckage. Beaten by an uncle who should've protected him. How he'd grown into the man she admired before her was still a mystery.

She cupped his jaw and made him look at her. "I'm sorry."

He seemed to let go of his anger on a deep breath and kissed her forehead. After finishing in the bathroom, they got dressed then went to Daneya's room.

Saden checked Mckenzie quietly, making sure not to wake her. "She looks good."

"Thanks to you." She took his hand and walked with him through the balcony doors to the terrace beyond. "When will you be back?"

"At nightfall. I should have a good idea of what Gabriel will plan to do by then. Go through the files you took and let Blade know if you find anything interesting."

Before he could turn to leave, she pulled him down for another kiss. He responded instantly, enveloping her in his strong arms and taking what she offered. They remained locked together for several seconds until a sharp gasp drew their attention.

Cherri was standing near the walkway to the balcony, staring at them in wide-eyed horror.

Daneya slowly let go of Saden and took a step to the side. "Cherri—"

"What's going on? What has he done to you?"

"Nothing, I promise. He's just…" She gave a small shrug, feeling a little like a teenager who got caught making out with her boyfriend. "He's not the man I thought he was at first."

"You mean you… This is voluntary?" Cherri waved a hand at Saden. "How could you?"

The disgust and accusation in her tone threw Daneya off-guard. It wasn't like her friend to jump to conclusions without asking for an explanation. Besides, Cherri had been the one to put a measure of trust in Saden from the beginning. "Let me explain. He's not exactly a criminal—"

"He's a Drakon, for God's sake!" she yelled. "A soulless murderer cast out by his own kind. The worst of the demons you hunt. Or have you forgotten you're a member of the DCM?"

A spark of anger flashed within Daneya. She looked to Saden whose face was set in stone, a mask she'd come to recognize as a way of hiding his emotions. "I haven't forgotten anything. I was just wrong before.

Life isn't always as black and white as we want it to be. Saden is a good man, and I trust him."

"What about Vincent?"

"Vincent?" she repeated.

"He cares about you and Kennie so much. I can only dream of having a man like him. Someone who would love and support me. He's willing to give you everything you deserve. A family, a *future*. How could you be so selfish and throw all of that away?"

Daneya gaped inelegantly, stunned by her friend's outburst. She'd never given Cherri or anyone else reason to believe she and Vincent might get involved romantically. Granted, it wasn't for lack of effort on his end. But he wasn't the one who had coaxed her secrets from her with acceptance. It hadn't been his patience and understanding that had made her see herself as a woman and not just a fighter.

Cherri did have a valid point, however. With Saden, there was no future. No chance of living the life she'd always coveted. Would she really want to, if Saden weren't a Drakon? She put the thought from her mind. There was no sense in dreaming of what couldn't be.

"Cherri, there's nothing between Vincent and me except friendship. With Saden it's…different. *I'm* different. Just listen for one minute —"

"Do you love him, now? Is that why you defend him?"

She paused, unsure of what to say to that. "It's not that simple."

"Yes, it is!" Cherri cried. Her eyes glittered with unshed tears. "You have no idea how lucky you are. How happy you could be. And you're wasting everything on this filth." She spun on her heel and stormed away.

Daneya turned to apologize only to stop when she saw Saden's face. It held a mixture of unease and…shame? She decided to switch tactics, scrambling to think of something to say that might diffuse the awkward situation. "Cherri doesn't know you like I do. I'm sure once I tell her the truth, she'll calm down."

His face was a mask again, hard and implacable. "Doesn't matter. She's right. You should be with someone who can give you what you need." He walked stiffly to the edge of the terrace.

"Saden, wait!" By the time the words were out, he'd already faded into the muted light of dawn. She ground her teeth as she made her way back inside. Alone, frustrated and thoroughly convinced she would strangle the next person who tried to tell her what was best for her.

* * * *

"It's about time you got back."

Saden solidified into his true form as he landed on the porch deck at the back of the manor. Blade jumped down from his perch on the banister, the setting sun lighting the bleached tips of his hair.

"I'm going crazy locked up in this house with two hormonal women. Especially ones that are off the menu. Don't get me wrong. Kennie's cool to hang out with and Daneya isn't so bad either, but a guy's gotta get laid every now and then."

Saden scowled. "Haven't you gone through all the beautiful women in LA yet?"

"Hey." Blade stretched his arms wide with a grin. "Beauty is only a light switch away, my brother, and I ain't picky."

He studied his friend briefly, looking for signs that Blade might still be standing on the precipice of insanity. They were evident, though not as pronounced as before. Saden had a feeling Mckenzie had a lot to do with that. She was a firecracker on a summer's day, and a reminder of why they worked so hard to do their jobs well. To safeguard innocents like her from the criminals they hunted.

It brought his mind around to another concern that'd been bothering him. "When you were getting your assignment from Serrakus, did you happen to overhear any information on mine?"

"What do you mean?"

He clawed a hand through his hair with a sigh. "Phoenix dropped by the other day." When Blade palmed the knife at his belt, Saden made a calming gesture. "Not as a threat. At least I don't think so. He said he came to warn me. Apparently, he heard Serrakus telling Lucius that Gabriel is my last job. And that the reason Serrakus didn't inform me of this is because he wants me to screw up so he can keep me on for a while longer."

"Whoa." Blade was silent for several seconds, then asked, "Do you think Phoenix is telling the truth? That guy can't be trusted for shit."

"I'm not sure. If he has some kind of ulterior motive, I haven't seen it yet. From what I know of him, it's not in his MO to purposefully get involved with other Drakons. He's a loner."

"All right, say he's not lying. If this is your last assignment, you can't afford to take any more risks. If you want my opinion, I think you should take the evidence you have now to Serrakus. I was looking over the files with Daneya earlier. There's definitely enough there to incriminate Gabriel. Let Serrakus decide what he wants to do about the others who are in league with him."

A slow smile spread across Blade's face. "Do you know what this could mean?" He tipped his head back and laughed, then gripped Saden's biceps. "You're free! No more groveling to a master and living a half-life. You've fulfilled your sentence. Sweet oblivion waits around the corner, my man. We should celebrate. Get your rocks off one last time. I'll get the girls, you bring the liquor. And don't give me crap about not being able to feel its effects. The burn as it goes down will be enough."

Saden shook his head grimly. "Daneya—"

"Fine. You can have her, I'll take the rest. Come on, man. Cheer up! This is what you've been busting your ass for. Don't tell me you're afraid to die now."

"It's not that." He paced to the other side of the porch then back again. Ever since Phoenix had come to him, he hadn't stopped thinking about finally taking the death he deserved. This was his chance to accept the only absolution he would get for his crimes. Only one thing stood in the way.

"I can't leave Daneya alone right now. There's no guarantee Serrakus will pursue Gabriel's operation. Daneya will try to bring it down herself. She's already got enough information to warrant the help of the DCM. Even with them on her side, she could get herself killed. We have no idea how many Djinn are working with Gabriel or how high this goes within the house of Avram. She'll be going up against factions from both races."

"Daneya's not that stupid. She wouldn't take on more than she could handle."

"Not stupid. Determined." He told Blade of Mckenzie's true parentage and why Gabriel had gone after Daneya the night Saden had first tracked him. The word Daneya had used infected his thoughts like an abhorrent disease. *'Obsessed'*. With anyone else, it might've been an exaggeration. With Gabriel, however, it was all too believable.

The knowledge sickened Saden more than he could deal with. Daneya had every right to demand revenge, and he knew she wouldn't rest until she got it.

Blade leaned back against the banister and let out a low whistle. "Well, fuck me sideways. She's got one hell of a bone to bitch slap Gabriel with."

Saden nodded at the eloquent summation.

"How did Gabriel find her? If she escaped years ago, he's had all this time to search for her. Why now?"

He shrugged a shoulder. "Daneya didn't say anything about it, so I'm assuming she doesn't know either."

The sounds of nature filled the silence that spanned between them. Eventually, Blade took a deep breath and crossed his arms over his chest. "You really love her, don't you?"

Saden opened his mouth to call the man a fool. It wasn't love that had him sacrificing his chance for freedom. It was his sworn duty. A promise to an old friend.

That excuse held up for about the blink of an eye.

He could no more deny his feelings for her than he could change who he was. She had set his fate the moment she'd found out about his past and still looked at him as if he mattered. Treated him like a man who was worth forgiveness and love. He would've given her anything for that, and all she'd wanted in return was comfort. From him.

When she'd asked him what he would take away after she left, his real answer had been everything. His heart, his devotion and sanity. All of it was hers.

If it meant suffering another decade or more of existence, he would do it. "Yeah, I do," he said simply.

Blade dipped his chin in acknowledgment. "Then let's do this."

"I can't ask you to do more than you already have. If this goes bad, it might be your ass as well."

"So what's new? I'm not exactly making myself into a martyr here. I care about what happens to Kennie, which means I can't let her mother go off and commit suicide in the name of revenge. Besides, I agreed to watch out for Daneya if anything happened to you. Might as well do this together."

Saden clapped Blade on the arm with a smile. "You're a good friend."

"Yeah, yeah. One more thing. I've been getting a real creepy vibe lately. Like somebody's watching us but I can't pinpoint who or where they are."

"Now that you mention it, there was interference from an unknown source at Gabriel's house when Daneya and I went to investigate. Someone was tranqing the leisonguardes there from a distance."

"Friend or foe?"

Saden shook his head. "I don't know. Keep doing routine scans in this area, though. If someone's spying on us, I want to find out who."

Blade nodded and led the way inside. From his room, he grabbed the four CDs Saden had taken from Gabriel's stash and the laptop he'd purchased for Mckenzie. While it didn't have Internet access for security reasons, she was able to use it for music and offline games.

In the kitchen, they found Daneya and Mckenzie sitting at the island eating the last of their dinner. A quick search with his Drakonem power told Saden that Cherri was in her room. Likely in an attempt to avoid him. Her argument with Daneya still occupied his thoughts.

He'd been an idiot to think what he was doing with Daneya wouldn't have consequences. Cherri was the one she'd be going home with when this was all over. And Mckenzie. What would her daughter say if she knew what a selfish bastard he was? How he couldn't let go of something he'd never had to begin with.

He had to end this now, before he drove a wedge between Daneya and the only two people who mattered to her. Yet, somehow, getting eviscerated seemed like a less painful ordeal.

Mckenzie waved excitedly and gulped down her mouthful of spaghetti. "Did it work? Are you feeling better?" She cast a furtive glance at her mom then started again. "I-I mean, how are you feeling?"

He leaned on the countertop next to her. "Your mom told me what you did. That was very brave of you. I am in your debt." When she blushed a deep red, he looked briefly to Daneya then back. "If it's okay, I'll tell you more about your power later and how to use it safely."

"Can he, Mom? Please?" She tugged on her mother's arm pleadingly, eyes as round as saucers.

Daneya sighed with exaggeration. "I guess. Don't think I love you or nothin'."

"Of course you do!" Mckenzie said brightly.

"All right, go play some games for now. The adults need to talk."

After Mckenzie took her plate to the sink, she skipped over to Saden and handed him a folded piece of paper, whispering, "The last one's for my mom, but don't tell her."

As she left, he reviewed the list of music CDs she'd made that he had promised to get for her then put it in his pocket. He looked up to find Daneya staring at him intently. Her gaze was searching, no doubt trying to gauge his reaction to the scene Cherri had made earlier. If he were smart, he'd have indicated right then how disastrous what they were doing was. Instead, all he wanted to do was drag her close and breathe her in. Take possession of her full lips the way he had the night before.

Blade cleared his throat loudly, snapping them both back to reality.

Daneya stood and took her own plate to the sink. "So did you find out what Gabriel plans to do now?"

Saden discreetly readjusted the bulge in the front of his pants while her back was turned, inwardly cursing his lack of self-control around her.

"He has a facility about forty miles from here where he's been since we broke into his house. From what I can tell, it's a two level building with one floor underground that he's passing off as a private research company under the ownership of humans. He's been transporting the women individually to a different location. So far, I've counted five that have left with three guards each. There are approximately twenty-five people in the facility at any given time, but I can't tell how many of them are captives."

"Twelve," Daneya said. She hurried back to the island and rifled through the files they'd stolen. "Take away five and that leaves seven women still at the facility. See here?" Saden and Blade looked to where she pointed at two different profiles. "Both are labeled as specimen 3-9, the only difference being the nine years that separates them. All of the others are labeled with a first digit that never goes above four, and a second that's never above twelve. I think the first number represents the facility they're in and the second a way to ID them out of a full dozen."

"Then there are four facilities with a dozen women in each at all times," Saden surmised.

"Exactly. This woman," she said, pointing to one of the profiles, "became specimen 3-9 less than one month after the other one was supposedly discharged. He's reusing their IDs whenever he replaces one with a new specimen."

Blade set the laptop on the counter then gave the CDs to Saden. "Let's see if these can give us any more information."

Saden sat next to Daneya and powered up the laptop. Over the years, he'd developed skills on working with computer hardware and software. It had proven an effective distraction from the bullshit of his life and a way of dealing with the loss of his power.

He put one of the discs in the drive and saw a password window pop up with a timer in the corner counting down from fifteen seconds. "Shit!" he breathed.

Only once had he seen the like before. It was a customized data destruction program with a personalized timer and password. If the correct password wasn't given within the allotted time, the program would not only destroy the operating system of the computer the disc was in. It would also delete the files on the disc and overwrite them with garbage files, ensuring they couldn't be recovered.

Twelve seconds and counting.

He wracked his brain for the full date Gabriel's wife had died and typed it in, ignoring Daneya's and Blade's alarmed inquiries as to what was going on. Nothing happened. The wife's name didn't produce results either. Something, damn it! It had to be something obvious. For all Gabriel's schemes, he was not a complex man. Saden scrubbed his face then leaned back, meeting Daneya's worried gaze.

A chill went down his spine. He typed in DANEYA. With two seconds to spare, the screen went to a desktop image with several folders lined up on the left-hand side.

"What was that?" Daneya asked.

He explained the type of program Gabriel had installed onto the disc, and likely the other CDs as well. When she asked what the password was, he could only stare at her. Caught between keeping his promise not to lie and protecting her from the truth. She was a smart woman, though, and her face blanched considerably as realization set in.

"You don't have to be here—"

She put up a halting hand. "I'm okay. Let's just get this over with."

Saden went back to the laptop, seriously rethinking his decision to take Gabriel in alive. The man was beyond obsessed. Setting his password to a patient's name then attempting to kidnap that patient from the middle of a DCM community was borderline addiction. Or possibly a compulsion to get back the daughter he'd lost. Either way, Saden was leaning dangerously toward delivering Gabriel's punishment himself.

He opened a folder labeled 'Final Proofs' then clicked on one of the files it contained. It was a video starring a woman around the age of thirty. She was sitting on a plain, twin-sized bed and appeared to be in the last weeks of her pregnancy. Her hands were splayed over her distended belly and eyes teetered nervously from the camera to some point to the left of it.

Gabriel's voice came from somewhere in the background. "Tell us who you are."

"My name is specimen 2-6."

"Your real name."

The woman bunched her fists in the loose gown she was wearing and frowned. "L-Lana?" It came out as a question, as if she couldn't quite remember.

"Why did you come to me, Lana?" When her expression remained confused, he prompted, "What made you decide to become a specimen?"

Her response was slow and deliberate, obviously rehearsed. "A friend told me about your kind and how you were dying out. She said you needed healthy surrogate mothers to help your race procreate and that I would be compensated for my time."

"And how long have you been here?"

"Almost ten years, sir. This will be my eighth baby."

"Very good, Lana." Gabriel's tone was sickly sweet and, at the same time, devoid of any tenderness. "You're looking forward to your reward, aren't you?"

She nodded perfunctorily then asked anxiously, "Can I go home soon?"

"Of course. Your contribution to my kind is greatly appreciated."

He continued with another question but the woman interrupted him with a low groan. She gripped her belly and rocked forward. A man dressed in scrubs came into the camera's view and began checking her vitals while another rolled a fetal monitor next to the bed. They quickly laid the woman onto her back and set about attaching an IV and several monitoring cables to her.

The camera panned out to allow the viewer to watch everything that was going on. Gabriel switched to a narrative standpoint and said, "As you can see, we have state-of-the-art equipment available to offer my specimens the best quality of care. A surgeon is on site at all times in case of emergencies and we have twenty-four hour access to the local pharmacy in case our supplies run low."

Saden ended the clip and went on to the next. The following two were nearly identical to the first with the same script and environment, the only difference being the ages of the women. The youngest was in her mid-twenties and pregnant with her fifth child. All were timid, giving him the impression that Gabriel was videotaping only the ones who'd already given up their will to challenge him.

Saden closed the folder then turned to Daneya. "Do you remember this going on when you were at one of the facilities?"

She shook her head. "He kept us isolated for the most part. The only time I saw the other women was for two hours a day in the underground gym and cafeteria. It doesn't matter, though. These recordings are all fabricated. None of the women I met wanted to be there. Except..." Her lips twisted in revulsion. "A few of them were seekers. Apparently, they'd been promised the opportunity to become preyunas to Gabriel's men if they completed their terms without complications."

"Did they say how long they had to serve before their term was up?" Blade asked.

"No. I couldn't stand to talk to them long enough to find out."

Saden opened another folder labeled 'Medical Records'. Inside were four more folders named after the states of California, Arizona, Nevada and Oregon. Each of those contained numerous files categorized by specimen and date. They listed the pharmacies, prescriptions and equipment used for each of the women.

Blade peered closer. "Looks like he's got a facility set up in all four of those states with connections to a pharmacy and medical equipment stores for each of them. Doesn't the house of Avram rule all of those areas?"

"The entire west coast," Saden confirmed.

"From the dates," Daneya chimed in, "he keeps the women for an average of ten years before disposing of them. That coincides with the testimony of the first woman in the videos. She said she was pregnant with her eighth child. It's conceivable that all of them give birth to about eight babies within the timeframe of their imprisonment."

Saden skimmed through the rest of the folders on the disc. They contained receipts, money logs and only the first names of the Vampyre families half of the babies went to, concealing their identities. The other half was simply reported as given to the Djinn. The same information with different dates was found on all three of the other discs.

Daneya sat back with her brow furrowed. "There's just one thing I don't understand. Why would Gabriel keep hard files of everything and risk exposure?"

Blade shrugged a shoulder. "Never assume intelligence. You'll always be disappointed."

"He's building a case," Saden said, even as his mind began piecing it together. "The receipts, the staged interviews. He's planning on informing the Rei'jin of the house of Avram once he has enough gains to justify the means. That's why he's forcing the women to lie and working with human medical companies instead of buying them out to ensure privacy. To establish a rapport with humans and make it seem like they would work in cooperation with Vampyres for the sake of Gabriel's goal. He wants to come out of hiding and expand his operation."

All of the color washed out of Daneya's face. "How would he explain killing the patients after their term?"

"He wouldn't have to once his operation was sanctioned. There are Vampyres with the ability to manipulate chemicals in the body, including those in the cerebrum where our memory lives. With the women's memories erased, there could be no substantial proof that they were ever involved with him. It's probably what he'll tell Lady Ilsa and her council he's been doing all along." Saden didn't mention the fact that wielding chemicals might be the very power her daughter had used to heal him. He could almost feel the calculated rage emanating from Daneya as it was.

Blade shifted beside him. "So what's your plan?"

"Gabriel has likely removed all evidence of his involvement at the nearest facility. From what I saw, he'd sent his leisonguardes and poignots with the females he was transferring, leaving only the Djinn to run the place. We'll need to infiltrate one of the others. Did you happen to follow one of their vehicles when you were on watch?"

"Only for an hour. It hit I-10 going east. I'd say it's safe to assume they were headed for the facility in Phoenix, Arizona. About a six hour drive from here."

"Then that's where we'll go." He slanted his gaze to Daneya. "I don't suppose I could convince you to stay here this time?" Her droll stare gave him his answer. "We'll leave tomorrow before dawn."

Blade inclined his head as he moved to leave. "I'll get my assignment done and be back by then."

Daneya went to the sink and began washing the dishes. Saden stood and watched her, trying to think of a way to broach the subject of their relationship.

Everything inside screamed at him to ignore his doubts and enjoy what she offered. Accept it for the brief interlude of happiness it was. It would be the last he'd get to experience it no matter the outcome of his assignment. But nothing in his life was that easy or without repercussions, and he didn't want her to share in the aftermath.

"Don't," she said. After placing the last clean dish on the rack, she turned around. Fiery resolve blazed in her expression. "You're going to tell me that what we've been doing is a mistake, right? That I would be better off with someone who could give me what I need."

Saden was taken aback by her blatant perception. "How did you know?"

"Because it's what Marco would've said if he were you. The two of you are so alike, it's no wonder you were the one he chose to look after me." She huffed in exasperation then walked slowly toward him. With her hair pulled back in a ponytail, the sharp angles of her face were accentuated, highlighting the spark in her eyes when she narrowed them. "Did you ever stop to think that maybe what I need is standing right in front of me? I get that you want to protect me and I respect the promise you made to Marco, but don't use that as an excuse to push me away. I'm a big girl who can make her own decisions."

"I just don't want to see you get hurt."

"Then don't try to live my life for me!" She clasped his waist with both hands and stared up at him. "I can't say what will happen tomorrow or next week. Whether

I'll ever see you again when this is over. All I do know is that, for the first time, I'm not afraid to be happy, and I owe that to you." Their breath mingled as she pressed her body to his. "Do you want me?"

Gods, yes! He was dizzy with the heat of her soaking into his skin through the fabrics that separated them. This was what he craved. What kept him from the edge of madness. Her passion, her courage and fortitude. For so long, he'd admired it all from a distance. Up close, she was absolutely mesmerizing. A force of calm in the storm of his existence.

And everything he couldn't have.

He gently detached her fingers from his shirt, hating himself more and more with each second that passed.

Daneya's face clouded over with a mixture of emotions that speared his gut. She lowered her head and took a step back. When she looked at him again, cool acceptance shone in her gaze. Wordlessly, she strode from the room, leaving suffocating silence in her wake.

Chapter Twelve

Saden curled his fists and clenched his jaw. It took every ounce of his strength to keep from smashing the CDs on the counter. It all led back to Gabriel. The events of their pasts that had brought them together. The twisted paths of their fates. All of it was linked to that murderous psychopath. Yet, Saden couldn't blame the man for everything. It wasn't Gabriel that had made Daneya care for him.

Would his life have been better without her in it?

He shook his fists loose then pulled out the piece of paper Mckenzie had handed to him. At the bottom of the list was written, The Best of Bill Withers. A talented blues artist and one of Daneya's favorite. She listened to him whenever she needed to unwind from a hard day. He recalled the many nights he'd spent sitting outside her bedroom window, hearing her sing along to the songs. Her voice alone could relax him no matter what mood he was in.

Mckenzie had chosen well. He slid the paper back into his pocket then gathered the laptop and information and went upstairs. After putting it in the top drawer of the dresser in his room, he headed for the front door of the manor, wanting fresh air to clear his thoughts. Mckenzie was sitting on the bottom step of the porch. A squirrel scampered away from her for the cover of a line of bushes to the side of the driveway. She glanced up at him with a small smile.

Saden sat down beside her and stared into the distance.

"I heard you talking to my mom," Mckenzie said quietly.

He looked at her sharply. If she held any disdain for him, he couldn't find it.

"Am I the reason you don't want to be with her? Because of what I am?"

"No!" The word came out a little too harshly. He took a deep breath then touched her chin, making her look directly at him. "It has nothing to do with you. I've done some things that can never be forgiven. My soul is damned. Your mom deserves better than anything I could give her."

"I don't get it. Even if you were bad, you've changed, haven't you? I know you think I'm just a kid, but I'm not stupid. I can tell you two like each other. Mom says when you care about someone, you should hold onto them. Don't you care about her?"

He chuckled lightly and crossed his arms, resting his elbows on his knees. "You're the smartest kid I've ever met. I care about you and your mom more than anyone else in this world, and I wish I could stay with you. What I did in my past makes that impossible, though. I'm a criminal with a sentence to serve. No amount of changing will erase that. Do you understand?"

Her thin shoulders slumped in defeat. "I guess."

"Hey." He bumped his leg into hers then gestured toward the bushes. "What were you doing before I came out?"

She brightened slightly at his inquiry. "If I concentrate hard enough, I can make animals feel warm. They come to me and want to play."

"That's good. Do you know what an aethra is?"

"It's the soul of a Vampyre, right?"

"Yes. It's also the source of a Vampyre's power which embodies his or her natural talents. Think of it as an extension of yourself that can be used for good or evil. You have to be careful when you send it out. Your power feeds from your emotions and can do harm if you lose control. The gift of healing is unique and treasured among Vampyres."

"Really?" Her beaming grin lit up her beautiful features.

He tucked a lock of her hair behind one ear. "You have a special talent. By altering the chemicals in a living being, you can boost its immune system and promote regeneration, allowing the body to heal itself rapidly. However, your power comes with a lot of responsibility. Giving life is only one side of it."

She chewed on her bottom lip in deliberation. "You mean I could take life away as well?"

"If you wanted to. You have to promise me you'll never use your power for that purpose." He put the full weight of his authority behind his tone.

"I promise," she said solemnly.

"Good. Now let me show you how to have a little fun." He spent the next half-hour teaching her how to send a portion of her aethra into the animals nearest them to sense their emotions. She caught on quickly and was soon able to cast her own feelings through the links she established. When a skittish doe pranced up to her and nibbled her fingers, she gasped in amazement. Her peal of laughter afterwards was like the sweetest music.

A faint sound made Saden turn to find Daneya standing in the doorway watching them.

Mckenzie followed his gaze then clapped excitedly, causing the doe to bolt toward the trees. "Did you see? Mom, did you see that? Saden taught me how to communicate with the animals, sort of."

Daneya joined them on the steps. "I saw." She peered at him over her daughter's head, her face unreadable. "He must be a good teacher."

Saden moved to leave but stopped when she reached around to touch his arm. To Mckenzie, she said, "Show me what else you can do."

Mckenzie worked more with her power under his guidance. Eventually, the tension he felt between him and Daneya faded and he relaxed in their company. It was soothing, in a way. He couldn't help imagining what it might be like to have this in his life. To be a permanent part of their family. To love them without fear of hurting them.

Hopeless dreams, he reminded himself cynically, and shut the door on those thoughts.

* * * *

It was four o'clock in the morning when Saden returned to the manor. A light drizzle cooled the pre-dawn air outside, lulling the sounds of nature and lending an atmosphere of tranquility to the coming day. That sense of peace would change soon enough, along with everything else. If all went according to plan, Daneya and her family would be free to leave within a day and he would be accepting the death that awaited him. Or choosing to stay on as a Drakon out of his stubborn desire to keep watch over Daneya.

And if something went wrong…

Saden forced that line of thought from his mind. He had less than a week to close his assignment and he couldn't afford to make any mistakes.

He made a quick run into town for gas and the music Mckenzie had requested. By the time he got back, Daneya was dressed, armed and waiting for him in the living room. They loaded into the car and hit I-10 on their way out of state. Daneya avoided him for the most part, staring out of the window at the passing scenery. The silence between them was near stifling.

This wasn't how he'd envisioned their time together would end. In anger or relief, yes, but not this rigid stalemate rife with unsaid words. He wanted to justify his actions. Explain to her why it was necessary to break off their pretense of a relationship now, while she still had the respect of her friend. More than that, he wanted her to know just what she meant to him. What she and Mckenzie had given him over the past several days.

None of that came out, however.

Instead, he broke the tension by going over the plan he'd worked out during the long hours of the night. "Gabriel is at his home for the time being, so we won't run into him. He'll most likely have Djinn guarding the facility since they can walk in daylight and a skeleton crew of leisonguardes and poignots inside. How much do you know of the Djinn?"

Daneya slanted him a glance through thick lashes. "I know they're spirits born of smoke and black fire who need bodies to contain their energy. Also, that they can reverse the effects of illnesses in their hosts but not heal their injuries. So once the host is down, it stays down, which forces the Djinn to leave the body. They can only enter a new body with the host's permission. So far, no one has been able to find a way to kill them permanently."

Saden dipped his head, impressed by her knowledge except for one point. "A Djinn can be killed. The black fire is their soul and can be destroyed by the blue fire of a Drakonem. The Drakonem are loathe to take them out, though, as it requires the death of the host. Usually by a shot or stab to the heart. The sudden shock temporarily immobilizes the Djinn and makes it sluggish when it's trying to release the host.

"When we get there, keep in mind that the hosts are almost always innocent. They may have accepted whatever deal the Djinn made them, but that doesn't mean they signed on for what the Djinn does while in control of their bodies."

"Careful. I do believe that's sympathy showing through your tough guy exterior."

He looked at her sharply and saw the teasing glint in her eyes. A corner of his mouth turned up in a grin. "Just remember what I said before. Stay close to me and kill only if necessary."

She appeared as if she might say something more then turned back to the window. Thirty minutes outside of Phoenix, he refilled the gas tank then set the specific coordinates for the facility into his GPS. According to the receipts on one of the CDs, the medical equipment was delivered to an area on the outskirts of the city. He found a back route and parked the car a quarter-mile away from the facility. It stood apart from a small complex of warehouses currently empty and up for sale.

After telling Daneya to stand by the car, he transformed to his dragon state and took to the skies.

Behind the building was a parking lot half full of vehicles, two of which were the same vans that'd been used to transport the prisoners. A single Djinn stood at the front entrance and another at the back with rotating cameras attached above the doors. Although there was an emergency exit on the roof, Daneya would never make it up there without alerting one of the guards.

He scanned the interior with his Drakonem power and sensed twenty-five people on the underground floor. Most of them were stationary and probably the women being held captive. Fifteen were on ground level and two of those positioned directly on the other sides of the entrances.

Gabriel hadn't taken kindly to the intrusion of his home.

There was no way he was getting Daneya in and out of there undetected. He flew back to the car, materialized to his corporeal form and relayed the information. "This building is identical to the one near LA, so I'm assuming all the facilities have the same structure. Do you recall where the security office was in the building you were held at?"

Her brow furrowed as she tied off the braid she'd pulled her hair into. "It would have to be on the first floor. The cafeteria, gym, infirmary and cells for the women are all underground. I'm not sure where anything else is located. Gabriel kept me locked up most of the time and leaving was…"

A nightmare. The unspoken thought was written on the lines of her face. "It's all right. We'll go in through the back. Stay near the cars in the lot until I take out the guard at the door. There's another one inside so wait for my signal, and try to keep your head down. I don't want you caught on the cameras." He readied to switch forms again when Daneya laid a hand on his arm. Her eyes beseeched his and held him frozen in place.

In a quiet voice, she said, "Don't make me wait for you like last time. In and out, remember?"

He cupped her jaw and brushed a thumb over her lips, unable to resist touching her. "In and out."

A few seconds later, he was airborne and flew to the roof of the building, tracking Daneya as she sprinted across the open land. When the Djinn's head was turned, she darted behind one of the vehicles. Saden took out the security camera on his way down then solidified in full view. The man stumbled back in surprise then hit the cement, going down from a glancing blow to his temple.

Saden took the key card from the band on the Djinn's belt and slid it through the electronic lock by the door. After opening the door, he hid on the other side of it.

"Stephen?" called the second Djinn from inside. "What the hell are you doing?"

As soon as he was out, Saden swung him around by the neck and slammed him face first into the wall of the building. The man rocked back and fell to the ground. Saden grabbed his key card as well then motioned for Daneya to join him. Inside was a long corridor with doors on either side. It was brightly lit and smelled of industrial cleaner. Luck was with him as the first door he tried opened to the security room with a wall of monitors to one side. The guard at the desk jumped up with a hand on the gun at his belt.

Daneya pushed past Saden, saying, "My turn." She smoothly knocked the weapon from the man's hand, kneed him in the gut then slammed an elbow into the back of his head as he bent forward.

Saden went to the terminal and told her to keep an eye out. It wasn't hard to access the main feed for the cameras and shut them down. Back in the corridor, they began checking the other doors but most wouldn't admit them with the guards' key cards. Gabriel obviously didn't trust all the people he was working with.

Daneya gestured for him to come over to a window along the left wall. On the other side of the reinforced glass was a nursery with several infant beds lined up in plain sight. Three of them were occupied and what appeared to be a female nurse was taking their vitals and recording them in metal files hanging at the foot of the beds.

Saden curled his lip in disgust. It appalled him that a woman could knowingly support what Gabriel was doing to other females. The fact that the surrogate mothers were human shouldn't have made a difference, though he knew it did. While Vampyres were raised to respect humans and treat them with equality, a great majority of them still considered themselves superior.

Before he could stop her, Daneya was in the nursery and attacking the poignot. The woman crumpled easily to the floor under Daneya's fists. It was over by the time he stepped into the room. Daneya grabbed the woman's key card and held it up with a grim smile. "This should get us into the offices. All of the assistants have access to them."

Saden had to admit he was glad she was there. When he dragged the poignot to a storage closet, movement from the window caught his attention. He yanked Daneya into the closet with him then shut the door, leaving an inch-wide crack for them to peek through. With her back against the wall, he brought his body flush to hers, ready to anticipate her move.

Sounds of another person entering the nursery drifted to them, and Daneya shifted to charge out as he'd known she would. He placed a staying hand on her neck and shook his head. They needed to do this with as little interference as possible.

A mewling cry came from one of the infants. There were shuffling noises and eventually the infant quieted down. It was a male nurse this time and his voice carried as he mumbled something unintelligible to himself. Saden could feel Daneya's pulse beating rapidly beneath his fingertips. When the soft click of the nursery door sounded again, he lifted her face to him and saw moisture brimming her lashes. Her eyes remained locked on the beds carrying the babies.

"They're innocent," she whispered. "They don't deserve to be used like this. Given to the Djinn." Her compassion rivaled the vehemence in her tone.

He gently wiped her eyes and kissed her forehead. "We'll get Gabriel and save them later, I swear."

She took a steadying breath then went with him to check the corridor. It was clear once more and they retried all of the doors with the nurse's key card. When they came to an office that was larger and far more elaborate than the others, he closed the door behind them, positive it belonged to Gabriel.

"Look for papers with current dates, full names, photographs. Anything that might help us track the Djinn he's working with." While Daneya searched through the bookshelves and filing cabinets, he powered up the desktop computer. It, too, was protected by a password, though there was no timer attached. He tried Daneya's name and a few other guesses without success. After a minute of deliberation, he asked, "Your birthday is September fourth, 1986, right?"

She glanced at the computer then rolled her eyes. "Not this again."

"It's worth a shot."

Her jaw flexed as she ground her teeth. "Yes."

When that didn't work, he said, "Do you remember the date he kidnapped you?"

"2003, January fifteenth."

Bingo. Gabriel's homepage appeared on the screen. Saden confirmed it with a nod, to which Daneya simply turned stiffly away and went back to her search.

He opened the Excel documents first. They contained more of the same information he'd found on the CDs from Gabriel's house. All except for the last one. "Fuck."

"What is it?" Daneya left her task to peer over his shoulder. In front of them was a spreadsheet with information in several columns. She pointed to the left column that began with the label *Infant 1-5-1, 03/19/1948*. "This looks like a list of the babies born to the women he's used."

"With the correct dates given for their births," he added. He moved her finger two columns over. "This has to be the list of people he's given them to. I recognize the name of the third one down. He's cousin to the royal family here. So is this one. And Roccuso Mires there is first general to korvaute Weiss, the commander of the leisonguardes for the house of Avram. Shit!"

Saden raked a hand through his hair. "This just got a hell of a lot more serious. Gabriel's got not only the Djinn, but a whole crew of powerful Vampyres behind him. From the dates, I'd say they even helped him set up his enterprise."

"Some of the babies are unaccounted for."

"No." He scrolled down to a division in the spreadsheet and found what he suspected. "Gabriel made two lists. One of the Vampyres he gave the infants to and one of the Djinn. None of these names on the second half are familiar to me. They have to be the Djinn who are involved."

Daneya straightened beside him. "This is what we need, isn't it?"

"That and a whole lot more." Quickly, he inserted a thumb drive into the computer and copied the documents. "If you found anything important, grab it now. It's time to get the hell out of here." When the transfer was complete, he stuffed the thumb drive and papers from Daneya into an inside pocket of his trench.

In that instant, the door to the office opened and a man wearing a white lab coat walked in. He had to be the other assistant they'd encountered, though his reactions were faster than those of the leisonguarde. Saden felt a vacuous shift in the air and realized the poignot's intent just as Daneya pulled a throwing knife from her belt.

"No!" he shouted and slapped the knife from Daneya's hand. At the same time, the air in the room was sucked toward the poignot then blasted back with a force that picked them up off their feet and threw them back several yards. A hardwood end table broke his fall and splintered beneath him. The yells of the assistant calling for guards sounded above the ringing in his ears. He crawled to where Daneya lay and cradled her face in both hands, swiping at the blood leaking from her nose. "Are you hurt?"

She coughed then pushed herself up. "I'm fine."

"Stay behind me," he said as he helped her stand. "Use weapons only at close range and don't let them corner you."

The pounding of boots in the corridor heralded the newcomers. Saden tapped into his Drakonem power and cast it out, erecting a wall of controlled, blue flames in the doorway to block the path of the guards. As he strode forward, he focused all of his concentration on bending the fire to his will. It moved into the corridor then split down the middle. One half blazed from floor to ceiling and proceeded to the left while the other half shifted to the right. It left a small space for him and Daneya to maneuver in.

He pulled Daneya with him and inched his way between the roaring flames toward the rear exit. Gunshots were fired above their heads, shattering the ceiling lights and raining glass down on them. They ducked down in a crouch.

"Lower the shield," Daneya told him. When he looked at her uncertainly, she leaned in close. "Trust me. Take care of your side. I've got mine."

Against his better judgment, he drew back his power and took a quick assessment of the situation as the flames dispersed. Four men stood in front of Daneya, six on his side including the poignot. Though he had full confidence in her skills, it didn't keep his attention from being divided.

A solid blow to his back brought him down to one knee. He spun around with a low kick and heard the satisfying crack of the nearest guard's kneecap. Saden cut off his scream with a fist to his face then dodged the next guy's attack. As soon as he gained his feet, three of the men came at him in full charge. He beat them back with a flurry of kicks and punches, relying more on instinct than sight to guide his moves. They hit the floor one by one.

Searing pain sliced through his left thigh and he turned to see the glint of steel flash in the hand of another guard. The man hacked with the dagger in clumsy sweeps. Saden waited until he overextended himself then trapped the guard's hand in both of his, twisting the blade and plunging it into the man's leg. Without pause, he shoved the guard away hard enough to knock back the rest of the men.

That bought him a brief respite, which he used to check on Daneya.

She was vision to watch. Her movements were smooth and lithe, her body flowing effortlessly in a deadly assault. Two guards lay at her feet, a third was going down beneath her strikes and the last was reeling from a vicious jab to his windpipe. Saden was about to go back to his own fight when he saw the fourth man pull a gun from his chest harness.

Daneya was too engaged to notice the new threat. He bellowed her name and dove for her, wrenching her behind him while sending a bolt of Drakonem power at the man's feet.

It was too much. His emotions doubled the force of the blast and he crashed with Daneya into the wall under a spray of choking debris. The ground around them rumbled and shook precariously.

Shit!

He realized he'd weakened the structure of the floor only seconds before it fell out from under them. Swiftly, he twisted in mid-air so that his back hit the floor on the lower level with Daneya on top of him. The breath was slammed from his lungs and his head bashed against the ground painfully. The world spun in a sickening rush around him.

Through the haze of dust above, he made out the silhouettes of two of the guards looking down at them. And the barrel of a gun trained on his head. He rolled with Daneya amidst more gunshots until they were out of view then scanned her for injuries, touching everywhere he could reach.

Her hands were steady as they took his and it was only when their eyes met that he was able to calm the fear-laced adrenaline pumping through his system. "I'm all right," she assured him.

The distant barking of orders from one of the guards snapped their attention. If they didn't find a way out soon, they would be trapped underground.

Saden jumped up and looked around. They were in what appeared to be one of the cells for the women. It had a clinical atmosphere with sparse furniture, a metal door and one wall made almost entirely of reinforced Plexiglas. A woman in her early twenties with long, flaxen hair was sitting on the bed. She stared at them with a combination of wariness and hope.

Saden told Daneya to stand back then focused a burst of power at the lock on the door. It swung open and he peered outside. Three guards were racing toward him from the far side of another long corridor. He glanced back to find Daneya standing beside the woman.

"What's your name?" Daneya asked.

The woman replied shakily, "I'm called 4-7."

"Daneya!" he said sharply.

Her eyes were imploring when they turned on him. "We can't just leave her here."

There was no arguing with the edge of determination in her voice. He knew her well enough to recognize when she wouldn't take no for an answer. Problem was, they might not be able to get themselves out of there safely, let alone a scared innocent. Not without killing a few of the guards on their way. Daneya could no more afford blood on her hands than he could. It would make her a target not only to Gabriel, but to the people he was working with as well.

Saden cursed inwardly. If death was on the menu, it would be by his doing. "Don't move until I get back."

The first two guards were on him just as he slipped out. They went down almost too easily. All brawn and no skill. The third, however, was built like a tank with the training to back him up. Saden traded blows evenly with the man, taking as good as he got. He was about to put an end to it when he saw Daneya in the corridor flanked by a small group of women. She was headed farther away from him, using the poignot's key card to release more of the prisoners.

The momentary distraction cost him. Pain ripped through his right shoulder as his arm was wrenched behind his back hard enough to tear muscle. The tank cut off his air in a choke hold then slammed him face first into the wall, immobilizing him. What he saw next sent a wave of fear crashing through him.

All of the women had fled into one of the cells, leaving Daneya to face the two guards that had appeared on the other side of her. For some reason, she wasn't moving. Held in an invisible grip while one of the men raised a gun and pointed it at her head. Saden drew upon all the power in his being, uncaring of the consequences. Before he could cast it out to incinerate the guards, a massive, tawny cat bounded from the room Saden and Daneya had fallen into and tackled the man with the gun.

A haze began to circle Saden's vision. He jerked his head back and heard the crunch of the tank's nose. When the hold on him loosened, Saden twisted around and finished the guy off, making sure he wasn't getting up any time soon. At the far end of the corridor, Daneya had snapped out of her trance and was urging the women from the cell where they had gathered.

A man with shoulder-length, dark blond hair left the guard he'd knocked unconscious and turned at Saden's approach. He was tall and firmly built wearing casual clothes with only a hunting knife at his belt. The golden panther that stood beside him watched avidly. Saden fisted one of his own knives, ready to attack if necessary.

The stranger held up his hands in a calming gesture. "I'm not your enemy. My name is Roshon, chief of the Thorien clan. Take the stairwell with the women up to the roof. My men are waiting to help them outside."

Saden was about to ask what a Rakshasas chief was doing there when the panther leaped past him and pounced on a guard he hadn't seen. Roshon ran after the cat, preparing to attack another guard who'd come from the room with the hole in the ceiling. Saden left them to their fight, his only concern now being Daneya's safety.

He went to the last door in the corridor and pushed through the crowd of women making their way up the stairwell. There were six in all, varying in their stages of pregnancy from barely showing to full bellies. What the hell had Daneya been thinking? He knew the answer to that even as he caught up to her on the last stair. Desperate triumph was shining on her face when she glanced at him. This was personal, and she wanted Gabriel to know it.

But it was also reckless. She was risking more than just their lives in her need for revenge.

He tamped down his anger and took her by the elbow out onto the roof. Another Rakshasa warrior was waiting for them. He guided them to the edge where Saden saw two more standing on the ground below.

"They'll catch the women when they jump," the man said.

It wasn't exactly safe for the pregnancies — however, there was no other option. Besides, many would probably lose the babies with no further recourse to Djinn energy, just as Cherri had. It was a sad inevitability, but necessary for the lives of the women.

Saden reluctantly let go of Daneya so she could coax the women's trust and help them over the side of the building. A plan formed quickly as he surveyed the parking lot. "The women will take that van over there," he told the warrior. "I need you to follow in my car. It's parked a quarter-mile southeast with the keys inside. Head to California on I-10. Stop only when you get to Riverside. I'll take care of any stragglers on your tail."

When Daneya was the last woman on the roof, he relayed what he wanted her to do then took dragon form and flew to the van. Its engine rumbled to life when he hit it with a burst of his power. After everyone was inside, he closed the driver's door for Daneya then leaned in close. "No pit stops. Straight to Riverside."

Her eyes were imploring when they searched his. "I had to. I couldn't leave all of them behind."

He gave a cursory nod and backed away, too wound up to speak. If anything had happened to her... His mind shut down that train of thought, not wanted to go there. Daneya was still alive and he was going to keep it that way.

From the air, he saw the chief burst through the front entrance of the building and swooped down to meet him. "Take your men and follow that van." He pointed to where Daneya was swerving around to the main road.

"What about you?" Roshon asked.

"I'll be watching from above." Once in the air again, he kept an eye on Roshon and his men and targeted the Djinn with bolts of fire aimed at their feet. It was easy to distinguish between the two by their clothing. The Djinn had no advantages of power or animals at their sides, leaving them to rely on weapons and protective gear.

There were five Rakshasas that he could make out—four men and one woman. They formed a line of two vehicles behind the van with Saden's car taking up the rear. When the Djinn gave chase in two more vehicles, Saden spread a line of fire in front of them on the pavement. The first car skidded in a tailspin and crashed into a ditch while the second shot through the flames. This one he hit with a blast of Drakonem power that killed the engine.

Fortunately, they were too far on the outskirts of the city for human enforcement to be a complication. He remained above them, soaring through the skies and only visible to the untrained eye as a shadowed blur.

Chapter Thirteen

Five hours later, the fear riding him at Daneya's disregard for her own life had turned to smoldering rage. He had to touch her. Assure himself that she was unharmed. Never in his life had he felt such panic as when that leisonguarde had held her in his power with a gun pointed at her head. All for the lives of women she didn't even know.

Though he understood her reasons, it didn't take away from the fact that she had deviated from the plan and put everything at risk. If they had failed, there would've been no second chances.

When Daneya pulled over onto an isolated dirt road just outside of Riverside, he landed near them and took back his corporeal form. Everyone except for the group of women got out of their cars. Daneya stood by the van and watched him as he strode purposefully toward her. Alarm sparked in her eyes when she saw his expression and she took a step back.

He knew what he looked like and didn't try to hide it. Didn't give a damn what the others thought of their relationship at that moment.

"Saden…" she started and put a hand up.

He ignored it, grabbed her by the arms and yanked her against him. His mouth came down hard on hers as he crushed her to him. She was stiff with shock in his steel grasp but he didn't care. All that mattered was the heat of her body against his and the feel of her lips surrendering to him.

He wrapped as much of himself as he could around her and deepened the kiss. When her muscles relaxed and she opened to him, he delved into her mouth with a passion he couldn't control. For that space in time, she was his and nothing could change that. Her courage, past and future. He was her protector, and he never wanted to feel that helpless again.

Gradually, the tension eased and he realized she was holding onto him as much as he was her. She pressed closer and entangled her hands in his hair, letting out a soft moan. When they finally pulled apart, he remembered the cause of his anger and shook her gently. "Don't ever put yourself in danger like that again."

A small smile was her only response.

The chief cleared his throat loudly. "I assume you have an idea of what you're going to do with the females you rescued."

Saden put a hand on Daneya's lower back as he turned around, not quite able to let her go yet. "I do. First, I want to know your part in all of this. Why did you go to the facility and how did you know we would be there?"

Roshon hesitated slightly. "Let's just say we have a mutual acquaintance who informed me of Gabriel Aikins' work with the Djinn. He also told me how to find you and what you're trying to do to stop Gabriel. In this, we are in agreement. The Vampyre must be exposed and his experiments on humans brought to an end for the sake of all demonkind."

"Who is this mutual acquaintance?"

"I think, in this situation, it's best not to look a gift horse in the mouth. Sometimes, allies can be found even among enemies."

Saden stared at the shapeshifter, trying to size him up. There was something familiar about him, in his fair features and lean build. Something Saden couldn't quite place. It didn't make sense for a Rakshasa, let alone a chief in charge an entire clan's warriors, to find interest in the affairs of Vampyres. While the two races had never gone to war with each other, neither had they joined in collaboration for any effort.

There had to be more to Roshon's explanation than he was letting on.

Daneya put his thoughts into words when she asked, "What could this mean for you? As far as I know, Rakshasas don't involve themselves with Vampyres."

"You're right," Roshon replied. "Just as Drakons don't usually work with vigilantes of the DCM." When Daneya and Saden both tensed, he raised his hands in placation. "Don't mistake my knowledge for a threat. I mean you no harm. If you'll forgive me, I've been spying on you ever since I was told about you a few days ago. Honestly, I thought the only way a vigilante would stand with a Drakon is if she was being forced to. Obviously, I was wrong. No offense," he said to Saden.

Saden knew the man had every right to his suspicions. He was a condemned criminal. The waste of demonkind and beneath the forgiveness and respect of others. Still, it rankled that anyone would think he was a danger to Daneya. "Offense taken."

"You have my apologies. You're not...what I expected in a Drakon. Be assured, I know nothing else about you, not even her name. What I do know is that the Djinn are rising in ways I can't explain and we would do well to work together. Over the past half-century, the Djinn have somehow found a way to turn my men into Vanaras upon their deaths and are using them to attack us."

"I thought Vanaras were self-made," Daneya interrupted. "A consequence of forsaking the afterlife."

Roshon nodded. "That is the way it should be. However, warriors I personally know would never do that are coming back from the dead. They're also hunting in packs, a phenomenon that's unprecedented. By the numbers I've come across, it appears as if the Djinn are building an army. I don't need to tell you what a legion of Vanaras and Djinn-possessed Vampyres could mean for all of us."

"You're also worried the Djinn might begin impregnating your own kind," Saden supplied. It was what would concern him if he were in the chief's shoes.

"I am. I know you have no more reason to trust me than I do you, but I'm asking you to let us"—he gestured to include his men—"continue helping in this matter. Whatever it takes, we want to see Gabriel's operation stopped."

Saden studied Roshon and his men. He could find no fault in their ambition, though as Roshon had said, it didn't exactly inspire trust. On the other hand, he could use a band of Rakshasas on his side. With the information he'd discovered at the facility, there was more at stake than just the welfare of the human females.

He looked to Daneya who gave an almost imperceptible nod. "All right, then. You can follow us back to my place. Your men will drive the women to the DCM compound near this area and drop them off as close as they can get without risking themselves. Daneya will call the director of the compound to notify him."

Daneya shook her head immediately. "I should go with them to make sure nothing happens."

Gently, he said, "If Vincent knew you were coming, he wouldn't let you leave." And he wasn't ready to say his goodbyes just yet. Not with the way things were between them. He pulled out his cell phone and handed it to her.

She took it without further argument. When she was done with the call, she told Roshon where his men could take the women and relayed Vincent's promise that no one would be harmed. From what Saden knew of the man, the promise shouldn't be an empty one. He went with Daneya in his car while Roshon assigned three of his warriors to escort the women then took one of the cars for himself and the fourth man.

Saden couldn't stop thinking about the acquaintance who'd tipped off Roshon and whether it was the same person who had tranqed the leisonguardes at Gabriel's mansion. Whoever it was, the person couldn't be considered a friend. Not with the vague comment Roshon had made about allies among enemies. For now, he would keep a close eye on the chief and hope that Blade might recognize him from his life before he became a Drakon.

* * * *

"So what do you think?"

Roshon glanced at Kent then put his SUV in drive behind Saden's car. "I'm not sure yet. This Drakon is experienced at his job, that's for sure. And I believe he means to do everything he can to bring down Gabriel. What I can't figure out is his connection to the human woman. It almost looks as if he—"

"Cares for her?" Kent finished.

"A man in his position has no right to involve himself with an innocent. Even if she is a vigilante."

"Because of what he is. Condemned."

The words were matter-of-fact but Roshon heard the undercurrent of cynicism in them. He winced as he realized what he'd said could've been applied to his friend as well. In a lot of respects, the two men were the same. Both had pasts they couldn't escape and a future with no hope. While Kent's situation was slightly different, and the reasons for his damnation a load of bullshit, it didn't change who he was.

A man apart from everyone else with no choice except to remain that way for the rest of his existence.

"I didn't mean—"

Kent waved him off. "Save it. I agree with you. He could've gotten the woman killed back there. He's tempting fate by involving the DCM in any way. Your brother was right to come to you about this. Saden's in over his head. Bringing Gabriel in won't stop what's going on. The Vampyre may have started his operation, but the Djinn are running it now, maybe more than he is. I recognized one of them as a servant to Forrest."

Roshon snapped his head around. "Forrest, the general of the Djinn in this area?" When Kent nodded, he let out a heavy breath. With Forrest in on Gabriel's scheme, they could be in potentially more danger than any of them realized. Roshon had never met the bastard face to face. Most of what he knew of him was from the handful of Djinn they'd captured over the years and

Kent, who'd had the misfortune of dealing with the leader before.

Forrest was a conniving ringleader among his kind. The one who convinced others by threat or promise to do his bidding while he stood in the shadows and collected the spoils of the wars he started. He was insane with power by several accounts and so far unstoppable. Roshon had long suspected him to be behind the recent rise of Vanaras, though he had no proof.

"Do you think Saden is aware of this?"

Kent rubbed his jaw in thought, his hazel eyes narrowing as he shook his head. "It's doubtful. We'll have to inform him before he takes whatever evidence he found to his Drakonem. Sadly, Gabriel is the lesser of the two evils. There's no telling what Forrest might do if that Vampyre is taken out of the equation."

Roshon agreed. It was likely Forrest would simply find another Vampyre to take over the operation. Possibly in a different part of the world where no one would find him again until it was too late.

Sometime later, they reached Saden's sprawling manor full of slanted roofs and wraparound verandas. Nothing like what Roshon would've taken for the temporary living place of a Drakon. It was designed more for a family, not a criminal. From the time he'd spent spying on Saden in his geis form, he was already familiar with the layout of the land. Also with the second Drakon who stayed there. What he hadn't expected was the shock of what he found inside.

When Saden and Daneya led them into the manor, a little girl shot out from a side hallway, shouting happily for her mom. Daneya swept her up and spun her around with a smile that could only come from a parent. The girl was almost her exact replica with burgundy locks and creamy skin, but there was a noticeable difference. Roshon could feel the faint ripple of power flowing through the girl.

Not human, or least not fully. A Vampyre. He and Kent both stilled in the foyer as that information sank in.

When the little girl's gaze fell upon them, her eyes rounded in wonder and seemed to fix on Kent. Roshon couldn't blame her. The man was a compelling sight. Large with angular features and an unmistakable edge of darkness. The black wolf at his side only added to the effect. Another woman came from the same hallway. This one was purely human with a homely face and a burst of strawberry blonde curls. Daneya ushered her and the girl up a flight of stairs to the second floor.

Saden took them to what appeared to be a living room, although half the furniture was covered in white sheets. He threw his trench over the back of a recliner then sat down while Kent and Roshon took the couch across from him.

"How did you become a Drakon?" Roshon asked bluntly, seeing no point in pleasantries after what they'd been through. When Saden raised a brow, he said, "You need our help, and I want to know what kind of man I'm working with."

Saden hardened his gaze and leaned back. "Gabriel was my uncle. At the start of his operation, he was discovered by a Drakon and tricked me into destroying his evidence. Three of the Djinn he was working with at the time were caught in the explosion. The bodies of their human hosts were found in the remains of the facility. I was charged with their deaths."

"So you have more reason than most to hate him."

"If you think I take no responsibility for what I did, you're wrong. Because of me, he was able to continue his experiments and ruin the lives of countless humans. It is for that reason I have an interest in what happens to him."

Roshon glanced at Kent then back to Saden with newfound respect. It took a brave man to admit to his faults, especially when they held as many repercussions as Saden's did. "I believe you. You wouldn't be the first to take the blame for someone else's actions. Sometimes I envy the humans their justice system, as wanting as it is. The Drakonem care nothing about fair trials or the truth of most situations involving humans."

Saden dipped his chin in acknowledgment.

"What of the vigilante? What's her reason for working with a Drakon?"

"You'll have to ask her. I won't betray her confidence."

"It's okay," Daneya said. All of them turned to watch as she strode into the room to stand next to Saden. She was a striking beauty even with her hair mussed and a thin layer of plaster covering her. "I used to be one of the women we saved from the facility today. When Gabriel came after me again, Saden rescued me, along with my daughter and friend. We've been here ever since."

Roshon quickly pieced together the missing details of her story. The little girl was a byproduct, then, of Gabriel's zeal to ensure the continuation of his race. It was no wonder she'd been adamant about freeing the captive females and putting her life in jeopardy in the process. "I'm sorry for what you must've gone through."

Daneya shrugged, her eyes trailing down to settle on Saden. "It hasn't all been that bad."

Her tone belied the affection he knew she was trying to hide. It was apparent what the two had for each other was more than simple lust. Judging from their kiss earlier, much more.

The blonde woman walked into the room, followed by the second Drakon. He might have looked as if he lived on the beach if it weren't for his eyes. They belonged to the kind of man who had seen death and caused it.

"This is Cherri," Saden introduced. "A friend of Daneya's. And Blade. He's been watching over the house for me." To Blade, he said, "This is Roshon, chief of the Thorien clan, and…"

"Kent," Roshon finished. "My second in command." He glossed over the events of the day, including the reasons why he and his warriors had come. When he'd approached his close-knit group of friends about it the morning after Cai's appearance, he'd made it clear that they were under no obligation to join him on this mission. Not a single one had blinked an eye. They were loyal to a fault and would give their lives in service to him, just as he would do for any one of them.

Blade left then at Saden's request and came back with a laptop which he set up on the coffee table. Saden filled them in on what he'd found at Gabriel's mansion then paused. The weight behind his next words was no warning, but a promise. "What I'm about to show you can go no further than this room. If it does, I will hunt you down and kill you."

Roshon almost grinned. Saden had a way of cutting through the bullshit that he admired. "You have our word."

Saden laid out a stack of papers from inside his trench coat onto the table then inserted a thumb drive into the laptop. An Excel document came up with several columns of information. "This is a list of all the infants that have been born under Gabriel's control and the individuals they were given to. Djinn and Vampyre alike. Some of the Vampyre names belong to members of the royal family here and high ranking officials of the leisonguarde."

Blade let out a low whistle. "Didn't see that coming. Talk about a twist."

The implications of the new information weren't lost on Roshon. In fact, he'd heard of entire clans of Rakshasas falling to similar situations. Unable to recover from the damage done, they'd been forced to give up their titles and submit to the reign of other clans just to keep the innocents caught up in the betrayal safe.

Those hard decisions had been made by people truly loyal to the survival of their clans, however. Saden no longer owed such loyalty to a race that had repudiated him. Roshon was curious to see what course the Drakon would take now, or whether it affected him at all. From Saden's grim composure, he had a good idea what the answer would be.

"I don't understand," Daneya said, creasing her brow in confusion. "We should be celebrating, shouldn't we? With this, we can justify the need for a full investigation. Everyone involved can be taken down, not just Gabriel."

Hesitation lined Saden's face, a mark of where he stood on the issue, though it was Kent who answered. "This proves that the inner structure of the house of Avram has been corrupted. A disgrace of this magnitude can't be dealt with quietly. Gabriel and his cohorts have completely disregarded all the laws the

Vampyre race was built upon after their separation from the Djinn. Once word of this spreads, there will be civil unrest. The royal family here will be considered weak and could face disempowerment by the other families. It could take them years to recover, leaving them vulnerable to the Djinn."

Blade scoffed. "Fuck civil unrest. It could cause a revolt. Their pride would demand nothing less."

"Well, then, can't you take this directly to the leader of the house of Avram?" Daneya asked. "Maybe he can work with the Drakonem and use this list to take out the guilty individuals discreetly."

Saden shook his head. "Lady Ilsa is only the figurehead. She can't make this kind of decision without the majority vote of her council, and many of the officials on this list are also on that council. Besides, the list only tells us who received infants, not everyone that might be involved. Even if I were to find the right people, informing them could still lead to the division of the house."

"And informing the wrong people could destroy everything you've done so far," Blade added. "It's a violation of our rules for a Drakon to consult any outsiders on an assignment he's given. Those people could claim that you fabricated the evidence and report your violation to the Drakonem. The case would be dismissed and you would be punished. Probably sent out of the country to another Drakonem."

Kent shifted in his seat. "It might not end there. The Drakonem don't care about governing houses or the people who fall under them. If your master were to continue the investigation without you, he could end up doing more harm than good."

A heavy silence fell over the room. Roshon had to admit he was at a loss as to how to proceed. The only thing he was sure of at this point was the growing respect he felt for Saden. To look at the circumstances from all angles while knowing he could be held accountable—again—for something that was beyond his control had to be maddening. Yet, he hadn't made one complaint about his lot. If the circumstances were different, they might've been good friends.

The blonde woman, Cherri, broke their reverie with a sudden outburst. "So what if the Vampyres become weak because of all this! Daneya and I are members of the DCM, Saden and Blade are outcasts and you two"— she waved a hand at Roshon and Kent—"aren't even Vampyres. None of us has anything to gain from helping them. And who knows, it could be a blessing. Obviously, if it was so easy to corrupt the officials of that house, it wasn't strong enough to begin with. They can rebuild and come up with better laws."

"It's not that simple," Saden said gently.

"I don't give a damn what's not simple for you! I want my life back! Daneya, tell him. This is not our concern."

Daneya stared at her companion with a mixture of doubt and disapproval. "Cherri—"

The other woman threw her hands up in exasperation. "Don't tell me you care about Saden so much that you would throw your life away. If Vincent found out about this, he would kick us out of the DCM. Is that what you want? You told me Saden swore to protect you years ago. Well, if he really wanted to keep his promise, he would let us go and face this on his own. He's nothing but a selfish coward."

"Enough!" Saden's roar echoed along the walls. After a visible effort to gather his patience, he said in a quieter tone, "Daneya's welfare has never left my mind, nor Mckenzie's or yours. Taking this evidence to my Drakonem and getting rid of Gabriel will only open the path for another to take his place. There's no guarantee that his replacement won't come after all of you to tie up loose ends. Risking the downfall of the house of Avram might not prevent that from happening either. One of the Djinn could assume control of Gabriel's operation and find out that Daneya was involved."

"He's right," Roshon said. "Kent identified one of the Djinn at the facility as a servant of Forrest, a powerful Djinn who's a leading general of his kind. I believe him to be behind the rise of Vanaras among my people. If he were to take control, there would be no stopping him. All of your lives would be in danger."

Tears welled in Cherri's eyes. She ran from the room, followed immediately by Daneya. The tense aftermath didn't last long. Blade grunted and started for the open doorway. "I think that calls for a beer. Anyone with me?"

Kent stood with his geis at his side. "I'll have one. Chief?"

Roshon gestured a dismissal. After the two had left, he sifted through the papers next to the laptop. "What are these?"

"Receipts of Vampyres paying Gabriel to be put on a list for an infant," Saden replied. "Apparently, they're in high demand."

He sneered in disgust then took a closer look at the man across from him. Saden seemed weary beyond the events of the day. There were shadows in his forlorn gaze and lines on his face that never aged. "What troubles you? Other than the obvious."

Saden let out a tired laugh and scraped his hair back. "This was supposed to be my last assignment. I could've welcomed death after this. Been pardoned my sins. Now, I'm looking at another ten, twenty years of service."

"You can still choose death," Roshon tempted. "Take the evidence to your Drakonem and forget about the consequences."

"And prove everyone right, that I'm nothing more than a soulless killer?" He shook his head. "Not my style."

Roshon chuckled lightly. "Nor mine. I've found there's a certain satisfaction in pissing people off. You have a gift for it."

"I'll try to take that as a compliment."

"You should." He sat forward, all joking aside. "It's that kind of quality that gives you an edge over your enemy. It'll also help you keep your woman safe."

Something indefinable passed through Saden's eyes and was gone in the next instant. "She's not mine. Never has been."

But he wanted her to be. The unspoken words were as clear to Roshon as if they'd been shouted in the still air between them. "She is…a dichotomy," he ventured. "To fight the very things she loves so much. I'm assuming the DCM doesn't know the truth about her daughter."

"Nor will they."

He held up a hand at the warning tone in Saden's voice. "Not from me or any of my men. Her secret is safe with us. Personally, I think it's good to see a vigilante who isn't one dimensional. Do you have an idea of what you want to do about Gabriel?"

Saden breathed a deep sigh. "No. While Daneya is my first concern, I can't forget about all the human females who are still under Gabriel's control. He'd get rid of them and start fresh if he thought he had to. It would take a united effort on the part of Drakons to get them free and I'm not sure that's possible, let alone whether my Drakonem would allow it. There's a reason why

Drakons are sent to kill and not to rescue innocents. We can discuss it further tomorrow. For now, it's late. I'll show you where your men can stay."

He directed Roshon to two spare rooms on the first floor and three on the second. Just as they were about to go back downstairs, the little girl appeared from the room at the beginning of the hallway and went to Saden. She was timid, asking if everything was all right. Saden gathered her in a hug as a father would a child and reassured her with soothing words.

It occurred to Roshon that Daneya wasn't the only one the Drakon would protect with his life. Unfortunately, it wasn't Saden's life at stake. It was his death. Roshon found he could empathize with the man more than he'd thought possible. Every week, he put his life on the line hunting the growing number of Vanaras, knowing that the only prize would be a warrior's death. If that were taken away and he somehow turned into a Vanara, he couldn't imagine the shame of living through that. Of putting his family at risk.

Quietly, he left Saden and the girl alone, taking comfort in the strength his geis offered through their link.

Chapter Fourteen

"He did *what*?" Gabriel yelled.

The poignot trembled like a simpering imbecile in front of him. "Th-the Drakon broke into facility three. We don't know how yet. Somehow, he managed to take six of the specimens with him."

"Was 4-7 one of them?" He'd had her transferred to the facility in Arizona along with the others in their first or second trimester. The rest he'd kept at facility four there in California, unwilling to risk the health of the fetuses with the stress of the trip.

"I-I don't know, sir. Rhys didn't give me the details when he called. He said he was on his way to facility three—"

"Gods damn it!" Gabriel swept everything from his desk, sending piles of papers and his computer monitor to the floor.

This shouldn't have happened. That cursed Drakon was supposed to infiltrate facility four, like Rhys had predicted he would.

Their plan had been fool-proof. Lure the Drakon to the facility by making it an easy target then force one of the women to attack him. A leisonguarde with the power of illusion would have superimposed his image onto the woman, tricking the Drakon into wounding or killing her. By the time the Drakon realized his mistake, it would be too late. Gabriel could claim the criminal had gone insane and this whole mess would be behind him.

Instead, his entire operation was in jeopardy. The Lady Ilsa and members of the other ruling houses would never accept his plans for the future of their race if they suspected he couldn't control the females he was using. He had to take care of this without anyone finding out. Get those females back before they could leak out any important information.

As it was, there was no telling what the Drakon had taken other than the specimens at facility three.

"Finish cataloging the finances and clean this up," he said to the poignot cowering in the corner of his library. "I'll be at facility four."

"But, sir—"

"Do it now!" He stormed out of his mansion to the separate garage on the side. When a pair of his leisonguardes tried to stop him, he told them to hold their posts and wait for his command. A short while later, he arrived at the facility and ignored the overabundance of guards and Djinn who'd been assigned to capture the Drakon. They were useless now. This Drakon was smarter than either Gabriel or Rhys had given him credit for. There was no way he would risk coming here after exposing himself at the other facility.

Gabriel made his way to his office where he pulled up short at the sight of Rhys accessing the computer at his desk. The man was disheveled and reeked of smoke and sweat. Dried blood was crusted on the side of his face amidst a smattering of bruises. He stood up instantly. For the first time since Gabriel had met him, an expression of guilt played across his hard features.

"You shouldn't be here."

"Cut the bullshit," Gabriel said angrily. "I think by now we both know the Drakon wasn't sent to kill me. He just wants to ruin me. Tell me everything that happened."

Rhys' jaw ticked nervously before he turned the monitor to Gabriel's view. "We found the Drakon in your office at facility three. He'd turned off the security cameras in the building before we could get him on tape, but I've managed to pull up the exact file he accessed on your computer. It's the production ledger with names and dates going back to the very beginning."

Gabriel nearly staggered back, the air punched from his lungs as he stared at the screen. It was impossible. The only ones who knew his password were him and Rhys. No one else would've been able to guess it unless they were aware of his intimate relationship with Daneya. Which again, didn't extend to anyone else. Not even Forrest.

He recalled the night he'd gone after Daneya over a week ago. How she, her daughter and friend had disappeared immediately after the two Drakons had interfered. Then there was the sighting of a dark-haired female at his mansion. At the time, he had assumed it was merely another Drakon working with the first.

Now...

What if it had been Daneya? Only she could've given the Drakon a clue to his password. Yet, it was inconceivable that she would involve herself with a criminal. The lowest of the very things she'd dedicated her life to destroying.

"There's more," Rhys said. "The Drakon wasn't alone. He had a female companion with him in your office. Five minutes after we engaged them, a group of Rakshasas appeared and helped them escape with six of the specimens. Seven of our men were critically injured."

"Rakshasas?" That was even more unbelievable. The race of shapeshifters would never intrude upon the affairs of Vampyres unless directly provoked. Forrest would've notified him if he'd had anything to do with this. "How can that be? Drakons are forbidden to work with others. Were you able to catch at least one of them for questioning?" If so, they might use that to their advantage.

Rhys hesitated, then answered, "No. All of them got away. We were trapped by the sun and the Djinn claimed they were run off the road by the Drakon's fire when they gave chase."

Gabriel shook with barely contained fury. With the information on the ledger and six specimens at his disposal, the Drakon could ruin him as well as everyone else involved in his operation. The house of Avram wouldn't recover from the blow. The treaty would be as if it had never existed and his people would once again be plunged into the depths of war with him as the catalyst.

Damn it! There had to be something he could use. Something he was missing.

A leisonguarde burst into the office, panting from exertion. "Sorry to disturb you, sir. There's a Djinn here demanding to see you. He says his name's Forrest."

Gabriel felt the blood rush from his face. One of Forrest's men must have informed him. The general was an unforgiving man and not likely to listen to excuses, no matter what the circumstance. "Give us a few minutes then show him in."

"No need." A slim man in his early twenties pushed past the leisonguarde with an air of authority. His trim brown hair and austere features suited his tailor-made outfit down to the wingtips on his loafers. Forrest wore his new Vampyre host well. The last Gabriel had seen him, he was in an aging human male with only a few years left to his prime.

With as much confidence as he could muster, Gabriel dismissed the leisonguarde then dipped his head to the general. "It's good to see you, Forrest. I see you found one of the offspring to your liking."

Forrest moved languidly to the armchair on the other side of the desk. Everything about his demeanor was as cool and calculated as ever. It was only in his eyes that one could see his true character, and it chilled Gabriel every time he looked into them. "My men tell me the situation with this Drakon has escalated. They say he made off with several specimens and possibly evidence that could incriminate you. Should I be worried?"

"Not at all," he replied smoothly. "I have the situation under control."

"Then tell me what your plan is to deal with it, since your last one went over so well."

Gabriel cursed inwardly. This was not a conversation he was prepared for. He cleared his throat and sat down in his desk chair, struggling to think of anything that wouldn't betray the seriousness of the situation. "Well, fortunately, I doubled the guard at all of the facilities, so it wasn't a complete loss. We now know that the Drakon is working with a group of Rakshasas, but eye-witness accounts alone won't be enough to discredit him. I think we…" His sentence trailed off as a thought occurred to him. Eye-witnesses may not be the only proof they had of the Drakon's infiltration.

Maybe…

"Hold on a minute." His fingers flew over the keyboard, typing furiously. If this worked, he might have all the leverage he needed to get rid of his nuisance.

Rhys peered over his shoulder to get a closer view of the screen. "What are you doing?"

"I'm activating the remote feed from the secondary security system. The one I had installed years ago upon your insistence, my good friend. I'm surprised it slipped your attention."

"The secondary cameras," Rhys said as understanding set in. "They should've kicked in immediately after the main feed was shut down.

"And so they did," Gabriel confirmed triumphantly. The screen segmented into eight parts, each one showing a different angle of the current events happening at facility three. He rewound the video to the beginning then watched carefully for a clear shot of the Drakon. When it came, he paused and zoomed in. Shock registered at first as a ghost from his past stared back at him from the monitor. It couldn't be. This man had died years ago.

"Sir, is that your brother?"

"No." Mathis was dead. Gabriel had arranged the funeral himself. Which meant the identical face on the screen had to be… "That's his son, Jeremy."

"Gods be damned," Rhys whispered.

A slow-burning hatred gradually replaced Gabriel's surprise. So, the little whelp thought he would come back for revenge. Play his hand at a real man's game. It was probably him who had reported seeing Gabriel dispose of the specimen's body weeks ago to his

Drakonem. Just waiting for Gabriel to screw up so he could make his move.

Gabriel forwarded the frames then locked on to the image of the woman at Jeremy's side. His hatred quickly turned to a boiling rage that seized his gut. It was Daneya Perodee. There was no mistaking the clean lines of her figure and stunning face.

So it was true. She had taken up with the Drakon. Chosen to sacrifice her self-worth for the company of a forsaken betrayer. What else had she given him—her body, her cries of pleasure?

He squeezed his eyes shut, blood pounding in his ears. None of that mattered. She was his. Had been from the day he'd first seen her in Marco's house so long ago. Even then, at such a tender age, her challenging spirit had awakened something inside him that'd been missing since his mate had passed away.

Marco hadn't understood. He'd foolishly thrown away his chance to become a father in spite of his mate's barrenness. Wasted his life in an effort to keep Daneya from Gabriel, but his actions had been in vain. Gabriel had found her years later and he would do it again. She belonged to him, and so did their daughter.

"Is there a problem?" Forrest asked in a dangerous tone.

Gabriel fasted through the rest of the video feed as his mind rapidly formed a plan. A slow smile spread across his face. "On the contrary, this couldn't have worked out better. The Drakon is a former adversary of mine. It will be a simple matter to convince the Lady Ilsa and her council that he set up a false accusation against me to get revenge by sabotaging my research. With proof that he's aligned with a member of the DCM and a group of Rakshasas, they'll have no choice except to report it to his Drakonem. My case will be closed on that offense alone."

"The idea has merit. When will you contact your authorities?"

"Right now. I don't want to give him any more time to use the evidence he's found against me."

Forrest rose and strode to the door. "Then I shall leave you to it. And, Gabriel, I don't think I need to tell you what will happen if this new plan of yours fails."

The threat hung in the air after Forrest's departure, but Gabriel was too excited to care. This would work. It had to. "Edit the film," he told Rhys. "Take out the images of the specimens. I want there to be no doubt that the Drakon is doing this out of personal vindication. Then go to the laboratory on my land and replicate the damage from the scene at the facility in case Korvaute Weiss wants to investigate. Inform the men of the version they are to tell if Weiss decides to question them. You have one hour."

"Yes, sir. What do you want me to do about facility three?"

"Repair it and make sure the specimens are settled. Things should go back to normal very soon. After I know the Drakon is taken care of, I want you to contact that woman of yours, Cherri. Do you think she'll be open to meeting with you again?"

Rhys grinned widely. "Absolutely. She's as desperate to have a child as a bitch in heat. I'll get on it as soon as I can." He was barking orders to the leisonguardes outside before the door closed behind him.

Gabriel poured himself a glass of vodka from his liquor cabinet and downed it in one swallow, relishing the sweet burn. He refilled it then tipped the glass in a silent salute to his nephew. Jeremy had proven more resourceful than Gabriel could ever have hoped for.

Not only would his very identity give cause for doubt among the council, but he would also play a key role in returning Daneya to her rightful position — submitting to Gabriel's control.

Yes, everything would go back to the way it should be. The way it was meant to be all along.

* * * *

Daneya threw back the comforter and sat up on the side of the bed. She glanced at her daughter sleeping soundly next to her then stood to go to the bathroom. Her body was restless, thoughts racing with the events of the previous day. After splashing cold water on her face, she stared at her reflection in the mirror, mind traveling back to her argument with Cherri.

Her friend had been right. She had no business falling for a man she couldn't have. When all was said and done, the past several days would be just a memory and everything would return back to the way it was. Comfortable and familiar.

Then why did that life seemed so distant now? The bustle of the DCM. Days spent drowned in her work and nights filled with worry over her daughter's future. For years, she'd told herself that her life was suspended only because of the threat Gabriel posed. That once he was eliminated, she could find happiness.

Did that still hold true?

Mckenzie would never be fully accepted for her heritage among the DCM community, which made Daneya an outsider as well. They could start fresh. Go to a place where no one knew of them and Mckenzie could practice her power without fear of discovery. Vincent was a good man, handsome in his own cavalier way, and might give up everything to follow her as Cherri so adamantly suggested.

However, Daneya knew he would eventually come to resent her for it. And what of love? Whatever a relationship is, it should at least begin with love, shouldn't it?

Daneya laughed quietly. She and Saden had begun with the exact opposite, and look how that had turned out. Her lips tingled in memory of his earlier kiss on the outskirts of Riverside. It had been so full of possession and need. In that moment, nothing else had existed. Not Gabriel or the Rakshasas or even their futures. The thought of going back to what she once had and never feeling that kind of freedom again was suffocating.

How could she find happiness knowing her sworn protector was watching alone from the shadows? Worse, that he wouldn't be there at all, depending on how he chose to deal with their current situation.

She threw on a robe then slipped from her bedroom with resolve and hurried to Saden's room at the other end of the corridor. Inside, she flipped on the light only to find the bed empty. A quick search of the weapons and living room revealed nothing more. She went back to his room and walked out onto the balcony. The night sky was still pitch black, broken only by the glow of the crescent moon and shimmering stars. Gentle winds teased her loose hair and carried the scents of the woods surrounding the manor.

Countless minutes passed, then the air beside her darkened. It shifted like a wraith made of fine mist then took the shape of a man. Saden appeared to her right. A tall figure steeped in darkness except for the green of his eyes reflected in the dim light.

He moved closer until only a few feet separated them. "What are you doing out here?"

A hundred reasons flitted through her mind, though they all came down to just one. "I don't care. About what others think or what my life should be like. I'm tired of worrying that one mistake could cost me everything. If you think I could turn away from you now with no regrets, you're wrong. This, between us, is the only thing I've been sure of in my whole life. Don't take that away from me before you have to."

He stared at her for long seconds, his face the same stoic mask he'd worn when they had first met. When he reached out to grasp her neck, she let him pull her against him. His other arm snaked inside her robe and enveloped her waist in a solid embrace. Everything about him was firm, unyielding, and it made her entire body ache with need.

This was what she had been missing all along. Not a normal life with a forgotten past. It was the acceptance of who she was in spite of her past that Saden gave her with just one touch. She could face the emptiness that would come afterwards. The knowledge of what she'd lost and might never find again. But not yet. She still had time, and she didn't want to waste it by thinking of tomorrow.

Their breath mingled as he leaned down, mouths only inches apart. "I don't want to be a regret."

"Then shut up and stop making me wait."

His rumbling laughter vibrated through her. He brought their lips together in a slow, languid kiss. The heat of his mouth was scintillating, his tongue provocative as it danced with hers. She pressed flush against his warm body and breathed in the smells of musk and leather. At her neck and hip, his hands tightened with arousing pressure. Through the rough fabric of his jeans, he rubbed his growing length against her abdomen.

It was a heady sensation to feel the evidence of his longing for her without the conflict of right or wrong. She hadn't realized she'd been holding onto it until Cherri had pointed it out. Told her to choose between Saden and their friendship. Daneya hadn't been able to do it. Her world was no longer black and white, and her desire for Saden no more wrong than the beat of her own heart.

To hell with what everyone else thought. This was her life to live.

He guided her backwards into the room, sliding her robe off and tossing it to the floor. She spanned her palms across his chest then pushed at his heavy coat. It fell away to reveal the thick lines of his muscles moving beneath his shirt. That went next, along with the belt harness for his knives.

When the backs of her knees hit the bed, she stripped out of her own shirt and lay down, baring her breasts to him. The hunger in his eyes sent chills racing over her flesh. The way he looked at her was captivating. As if she were a treasure he wanted to explore inside and out. It made her blood rush as he began to trace every inch of her skin with his hands.

He followed her down and took one of her puckered nipples into his mouth, sucking greedily and rolling it gently between his teeth. This time was different from the others. There was no hurry to his movements. No haste to find completion. Every sensuous touch was a slow burn that heightened her senses. She ran her fingers along the hard ridges of his sides up to his shoulders and arms, wanting to memorize the feel of him. It seemed impossible that anything she might find with another man could compare. A thought she didn't want to contemplate.

Would he find this again with someone else? Make love to another woman the way he did with her?

Without realizing it, she voiced her thoughts, the words tumbling from her mouth before she could stop them. She wanted to squirm in embarrassment when he reared back with a frown. It wasn't like her to dwell on hypotheticals, yet she couldn't help but wonder.

He studied her for long moments then buried his face in her neck. "We shouldn't talk about this right now."

The way he said it piqued her curiosity further. Not because she was jealous. Rather because she didn't want him to be alone for the rest of his existence. His tone was so empty. Final. She combed her fingers through his hair and said quietly, "I want to know."

When he rolled over with a groan, she propped her head on one hand to stare down at him. His expression was both hesitant and intense. "There was no one before you and there will be no one after."

The first part was believable. What his Drakonem had done to him would've left lasting effects no matter how strong he was. The second part, however… "You can't cut yourself off entirely. There might—"

"It's not like that." Saden reached up to tuck a lock of her hair behind one ear. A sad half-smile lifted a corner of his mouth. "Drakons are forbidden to create permanent ties to anyone in this realm. It's considered a detrimental interference into the lives of decent people and a punishable offense."

"So what we're doing really will carry consequences."

"If my Drakonem were to find out. Yeah."

Daneya looked away, a sudden pain piercing her chest. None of it was fair. The sacrifices he was about to make. His concern for her welfare when he was the one who would suffer most. Meanwhile, he took all of it in stride as though he'd expected nothing less from life. It infuriated her that there was nothing she could do about it.

He cupped her jaw and forced her to look at him. "Hey, it's okay."

"No, it's not."

Whatever else she might've said was trapped behind her lips as he pressed them to his. She gave in reluctantly and allowed him to pull her close. Gradually, his warmth seeped into her, melting her bitter anger. As he deepened the kiss, she shifted her body on top of his and sank into the feel of his arms banding around her. When she swiveled her hips, the material still separating them brought her back to awareness. She wanted to be as close to him as she could get. Tangled in his skin and lost in his touch.

After easing her way down, she unfastened his pants and pulled them to his knees, careful to avoid the bandage covering the wound on his left thigh. His solid length bounced invitingly against his hard abdomen, beautiful in its masculinity. She couldn't remember wanting anything more than the way she wanted him now. While she stood to strip out of the rest of her clothes, he quickly took off his boots and jeans. In the next instant, she was on him again, straddling him just above his knees and taking him into her hand.

The loud groan he let loose was exhilarating. To hold his pleasure in her grasp gave her a sense of power that sent heat coiling deep within her womb. Her sex was damp and throbbing, eager for the feel of him driving into her.

She moved forward and raised herself above him, guiding his tip to her entrance. They both gasped as they came together, his swollen cock filling her completely. His gaze when she met it was half-lidded and consuming. An anchor that tethered her to him. A low moan fell from her lips and she arched into his hands as he kneaded her breasts. Slowly, she slid up and down his length, the friction of their skin generating a blaze that flushed through her sensitive core.

He urged her forward and took possession of her mouth in a searing kiss. The change in angle rubbed his bluntness against that intimate spot inside her, causing jolts of electricity to fire through her blood. His hands gripped her waist and hips surged up to meet each of her thrusts.

Daneya panted heavily, caught in a whirlwind of sensation. In that moment, she knew there would be no one who could replace him, and she didn't want to try. Despite what everyone else thought, she hadn't spent the last nine years alone out of personal choice. It just wasn't in her to settle.

For a missed opportunity. For something that might be if she gave it a chance. With Saden, there was no second guessing. He had been a part of her life before she'd ever met him and she would give all that she could to keep him with her.

If only…

Her thoughts scattered as Saden flipped them over and spread her legs beneath him. He clutched her hips and delved past her threshold, setting up a vigorous pace. It was all she could do to hold onto his shoulders as the pressure building within became overwhelming. Her pleasure rose swiftly to a peak, the force of her climax crashing wave after wave of ecstasy over her body.

Saden leaned forward to swallow her cry, quickening his strokes until he released a raw groan. His cock pulsed with his orgasm and muscles tensed around her.

She floated in a haze of bliss, too content to move. After a while, Saden lifted her to the top of the bed and covered them with the blanket. The first wisps of pre-dawn light brightened the darkness through the open balcony doors. In the silence, she laid her head on his chest and listened to his heart beating. Sleep should have taken her but the thoughts she'd been avoiding gradually crept in. It was the start of a new day that would decide their fate and she knew Saden could no longer put off his decision.

"Do you know what you'll do yet?"

Saden heaved a deep breath and kissed her forehead. "I'll have to work out a deal with Serrakus. If he agrees to let me organize a group of Drakons to investigate Gabriel's accomplices, I'll hand over Gabriel and extend my sentence. Taking the accomplices into custody one at a time over a period will minimize the attrition of the house of Avram."

She frowned up at him. "Extend your sentence. You sound as if you would be done if it weren't for this setback."

A long pause followed, then he replied, "It doesn't matter now. I couldn't rest until I knew you and Mckenzie were safe."

Rest. It was such a peaceful word when in reality, the end of his sentence meant death. Her emotions warred with logic. While she didn't want him gone forever, knowing what he would endure under the control of his Drakonem seemed just as severe. It would be so much easier if she could join his team to take down the accomplices, but that wasn't an option. They might report his relationship with her and all of this would be for naught.

"Will you keep in touch?" she tried. "Let me know how things go."

Before he could answer, the bedroom door swung open and Blade stepped inside. He was fully dressed with a grim expression. "Playtime's over, kiddies. I've detected three Drakons on their way here and by their speed, I'm bettin' they're warders come to bring you in."

Saden jumped out of the bed and tugged on his jeans and boots then tossed Daneya her clothes. "How far out are they?"

"Three minutes. Maybe less."

"Get Roshon and his men out of here. Daneya, Cherri and Kennie will go to the DCM compound."

Blade nodded then took off. Daneya's heart pounded with adrenaline-laced fear as she got dressed. She couldn't understand what was going on. Saden wouldn't send her away unless it was absolutely necessary. "What's happening?"

Saden snatched her robe then clamped a hand around her wrist and pulled her from the room. "Warders only come out when they're sent to retrieve a rogue Drakon."

She had to jog to keep pace with him. "Why are they coming after you? You haven't done anything wrong."

"I've done plenty." In Daneya's room, he handed her the robe then picked up Mckenzie. "Grab a gun. You might need it."

Instinct kicked in and she covered herself with the robe then tucked her favorite gun into one of the pockets. They took the stairs two at a time, followed by the Rakshasas.

Mckenzie clung to Saden's neck, her face pale and eyes wide with fright. Her voice was small and barely audible over the clamor of confusion. "Mom, where are we going?"

"It'll be all right, sweetie. Don't worry." She couldn't say more than that, unsure of the plan herself.

Roshon ran to meet them from the area of the living room. "Your friend tells me I'm to take my men and head out."

Saden paused long enough to extend a hand to the chief, who shook it falteringly. "It seems our paths end here. I can't thank you enough for what you've done. Blade will be in contact with you later."

Roshon furrowed his brow but didn't argue. "Good luck to you, then."

By the time they reached the garage, Blade and Cherri had caught up to them. Saden opened the garage door, kissed Mckenzie's cheek then loaded her into the back seat of the sedan with Cherri. When he tried to pull Daneya to the front passenger seat, she twisted her arm out of his grip and planted her feet on the floor.

"I'm not going anywhere until you tell me what's happening." She could almost hear him grind his teeth in impatience.

"My Drakonem wants me back. I don't know why and the warders aren't likely to stop and answer my questions. They're dangerous and will hurt any innocents who get in their way. I can't guarantee your safety."

"When will I see you again?"

"Saden, they're here!" Blade shouted from behind the wheel.

Saden's expression changed to one that made her chest seize with emotion. He crushed his lips to hers then shoved her into the front seat and slammed the door behind her. She was about to open it again when a large figure appeared several yards in front of the car. The ground exploded at his feet, throwing him back at the same time Blade punched the gas and swerved around him.

Daneya rolled down her window and climbed halfway out of the seat to look back. Another figure materialized out of the gray light of dawn and cast a bolt of blue fire at Saden. He dodged it and sent one of his own, though it was already too late. A third Drakon took form some distance away and shot out a blinding arc of fire. It struck Saden in the back, hurling him to the ground.

"No!" Daneya screamed. She saw Saden rise to his hands and knees then crumble once again when all three Drakons hit him repeatedly with bursts of fire.

Within seconds, the horrifying scene faded into a background of flames that engulfed the garage and slowly extended to the rest of the manor. She looked at Blade, unable to keep the accusation from her tone. "They're killing him. Aren't you going to stop it?"

Blade glanced at the rearview mirror, his face a rigid mask of stone. "I can't. The warders would take me in as well if I tried. They can't kill him. Serrakus is the only one with the power to do that."

When they reached the main road, Blade took a left while the Rakshasas' vehicles turned in the other direction. Daneya's mind was reeling from what had just happened. This couldn't be how she and Saden parted. There were still things to be said and done. What of the deal he'd planned on arranging with Serrakus, or the Rakshasas? She couldn't go back to the DCM now.

Somehow she knew if she did, all of this would be over and her connection to Saden lost.

"Why would his Drakonem demand he go back like this?"

Blade shrugged. "It could be any number of reasons. Because he healed you, involved the Rakshasas. Serrakus might've just gotten fed up with waiting for him to complete his assignment."

Her thoughts traveled back to the conversation she'd had with Saden earlier in his room. "Or because Serrakus found out about his relationship to me."

His face softened a measure. "My man knew what he was doing when he took you from Vincent's house. He was prepared to take the consequences. You were always more important to him."

The words were meant to be supportive, yet they filled Daneya with guilt. Was she partially to blame for the warders' attack? The idea caused acid to churn in her stomach. "What will Serrakus do with Saden?"

Blade's hands gripped the wheel until his knuckles turned white. "I don't know. Serrakus must be really pissed off to send three warders. Saden might be gone for a year at least."

"A year!" she exclaimed. "For punishment?"

His expression told her it was nothing unusual. "Time is irrelevant to the Drakonem. They can keep us for as long as they want if they choose to. I'll find out what I can."

A year, she repeated silently, feeling ice creep into her veins. So this was it. The point where she returned to her old life and forgot about Saden. She'd known it was coming. Saden had given her no illusion that he could prevent it from happening. Somewhere along the way, though, she had refused to acknowledge it. Her life had changed and she wasn't ready to go back to the way things were.

No. Screw that, she thought bitterly. She didn't want any part of her previous life, now or ever. Those days were gone. Saden had made her a different person and she still needed him. In her life, at her side.

"Don't go there," Blade said quietly. When she remained silent, he focused his gaze on her. "I can tell what you're thinking. You've got to let him go. It's what he would've wanted."

"What if I don't want to believe that?"

"You have to. Those warders saw you before we left and they'll report it to Serrakus. Saden will be lucky if he doesn't get transferred to another region and a new Drakonem." He lowered his voice so that only she could hear him above the hum of the engine. "Everything he did was for you. If you care about him, you'll go on with your life and find happiness."

Tears stung her eyes as she bit her lip in frustration and stared out of the side window. Images of Saden falling to the warders in his effort to distract them flashed before her blurred vision. No matter how hard she tried, she couldn't think of a way around the situation. Saden was going to be trapped in a realm she had no access to for who knew how long and she still needed protection from Gabriel. The DCM was the only place that could provide it.

Daneya wiped her eyes briskly. "What of Gabriel?"

"I'll take the evidence we found to Serrakus. Even if he closes the case on Gabriel, I'll find a way to reopen it or bring new charges against the bastard. You have my word."

She gave a cursory nod then glanced at her daughter's tear-streaked face. Mckenzie was wrapped in Cherri's arms, her lower lip trembling. Cherri's expression carried a mixture of concern and satisfaction. "Maybe this is for the best," she whispered.

Daneya had to look away. She couldn't contemplate that right now. Not with Saden in the hands of his sadistic Drakonem.

Sometime later, Blade pulled into the rear lot of a gas station roughly five minutes from the DCM compound. Daneya got out of the car with him and met him by the trunk. He handed her his cell phone, saying, "Call Vincent. Tell him to keep you at the compound for the next month. It won't be safe enough for you at his house."

"Will I see you again?"

"No. I'll keep the promise I made to Saden to watch over you and Mckenzie, but it'll be from a distance. I can't risk Serrakus finding out that I'm still in contact with you." He hesitated, then said, "Tell Kennie she's going to be a hell of a warrior one day. I'll miss her."

Daneya smiled tightly then stared down at the phone, her throat too tight to speak. When she looked up again, there was only empty space in front of her.

Chapter Fifteen

The call to Vincent was short and succinct. To her surprise, he arrived in less than ten minutes, apparently never having left the compound after the previous day. Warm comfort seeped into her at the sight of his familiar face. Even with a cast on one arm and sweats instead of a suit, he looked better than she remembered.

No questions or complaints fell from his lips. He simply marched up to her and encased her in a firm hug. After the morning she'd had, his solid presence nearly unraveled her determination to keep it together. She sank into his embrace and allowed the brief respite to calm her nerves.

When they drew apart, he brushed the moisture from her cheeks she hadn't known was there. "Is Mckenzie with you?"

She tilted her head toward the car. "And Cherri. We'll need to stay at the compound for a while. It won't be safe for us anywhere else."

Again, he made no enquiries about her circumstances. Merely gave a nod then told her to follow him. They drove to the back of the DCM compound where a separate area housed new recruits in a series of town houses. She and Cherri had lived in one for years while they were both being trained in their respective fields. The apartments were basic and efficient for short- or long-term stays.

Vincent led her to the last set of town houses on the right. As soon as she got out of the car, a streak of pale skin and red hair shot from the front door of the middle apartment and barreled into her. Erin threw her arms around Daneya's neck and squeezed as if her life depended on it, letting out breathless peals of laughter.

"I'm so glad you're back! I've missed you like crazy. We all have. Floyd and the others wanted to be here but Vincent has them out on patrol. They'll come by later. How are you doing? Where's Kennie and Cherri?"

Daneya mustered a thin smile. It was good to see her friend after being away for so long. Although Erin was petite and—in the words of most of the men at the compound—a bombshell, she was loyal to a fault and an expert at tactical maneuvers. They had met during Daneya's second year there and been friends ever since. She and Floyd had one child who'd grown up with Mckenzie. The pair was inseparable whenever they were together.

"Erin," Vincent called gruffly from the other side of the car, "quit running your mouth and help out." He pulled Mckenzie from the back seat and hefted her into his arms.

Erin immediately rushed to him and began fussing over Mckenzie who remained oddly quiet. "Hurry and come inside. Everything's ready for them."

With a frown, Daneya moved aside to let Cherri pass by on her way into the apartment. "How did you know we would have to come here?"

Vincent surrendered Mckenzie to Erin then guided Daneya to the door. "This is closer than my house and going to yours is out of the question. I had Erin fix up the place as soon as I got your call."

It seemed everybody was making the decisions regarding her welfare, whether she agreed with them or not. Currently, it was the latter, but she was too tired to care, both mentally and physically. Saden had kept her up all night, in her thoughts then later in his bed. The memory of the heat of his body surrounding hers echoed along her skin like an invisible blanket. It didn't extend to the rest of her, however, or keep the chill from her bones.

Inside, she followed Erin to the downstairs bedroom. It held the basic necessities. A twin-sized bed, plain dresser and nightstand with an alarm clock and cast iron lamp on top. After Erin tucked Mckenzie under the covers of the bed, Daneya sat beside her daughter and kissed her forehead. "How are you feeling?"

Mckenzie didn't say anything at first. Her face was ashen against the tangled locks of her auburn hair. "We're not going to see them again, are we?"

A dull ache throbbed in Daneya's chest. She wanted to tell her daughter everything would be okay. That Saden would be fine and Blade was watching over them. But the words clogged in a tight knot.

Truth was, she wasn't sure of anything. Not anymore. Her life had been hurled precariously out of control and with Saden gone, there was no anchor to keep her steady. She filled her voice with reassurance despite her emotions and drew her daughter into a hug. "We'll never forget them, I promise. Now go to sleep. I'll wake you in a few hours for breakfast."

On her way out, Cherri took her hand with a sorrowful expression. "I'm sorry. I really am. If you need me, I'll be in the room upstairs."

"And I'll come back later," Erin said. "I'm teaching a class on small arms maintenance. The fridge is stocked and the landline phone is connected in case you need to call me. Get some rest. You look like you're about to fall over." She pecked Daneya on the cheek then left the apartment.

Daneya wandered into the living room in a light fog and sat heavily on the couch. The ensuing silence was thick. Every muscle in her body was sore from tension. Just as her eyelids started to droop, Vincent entered the front door carrying a bottle of whiskey in one hand and two tumblers in the other. She chuckled and made room for him on the couch. The man had read her mind.

"I'm staying in the apartment next door," Vincent said with a grin. "Thought you could use this."

"You thought right." She took a half-full glass, downed the contents in one swallow then handed it back for a refill. Liquid fire spread heat like a soothing balm along her insides. It was almost enough to warm the bleak cavity in her chest. Almost. "Why aren't you at home?"

"My house needed some repairs after…well, after the incident." He finished off his glass, scrubbed his face then leaned back with a sigh.

It was then Daneya noticed the wear on him that hadn't been there before. The lines around his eyes and stubble on his jaw. His once cultivated appearance was now haggard, showing every day of his thirty-six years. When he looked over at her, his bloodshot eyes told her that the past several days had taken their toll.

He straightened and set his glass on the coffee table. "I won't ask you to tell me where you've been or who the man was that you left with. I've been around you long enough to know when to push and when to keep my mouth shut. You should know, though, that I have missed you. And Kennie. Things have been...hard without you here."

A wave of guilt washed over her. She should've called him, if for nothing else than to let him know she was alive and well. Saden wouldn't have stopped her. After studying Vincent for long seconds, she decided to come clean. She owed him more than the silent treatment, no matter how reluctant she was to speak of where she'd been.

The story came out slowly, or most of it. There was no need to go into detail about certain aspects, like the extent of her relationship with Saden and her past connection to Gabriel. Some things were better left unsaid.

Vincent remained uncharacteristically quiet the entire time. His only response was to affirm that the women from the facility were under careful watch in three of the townhouses farther down the row. When she was done, he stared into his glass for a time. "This is the same Drakon you met during your last job?" At her nod, he swilled his liquor and took a sip. "You make him sound like a decent guy."

"He is."

"Will you be seeing him again?"

From his tone, she knew there was more to his question than he was saying. Slowly, she replied, "That won't be possible. He's gone back to the Drakonem realm."

"What of this Gabriel Aikins? Is he taken care of?"

"He will be. For the next month, though, it'll be safest if Kennie, Cherri and I remain on the compound."

Vincent gestured his agreement. On his feet again, he began to pace the length of the living room in front of her. "Of course. Meanwhile, I'll take down the information you were able to gather and start forming parties to locate the facilities in each state. If necessary, I can contact the director of the closest DCM unit to us and ask his assistance. It will probably be best to organize enough teams to infiltrate the facilities all at once. That way the Vampyres will be taken by surprise and won't have the chance to relocate the women or form an attack against us."

"You can't do that. It's too dangerous." When he lifted his brows, she realized how out of character she sounded. The old Daneya would have jumped at the opportunity to be part of the rescue effort. She would've been on the front lines leading one of the teams herself. And while everything in her wanted to do just that, she knew now it would be a reckless endeavor that only a fool might attempt.

As humans, they were vastly outmatched and she no longer had a protector watching out for her. Blade was going to have his hands full trying to pick up where Saden had left off.

"These aren't just Vampyres we're going up against," she continued. "The Djinn can walk in daylight and after breaking into the facility in Phoenix, there's no telling what fortifications Gabriel has made since then. We could be fighting more than simple Djinn in human hosts. They have generations of Vampyre and human offspring at their disposal as hosts. We can't compete with that combination. Our members are used to fighting the Djinn on our terms, not those with Vampyre capabilities.

"Judging from their numbers, I would say each facility could be guarded by twenty, thirty men or more. The advantage would be theirs no matter how strong we went in."

"Well, I can't just sit back and do nothing," Vincent said, his temper rising. "And I can't believe you're suggesting it. What did that Drakon do to you to make you so cautious all of a sudden?"

She slammed her tumbler down on the table hard enough for whiskey to slosh over its rim. "If caution means saving lives, than yes, he has changed me! I saw what we're up against. If it weren't for Saden and the Rakshasas, I'd have died at that facility. We have no choice but to let Blade take care of things his way first. One month. That's all he asked for. If nothing's been done by then, we can involve the DCM."

He stared at her for a long period, jaw ticking in irritation. Finally, he resumed his seat on the couch and rubbed his temples. "God, you're right. I'm sorry. We're not prepared for this kind of threat. For now, we'll just keep an eye on the facilities." After another pause, he asked, "You said this Drakon is a former Vampyre, right? Was he able to give you some pointers on how to manage Kennie's power?"

Daneya's mouth dropped open in shock. How could he know about Mckenzie? She'd said nothing regarding the recent development of her daughter's power.

Vincent smiled sheepishly. "When you joined the DCM, I looked into your background a little further than I should have, perhaps. Found out that your sister was married to a Vampyre and that after her death, you were abducted from your foster home at age seventeen. For two years afterwards, you were off the grid. Then you showed up here with a baby and an almost fanatical drive to rid the world of demons who crossed the line. It wasn't hard to piece together the missing information."

Before she could focus her anger into a response, he held up a hand in defense. "It was a violation of your privacy, I know. I hope in time, you can forgive me. I just want you to know that I don't care about who fathered Kennie or what happened in your past. If anything, I admire you more for it. Not many people can recover from something like that the way you did."

"Who else knows about her?"

"No one, I swear."

Daneya breathed a deep sigh, unable to hold onto her anger. "It's all right, and kind of a relief to have someone else to talk to about her secret. But how did you know she'd come into her power."

He shrugged. "I didn't. It was bound to happen sometime, though. What is it, particularly?"

She smiled with a surge of pride. "She can manipulate chemicals in living things which allows her to heal. It's really amazing."

"I'll bet." He slanted a glance at her then bowed his head. "Listen, I've been thinking a lot lately about what it will mean for Kennie to grow up in the DCM. It would be tempting fate to hope her secret wasn't discovered later on, and likely by the wrong member. She should be raised in an area where she won't be persecuted for it. I want to help you do that. My parents left me a horse ranch in Oregon just outside of the small town I grew up in. The people there are friendly. Community's a little behind on the times, but it fares well. We could all live there. Even Cherri, if she wanted to."

Daneya stilled, her mind trying to register exactly what he was proposing. "Are you saying you're willing to give up everything you have here for me and Mckenzie?"

"I wouldn't be losing much. More like starting a new life. We could go on reserve for the DCM and run the ranch full-time. My brother works it now with a few farmhands. He says he wouldn't mind the company." His gaze when he looked up was half nervous, half expectant. "I love you, Daneya. And I love Kennie like my own daughter. I could make you happy if you gave me a chance."

His voice held a vulnerable quality that stirred a well of emotions inside her. This had been the last thing she'd expected. Vincent was a man of strong integrity, and the sincerity in his eyes gave her no room to doubt his honesty. Still, it was an offer she was unprepared to deal with in that instant. "I-I don't know what to say."

"Don't say anything yet. Think about it for a while and give me your answer when you're ready. I'd rather wait a week for the right one than get the wrong answer now." He leaned forward and pressed a lingering kiss to her cheek. "I'll check in on you tonight."

After he was gone, she nursed her drink quietly. Vincent's words circled her thoughts, making more and more sense with each passing minute. Could this be her path to happiness? They were so much alike and Mckenzie deserved a father who accepted her completely. Maybe Cherri had been right all along.

With Vincent, Daneya would never feel the pain of loss as keenly as she did with Saden. Never worry about the future or be haunted by the past. She didn't love him as she should, but perhaps that would come in time. When all was said and done, she couldn't deny that Vincent was probably the closest she might come to fulfilling her dreams.

Still…

She scrubbed her eyes then found a spare blanket and pillow in the linen closet and made a bed for herself on the couch. Gradually, her tension eased, and the strain of the morning faded to the background. Visions of Saden chased her thoughts until she eventually fell into a fitful slumber with Vincent's request not far from her mind.

* * * *

Sounds of mellow blues drifted softly through the apartment. Cherri followed them downstairs to the kitchen where she found Daneya sitting at the small, round table. The guns Vincent had brought over for her to work on lay dismantled and spread across its surface. Untouched since dinner hours ago. There was a distance in her eyes that came all too frequently of late.

It frustrated Cherri increasingly to see her friend dwell on what, in her opinion, was nothing more than a horrible mistake. Saden had no place in their world, just as he'd had no right to take them from it. Because of his failure to do his job, they were stuck here in limbo. Trapped by the threat of Gabriel who should've been taken care of by now.

Then there was Vincent.

Daneya had told her of the offer he'd made almost a week ago. How he wanted to whisk her away to a better life for her and Mckenzie. It was like a fairy tale. Only in this story, the poor prince had barely a leg to stand on. He still awaited an answer, ever optimistic that it was the one he hoped for.

Cherri wanted to slap her friend for being so tentative and cruel. Vincent deserved more than a position on the sidelines. Between him and Saden, there was no comparison. How could Daneya keep him dangled on the edge of a cliff with her indecision?

Well, Cherri was tired of trying to make her friend see what was right in front of her. She had her own life to live and planned to get on with it as quickly as possible. She walked into the kitchen and cleared her throat loudly.

Daneya jumped in startlement then scraped back her mess of burgundy locks, eyes bloodshot from too little rest. "Hey, I didn't see you standing there. You look nice. Are you going somewhere?"

Cherri looked down at her long skirt and sleek, cashmere sweater she'd forgotten to hide beneath a coat. It wouldn't do to raise suspicions before she even got out of the apartment. "I'm going to meet some friends at the mess hall. I know I'm a little overdressed but I haven't been out in so long, I thought I'd splurge a little. Will you be up late?"

"Yes. No." Daneya chuckled lightly and glanced down at the guns as if just noticing them. "I have no idea."

"Will Vincent be joining you later?"

"He's busy with work. Don't worry about me. Go out, have fun! God knows one of us should."

Cherri squeezed Daneya's arm then grabbed her jacket and hurried out, confident Daneya wouldn't insist on staying up until she got back. Which, with any luck, would be quite a while. She got into her car, grateful that Vincent had returned it to her, and headed for the security gate.

The anticipation she'd been reining in for the past few days bubbled over into excitement. It turned out that Rhys hadn't forgotten her. In fact, it was much the opposite. In their recent chat with each other online, he'd admitted to being worried sick about her.

Convinced that either the worst had befallen her or she'd had a change of heart.

His eagerness to drive the two hours from his house just to visit and pick up where they'd left off had filled her with giddy relief. The stress of the past few weeks, the fear of having lost the only man who could make her wishes come true, had been sloughed like so much waste.

This time, she wasn't going to let anyone interfere with her desires. She had more right to them than most and damned if she would let them fall to the wayside.

She pulled into a dog park fifteen miles out from the compound and parked beside a dark green suburban. The park was empty at this hour save for a lone figure who stood by the small lake at its center. Rhys' face became clear in the dim light of the moon and stars above as she walked toward him. He was even more appealing than she remembered. His massive build might've been intimidating if not for the softness in his light brown eyes. They seemed to draw her into their depths and hold her in a sea of warmth.

He cupped her jaw and leaned down to bring their lips together, tickling her with his mustache. "*Mon cheri*," he whispered before guiding her tongue in a slow, erotic dance.

She was breathless by the time they pulled apart. Heat scalded her cheeks, in part due to the play on her name—a habit of his whenever they chatted online or over the phone.

"Thanks for meeting me out here," Rhys said. "I thought it would give us some privacy to talk. Sit with me?" With a hand at her back, he steered her toward a nearby bench. "So you had quite an adventure after the last time we met."

"Not an adventure, really." She smiled to hide her anxiety over the issue. While lying wasn't in her nature, she'd grown accustomed to it with her job at the DCM. As far as Rhys knew, she'd been out of town for a work-related emergency. "More of an inconvenience. I'm sorry I didn't contact you sooner."

"Don't apologize. I'm just glad you're back."

"Me, too."

His expression grew serious as he took her hand, his voice pensive. "There's something I have to tell you, and I'm not sure you'll like it. It has to do with the promise I made to you."

Cherri felt her heart plummet. She knew without asking just what promise he was referring to, and it made her skin grow cold. "You can't fix me."

"I can," he said quickly. "We could start a family together like you wanted. It'll just be different from what you had in mind. I don't know if you'll accept me once you hear the truth."

The suspense was killing her. Rhys was normally so straight forward. It pained her to see his confidence shaken. "Whatever it is, we'll deal with it. You won't lose me."

"I hope you're right." He kissed her hand like a courtly gentleman then took a deep breath. "For us to be together, I had to do some research on you. I know that you're a secretary for the DCM and that you've been with them for almost nine years. Your roommate is a vigilante and you're currently living at the compound. I know all this because I'm a Vampyre."

She was on her feet in the next second, stumbling back in shock. Her palm flew to her mouth in horror. How could this be? She'd been so careful, and Rhys had seemed so ordinary. In all their conversations, not once had she gained the impression he was anything other than a normal guy who desired a committed relationship. Yet, what kind of Vampyre trolled human dating sites unless he had an ulterior motive?

Rhys stood with his arm outstretched then let it drop to his side. "I won't stop you if you want to leave. All I'm asking for is five minutes to let me explain. As a member of the DCM, you have to know that not all demons are evil. I'm one of the good guys, or I've wanted to be ever since I met you." When she didn't respond, he lowered his voice. "You said you trusted me once. Give me the chance to earn it back."

The honesty in his tone compelled her to stay. Even after his revelation, she had to admit that some part of her still wanted him. Craved the life he'd promised her with children of her own.

At her slight nod, he sat down again, gaze never leaving hers. "I work for a Vampyre named Gabriel Aikins. He's a revolutionary among my kind. We were dying out from our war with the Djinn. Gabriel found a way to increase our numbers and form a truce with the Djinn to end the fighting."

"I know exactly what he's doing to increase your numbers," she spat, body shaking with the fury of her memories. "It violates every law your kind has regarding the treatment of humans. And it's why I can't carry a child." She clutched her belly and blinked back the tears threatening to spill over her lashes.

"Then we're on the same page. I won't lie to you. At first, I thought it was the answer to our problems. The Djinn were getting bolder, sacrificing as many of their human hosts as was necessary to capture my kind and force them to become hosts. The combination of Djinn and Vampyres rising against us was devastating. I've had to kill my own comrades locked inside their bodies by the Djinn after gods know what torture they endured.

"Gabriel told me—all of us—that the Djinn would cease their attacks if we supplied them with willing hosts, and he was right. It seemed a small price to pay for human females to bear our offspring for a while. One decade. Their memories would be erased afterwards and they would go on with their lives."

Bile crept into the back of her throat. "That's what you meant when you said you've helped women overcome obstacles in childbirth. They weren't healed by some special operation. You sired their offspring."

His expression became strained as he inclined his head. "I'm not proud of what I've done. The shame of my actions will haunt me for the rest of my existence. It wasn't until recently that I found out Gabriel was having the women killed after their term. I didn't want to have anything else to do with him or his operation, but by that time, I was already too involved to get out.

"I wanted to start a new life that was free of the taint I had cast on my own. That's why I began searching for a human mate. When I found you, I couldn't let you go even though I knew you were part of the DCM. You were so kind and loving. I want to bond with you. Make our relationship permanent. It would change your body and allow you to carry children again. That is if you're still willing."

Her head was spinning with the details of his story. All of it made sense, as terrible as it was. The remorse he claimed was reflected openly on his face. She should curse him. Run away and report his identity to Vincent. Yet, she couldn't bring herself to do it. His proposal rang in her thoughts and caused her gut to flutter with a new kind of anticipation.

To mate would bind them irrevocably with only death to part them. Nothing could prove the sincerity of his promises to her more than that single act.

Was he really telling the truth?

"If you want to bond with me, then you must want me."

He closed the distance between them to cradle her face in his hands. "I do. For you, I would give up everything."

Her mouth went dry as he poured the passion of his words into a kiss. Heat coursed over her skin and set fire to her blood. She could've drowned in his intensity if not for the nagging question that still remained. With no small effort, she pulled away to meet his gaze. "What will you do about Gabriel?"

"I've already spoken to him. He says he will release me from his service on one condition." There was trepidation in his eyes when he paused.

"Tell me." Whatever it was, it couldn't be as bad as what he'd already confessed to. If she was willing to forgive him for that, Gabriel's condition should be a breeze.

"He says he wants your roommate, Daneya. That they were involved at one time and had a child together."

Cherri jerked out of his grasp. The elation she'd felt just a moment ago splintered like shards of ice. This couldn't be. There had to be another way.

"It's the only way he'll let me bond with you," Rhys rushed on to say as if reading her mind. "He wants you to prove your loyalty to our race. I'm aware of what he did to her in the past, but he wants to change. You have to believe that. He regrets treating her badly just as I regret what I did to those women before I met you. When I told him you wouldn't put your friend in danger, he swore to me his only concern was for

Daneya's welfare and that of their child. I can't fault him for wanting to make amends and the child deserves to be brought up in a Vampyre community where she can learn to use her power."

Again, his argument made perfect sense. Even in the small town where Vincent wanted to take Mckenzie and Daneya, Mckenzie would still be an outsider. Possibly an object of ridicule and hatred if the humans there ever found out about her. No matter Gabriel's intentions, however, Daneya would view it as betrayal if Cherri were to turn her over. It could cost her their friendship.

On the other hand, she could lose Rhys and all that he offered if she didn't. It all boiled down to how far she was willing to go to hold onto her dreams.

"Daneya won't accept him. She's built her life around protecting herself from him."

"Gabriel has agreed to let her go with the child if she refuses him," Rhys said. "After a certain amount of time, of course. It's all taken care of. Give her a call and tell her to meet us here with the kid so I can talk to her."

Cherri's brows shot up. "Now? I-I wouldn't know what to say. Daneya won't bring Kenny out this late. She won't even come herself after what happened."

He stepped close again and feathered his fingers through her hair, lowering his voice a few octaves. "It has to be now. Gabriel wants an answer by tonight. I know you can think of something. Do this for me, for us and the children we'll have."

Her next argument was swallowed in a searing kiss. When he crushed her to him, her thoughts scattered and her heart beat wildly in her chest. This was what she had been waiting for. A lover and provider. A man who could make up for all those years of loneliness and suffering. Who could give her the life that had been stolen from her so long ago.

Was it so wrong to want it at the price of her friend's freedom for a short while? Surely, Daneya wouldn't begrudge her a lifetime of happiness if it meant spending a few weeks with the man she abhorred.

Just a little while. That was all Gabriel was asking.

An idea was forming before Cherri reluctantly broke away from Rhys. "I think I know of a way to get her here. I'll need you to keep quiet while I call." As soon as he gestured his approval, she pulled her phone from her jacket and dialed the new cell Vincent had provided Daneya with.

"Cherri?" Daneya answered. "What's up? Is everything all right?"

Cherri altered her voice to a hoarse, wavering whisper. "I need you to come get me. I'm hurt and can't make it back to my car."

"What? Was there a break in?"

"No, I… I lied to you. I'm sorry. I went to Two Pines Park to get some air."

"Don't move," Daneya said quickly. "I'll call an ambulance—"

"No ambulance. It was a demon attack. The hospital will ask too many questions and I don't want anyone at the compound to see me like this. Just bring Kenny, please. She can heal me."

Dead silence filled the line for what seemed an eternity. Cherri chewed her lip nervously, certain Daneya would see through her ruse.

"Okay," Daneya said finally. "We're on our way. Try to get to a safe spot. I'll find you."

Cherri's hand trembled as she put away her phone. Doubts wove through her mind, spreading a chill that encased her entire body. There was no turning back now. Whatever happened next would be on her. "Promise me she won't get hurt. This is only a meeting, right? To explain to her why we're doing this."

Rhys gathered her in his strong hold and rubbed her back soothingly. "You've done the right thing. I'm so proud of you, and I can't wait to make you my mate. This will all work out, you'll see."

She nodded, more to convince herself than him. It didn't take long for the sedan they'd used to escape Saden's house to pull into the parking lot. Daneya got out with Mckenzie, grabbed her daughter's hand and started running into the park toward them. Cherri could tell the moment her friend suspected something was amiss when Daneya's steps faltered and slowed significantly.

From ten yards out, Daneya asked, "Cherri, what's going—?" The rest of her sentence never made it out as she stiffened then toppled to the ground.

Sooner than Cherri could react, several figures shrouded in black clothing fell from the nearest trees and jumped out from behind bushes. They crowded in around Daneya's prone form and rolled her over. One of them snatched up Mckenzie and stifled her terrified scream.

"No!" Cherri cried.

Rhys caught her from behind and trapped her in his arms. "Shh. It's okay. They won't be harmed. It had to be like this. You know Daneya wouldn't have come willingly if we'd given her a choice. Let the men do their job."

She struggled for only a few more seconds then slumped in Rhys' hold. Somewhere in the back of her mind, she knew he was right. Daneya wouldn't have listened to reason no matter what Cherri might have said. Her hatred of Gabriel went soul deep. Maybe this was a mistake. If only she could have more time. Possibly ease Daneya into it. There had to be a better way. "Rhys, she won't understand."

"Calm down, *mon cheri*. You have to trust me. It's already done."

She watched with tense remorse as Daneya and McKenzie were carried to Rhys' suburban. "What do we do now?"

"We'll follow them in your car. Is it equipped with a tracking device the DCM might be able to find you with?" When she shook her head, he gave a smile that seemed a little too satisfied under the circumstances. "Good. Let's begin our life together, shall we?"

Cherri took his hand and went with him to her car, silently telling herself everything would turn out all right. It was all happening so fast, but it was the only way, wasn't it? Daneya had to forgive her eventually.

At least that's what she hoped, and repeated to herself over and over again as Rhys drove her to her new future.

Chapter Sixteen

Saden hung suspended from the ceiling by thick, iron shackles around his wrists. Pain lived in every fiber of his being. Not an inch of his skin was unmarked and his shoulders throbbed from having to support his full weight. They would dislocate soon, as Laurs had intended while chaining him up two nights ago. A particular cruelty considering Serrakus was the only one with the power and authority to heal and he would be gone for several days more. Off on his vacation enjoying the most depraved sins humankind had to offer.

Sweat trickled through layers of dirt into his countless wounds, some fresh and others caked over with dried fluids. The heat of the windowless cell was near suffocating, scorching his bruised lungs with each breath. Complete darkness was his only comfort, for the coming of light meant another round of torture.

This punishment was only the beginning of his suffering for the offense of using his power to heal Daneya. After a month or two, Serrakus would begin punishment for the second crime of failing his assignment. The third was for interfering in and endangering the lives of humans and Rakshasas, for which he would pay most dearly.

The Drakonem had gleefully refused to listen to the evidence Saden had found on Gabriel. If Saden hadn't already been expecting that response and aware of the reason why, he'd have earned himself another penalty for trying to strangle Serrakus. As it was, he consoled himself with the knowledge that Daneya and Mckenzie were safe and that Blade wouldn't stop until he found new evidence to incriminate Gabriel with.

The quiet of his temporary solitude was disrupted by the constant dripping of blood from his lacerated back. Time was irrelevant in the dungeons. Days and nights bled together, marked only by the appearance of the Drakon whose job it was to supply water to those in confinement. Saden had learned early on that the gift of water was simply another form of torture. The single cup provided was enough to wet one's throat and leave them yearning for more.

His thoughts turned to Daneya and their last night together. Her fiery resolve to be with him despite what he or anyone else thought had meant more than she would ever know. She'd taken him from a lowly criminal forsaken by his own family and kind to a man worthy of respect with just her words. Her touch. Even now, in the depths of his prison with the additional years he faced under Serrakus' control, he couldn't regret giving up his death for her. Or enjoying every moment she'd given him a measure of peace.

In his life, it wasn't the gratification of living up to his parents' expectations or the honor of serving his race that he would take to his grave. It was the small, seemingly insignificant things that had made it worthwhile. His vow to keep Daneya safe. Their connection, which defied all logic, and the opportunity to help Mckenzie handle her power. It was more than he had a right to claim pride to, and all that mattered in the end.

The door to his cell creaked open. He cringed away from the torchlight spilling into the darkness and burning his eyes. The tension in his body fled when he heard the bare footsteps of Serrakus' slave pad across the stone floor. In their Drakonem's absence, the young Dresidien had been assigned to provide water to those Drakons enduring punishment.

Saden could tell from these brief interludes that the slave's spirit hadn't been completely snuffed by Serrakus' treatment. There was still fire blazing behind the phantom's cowed eyes and an edge of confidence to his movements. Sooner than later, Saden was determined to keep his word and show the Dresidien how to escape and make a kill as he'd done years ago. It was the only way to be released from Serrakus' sick dominance.

The slave, dressed in only a thin pair of pants, put the torch in a sconce then propped a step ladder in front of Saden's naked form.

Saden licked his cracked lips and asked, "What's your name?" It came out as a barely intelligible croak, better the second time when he tried again.

The phantom jerked in startlement, spilling some of the water from the cup. Warily, he answered, "Demetrius."

"I'm Saden. Do you know how to use weapons? Knives or a gun?"

"My father taught me how to hunt. I'm good with a bow and arrow."

Saden's lips stretched in a faint grin. He'd forgotten how remote most of the Dresidien tribes were. Their isolation gave them little need to train in the arts of combat. "Good enough. If I could show you a way to prove yourself as a Drakon, would you risk it?"

Doubt flashed in Demetrius' black eyes as he lifted the cup to Saden's mouth. "I don't think you could do much of anything right now. You look like…"

He swallowed the stale liquid then said what the Dresidien was too polite to admit. "Shit. I know, but don't count me out." With no broken bones and no damage to his internal organs—yet—he could still get around if necessary. "You'll learn that a little pain doesn't take you out of the fight."

"I haven't given up," Demetrius said defensively. "Serrakus says I'm weak but I could do the job if he'd let me."

"I know you could."

After a heavy pause, the Dresidien asked, "Why would you help me?"

Saden flexed his muscles to take the strain off of his shoulders. "Because I've been in your position. Serrakus will fly off the handle like a little bitch but it'll be worth it. Are you up for that?"

Demetrius grinned widely, white teeth glistening against his copper skin.

The door to the cell slammed open and a loud voice echoed along the walls. "Leave us."

Demetrius scrambled to remove the step ladder and gave the newcomer a wide berth on his way out, closing the door behind him. Saden didn't recognize the stranger. Whoever it was stood with his back to the flames, providing only a tall silhouette.

Without warning, his shackles unlocked and he fell to the floor in a broken heap. New pain lanced through his body, so fierce it took all he had to keep from screaming in agony. What felt like thousands of tiny blades tearing his skin streaked along his arms as blood rushed back into them. His fingertips clawed inwards, each a blazing pinpoint of fire. He could thank Laurs for that. The sadistic fuck had plucked off his nails with a pair of pliers.

When Saden could finally unclench his muscles and roll to his side, he took in the sight of the man standing above him with a shroud of silver, flowing hair. It was Lucius…in his cell. What the hell was he doing there in Serrakus' absence?

Lucius knelt down, a look of quiet contemplation on his aristocratic features. "It has been a while since we last met, hasn't it, Saden?"

He sat up and held his throbbing hands to his sides. The first and last time he'd seen Lucius had been a week after Saden had defied Serrakus and earned the right to become a full-fledged Drakon. In a cell much like this one, and he in the almost same condition. Lucius had come to explain what he'd known Serrakus never would, though why he'd bothered was still a mystery. There'd been nothing to gain from imparting his knowledge, for him or for Saden. "What do you want?"

Lucius wasn't the slightest bit put off by Saden's gruffness. "I've been intrigued by your exploits on your latest assignment."

"You were tracking me?" It was possible, and not unheard of, for Drakonem to use their Drakons as spies. However, Lucius hardly had a reason to take any interest in him. He didn't even belong to the Drakonem.

"In a way. Among other things, I wanted to find out what my brother saw in you that was worth invoking the wrath of the gods. You see, he told me about his plan to set you up for failure. I'm sad to find that it worked, although not quite as he or I expected. My curiosity did not go unrewarded, though. It was very entertaining to watch your love for that human female grow. She is a remarkable creature, I'll grant you that."

Saden let out a low growl. "If you think to threaten me by telling Serrakus —"

Lucius' brows shot up. "Just the opposite. Informing my brother of this wouldn't make for a very good ending to your story. He lacks a flare for the finer things in life. A trail of intrigue. An unexpected twist. Events that make our existence a little more…tolerable.

"Alas, as you can probably guess, it can get quite monotonous being confined to this realm, century after century, for the better part of each year. Trapped in a routine of simple pleasures and death. It isn't very stimulating, wouldn't you say? Rather leaves one with no other choice but to live vicariously through others. For a short while there, you were my other. Care to be again?"

He shook his head in confusion. "What do you mean?"

"Do you recall what I told you during our first meeting?"

The memory came to him as clearly as if it had been yesterday. He remembered because it had given him hope until he'd soon realized the odds against him. Lucius had told him there was a reason the gods decreed that the worst criminals in demonkind be made Drakons. That everyone deserved a chance at salvation without the permanency of death.

Just as Drakonem had been created with the great treasure of worshiping the gods, so Drakons were reborn with the infusion of a Drakonem soul which sealed in their own treasure.

Every Drakon's treasure was unique, for it was dependent on the key to their crime. In most cases, it was a sin. Jealousy, wrath, greed. For Saden, it had been his innocence. His blind faith in the good intentions of his uncle had led to his undoing. In theory, a Drakon could be released from his sentence and forgiven his crime if someone were to give up that particular treasure for him. For instance, a crime of greed could only be pardoned by the absolute sacrifice of greed in another. The same went for innocence.

It was foolish to think anyone would give up one of their few cherished qualities that could never be regained for a murderer. And Saden had only been a fool once.

"You told me my treasure was innocence. That I could be absolved of my crime if I found someone willing to forfeit their own innocence for my freedom."

Lucius' pale eyes glinted with mischief in the flickering torchlight. "Very good. Tell me, would you allow someone to do that if you thought they might?"

"No." The answer was immediate. He knew the repercussions of losing such a precious gift. It was a fate he wouldn't wish on his worst enemy. When Lucius narrowed his gaze, it dawned on Saden what he was implying. "You're thinking of Daneya."

"The woman does seem a prime candidate for saving your soul."

And scorpions could crawl out of his ass. "Not a chance. Besides, her innocence was taken from her a long time ago."

"Everyone carries a measure of innocence in them. Even you."

While that might be true, Daneya was out of the question. His time with her was done. She deserved to move on to a life far better than anything he could offer. "I said no."

Lucius breathed a deep sigh, a streak of irritation crossing his features. "Well, that is going to make for a dull ending, but your story isn't over yet. I'll give you twenty-four hours to gain hard evidence to complete your assignment. You'll need actual confessions, not just those files you found. I can infuse you with a piece of my soul to temporarily hide you from Serrakus should he try to track you. There is only one stipulation you must agree to. I want you to ask Phoenix to help you."

Saden let out a raw bark of laughter. "Even if I could get it done in one day, Phoenix would never join me, and I wouldn't ask him. He's too much of a liability. I couldn't trust him at my back." Especially not with that Djinn inside him. There was no telling what he might do when they came face to face with the Djinn Gabriel was conspiring with.

"Did I mention Gabriel Aikins is holding your human at one of his facilities? Oh, and her daughter as well."

"What?" he roared. A blast of adrenaline shot through his system and shook his entire frame. He curled his hands into fists, using the pain to focus his rage. "Heal me. I'll get the evidence." And Gabriel. His uncle had gone too far. Saden was going to make sure he never crossed that line again.

Scorching, white heat engulfed him as Lucius used his power to accelerate the regeneration of his flesh. Unlike Serrakus who took pleasure in prolonging the agony of the process, Lucius was done in a few heartbeats. Saden swayed afterwards, feeling weak and slightly disoriented.

Lucius stood and pointed to a pile of clothes and pair of boots next to him. "You'll need these."

Saden forced his trembling limbs to cooperate. The outfit was what he'd been wearing when the warders had come to collect him. He didn't ask how the Drakonem had found it, or what his intentions were for wanting to include Phoenix. All that mattered was getting to Daneya and Mckenzie. "Do you know where I can find Phoenix?"

A wide grin spread across Lucius' face. "He's at the Amber Heart Opera House."

Saden dipped his head, familiar with the location of the building. To his surprise, he caught Demetrius eavesdropping in the corridor outside. Before the Dresidien could bolt, he snatched Demetrius' arm and turned back to Lucius. "He comes with me." It was likely the only opportunity he'd have now to keep his promise to the phantom. When Lucius started to argue, he cut him off. "Either he goes or I stay."

It wasn't a gamble, really. The Drakonem had already gone to too much trouble to see this through. Lucius reluctantly placed a hand on Demetrius' chest to transfer the sliver of his soul. Saden had to clamp onto the terrified phantom while he explained what was going on. No doubt Demetrius associated this with his Drakon initiation. Serrakus wasn't known for his gentleness during the painful process of linking his soul to that of a new Drakon.

"I would advise you to hurry," Lucius said as he lowered his hand. "The clock is ticking."

Saden took Demetrius by the wrist and headed farther into the bowels of the dungeon, keeping an eye out for warders. At the end of a dank hallway, he used his power to create a temporal rift. They stepped through the seam in the atmosphere to the back alley of an apartment complex in downtown LA. From the barrage of noise and blush cast to the sky, he figured it was nearing dusk. Normally, he would find a discreet area to change forms in but at this point, he didn't care who saw them.

"We need to fly," he told Demetrius. "Concentrate on the power Serrakus gave you. It should feel like a buzzing sensation on the edge of your consciousness. Imagine it expanding to surround your body. Your molecules will fade and reshape themselves into the form of a dragon. Let the change come naturally." When the phantom's dark skin began to dissolve, he said, "Now reach out with your senses and feel my heat. It's like a signature that differentiates me from every other living being. Lock onto that and follow me up. Got it?"

Saden altered his own form swiftly and rose up high into the air, waiting to make sure Demetrius had accomplished the change. It didn't take long for the phantom to adjust to using his new shape. They sped through the skies toward the opera house some distance away.

At the front of the building, a large crowd divided into two lines was slowly making its way inside. A quick scan of the building's interior told him there was bustling movement at the back. The night's performance would be starting soon. Phoenix wasn't hard to find. His core energy was brighter than the rest due to the ancient Drakonem's soul within him. From his position, Saden guessed he was somewhere up in the rafters near the stage.

He circled behind the building and landed close to one of the back access doors. Seconds later, Demetrius performed a graceless hit and roll, cursing as he skinned his palms and knees. Saden pulled him to his feet and guided him to a dumpster, telling him to stay out of sight until he was finished dealing with Phoenix. The last thing he needed was to carry the rookie back to the Drakonem realm because of an unpredictable psychopath.

Phoenix wasn't known for playing well with others.

He aimed a tendril of power at Phoenix's energy, strong enough to cause a small spark and get the man's attention. A minute later, the Drakon came through the back door with a knife gripped in one hand.

Saden raised both of his in a calming gesture. It struck him as bizarre to see the likes of Phoenix in a reputable opera house. The clash of style and culture in the two seemed more at odds than a soccer mom at a BDSM convention. Phoenix had to be there on assignment, although no Drakon in their right mind would risk exposure in such a public place. The man may be volatile, according to the rumors about him, but he was no idiot.

Phoenix returned the blade to a side harness and crossed his arms over his chest.

Saden lowered his hands. "I, uh…" *Gods,* he couldn't believe he was saying this. "I need your help."

Phoenix merely arched his winged brows.

"I was given twenty-four hours to complete my assignment," Saden continued. "It'll involve taking down several figureheads in the house of Vampyres in this area. Since you're already familiar with my case, I figured you might want in on the collection of criminals. At the very least, you can get in a little bloodshed and win Serrakus' favor for a while."

Phoenix seemed to mull this over then turned to make his way back inside. "Good luck with that."

"Wait." Shit! He may have underestimated the man. "You were right about Daneya. Is that what you want to hear? I should've found a safe place for her instead of keeping her with me. My target has her now and I can't go back to the Drakonem realm until I know she's out of danger. Gabriel has powerful allies. I won't be able to bring him down on my own."

"Not my problem."

The deadpan response set his nerves on edge. "Is it because my target is in league with the Djinn?" he asked through his clenched jaw. "Is that why you won't help? I should've known you have some sick affinity for them. Or maybe the one inside you is pulling all the shots. Made you a weak puppet that can't think for itself." His back was slammed against the building in the next instant.

Fury burned in the depths of Phoenix's gray eyes, his teeth bared as he leaned in close. "You think I hold love for the Djinn? They've taken more from me than you could ever conceive of. How dare you think to pass judgment on me or the Djinn I carry. She's an innocent—"

The rest of his sentence was cut off by some inner turmoil twisting his features. Saden's anger melted in spite of his effort to hold onto it. This wasn't the first time Phoenix had intimated that the Djinn inside him was different from the rest of its kind.

Saden had heard that at one time, over a millennium ago, there had been three types of Djinn. Evil, tricksters, and those who were benevolent. When the Vampyres had gone their separate way, however, all of the Djinn had become evil in their quest for revenge.

Could Phoenix really be housing one that hadn't been corrupted by greed? The idea was ridiculous and yet there was no deceit in his expression. Only pure rage and...suffering.

Phoenix shoved himself back with a look of disgust. "You know nothing."

As the man stormed away, Saden swallowed his pride and switched tactics. "I'm sorry if I offended you." Phoenix didn't stop. Saden was going to lose him if he didn't think of something fast. "Lucius set me free. It wasn't Serrakus." That was enough to make Phoenix pause. "He's been spying on me. Apparently, he's got some sort of interest in my story and wants to see it played out. The twenty-four hour release is dependent upon your involvement. For whatever reason, he wants you to help me."

The man didn't move or respond at all. Saden thought about Daneya and Mckenzie as a sliver of panic pierced his chest. "Like I said, I *need* your help. I'll beg if I have to."

Finally, Phoenix shifted to face him. His gaze seemed distant, as if he were concentrating on something far away. "All right. You win."

Saden frowned, not quite sure it was him Phoenix was talking to. "Excuse me?"

This time, the man looked directly at him. "Not you, but I will help. What do you want me to do?"

He let out a breath he hadn't known he was holding. "Follow me. I have to check in on a friend first. Demetrius, come out. We're leaving."

The Dresidien walked timidly out from behind the dumpster and wisely steered clear of Phoenix. Saden led them in dragon form to his house. His anger resurged as he landed in the driveway and took in the damage done by the warders. The slanted roofs above and near the garage had been destroyed by the fire. The stone walls of the living room and kitchen areas were still standing, though they appeared more as charred bones than the lovingly crafted frame of the manor.

Inside, layers of plaster and other debris lay scattered among the antique furniture. Some intact and some beyond salvaging. It would take months to repair the damage. Months he didn't have thanks to Gabriel's lies.

The only compensating factor was that the property belonged solely to him, and would still be there after the years of his punishment.

Still, it was devastating to see the work of his father ruined because of him. Just another failure to add to his growing collection.

Blade stepped out from the hallway leading to the other end of the manor. His mouth dropped open in shock. "Saden? What the hell? I thought Serrakus grounded your ass." He strode over to Saden and gripped him in a tight embrace. "Damn, it's good to see you," he said with a grin.

"I'm only out on temporary release."

"And you've brought company." His face sobered as he took in the pair waiting in the foyer. He walked over to Demetrius and extended a hand. "I take it Saden smuggled you out. I hope there's no hard feelings between us."

The phantom shied away stiffly. Understandable considering Blade was the one who'd brought him in to Serrakus. "He said I could prove myself as a Drakon."

"You will," Saden assured. "What you're going to do with us will force Serrakus to put you into training to go out in the field. You won't be his slave anymore."

Behind Demetrius' doubt, Saden saw raw hope in his expression.

"What about the other one?" Blade asked, jerking his chin at Phoenix.

Saden explained his deal with Lucius, making sure to add that Phoenix was there doing him a solid. Truth was, he felt a sense of gratitude toward the man. If their roles had been reversed, Saden couldn't say he would've agreed to put his ass on the line for Phoenix.

"Well, fuck me with a chainsaw. Miracles do happen. Come on, the others are here." He took them down the hallway to the dining room.

At the massive oak table sat Roshon, Kent and the three other Rakshasas who'd intervened at Gabriel's facility. Their geis rested on the floor and the backs of a few chairs around them. A smile lifted the corners of Saden's mouth, followed by a rush of welcome relief. "What's going on?"

Before anyone could answer, the Rakshasas jumped to their feet and drew weapons. All except for Roshon and Kent, who stood with twin looks of disbelief.

"You bring a Djinn into your own home?" the female shifter sneered to Saden, though her eyes never left Phoenix.

Roshon inserted himself between Phoenix and his group. "He's not our enemy here. This is Cai. He was…*is* my brother."

Blade barked in laughter then grunted when Saden backhanded him in the gut. He rubbed the spot and mumbled under his breath, "Damn, man."

"Phoenix is doing me the service of being here to help us with Gabriel," Saden said. "If anyone has a problem with that, they can leave now." The shifters at the table sat back down, though he had a feeling it was more out of respect for their chief than his authority over the situation. Either way, he didn't care. So long as everyone kept it together until his job was done.

Roshon held out a hand to Saden. "It's good to see you again. Blade found us a few days after you…after what happened. We all agreed to do what we can. Why don't you get yourself cleaned up and we'll talk when you're ready?"

Saden shook his hand, grateful beyond words. For the chief to put aside the differences in their stations and races spoke volumes about his courage. Any other man might've outright refused to have anything to do with Vampyres and their dilemma, whether or not it could potentially affect his clan in the future. With Roshon and his men there, Saden believed for the first time he actually had a chance of pulling off his assignment and rescuing Daneya and Mckenzie.

"I'll be outside," Phoenix said, then turned to leave. It looked as if Roshon wanted to say something but held his tongue.

Saden took Demetrius upstairs to Daneya's old room. From the dresser, he pulled out one of her combat outfits and held it up to the phantom. "These might be a little tight but they'll have to do. You're too thin for my clothes. You'll find a bathroom through there. I'll be back for you shortly."

Demetrius grabbed his arm before he could leave, mouth opening and closing before he managed to get out, "Thank you."

Saden nodded then left.

Blade was waiting for him in the hallway and walked with him to the other bathroom. "Brothers. Huh. Who'd have thought Roshon could be related to that?"

He stripped out of his clothes and started the shower, mindless of his nudity. They'd seen a lot more, and worse, of each other. "You're talking to the nephew of the bastard who started all of this," he reminded his friend. "In comparison, I'd say their connection is only mildly disturbing. Makes me wonder if it wasn't Phoenix who alerted Roshon to our situation in the first place."

"Nah, it couldn't have been," Blade said, though uncertainty colored his tone. "It was probably Lucius, or his spy. It's no secret the Drakonem gets his jollies off by meddling in others' affairs. Granted, this is the first time I've heard of him taking an interest in Drakons besides his own. Still, I'd count yourself lucky."

Saden didn't deny that, nor did he trust Lucius' intentions, regardless of how convenient they were. He would deal with that later, however. The pressure of the water soothed his tight muscles, sloughing away layers of blood, dirt and sweat. Laurs' whip echoed like a thundering crack in his memory. What he'd endured over the past week was going to seem like a picnic compared to what was in store for him on his return. Laurs would have to compensate for his failure to watch over Saden or end up in a cell himself. The fact that it was Lucius who had gone behind Serrakus' back wasn't going to matter.

Again, Saden cleared his mind.

"So, about Daneya—" Blade began.

"Lucius already told me."

"He did?"

"What I don't know is how Gabriel managed to kidnap her and Mckenzie from a DCM compound. That is where you took them, isn't it?" He didn't try to hide the anger in his voice.

"Yeah, look, I'm sorry," Blade said falteringly. "They were there when I checked on them a few nights ago. The next morning, they were gone. That Vincent guy damn near tore up the whole compound searching for them. The real kicker is…Cherri had gone missing that same night. Both hers and Daneya's cars were taken. Somehow, Gabriel was able to lure them all out. I found them at the facility here. Roshon and I were planning to break into it tonight."

Saden closed his eyes and tried to block the images crowding his mind. Daneya bound and gagged, helpless against Gabriel's advances. Mckenzie frightened and alone. Something about Cherri's absence bothered him. Why had she taken a separate car? Daneya was too smart to split up, let alone risk taking Mckenzie with her for anything less than a direct threat to her family.

As much as he wanted to race to the facility now and get them free, he knew there was other business to take care of first. The house of Avram would just have to suffer the fallout of losing more than a quarter of their officials at once. Making Gabriel's operation known was the only way he could ensure Daneya and Mckenzie's safety long after he disappeared from this realm again.

"That'll have to wait. We need to find an official on that list of buyers for the offspring and force him to confess his association with Gabriel to the Lady Ilsa. Only she has the power and influence to make sure none of this gets swept under the rug by the wrong people on the council." He finished washing his hair then stepped out to dry.

Blade cast him a dubious look from the door. "From what I've gathered, one of the council members is holding some sort of formal reception at her mansion tonight. I'm sure the Lady Ilsa will be there. Maybe we can follow her afterwards and—"

"No. We'll go there and get it done." Since Serrakus had taken away his ability to track Gabriel, it would be a gamble on whether or not the Vampyre would be at the reception to interfere with their plans

"And get our asses handed to us," he said with an incredulous laugh. "In case you haven't noticed, there are eight of us and one kid who's probably never held a gun in his life. That mansion is going to be crawling with leisonguardes. Even if we could get to the Lady, she'll be surrounded by her personal guard. They're not going to stand by while a group of Drakons and shifters torture one of their own until he confesses."

Saden slammed his fist on the sink counter. "Twenty-four hours, Blade! That's all I have! There's no time for caution or reconnaissance. Unless you've got a better idea, we do this my way." When no response came, he wrapped a towel around his waist and shoved past Blade to his bedroom.

The rumpled sheets on the bed made him pause. Daneya's scent still clung to them faintly, the natural perfume of her body hanging in the air like a cold reminder of what he'd lost. With no small effort, he forced himself to move to his closet where he pulled out a clean set of clothes.

"All right, your way," Blade said as he walked in. "We'll work out the details with the others. Meanwhile, you want to tell me just what happened with Serrakus? You told him about the evidence, right?"

He flexed his jaw as he recalled his conversation with their Drakonem. "He said Gabriel had video footage of the break-in at the facility in Arizona. Apparently, Gabriel submitted this to his superiors and claimed I had originally set up a false accusation against him out of a personal vendetta. That I tried to take my revenge on him by destroying him and his research. Because I couldn't find sufficient evidence on him at his house, I resorted to the aid of Rakshasas and a member of the DCM to set him up."

"That's bullshit. Serrakus knows you weren't the one to file the charge against Gabriel."

"Doesn't matter. My involvement with Daneya, Roshon and his crew was enough to have the entire case thrown out. Which is why nothing short of a confession is going to be enough to incriminate Gabriel.

It'll have to come from a high-ranking official. One the Lady trusts."

"Damn." Blade scrubbed his face. "This could get deadly. It may not be right to include Roshon and the others. This isn't their fight."

Saden grabbed an extra pair of boots then made his way back down the hallway outside. "That's what I plan on telling him. I don't want to be responsible for his death or anyone else's."

He knocked on the door to Daneya's old room before entering. Demetrius was dressed and smoothing the wet locks of his raven hair. His visible skin was a deep ruddy color with occasional light abrasions, as if he'd taken coarse sandpaper to it. Saden didn't bother to ask. He already knew the reason. During his time as Serrakus' slave, he had scrubbed his flesh raw every time he'd showered. And for years afterwards, trying to erase the memories of Serrakus' rough touch.

Eventually, they would fade from Demetrius' mind, though not without leaving permanent scars.

He handed the boots to Demetrius then looked to Blade. "I can't ask you to come either. Serrakus will find out about this and punish anyone who's with me."

Blade snorted. "If you expect me to sit around and let you guys have all the fun, you can kiss my ass. Besides, somebody's gotta watch your back with Phoenix at your side."

Saden smiled and clapped his friend on the shoulder. He led the way up to the weapons room on the third floor to grab extras for Demetrius. The coming night weighed heavily on his thoughts, haunted by Daneya's last words to him.

"When will I see you again?"

At the time, he'd have given anything for one more hour with her. Now, he'd be content to remain indefinitely in Serrakus' dungeons if it meant knowing she and her daughter were safe. He wouldn't fail them this time. Even if he had to kill Gabriel himself and whoever got in the way. He would stain his hands with blood before he let any more harm come to them.

Chapter Seventeen

Daneya stalked the confines of the small room in her bare feet. Everything she could use as a weapon had been stripped from it, leaving only the twin-sized bed and a metal chest for the plain clothes she'd been issued. The connecting bathroom was no more than a narrow closet with a standing shower, sink and toilet, all within arm's reach. The mirror had been taken out upon her arrival.

She glared at the Plexiglas wall, feeling exposed and vulnerable without her guns and knives. Anything she could use to attempt an escape with. Every once in a while, her memories closed in on her, causing a sense of claustrophobia that was almost too much to bear. The oppressing isolation and familiarity of it all wracked her to the core of her being. Made her feel as if she were that frightened child again whom Gabriel had kidnapped so many years ago.

She was different now. The confidence of her training and experience in combat gave her an edge, yet it wasn't that which kept her going. It was the thought of

Mckenzie doubtlessly suffering far worse than anything she might endure.

Her Kennie was strong willed and resilient, but this situation was one no nine year old should be forced to comprehend. Just imagining what her little girl must be going through, alone and afraid, brought every motherly instinct to the surface and fueled the flames of her rage.

In the two days since she'd been imprisoned in this barren room, she'd had only one visitor. Gabriel had wisely stayed on the other side of the Plexiglas and only long enough to assure her that Mckenzie was unharmed and bunking with one of the other women. When she had demanded to see her daughter, he'd merely laughed, saying she would have to prove her loyalty to him first. Adversely, it wasn't his words that had shaken her. It was her sudden impulse to do what he wanted.

She *had* to see her daughter. Had to hold Kennie in her arms and know for certain she was all right. Their separation was like a living shackle around her neck growing tighter with each passing second. Problem was, Gabriel had never been fooled by her false intentions.

For the first time in years, she found herself wishing for the protection of another. The man who shadowed her thoughts and filled her dreams. Saden was like an aching hole in her heart. An anchor no longer within her reach. She longed for his cool confidence and strong arms. She… The island of self-imposed solitude, as Cherri had so often labeled her.

Cynical laughter bubbled up in her chest at the thought of her best friend. Of all the people to betray her—Saden and Blade with their criminal backgrounds

and the Rakshasas with their mysterious appearance —
it had been the one person she'd trusted most.

Cherri had come to see her multiple times to explain
and beg her understanding. Even with all the facts, she
couldn't fathom how the woman could fall for such a
twisted web of lies. Or how Cherri's loneliness had
grown so great that taking a Vampyre lover in league
with their enemy had become a viable option.

Daneya recalled her friend's increasing strange
behavior over the past month. How Cherri's normally
excessive optimism had turned to long periods of
brooding and occasional outbursts. Had she missed all
the signs? Was it her fault for not seeing what was
going on? Perhaps. But none of that could account for
Cherri's actions.

The door to her room opened slowly and in walked
the devil herself. Cherri's expression was pensive, her
eyes flicking back to the door before settling on Daneya.
In her hands was a tray stacked with finger foods,
which she placed on the chest. Not even silverware was
allowed in Daneya's presence. Cherri offered a watery
smile as she sat next to the tray. "Have you thought any
more about what I said?"

Daneya took a breath to steady her nerves, resisting
the urge to strangle some sense into her friend. "There
is nothing to think about. I will never accept Gabriel.
You should know that by now."

"I know you have plenty of reasons to hate him. I do,
too. He wants to change, though, just like my Rhys."

She glanced at the glass and saw Cherri's new
boyfriend waiting outside as he always did during their
visits. "I don't get it. Why are you still here? Didn't he
promise to take you away from all this?"

Disappointment flashed across Cherri's face. "Gabriel
won't let us bond until he knows you'll listen to him.

He wants me to convince you to give him a chance. That's all he's asking for. Can't you agree to at least that?"

Daneya let out an exasperated huff. "People like them don't change! They're murderers and rapists. Is that the kind of father you want for your children? Damn it, can't you see? He and Gabriel are using you to get to me."

Cherri pursed her lips, her cheeks reddening with anger. "You always were so high and mighty. Only ever thinking of yourself. How dare you pass judgment on me when you were the one to lust after a Drakon. For all you know, he could've filled your head with lies just to get a piece. And you fell for it after the first day. Don't think I didn't notice the way you would look at him. At least Rhys loves me and can give me a future."

"Saden is nothing like Gabriel or your precious Rhys," she said through gritted teeth. "If he had wanted to take advantage of me, he wouldn't have pushed me away after you accused him of tricking me into his bed. And in case you don't remember, *he can't give me a future because of Gabriel!*" Her shout rang out in the ensuing silence. She lowered her voice and tried again. "Saden wasn't the one who took my life from me. He saved it, and yours."

"If he's so great, then why is he being punished now?"

Daneya sat on the edge of the bed and shook her head. "I don't know. Something went wrong. I'm not going to condemn him for it, though." Especially not when she might have been partly to blame.

"Please, give Gabriel the opportunity to explain himself," Cherri said after a period. "I've spoken to him and he promises to release you and Mckenzie in a month if you still feel the same way. You can go back to your normal life and forget about all of this. If you ever cared for me, you'll do this. It's the only way Rhys and I can be together."

She stared at the woman she'd known for a decade. The one she'd convinced Marco to take with them from the first facility. The friend who had been at her side through thick and thin over the years. And realized she didn't know her at all. Not anymore.

The person in front of her was just another seeker willing to give up everything and everyone in her life to create a new one. Nothing Daneya said was going to make a difference at this point. So she said the only thing she could without losing her temper. "I want you to leave."

"Come on, sweetie, be smart. Fake interest if you have to. You've been doing it with Vincent for long enough. It should come naturally to you."

"Get out!" she snarled.

This time, Cherri reared back in fear. She got up, knocked on the door then slipped out as soon as Rhys opened it for her.

Daneya put her head in her hands and fought the tears threatening to spill over. It seemed her life had come full circle, landing her in the same position as when this had all started. Alone and under the control of a madman. Blade was still out there somewhere. Her only hope of getting out of this alive. However, there was no telling how long it might take him to find her and Mckenzie and get them free, if he tried at all.

Daneya couldn't blame him if he decided the consequences were too great. Marco had saved her and earned a permanent position as a warder on another continent for his troubles. How could she expect a man who barely knew her to risk that kind of penalty?

The door opened again to admit the last person she wanted to see. She jumped to her feet and backed up to the wall as Gabriel sauntered into the room. His dark brown eyes fixed on her intently, a thin smile curving his lips. "So, it's true. You did fall in love with my nephew. I didn't believe that little whore at first. I thought you had better taste."

It took all she had to keep her expression impassive. She should have known he'd been listening in on her conversations with Cherri. All of the rooms were equipped with cameras built into the ceilings.

Gabriel walked closer until only a few feet separated them. "Don't worry. I've chosen not to hold it against you. We all make mistakes. As long as you understand you're mine now."

She jerked away from his hand on her waist then stilled when his fingers dug in hard enough to leave bruises. A wave of nausea hit her when he leaned forward to whisper in her ear.

"Easy, wildcat. I've waited a long time to get you back and I'm not going to let you or anyone else spoil this for me. From now on, you will submit to me. Or you can choose which one will die for your disobedience. Your best friend, or our daughter."

Blind fury coursed through her. Out of pure, gut reaction, she brought her knee up in a vicious blow to his groin. He twisted a fraction of a second before it connected, taking the brunt of the blow on his inner thigh. Not quite her mark but still high enough to send him reeling back in agony.

Gabriel gradually straightened and cast her a leering glare that sent a chill racing down her spine. "Just like I remember. We're going to have so much fun."

The back of his fist cracked along the side of her face, bouncing her off the wall to the hard floor. Pain exploded in her skull and the taste of coppery blood filled her mouth as she struggled to regain her balance. Above the ringing in her ears, she heard Gabriel calling out orders. The rough hands of two leisonguardes gripped her and tossed her onto the bed. Her arms and ankles were tied down in the leather straps attached to the metal frame.

Gabriel pushed the guards out of the way then hovered over her, caging her in with an arm on either side of her head. "Tell me. Is our daughter as feisty as you are?"

Daneya wrenched at her restraints. "If you hurt her, I swear to God, I'll kill you!"

He chuckled deeply and tangled his fingers through her hair, pressing his weight on it. "She'll learn to obey me as well if she ever wants to see her mother again." He crushed his mouth to hers, grinding her teeth into the cut on her lower lip.

She turned and spat when he finally let her go.

"Give her two cc's of Rohypnol," Gabriel said to one of the men. "Keep her sedated until I get back. I want her ready for transport by then. Are the preparations complete at my house?" When the guard nodded, Gabriel sent one last glance at Daneya. "Good. I want her comfortable."

Daneya fought against the restraints on a sudden rush of panic. She couldn't go to his mansion. No one would find her, let alone think to look there. If Blade or Vincent did search for her, the facilities would be their first choice, giving Gabriel all the warning he would need to make sure she stayed hidden.

And what of Mckenzie? Gabriel hadn't mentioned moving her as well.

The guard left with Gabriel then came back with a loaded syringe. The second man held one of her arms still while he plunged the fluid into her.

Warmth sped through her bloodstream as the drug attacked her nervous system, swamping her with a sensation of weakness. A single tear fell past her control and slid down her cheek. This wasn't happening again. She couldn't lose everything she'd worked so hard to get. Her freedom and independence. Her daughter…

An image of Saden appeared behind her drooping lids and she called out to him. Or thought she had. Her mind was a fog of confusion. Blackness teetered at the corners of her vision, pulling her down into a numbing abyss. The last thing she remembered was Saden's hand wiping her tear away, or maybe that was a trick of her mind, too.

* * * *

"We've got to move soon," Roshon said from beside him. "The guests are starting to leave. Have you been able to find Lady Ilsa yet?"

From their perch on a hilltop overlooking the mansion, Saden strengthened the net of his power and sent it out farther. It told him how many people were in each room and where, but couldn't identify them. The royal blood in the Lady's veins made her life force no more powerful than the rest.

Dozens of pinpoints of energy were in what had to be the ballroom on the first floor of the left wing. Those moving in a predictable pattern to certain rooms in the right wing and back were poignots scrambling to serve the guests. On the second and third floors were pairs and triplets of Vampyres occupying the rooms for approximately an hour at a time. Probably invigorated by the night's events and seeking a little private gratification before going home.

The only thing going in his favor was that he'd spotted Gabriel going into the mansion a few hours ago with an escort of leisonguardes and hadn't seen him come out since. Which meant the korvaute was still in there somewhere. With any luck, they could kidnap one of the officials, force him to confess to the Lady and apprehend Gabriel before news of their presence reached the facility Daneya was being held at.

Saden shook his head in frustration and glanced at Roshon. "My power can't distinguish between the individuals. She could be anywhere in the left wing. All I can recall about her is that she doesn't like to stand on ceremony." He was about to concentrate again when he noticed Roshon staring oddly at his eyes.

"Do they…always do that when you use your power?"

Quickly, he withdrew the Drakonem power, realizing the man had likely never seen the glowing white-violet hue it turned a Drakon's eyes when activated. "Sorry."

"No no, it's all good. Just give me a bit of warning next time."

"Don't worry. You'll get a heads up when I plan to shoot my laser beams," he said casually.

Blade burst into laughter when Roshon inched away, his expression a comical mixture of alarm and doubt. The grin Saden was fighting slowly leaked out.

Roshon scowled darkly. "See, that's just not funny right there. How the hell am I supposed to know what you guys are capable of?"

"Aside from taking dragon form and feeling the presence of others within a few miles radius, we can only call fire and cause explosions," Saden explained.

"Only." He snorted. "I'll keep that in mind.

The sky darkened behind them as a large, undulating shadow swooped down. It condensed and reshaped itself into the form of a man until Phoenix's distinct features became visible. His wavy blond hair was highlighted by the moonlight against his black outfit. The resemblance to Roshon was striking now that Saden knew of the connection between them.

He strode over and knelt down next to them. "The Lady has gone upstairs to the third room from the left on the second floor with two of her mistresses. Four leisonguardes are standing outside her door. Two guards are at every entrance on ground level and more are standing at the foot of the main staircase. Our best bet would be to sneak in through the servant's entrance and take their separate stairwell up."

"How did you…?" Blade began, then waved a hand. "Never mind. I don't want to know."

Saden inwardly agreed. No need to question how the wizard behind the curtain got his information. Just as long as he was on their side. "Good work. If I remember correctly, it's customary for the Lady to stay until most of the guests are gone. Now all we need is a viable target."

He gazed down at the driveway of the mansion below. A family of four was loading into their car accompanied by two poignots. Five minutes later, a prominent official came out with his mate hanging on one arm and what appeared to be their teenage son at his other side. The four leisonguardes and two poignots flanking them told Saden they had to be closely related to the royal family. He sensed a slight difference in the boy. A less complex field of energy that could only be the result of partial human genetics.

"That's our target." Saden pointed to the departing group. "He has to be one of the officials on the list.

Phoenix and I will go after him and drive his limo back around to the servants' main entrance. Blade and Demetrius will come with us to confront the Lady. Roshon, I need you and your team to find and guard all access ways to the second floor. Make sure none of the leisonguardes downstairs interrupt us. Remember, we want to keep this as covert as possible. I don't want anyone following us to the facility once we're done here."

Roshon dipped his chin in assent. "I'll have the geis watch the outer perimeter. They'll inform us if anyone fitting Gabriel's description leaves the mansion."

He gripped the chief's arm, silently giving thanks for his presence even after he'd been informed of the odds against them. "Be careful."

"And you. Now let's go piss some people off."

Saden nodded then turned to Phoenix only to find him gone. The Drakon was already flying swiftly along the road leading away from the mansion. "Damn it!" He took off in the same direction.

Five miles out, he caught sight of the target's limo pulled over onto a narrow dirt path a short distance from the road. The leisonguardes' vehicle was lying upside down ahead of it with smoke coming from the engine. Phoenix was like a deadly wraith in the circle of men surrounding him. His movements were a blur of lethal precision, his body in constant, sinuous motion. So fast, it was hard to distinguish him from the others.

One by one, the guards fell at his feet. The last let out a choked howl as Phoenix kicked his knee, bending it an unnatural angle. Almost simultaneously, the man was lifted by the throat then slammed to the ground on his back and finished off with a solid punch to the head.

Saden surveyed the damage as he landed next to the wreckage. "You were supposed to wait for me."

Phoenix casually dusted off his shirt. "I got bored."

He eyed the other Drakon warily then looked at the guards. Not a single one moved or so much as twitched. "Are they still alive?"

Phoenix shrugged a shoulder. "Technically."

The indifference in his voice was unnerving considering their circumstances. Saden quickly re-evaluated the man who stood before him without a scratch on his body. If he hadn't just seen Phoenix take out four highly trained leisonguardes in less than a minute and before they could attempt to use their powers, he'd never have believed it.

He was beginning to think the man was still alive not because of the Djinn, but because Serrakus really didn't want to lose him.

The front doors of the limo opened and the two poignots stepped out, each holding a gun that shook in their trembling hands. Saden took pity on the servants, knowing they were only following the orders of the coward who employed them. A simple spark of blue flames at their fingers had both shrieking and dropping to the ground in terror. He gathered their weapons and told them to stay put.

Phoenix walked to the back of the limo and began yanking the family out. When he dumped the woman unceremoniously on her rear end, the teenaged boy seemed to grow a spine and attacked him. Phoenix snatched one of the kid's wrists and wrenched it behind his back then shoved him against the side of the limo. "Make another move and I'll rip your arm out of its socket."

The kid's face blanched under his mop of brown hair.

"Phoenix, take it easy—" Saden started before he was interrupted by the blustering official.

"Release my son immediately! You have no right to treat us like this. Do you know who I am?"

Saden approached with his teeth bared, causing the portly official to stumble backwards. "No, actually. Why don't you tell me?"

The man's face flushed a deep crimson and his jowls flapped as he sputtered indignantly. "I am Reginald Crenshaw, second cousin to the Rei'jin of the house of Avram and a board member on the council. If you think to kidnap me and my family for ransom, you won't live long enough to regret it. I'll see that you suffer before you pay for your crimes."

He recognized the name from the list and fisted the front of the man's shirt. "It's already too late for that, but I promise to return the offer." After shoving Crenshaw back into the limo, he grabbed the woman by the arm and dragged her over to the poignots. "Unless you want to bury your preyune, I suggest you stay here until someone comes for you. Phoenix, bring the boy over here."

"I've got a better idea. We can use him as leverage."

Saden suppressed the urge to argue. As much as he hated the thought of putting a child in danger, Phoenix was right. After confiscating the rest of the weapons and any cell phones he could find, he climbed into the back of the limo and sat opposite Crenshaw. Phoenix took the wheel with the kid sitting beside him in the passenger seat then headed back toward the mansion.

"My name is Saden. I'm the Drakon that's been investigating Gabriel Aikins' illegal enterprise. I know that you and several others have agreed to keep his secret and fund his operations in exchange for Vampyre offspring. Babies he's harvested from hundreds of human females against their will with the help of the Djinn. I also know your so-called son is one of those offspring."

The kid looked to his father questioningly. "Dad?"

"Don't pay any attention to him, Keefe. He speaks blasphemy. Gabriel Aikins was acquitted of all charges to his name. No one will believe this ridiculous story you've concocted."

"No?" He pulled a folded stack of papers from the inside pocket of his trench coat then found the two he was searching for and handed them to Crenshaw. "Do you deny that's your name on the list for infants received by Vampyres in the past twenty years? And the receipt for the personal check you made out to Gabriel in 1997 in the amount of one hundred thousand dollars. Sixteen years ago, the same age as your son, isn't it?"

Crenshaw's beady eyes skimmed over the papers then met Saden's levelly. "This doesn't prove anything. You could've fabricated these out of desperation. It still comes down to your word against mine. Who do you think everyone's going to trust? Me, or some psychotic killer who's already failed his mission once?"

Saden jerked the man forward by the shirt, pulled out one of his knives and pressed it tip first into Crenshaw's protruding gut. "This psychotic killer has just had a really bad week. I'm tired, cranky and sick of the *gods-damned* lies people like you base your whole pathetic lives on. Right now, nothing would give me more pleasure than twisting this blade in your fat belly and stringing you up by your intestines. So I suggest you stop *fuckin'* around and admit the truth."

Crenshaw merely laughed. "You won't kill me. I know about the consequences you'll face for taking an innocent life. Just as I know what will happen to me if I incriminate myself. Death would be the better option. You've got nothing."

Saden flexed his jaw, past his threshold for patience. "You willing to bet your son's life on that?"

Apprehension flashed in the man's eyes then was gone in the next instant. He leaned in farther and lowered his voice, saying, "Go ahead and kill him. This little plan to prove Gabriel's guilt will fall through, and when it does, I'll be able to get a dozen more sons if I want to."

Saden raised his hand to strike the smirk off the official's face when Phoenix's words made him pause.

"Let me know when, boss."

He released Crenshaw to peer over his shoulder and saw the glint of steel Phoenix held to Keefe's throat. The kid was paralyzed in his seat with beads of sweat forming on his temples. In the rearview mirror, Saden caught Phoenix's gaze. Instead of the crazed look he was expecting, it was utterly calm and steady.

"I'll take care of the bodies while you find another target," Phoenix said.

Saden nodded, hoping like hell Crenshaw would fall for the bluff. If it was a bluff.

Phoenix slammed on the breaks, wrenched the kid's hair back to expose his neck and brought the blade down in a vicious arc. The boy cried out just as Saden was about to intercept the knife, but it was Crenshaw who stopped all of them.

"Wait!" The official's expression held a desperate combination of anger and fear. He swallowed repeatedly, eyes glued to the boy. "I'll give you what you want. Please, let my son go."

The one-eighty in the man's attitude nearly threw Saden off. As the car started again, he saw Phoenix wink at him in the mirror. "We're going to keep him for insurance," he told Crenshaw. "Do what I say and I'll make sure he gets back to your preyuna. You're going to work out a deal.

"I want you to testify in front of the Lady Ilsa. Tell her everything you know about Gabriel's operation and involvement with the Djinn, including your own. In exchange, I'll allow you to beg her for mercy and spare you the sentence of a Drakon. Keep in mind, I'm aware of all the facts and I'll know if you lie."

"What makes you think the Lady will believe me? My confession could destroy her standing among the other royal houses in this country, and possibly the two overseas. She'll be viewed as weak."

He recalled vaguely his father's temper whenever the Lady's decrees had interfered with his work. The details were sketchy, though one thing remained clear. Lady Ilsa did everything out of personal pride. It was her pride that would demand she take care of an internal issue before the other houses became aware of it. Even if it did jeopardize her reputation. "She'll believe you. She won't have a choice."

"We're here," Phoenix said.

Saden pocketed the papers then got out with Crenshaw. "You're going to take us up the back stairwell to the second floor of the left wing. I have men inside and out of the building ready to move on my command, so don't try anything." When they came to the servant's door, he let the official and kid walk through then held Phoenix behind to ask, "How did you know…about Crenshaw?"

The Drakon's expression was once more nonchalant, almost deadpan. "That boy is Crenshaw's biological son. His legacy. There was no way he would've given that up."

Son of a bitch. No wonder Crenshaw's payout to Gabriel had been higher than most of the rest. He'd impregnated one of the human females himself to gain an unquestionable heir to his estate.

It was slightly disturbing that Phoenix had picked up on that so easily. Then again, he supposed that surviving several centuries in their occupation would make anyone an expert on reading others. Grudgingly, he had to admit Phoenix was turning out to be a more valuable ally than he could've anticipated.

Chapter Eighteen

Blade, Roshon and his men met them at the door. They entered a large kitchen full of poignots who instantly became flustered at their appearance. Crenshaw was surprisingly collected for what he was about to do and ordered the poignots to disregard the intrusion and continue their duties. They found the servants' staircase without further disruption and climbed it to the second floor.

Saden tamped down the urge to find Gabriel immediately and take him into custody. His twenty-four hour mark was getting closer and everything was riding on his ability to get the korvaute and the proof of guilt to Lucius in time. There was also the danger to Daneya. If Gabriel discovered Saden was back, he could take her and Mckenzie on the run with him. Saden might not be able to find them before his time was up, but he needed the proof first, and the Lady on his side.

Roshon and his team dispersed to keep watch over the crowd downstairs and entryways to the second floor. The long corridor remained empty until they neared the end. As Phoenix had said, four guards stood outside the third to the last door on the left. Crenshaw took the lead and approached the group, claiming he had vital business to discuss with the Lady.

One of the men stepped forward, eyeing them suspiciously. "The Lady is busy. You'll have to wait downstairs."

When Crenshaw tried to argue, the man merely pushed him away then ordered another guard to escort them all to the ballroom.

"Screw this," Blade muttered and charged the man coming at them.

Saden cursed and shoved the official toward Phoenix. He dodged the first guard's fist then swung his own, hearing the satisfying crunch of the man's nose beneath his knuckles. The man stumbled back, giving Saden the advantage he needed to take him down with a combination of punches to the face and stomach. Another guard launched at him from the side with a knife in hand. He grabbed the guard's wrist and twisted then brought his other arm around the man's neck in a choke hold. A glance in Blade's direction showed his friend taking on the last guard standing.

Saden grunted as a sharp elbow struck his ribs. The guard in his hold used the momentary distraction to wrestle out of his grip then spun around to slam the heel of his palm into Saden's chest. More than simple muscle was behind the force of the blow. Saden crashed through the door at his back, flying with it several feet into a room. He landed hard, the back of his head cracking against solid wood.

The guard followed him down with his palm reared to strike again and this time Saden could feel the man's power building for another vicious blow. At the last second, he punched the guard in the throat then shoved him over, switching their positions.

"Stop this, now!" a female shouted.

The shrill voice rang out above the noise and carried with it a command that seized every muscle in Saden's body. He was paralyzed from the neck down, unable to move or make a sound. The abrupt silence that filled the air told him everyone else was also trapped in the power of the woman's voice.

On a massive four-poster bed in front of him were two women scantily dressed in sheer fabrics that draped over their voluptuous curves. A third was lying on her back completely naked save for her long fall of raven hair and sparkling gold jewelry that hung at her throat, wrists and ears. Obviously the Lady Ilsa. She was a striking beauty with smooth, pale skin and supple legs parted for the stunned mistress who knelt between them.

When she moved to stand, the other mistress hastily snatched a shimmering gown from the floor and helped her into it.

Lady Ilsa glared at them imperiously. "What is the meaning of all this?"

The guard locked in frozen combat with Blade spoke up from somewhere near the doorway. "These men attacked us without cause, Your Highness. There are more out in the hallway."

The piercing gaze of her coal-lined eyes landed on Saden. "Is this true? Who are you?"

Saden felt his vocal cords relax, though the rest of his body stayed in its paralyzed state. "I'm the Drakon who was sent after Gabriel Aikins."

"I thought that mess was taken care of."

"He lied to you and I can prove it. Your cousin, Reginald Crenshaw, is waiting out in the hall to give you the truth."

The very air was still as she mulled over his words. "I'll give you five minutes to justify your accusation. You'd better make it worth my time. Unlike my commanding leisonguarde, I would have no problem freezing you again and allowing my guards to send you back to your Drakonem in pieces."

Her hold on them was withdrawn and Saden gained his feet to take up position on one side of the room. Blade and Demetrius joined him with Keefe in tow while the two leisonguardes still conscious stood at the other side.

"Did you know she could do that?" Blade asked quietly.

Saden shook his head. He'd never encountered anything like the Lady's power. She'd have made an impressive warrior if not for her royal blood.

Phoenix came in last and shoved Crenshaw to his knees before the Lady. When one of the guards prepared to jump in, it was Crenshaw who raised a hand to stop him.

"My Lady…" Crenshaw licked his lips nervously and glanced at his son. "My Lady," he repeated, "the Drakon is right. Korvaute Aikins has been lying to you for years. I know because I helped him hide his secret. He's been kidnapping human females and using them to breed more of our kind. The hybrid offspring are given to those who are in his trust. Leisonguardes and other officials like me. I'm not sure how many there are, but I've heard him speak of making deals with officials in the houses of Sekelsky and Nitz."

Saden sucked in a breath. He'd had no idea Gabriel's scheme had spread so far as to include the other two houses of Vampyres in the United States.

"The hybrids are raised as our own and know nothing of their true parentage," he looked again to Keefe and said in a strained voice, "My own son is one of them. I…I sired him off one of the humans to produce a blood heir so that he could continue my line."

"No!" Keefe cried out and lunged for his father. Saden caught and held him as he struggled. "You're lying! How could you do this?"

Crenshaw shook his head pleadingly. "You are my son."

"Your *bastard* son!" Tears of rage glistened in the boy's eyes. "Does your preyuna know about this?"

Saden guessed the kid's reference to his mother as Crenshaw's 'preyuna' was both a way of dissociating himself from his family and an insult to his father. Crenshaw flinched visibly, his refusal to answer confirming the truth.

Lady Ilsa spoke next. "How is that possible? You've been mated for more than four centuries. I saw your preyuna with us earlier tonight."

"Gabriel found a way for us to breed without having to bond with the females. It's very possible with the help of the Djinn." The Vampyres in the room let out a chorus of gasps. Crenshaw went on to explain the process in vague detail, skimming over the worst of it. He also included the fact that Gabriel was giving half of the offspring to the Djinn to be raised as their willing hosts.

When he was done, Lady Ilsa sat down slowly on the foot of the bed. "That's why the Djinn agreed to a truce with us, isn't it? Of course. It makes sense. Gabriel formed the truce just a few years after he claimed to have found a solution to our dwindling population."

"Your Highness," one of the guards began. "You can't know he's telling the truth. This could all be some elaborate plan the Drakon formed to win back the favor of his master. He's a disgraced murderer who probably seeks to bring down your house."

"Perhaps," she said distantly. To Keefe, she asked, "When did you come into your power, boy?"

Saden released the kid and watched his face turn a bright crimson. "Last year, my Lady. My parents told me to lie and say it had developed sooner. They said they were only protecting me from the shame of coming into it late."

"Half-breeds don't fully develop until their teenage years," she mused almost to herself. "I assume you have more evidence to back his claims," she said to Saden.

He pulled the papers from his trench coat and handed them to the Lady.

The guard stirred restlessly. "Your Highness, please. This traitor is an insult to our house. Let us give him what he deserves."

"Unless you too have something to confess, I do not need your input," she snapped. After skimming over the documents, she said, "Get Commander Weiss and korvaute Aikins. Tell them to come immediately." When the guard left, she turned back to Saden. "We will confront him together. As you have brought this matter before me and not your Drakonem, I will have the final say in his sentencing *if* I find him guilty. And if I discover you have lied to me, I will contact your Drakonem and see that you and your companions suffer the consequences. Am I clear?"

He bowed his head, already devising a contingency strategy in case this didn't work. One way or another, Gabriel was coming with him and the facilities would be put out of commission. Even if he had to inform Vincent of their locations and let the DCM take care of it.

The guard came back on the heels of an older Vampyre who outweighed Saden by about fifty pounds of pure muscle in breadth. His authoritative demeanor matched the iron lines of his visage and the only indication of his age was in his peppered hair and weathered skin. He took a quick assessment of the room then focused on the Lady. "What's going on here?"

"Thank you for joining us, Weiss. Where is korvaute Aikins? I sent for him as well."

"Aikins left ten minutes ago. Said he had some urgent matter to attend to."

Saden felt his insides grow cold. Had Gabriel detected his presence? The man could be on his way to the facility where Daneya and Mckenzie were being held. If he took off with them, there was no telling where he might go. Saden started for the door only to pause when the Lady's voice cracked through the air like a whip.

"Where are you going, Drakon? I didn't give you permission to leave."

He spun around, reining in his impatience. "Gabriel is probably aware that I'm here and headed to his facility to destroy the evidence of his crimes. I need to go after him."

"I can send a troop of my guards to his laboratory now. It's not too far—"

Saden made a chopping gesture to shut her up. "Not the one on his land. He's got four private facilities spread throughout your region and the closest is in this area. By the time you form a troop, he'll be gone, and the only ones you'll find there are Djinn."

"I can't let you apprehend him alone."

"Lives are at stake and I'm not going to stand here arguing with you about it!" he yelled.

Just as Weiss tensed to jump at him, the Lady raised her hand. "Stop. I'll let you leave as long as you take Commander Weiss and my two guards with you."

"Lady Ilsa," Weiss said in a warning tone. "I don't trust any of this."

"Neither do I, but I've had my suspicions about korvaute Aikins and I want to see this put to an end. You will go with these men. I expect to hear from you before the sun rises."

Saden didn't wait for the commander's response. He strode swiftly from the room toward the kitchen entrance where they'd come in.

Roshon emerged from a shadowed alcove and fell into step beside him. "I take it we're leaving."

"The Lady's on board so far, but apparently Gabriel left—"

"Just after we entered this place," Roshon finished. "My geis told me he saw a man fitting the Vampyre's description at that time. I'm not sure if Gabriel spotted us. Lorna sent her eagle to follow him. I thought it best to inform you after your meeting with Lady Ilsa."

Saden flexed his fists in an effort to suppress the anger rising within him. Roshon's discretion had been well placed. The Lady undoubtedly would've viewed shapeshifters in the mansion as an additional threat. He could already hear Weiss behind him demanding to know who he was talking to. Besides, with a winged geis on his trail, Gabriel couldn't elude them.

The female Rakshasa met them at the top of the stairs. "My geis tells me the Vampyre she's following is headed in the same direction as the facility."

Saden nodded curtly then said to Roshon, "Phoenix, Blade, Demetrius and I will fly. I'll need you to take the pompous ass behind us and his two guards with you and meet us there."

"Pompous ass and hemorrhoids. Got it. Any chance I can convince you to wait until we arrive?"

He clapped the commander's arm as they stepped outside. "Don't worry. I won't take all the fun. Watch your back and if you have to, pull your men out of there. You have families to go home to."

"And you have one to save, whether you want to admit it or not. We'll be at your side."

With a faint smile, he turned around, ignoring Weiss' questions. "Phoenix, Blade, let's go. Demetrius, stay with me like I taught you."

They took to the skies with Saden in the lead. Thirty minutes later, they landed at the edge of the facility's parking lot. Like the one in Arizona, it was located on the outer rim of a block of warehouses. The surrounding streets were empty at this hour. Every window in the facility was lit up from the inside, showing the silhouettes of several figures moving about through the cracks of their heavy drapes. At the back entrance, a truck was parked near the propped-open door. Two poignots in lab coats were busy loading boxes and what appeared to be computer towers onto its bed.

The heightened activity confirmed Saden's assumption that Gabriel had somehow become aware of his conference with Lady Ilsa. That left them with no choice but to go in full bore with only half his team. Otherwise, the hard evidence and the women could be gone by the time Roshon arrived with Weiss.

He pulled up an image of the building's inner structure in his mind. "I need a distraction while Demetrius and I take the emergency stairs through the access door on the roof."

"We'll go in through the back door," Blade said, jerking his head to Phoenix.

"Meet us on the underground level when you can." He gave Phoenix a critical look. "Are you solid?"

Phoenix smiled grimly. "It's what I live for, isn't it?"

The reply was more chilling than comforting, though it would have to do. They streaked across the parking lot, blending into the darkness where they could. Blade effortlessly crept up behind one of the poignots, snatched him from the truck bed and put him in a sleeper hold. Phoenix took a less subtle approach to the second poignot and bashed his face into the side of the brick wall. The assistant crumpled in a boneless heap to the ground.

As soon as Blade and Phoenix entered the facility, Saden glanced back at Demetrius. "Remember to keep a weapon ready at all times. Use your gun as a last resort and always strike first. You need to be responsible for the death of at least one of these criminals to become a full Drakon. Don't worry about Serrakus or the morals you were taught growing up. Let the heat of the kill come to you, and remember, these bastards have more innocent blood on their hands than you ever will. You ready?"

The young phantom nodded shakily, eyes dancing with both anticipation and dread. They flew to the roof and materialized in front of the metal door. Saden stilled in wait. If he knew Blade, there would be some sort of signal…

A loud explosion just below them shook the gravel at their feet, immediately followed by the blare of a security alarm.

And there it was.

He sent a small blast of power at the lock on the door then yanked it open and rushed in. Two flights down, they entered a corridor identical to the one at the previous facility. A pair of leisonguardes was herding three full-term pregnant women at gunpoint toward the elevator in the middle of the corridor.

"Get the women back into one of the cells," he told Demetrius, then raced toward the clustered group. The female guard nearest him saw him first and aimed her gun at him. She let out a shriek and dropped it when Saden called forth a burst of flames at her hand. Just as he was almost on her, she turned and threw one of the women at him.

Saden's protective instincts kicked in and he twisted in mid-air to cushion the woman from the fall with his own body. He rolled the woman over delicately, careful not to lean on her distended belly, and let Demetrius drag her out from under him.

In the next moment, stabbing pain ripped through his right arm almost before the blast of a gunshot rang out. High screams reverberated along the walls. He ignored the throbbing burn in his arm and jumped to his feet. The female guard swung at him in a wide arc. Saden grabbed her arm and used her momentum to flip her over his shoulder. As soon as she hit the floor, he cracked her skull against the tiles with a hard punch, knocking her unconscious.

Something slipped over his head then and latched around his throat. A thin strip of wire that choked off his air supply as the other guard used it to yank him up. The wire dug into his tender flesh, crushing his trachea and breaking through the skin. A haze of darkness teetered on the edges of his vision.

He shifted around then threw himself backwards, slamming the man behind him into the wall. At the same time, he butted his head into the guard's nose and took advantage of the brief disorientation to pull free. The guard went down quickly after that.

Saden took off his trench to alleviate the weight on his arm then swayed precariously and leaned on the wall, waiting for his balance to return. Demetrius came into focus before him with an anxious look on his face.

"Are you okay?"

He touched fingers to his throat and grimaced when they came away smeared with blood. "It's nothing," he said in a voice more ragged than expected. "The women?"

"I put them in one of the unlocked rooms."

Saden nodded his approval then straightened when movement caught his eye from farther down the corridor. Fury shot through his veins like a flood of adrenaline.

Gabriel emerged from one of the cells with Daneya's limp body in his arms. She was dressed in a white cotton gown that emphasized the abnormally pale tint to her skin. It was only by her half-lidded eyes and feeble gropes of her hand at Gabriel's chest that Saden was able to tell that she lived.

A leisonguarde stepped from behind Gabriel and lifted his hand, palm out. Saden could feel the man's power mounting around him, creating a vacuous space in the air. His lungs contracted in response as if they were being squeezed from the inside. He'd gone after a Vampyre with this kind of ability in the past. It was a slow-acting form of suffocation best used as a distraction or fear tactic. Also easily circumvented with another type of distraction.

Especially if one was a pissed off Drakon with too much experience in handling torture.

Saden pulled a knife from his trench, flipped it over then hurled it at the guard. The blade sank hilt-deep in the man's shoulder. Air rushed back into Saden's lungs as he gripped the man's shirt and tossed him several yards away. The pathetic attempt to get rid of him so Gabriel could make his escape with Daneya only fueled his anger. He turned on his former uncle, barely resisting the urge to call forth the Drakonem power within and set him on fire.

"Put her down."

Gabriel's gaze flicked from Saden to the fallen guards in blatant calculation of his odds. Slowly, he laid Daneya on the floor. "I should've known it was you from the beginning. You still don't know when to accept your fate, do you?"

"Likewise. It's over, Gabriel."

"Ahh, but I've already won. I know you spoke to Lady Ilsa earlier at Mazel's mansion. One of my men spotted you going up to see her with that worthless official, Crenshaw. It's too late, though. Even if she decides to reopen the investigation on me, there will be nothing left here to support your accusations by the time her guards show. I've given orders for all the facilities to be evacuated. You won't have a shred of evidence to use against me."

"What makes you think I want to bring you in alive?" Saden asked with a malicious grin, half bluffing and completely prepared to follow through if necessary.

Apprehension sparked in Gabriel's eyes. "Your Drakonem dropped my charges. He couldn't have given you permission to kill me."

"I never said anything about permission." He jumped at Gabriel, feigning with his right arm then swinging an uppercut with his left. Gabriel folded at the waist and clutched his stomach. Just as Saden was about to smash his knee into the man's nose, Gabriel snapped upwards to bash the crown of his head into the underside of Saden's chin. Saden reeled back in shock as he bit through his tongue, mouth pooling with blood. Apparently, his former uncle had sharpened his fighting skills since the last time they'd seen each other.

He was taken by surprise again when Gabriel landed a solid kick to his chest, sending him stumbling backwards. Gabriel charged him after that and rammed his shoulder into Saden's gut. Saden leaned in then brought his elbow down in a piercing jab to Gabriel's spine. The impact forced the man to loosen his grip, giving Saden the purchase he needed to throw Gabriel's weight against the nearest wall. As Gabriel slumped down in a daze, Saden reared his fist only to pause at Demetrius' loud bellow.

"Saden, watch out!"

He ducked in reaction just before a gun fired. Behind him, the guard who'd accompanied Gabriel dropped lifelessly to his knees then face-planted on the floor. In the middle of his forehead was a small, bleeding crater from the exit of the bullet. The knife he'd held in his frozen grasp clattered onto the tiles. Demetrius stood a few yards away staring wide-eyed at the body, a gun shaking in his white-knuckled hands.

Saden shifted to stand when he felt a tug on his harness and looked down. Gabriel had seized his other knife and moved to strike at him. He leaped to the side, but not fast enough to avoid the blade. It sliced across his ribcage, tearing a searing line of fire into his flesh.

Gabriel threw the knife then scrambled to his feet and raced down the corridor toward the stairs.

As soon as he disappeared behind the door, Saden let out a curse and lifted his shirt to inspect his wound. The cut ran the width of his midsection and was deep enough to expose his bottom ribs. It wasn't the pain he was worried about, though. It was the loss of blood from his injuries.

All of that fled his mind, however, when Daneya stirred groggily. He returned his knife to its harness and rushed over to cradle her head in his lap. Her dark lashes fluttered open to display dilated pupils. Splotches of high color stained her otherwise pale face. The beat of her heart thrummed too rapidly beneath his fingers at her throat. He shook her gently, trying to get her gaze to focus on him. "Leisontee?"

She crinkled her brow in confusion. "Saden?" His whispered name was barely a coherent murmur on her lips.

Damn it! The son of a bitch must have drugged her.

Blind rage suffused him as scenarios of what Gabriel might have done to her swam through his thoughts. This was his fault. He should've brought the evidence he'd obtained against Gabriel at the first facility to Serrakus immediately. He should've secured Daneya and Mckenzie at the DCM compound when he'd had the chance. Or, better yet, taken them there at the start of all this instead of foolishly believing they were safer with him.

No regrets.

Her promise to him echoed through his mind. A conviction that was as empty now as the oath he'd made to always protect her. Because of his failure, she would have nothing but regrets, and more painful memories to add to her collection.

"What do we do now?" Demetrius asked hesitantly.

Saden reined in his self-loathing and bent forward to place a soft kiss on Daneya's temple. "Take her." He lifted Daneya in his arms and handed her over.

Demetrius took her then glanced at the dead guard. "H-he was coming at you. I didn't have a choice."

With a grimace, Saden squeezed the phantom's shoulder for reassurance. In truth, he was lucky Demetrius was there. Never had he been so carelessly distracted by his target. "You did good. You got your kill. Now I need you to hide her somewhere outside and stay with her. I'll find you when I'm done."

They started toward the emergency stairs. Just as they passed the elevator, a massive explosion rocked the building, centering from behind the elevator doors. Saden pushed Demetrius to the wall then took out his knife. When the doors were pried apart manually, smoke billowed out to the ceiling, surrounding a tall figure that rolled out gracefully to a standing position. It was Phoenix, covered in soot and coughing repeatedly as he waved away the smoke.

Saden checked the interior of the elevator and found it empty and slightly tilted from the crash. Its roof contained a large hole where Phoenix must have blown the electric motor to disengage the cable. The maneuver was a smart one, leaving the stairwell as the only access point to and from ground level. "Where's Blade?"

"Coming," Phoenix replied gruffly and gestured to the end of the corridor. "We got split up. Did you find your little girl as well?"

He frowned at the odd phrasing. "Not yet. Will you go up with Demetrius to make sure he gets out safely?"

"What about his goal?"

"It's taken care of. Daneya is his priority now." He thought he saw a hint of approval on Phoenix's face but it was gone in the next instant.

At the entrance to the stairwell, Blade burst through the door just as Demetrius was headed in. Though blood trailed from a shallow cut on one cheek and he walked with a slight limp, there were no other visible signs of damage. "Hey, you found your woman! Wait, is she all right?"

"She will be," Saden answered grimly. "Did you pass Gabriel on your way down?"

"Haven't seen him. It looks like most of the Djinn are abandoning ship, but the leisonguardes will be joining us soon."

"Go!" he snapped at Demetrius. When the phantom left with Daneya and Phoenix, he began checking each of the cells for Mckenzie. "Get the women out of their cells and ready to take upstairs."

"Didn't you hear me?" Blade said, hurrying after him. "Those guards are gonna be coming soon. We won't be able to get all the women out of here safely before Roshon and his men show up. At best, we can only afford to get Kennie and Cherri."

"Then we stand and fight. We need those women alive to testify against Gabriel and I can't risk him killing them if we leave them here."

"You sure about this?"

Saden turned sharply to his friend. He couldn't blame Blade for wanting to leave now. The odds were stacking up against them rapidly. "Are you having second thoughts?"

Blade bared his teeth in a wide grin. "Hell no. This is just gettin' good."

He smirked and continued to make his way down the corridor while Blade used his power to break the locks on the doors. It was in the last cell that he finally spotted Mckenzie. Relief flooded him when he saw she was unhurt. He released the breath he hadn't known he was holding and willed his heart to return to a normal pace. If anything had happened to her, there's no telling how much blood he would've bathed in before his twenty-four hours were up.

Her room was a luxury pad compared to the others. Complete with carpeting and wood furniture that muted its clinical atmosphere. She was standing in the middle of it and appeared to be arguing with Cherri, who looked none the worse for having been taken captive. The woman was dressed in stylish street clothes and wearing about a pound of makeup and jewelry.

Saden blew the lock and walked in. Mckenzie blinked in surprise then ran into his arms. Her hold was like a death grip around his waist, pulling at his wound, but he didn't care.

"I knew it!" she cried. "I knew it was you! Did you find Mom?"

He gently disengaged from her tight grasp and knelt down to wipe his blood from her cheek. "She's waiting for you outside. Are you hurt?"

Mckenzie's soft features hardened into a brave mask as she shook her head, even though Saden could feel her trembling. So much like her mother. He met Cherri's wary gaze with a critical eye. The woman was hiding something. It was evident in her bearing and posture. "What about you?"

Cherri offered a thin smile. "I'm glad to see you."

"No, you're not," Mckenzie refuted hotly. "She's not," she repeated to Saden. "We wouldn't even be here if it weren't for her. She lied to Mom so Gabriel could

353

kidnap us. They were waiting for us at the park. Her boyfriend works for Gabriel."

"She's a little confused."

"I'm not confused! I've seen you kiss him. You tried to make me think my mom wants to be here with Gabriel but I know that's not true. She told me he's evil. You care more about him than you do about us. Saden, you have to believe me."

"Shh," he said soothingly. "I believe you." The underlying fear in Cherri's eyes fit it all into place. She had been the instrument Gabriel had originally used to find Daneya after nine years and the means for Daneya's recent capture. Her anger and impatience over being confined at his manor for more than a week made sense now.

As far as he was concerned, she was no better than a seeker and deserved to face her fate alongside Gabriel. She was a part of Daneya's family, though, and he wouldn't disregard that if their friendship still held true.

"Let's go," he said to Cherri in a tone that brooked no argument.

Chapter Nineteen

Outside, Blade was still working on coaxing the last of the women from their cells. Those that stood around him were skittish with fear except for a few who appeared ready to fight for their freedom. Even they, however, wore their bravery like a thin shield over their obvious terror. Saden could see it in their eyes. It sickened him to find most of their spirits broken by a race he had proudly claimed his own once.

It would be easy to blame Gabriel entirely for the corruption of Vampyre laws and integrity, but the truth was, he had only been the conduit through which they had found their so-called salvation. The man who had delivered them from the potential threat of annihilation brought on by their own righteous ignorance.

While the Djinn had started the war, it had been the Vampyres who had kept it going throughout the centuries. Recklessly sacrificing their warriors in battle in an effort to not only beat back the Djinn, but to eradicate them completely. A feat that was strategically impossible.

Saden recalled the lesson his father had taught him as a boy. That sometimes battles were won simply by staying alive and knowing when to back off. A lesson most of their race hadn't learned, and was paying the price for now.

Mckenzie shouted Blade's name as she barreled into him. He swept her up and swung her around with a deep laugh. "Hey, two bit. Did you miss me?"

She answered by plastering herself to his front and burying her face in his neck. Saden felt a pang of sympathy for his friend. While Mckenzie had unwittingly become as close to a daughter as he would ever know, it was Blade who had real experience at being a father. The fact that he could care so much for a little girl he barely knew after losing his own child and mate spoke volumes about his strength.

Saden couldn't say he might turn out the same if he were to lose Mckenzie and Daneya. Insanity would be a safer bet than the high ground Blade had taken.

He opened the two remaining cells and forced the women outside, ignoring their frightened attempts to shy away. "Come with us or stay and die," he told them gruffly. They were running out of time and couldn't afford to wait on Roshon and his men.

After herding the women down the corridor, Phoenix burst from the narrow landing of the emergency stairs. He slammed the door closed behind him then turned to Saden. "That way's no good. I had to distract the guards from Demetrius. They'll be here soon."

"That was the only exit," Blade said. "I'm all for fighting but what do we do with the women?"

Saden recalled Daneya mentioning an underground cafeteria and gym at the facility she'd first been taken to. Although neither room was ideal, it would at least give them a little more space to maneuver in. "Follow me."

He took them past the elevator to a door on the opposite side of the cells. It opened to what looked like the cafeteria with six wooden tables and chairs placed randomly in the center and a long, metal serving line against the back wall. Several tall cabinets lined the side walls and at the far left corner was a pair of double doors he assumed led to a kitchen area.

"They're coming," Phoenix warned. His eyes had faded from their normal gray hue to a glowing, ice-violet as he sensed the guards.

Saden grabbed Mckenzie's hand and started across the expanse of the room. "This way!" He blasted the lock on the double doors and kicked them apart then stood aside while the women hurried past. Inside, he knelt down and made Mckenzie focus on him. "I want you to stay in here until either Blade or I come for you. *Do not* come out by yourself no matter what you hear. Understand?"

"But they'll kill you," she said, her voice tremulous and wide eyes swimming with concern.

Her fear for him made his chest ache with emotions he'd once thought dead to him. After smoothing her wild hair, he kissed her forehead and said, "I'm not that easy to kill. Trust me, okay?"

She bit her lip and gave a small nod. He shut the two doors behind him just as Gabriel stormed into the cafeteria with a group of six men. Five more entered a few seconds later from a door that was farther down the corridor outside. By their energy, he could tell only seven of them were leisonguardes. The other four were Djinn who must've come back for the fight.

Gabriel sneered at him with unveiled contempt. "You should have stayed in the hell realm I sent you to."

"Oh, I'm going back, but I'm taking you with me."

"Get them!" Gabriel barked to his men.

Saden summoned a wall of blue-white flames in front of the men just long enough to temporarily blind them and throw them off-kilter.

The three nearest Phoenix on the other side of the room were already too close to react and charged in all at once. The guard in the middle went at him swinging. Phoenix responded with a fluidity that was remarkable for his size. His movements were sinuous and precise. A testament to his deadly reputation.

He smoothly leaned to the side and caught the man's wrist in one hand then slammed the heel of his other into the back of the man's elbow. The joint was torn apart as bone ripped through flesh, causing the guard to let out a high-pitched scream and hunch forward. Phoenix kicked him in the chest and sent him skidding across the floor.

The two still standing came at him from both sides. At his left, the guard did a spinning kick that he blocked easily, though it left him vulnerable. The second man rushed him from behind and punched him in the base of his skull. He stumbled precariously but quickly regained his equilibrium and spun around, lifting himself up to smash the point of his elbow down onto the guy's collarbone. Saden could almost hear the bone shattering as the man dropped to his knees howling.

Phoenix immediately turned to see the gun the other guard was aiming at him. He went in low before a shot could be fired and grabbed the guy's wrist to get in two swift kidney shots. That allowed him to step into the man, grip the gun from the inside and use it to shoot the guard with the broken collarbone in the leg.

The whole scene occurred in a blur of speed. Saden pulled his attention away when one of the guards to his side lunged at him with a double-edged dagger. He leaped back to dodge the blade as it was curved through the air toward his midsection then again at his throat. At the third attempt, Saden took advantage of the man's overextension by gripping his forearm to yank him close and head butt him. Another hard yank enabled him to snatch the back of the guy's neck and hurl him into one of the cabinets against the wall.

Motion from the corner of his eye made him turn, but he was too late. A Djinn in the vessel of what looked like a human bulldozer barreled into him. He felt the room tilt as he was picked up by the belt and neck then slammed down onto one of the tables. The wood splintered on impact, breaking beneath him. Everything went white as jarring pain ripped through his back and head. Air was punched from his lungs and his mind fogged over for several heartbeats.

It was only the sound of a bullet ricocheting off the floor next to his ear that forced him back to awareness.

He rolled over, snatched the knife from his harness and lashed out at the nearest body. The blade sank hilt deep into the Djinn's calf, bringing him down to one knee with a sharp cry. Saden ignored the strain of his bruised muscles and put the brunt of his weight into a blow to the man's jaw. Another round was fired and missed. He gained his feet and put the Djinn in a choke hold, using the guy's massive build as a human shield.

Instead of trying for another shot, the guard tossed his gun then lifted one hand. Saden saw the concentration in the man's gaze and knew what he intended, yet couldn't react fast enough.

Just as he tapped into his power, the guard overrode it with his own. Agonizing spasms seized his body as it was riddled with high voltage, electric currents. The strength of his convulsions dropped him to the floor, his eyes rolling back and teeth vibrating violently. It felt as if thousands of razor blades were shredding his insides while his bones threatened to shatter.

A sharp, heavy weight bore down on his chest then more pain exploded in his jaw. Over and over again, he was struck in the face until consciousness began to fade.

Suddenly, the punches stopped coming along with the electric shocks. It took him long seconds to fight through the drowning haze surrounding his mind. Cramps flared in his muscles as he sat up and pried open his eyes. Beside him, the Djinn lay on his back with a shuriken embedded in one shoulder and another just above his heart. On the other side farther away, the guard was on his knees cradling one of his hands, a shuriken sticking out of his palm.

Blade.

Saden glanced across the room to his friend who shot him a devious grin. Blade had stripped out of his trench coat and sported more than a few deep cuts and bruises, though he was far from out of the game. He held a knife in each hand and wielded them with expert precision — living up to the Drakon name he'd been aptly given.

The guard Saden had thrown against the nearby wall cabinet came back at him with a chair. Saden ducked easily then swept the guy off his feet with a low kick, simultaneously sending out a spark of Drakonem power which instantly igniting the wood.

To his surprise, the flames were snuffed out before the wood fell on top of the man. Not from the same vacuous power used by the leisonguarde he'd taken down in the corridor, but rather from what felt like a confined impact of a severe cold front hitting the flames. His skin tingled and breath fogged in proximity to the area.

He'd only heard of the rare technique once. The ability to cause a localized manipulation of air particles that changed the temperature to severe degrees of cold or hot. The oxygen feeding the flames had literally been liquefied. Taken well past the freezing point.

Shock froze the features of the guard on the floor, telling Saden the power had come from someone else. He looked over to find another leisonguarde with a buzz cut standing close, staring at him with bold confidence.

This man was different from the others. There was the mark of authority in his hard countenance and light brown eyes. His thin lips curved up in a humorless smile half hidden by a mustache. "Want to test your power on me?"

Saden glanced past the man to where Gabriel stood by one of the doors, watching the entire scene unfold. No doubt waiting to see whether he should bolt or not.

When their gazes met, Gabriel sneered and waved the gun clutched in his hand at buzz cut. "What are you waiting for? Take him down."

Quickly, Saden assessed the situation and changed his stance. The order hadn't been to kill, which meant Gabriel wanted to save that pleasure for himself. A good thing considering Saden's power against the guards' was like fire on ice, a combination that could destroy everyone around them if they weren't careful.

He recoiled from the guard's advance, dodging the swing at his face to come back with a punch to the man's ribs. Movement from the corner of his vision alerted him to the charge of the second guard who had gotten over his shock. He took a step back, spun around and slammed his elbow into the guy's temple, sending him reeling into buzz cut.

In that brief moment, something else caught his attention. Something that made him freeze in terror. Mckenzie was in the room near the back wall, leaning down to pick up a gun that had been dropped by one of Gabriel's men. Her eyes as she straightened were wild, trying to take in everything at once. A few yards away, Cherri stood with the same panicked expression, only her fear seemed to stem from a different source. She was staring past Saden at the guards behind him.

He took a step toward Mckenzie and shouted, "Kennie, get out—" The rest of his sentence was cut off by a hand on his right arm. A thumb dug into the bullet hole there and cold so deep it blazed like a hot iron seared through his flesh all the way down to the bone. It rocked him with a wave of weakness that spread the entire length of his body.

Before he could react, he was yanked around to meet buzz cut's gaze. Rending pain tore through the muscles in the side of his abdomen as he was stabbed with a thick blade.

The guard moved in close to murmur, "Not so invincible after all, are you?"

Saden felt his strength fading rapidly. His limbs were heavy and heart pounded out a sluggish beat in an effort to compensate for his blood loss. He went down under the guard's hard shove, jerking when the blade was wrenched away. In a last ditch attempt, he summoned a column of fire to envelop the guard but it was snuffed out almost immediately.

Gabriel came into his line of sight to loom over him with a gun hanging loosely from one hand. "Thank you, Rhys. I'll take it from here." He placed the sole of his shoe on Saden's windpipe with menacing pressure then slowly aimed the gun at his head, as if he had all the time in the world. "I should have killed you when you were a boy. Your sister is the only legacy worthy of your parents. She'll be glad to know you're taken care of once I tell your Drakonem about this."

The zeal in Gabriel's eyes was sickeningly familiar. It was the same feverish glee he had shown when he'd tried to beat Saden to death to cover up his treachery. Saden struggled against the foot at his lacerated throat. Although the hole in his side was just a flesh wound, the knife had gone straight through. Combined with the effects of his other injuries, what little energy he had left wasn't going to last long.

He called forth a surge of power and readied to send it out in an explosion, his only chance at killing Gabriel. The gun would likely go off, incapacitating him in the process, but it was a risk he had to take.

"Stop!" Mckenzie's scream rang out high above the din of combat.

Almost simultaneously, Gabriel lurched forward and clawed at his chest. His face contorted in a rictus of pain before fury set in and his gaze fixed on Mckenzie. Seconds later, all sounds of fighting ceased as everyone's attention was drawn to the spectacle of a small girl holding a gun on Gabriel. The weapon shook in her trembling hands and her eyes flicked nervously from Gabriel to Saden and back.

It dawned on Saden then what she had done. Used her power on Gabriel to affect his physiological state, probably creating a small seizure similar to a heart attack or stroke. An ability that should've been far too advanced for her limited skills. Not even Gabriel could've accomplished that at such a young age, despite the fact that their powers were alike.

Every protective instinct Saden possessed made him want to eviscerate Gabriel, yell at Mckenzie to run and hide, do something! Yet, there was nothing he could do without endangering her life as well. While Gabriel still held him at gunpoint, nearly every other Vampyre and Djinn in the room was focused on Mckenzie with deadly intent. Ready to take her down if she made another move against their leader.

Saden glanced around the room to find Blade and Phoenix both tensed to strike. He moved his head in a barely perceptible shake, silently warning them to back off. Even if they managed to distract Gabriel and most of the guards, they wouldn't be fast enough to protect Mckenzie.

"Try that again, brat, and I'll make sure you suffer before you die," Gabriel snarled.

Cherri hesitantly approached Mckenzie with her hands raised. "Don't do this, sweetie. Please, for your mom's sake. She couldn't bear losing you, and neither could I. Just give me the gun."

When Mckenzie didn't respond, she glanced at Rhys then began again. "Gabriel really isn't evil. It was all a mistake. He just took things too far. The Djinn were a bad influence on him but he's ready to make it right. You and your mom don't have to be afraid. He wants to take care of both of you." This time, she shot an expressive look to Gabriel as if urging him to go along with her lies.

Gabriel smiled thinly. "You should listen to her, little girl. All I ever wanted was to keep my race alive. *Your* race. Without me, you would never have been born. And now you're willing to throw your life away for what? A criminal and murderer like him?" He took his foot from Saden's throat and cocked the gun then turned back to Mckenzie. "If you kill me, an innocent man, the Drakonem will come after you and your life will be over. Is that what you want, to follow in the footsteps of this trash? I guarantee you'll never see your mother again."

Mckenzie met Saden's gaze with wavering confidence. Tears shimmered on her lashes and her bottom lip quivered with the conflict he could see on her delicate face. He knew she was struggling to do what she thought was right. What her mom would've done. Pride flowed heavily in their veins.

However, he also knew Gabriel hadn't lied about the consequences. She would be held responsible for taking the life of an innocent since Gabriel had yet to be found guilty of his crimes. There would be no trial or review of extenuating circumstances, as there never was when the Drakonem were involved. Killing in defense of a Drakon—a Drakon whose job it had been to bring Gabriel in alive for questioning—would only extend the length of her sentence.

No.

He couldn't allow her to throw away her future for his sake or anyone else's. She was everything clean and pure in a world he'd given up on long ago. He would rather spend eternity as a Drakon before watching her fall down the path he had taken in ignorance.

Saden's voice was raw when he spoke, the skin around his neck bruised and weeping blood from the reopened wound. "Put the gun down, Kennie. I can't let you do this."

She pressed her lips together and shook her head. "You said—"

"Fuck what I said! Put the gods-damned thing down and go back to the kitchen!" Self-loathing filled every fiber of his being for the hurt that welled in her soft eyes. The moisture in them broke and streamed down her cheeks in large droplets. At that moment, he almost wanted Gabriel to put a bullet in his head.

Phoenix's voice cut abruptly through the tension. "Gabriel's right, Mckenzie. Why should you risk everything for a man you barely know?"

Anger suffused Saden at the unexpected contempt in the man's tone. He tried to surge to his feet only to be kicked in the spine by Rhys. The impact jarred his side, sending streaks of white-hot agony through his torn muscles so great, consciousness teetered on the edge of his control. When he could finally unclench his jaw, he glared over at Phoenix and growled, "Shut the hell up."

Completely ignoring the interruption, Phoenix waved a hand at Saden. "He's only a criminal, right? A lowlife piece of scum who kidnapped you and your mom and held you both prisoner just like these men. He doesn't deserve your sacrifice. Doesn't even know how to trust or love."

Blade roared and launched himself at Phoenix but was held back by the guards nearest him.

Cherri spoke quickly over the commotion, imploring Mckenzie again with soothing words. "Please, sweetheart. I promise no one is going to hurt you. This really is for the best, you have to believe me."

A choked sob slipped past Mckenzie's lips as she let Cherri take the weapon from her grip.

Gabriel handed his gun to Rhys to watch over Saden while he strode toward Cherri and relieved her of the weapon. With a cold smile, he traced Mckenzie's cheek with his fingers and said, "Good girl. Now it's time you learned where your true allegiance lies." Swiftly, he walked back to Saden and pointed the gun at his head. "This time, stay where you belong."

Saden called forth his power, knowing he was defeated yet unwilling to give up. The blast of frigid air that swallowed the flames he summoned was no surprise. What he hadn't expected was the curdling shriek that echoed through the room in place of a gunshot.

"No!" Mckenzie's cry was like a tortured crack of thunder in his ears.

Gabriel's hands instantly flew to his head as his body began to jerk spasmodically. Trails of blood leaked from every orifice on his face and within the span of a few breaths, his eyes glassed over with the vacant stare of death.

"Sir?" Rhys dropped his gun to catch Gabriel's limp body as it slumped to the floor. In the next second, rage twisted his features and he sprang at Mckenzie.

Cherri stepped between them and shouted, "Rhys, stop!"

"Get out of my way, stupid bitch." From the sheath at his belt, he pulled the same knife he'd used on Saden, still coated with his blood, and plunged it into her chest.

Saden lurched to his feet and yelled, "Kennie, run!" Power shot out of him like a living extension of himself as he raced for Mckenzie. It crashed into Rhys in the form of a ball of fire, exploding on impact. At the same time, Saden barreled into Mckenzie and rolled with her to the back wall.

The room erupted into chaos as the fighting resumed in full force. Moments later, Roshon came in with his men and joined the fray, their geis weaving in and out of the crowd like lethal shadows. A part of him wanted to jump in and do what he could to finish off Gabriel's men, but his mad lunge had torn the seams of his wounds. He was running on fumes and losing energy with each breath.

That and the image of Mckenzie being targeted by nearly every leisonguarde and Djinn in the room kept him where he was, on the floor using his body as a protective barrier between her and the combatants.

She pressed herself tightly to his back and wrapped her arms around his midsection. The pain of her tight hold was nothing compared to the relief he felt knowing she was safe.

The remainder of the battle didn't last long. When the two Djinn still standing realized it was over, they vacated their human hosts to avoid capture. Their spirits of smoke swirling around twin spirals of black fire were just thick enough to push through one of the doors leading to their escape. No one bothered to stop them. Although Drakons had the ability to destroy them using their Drakonem power, doing so without permission would be the same as killing an innocent.

After the last of the guards were subdued, Blade picked his way through the fallen bodies over to Saden. His limp was now severely pronounced and he favored his left side, but his shit-eating grin didn't waver.

Roshon strode toward them and assessed Saden critically. "How are you doing?"

Saden took mental stock of his wounds. Every part of him ached with intense throbbing and the loss of blood had sapped what little strength he had left. If he were mortal, his condition would be critical without immediate medical attention. Yet, a feeling of inner peace filled him that he couldn't explain. An alien sense of wholeness that encompassed his entire being. For the first time since becoming a Drakon, the sliver of Serrakus' soul inside him was no more than a faint pulse in the background.

He put aside the unnerving sensation and replied in a torn voice, "Peachy."

"Yeah, well you look like shit warmed over. Couldn't wait till we got here, could you?"

Saden grunted and took Roshon's extended hand, pulling Mckenzie up with him. She clung to his uninjured side and remained silent. "What the hell took you so long?"

A commotion at the front of the room made them turn. Commander Weiss pushed his way past Roshon's men, followed by the two guards who'd been assigned to him "I demand to know what's going on here!" he bellowed. He focused on Saden with an imperious expression.

"The goal was to apprehend Gabriel Aikins, not kill him."

"Question answered," Roshon murmured, shooting Weiss a look of disdain.

Saden barely reined in his temper, in no mood to argue with the korvaute. "You'll find proof of his crimes in the files by the back door to this facility and through that room," he said, pointing to the kitchen area. "There are a dozen human females who can testify to his real operations. Chief Roshon will remain in charge of them until you're done with your investigation. After that, they'll be released to the director of the DCM unit in this area. A man named Vincent Condretti."

Unfortunately, turning them over to Vincent immediately was not an option. The DCM would never allow them to be interrogated by the same race who had taken them captive, and Saden needed their testimonies to prove his case.

Roshon didn't blink at the delegation of a responsibility that had nothing to do with him. Instead, he merely nodded in acquiescence, for which Saden was grateful. Those women needed someone to watch out for their welfare, and Roshon was the only one he trusted who had the means to do so.

Weiss' broad face turned red with anger. "How dare you think to give me orders! You have no place in the chain of command that rules—"

"I don't give a damn about your politics," Saden cut in. "Either take the deal or I'll call Condretti right now and inform him that you're holding human women against their will. I won't leave them with you unprotected."

It was a bald accusation of the house of Avram's inability to uphold demon laws in regards to humans and one which Weiss obviously took personal offense to. But Saden couldn't bring himself to care. Gabriel had fooled over half the Vampyre authorities above him and corrupted the rest.

The house of Avram had a lot to answer for.

The commander's jaw ticked as he calculated Saden's threat. "You're staying here until I've completed a full investigation. I will not allow you to leave until I know exactly what went on here."

"I take full responsibility for the deaths of Gabriel and the one called Rhys." He tipped his head in the direction of a pile of ash on the floor a few yards away, all that was left of Rhys' corpse. "That's all you need to know from me."

Before Weiss could launch into his next argument, Blade took him by the arm and steered him toward the kitchen.

Roshon cast a look of approval at Saden. "You should've been a korvaute among your kind. You wear authority well."

Saden lifted a corner of his mouth. "There are many things I wear. Authority was never one of them. You don't mind seeing to the treatment of the females?"

"Not at all. My leader won't be pleased to know I'm assisting Vampyres, but I want to see this through. What will happen to you?"

His response was interrupted by Mckenzie. She left his side and went to Cherri's prone form then knelt to cradle the woman's head in her lap. Saden bent on one knee beside her and watched the tears streaming down her cheeks. It killed him inside to see her cry over the death of the woman who had helped raise her, despite Cherri's betrayal. No one so young should have to experience that kind of loss.

Mckenzie looked up at him and said in a small voice, "She tried to save me."

"She loved you. That's all that matters. Your mom is waiting for you outside. Blade will drive both of you back to the DCM compound."

With a brief nod, Mckenzie smoothed the curls from Cherri's face and leaned in to kiss her forehead. Saden was amazed again at the girl's calm maturity under pressure. The courage she had shown in the face of danger, the sacrifice she'd made for him, was utterly humbling. She was every bit the warrior her mother was.

And he had to know.

"Kennie, why did you kill Gabriel knowing what could happen?"

Her soft brown eyes seemed to reach into him, touching a part of him only Daneya had found. "They were wrong about you. You do know how to love. You love me, don't you? And my mom. I couldn't let Gabriel kill you."

He gathered her in his arms and crushed her to him. He had no right to what he felt for Daneya or Mckenzie, yet there was no denying it. Serrakus would have to be satisfied with extending his sentence indefinitely for the murder of Gabriel. Saden would not let him have Mckenzie. Not as long as he drew breath.

"Looks like you found your treasure," Phoenix said from behind him.

Saden gently pulled away from Mckenzie then stood to face the man. Fury, pure and unmasked, flowed through him as he reared back a fist and smashed it across Phoenix's head. He moved to strike again but was stopped by a sudden, burning pain in his chest. The heat of it spread like wildfire throughout his body, crippling him with its intensity.

Serrakus' call was stronger than he'd ever felt it, and he was too weak to withstand the summons. His vision blurred as he hit the tiles, mind fading to escape the agony. The last thing he remembered was hands grasping at him before darkness flooded in and the world fell away.

Chapter Twenty

"So, we are in agreement." Lucius stood in the center of his office in the Drakonem realm, staring through the opening of the temporal rift he had erected and awaiting a reply. His powers as a Drakonem were not limited by space as were a Drakon's. This allowed him to create a gateway to any part of the world through which he could communicate with demons in the human realm. It was how all of his kind exchanged information with the authorities of the demonic races regarding their laws and the punishments of violators.

Currently, he was accessing the weakened field of space found in Lady Ilsa's private study at her mansion where Serrakus usually conducted his business affairs with the Lady. At the moment, however, Serrakus was busy in his own office punishing the focus of both their attentions and giving Lucius the opportunity to take the advantage.

Lady Ilsa sat at her desk, fingers steepled in front of her mouth and exotic features pinched in contemplation. Behind her, a large Vampyre in the seniority of his years with grizzled hair and a granite face paced in agitation. He glanced irritably at Lucius then shook his head. "I don't like this. Placing a Drakon in a position of authority in the house of Avram is too dangerous."

"Former Drakon," Lucius reminded him. "As I said earlier, Saden has been...exonerated, so to speak. His past sins have been wiped clean. He is now as free as you are." Or would be once Serrakus was forced to admit the truth.

What had started as bored curiosity had turned into an unforeseen opportunity for Lucius. It could not have worked out better. When that little halfling, Mckenzie, had sacrificed her innocence by killing Gabriel Aikins in defense of Saden, she had given Saden back his treasure. Redeemed his soul and thereby liberated him from the burden of his past sins. The very act was monumental in its rarity and for the grim consequences it entailed.

Each Drakon's treasure was precious, for it was the reason the demon had become a Drakon in the first place. The sacrificing of that treasure by another on behalf of the Drakon often placed that other person in the same predicament.

When Mckenzie had traded her own innocence for Saden, she had become the criminal he was. No one was aware of it yet. Saden had claimed responsibility for Gabriel's death. A ploy which was only delaying the inevitable. Eventually, the truth would come out and Mckenzie would be taken into custody.

But Lucius knew the truth now, thanks to Allorha, and he planned on using his knowledge to sway the outcome of the events to reap his own benefits. He'd originally thought it would be Saden's beloved human, Daneya, who would give Saden back his treasure.

However, the human's daughter worked out just as well.

The gruff Vampyre, Weiss, curled his lip in repugnance. "I don't know how he convinced Serrakus to give him back his freedom, but he will never be accepted among our kind again. He is a dishonored murderer undeserving of our tolerance."

"He's also our best chance at rectifying the mess Gabriel has made of my house," Lady Ilsa interrupted impatiently. "The files we found at Gabriel's facility are mostly encrypted, yet Saden somehow managed to discover what was on them and unravel korvaute Aikins' secret operation. We need him to tell us what else we don't know so we can put this travesty to an end without further embarrassment.

"As things stand, we have no idea how far Gabriel's influence has reached, much less which leisonguardes we can trust to capture those who were in collaboration with the Djinn."

"This is not a light decision, Your Highness. We should bring it before the council and let them have a say as to whether we should recruit a Drakon or not."

"According to the list Saden gave us, nearly half of our council has been compromised!" she replied furiously. "I can only ask for so much assistance from the other royal houses without raising their suspicions. If they find out it was one of our own who initiated contact with the Djinn and has been voluntarily giving the Djinn our offspring, I could be stripped of my jurisdiction."

The Lady smoothed her already straight, raven locks in a calming motion. "I need them to think this was an act of infiltration purely orchestrated by the Djinn."

"There has to be another way," Weiss grumbled.

"If you can think of one to take care of this situation as quickly and quietly as possible, please, let it be known."

The chief let out a low growl of frustration.

"I will need to speak to Serrakus to verify Saden's release from his Drakon sentence," the Lady said to Lucius.

"And you will. I'll notify him immediately of your request." As soon as he put all the pieces into play. There was still one more crucial part to his plan. "Oh, and let's keep my offer of assistance between us, shall we?" he added almost as an afterthought. "I wouldn't want to turn my good intentions into a battle of competition with my brother, Serrakus."

Of course, that's exactly what it would become when Serrakus caught on to what he'd done. With Saden installed in the house of Avram as the Korvaute in charge of bringing those involved with Gabriel to justice, he would be in a position to work directly with Lucius. Through that inside connection, Lucius would be able to gain information on the violators and send his own Drakons to help Saden apprehend them. Thereby allowing him to claim rights to their souls and make them Drakons under his control.

It was a foolproof way to ensure he got credit for them no matter which Drakonem's territory they were captured in.

Serrakus was going to be livid when he found out. By then, however, it would be too late. Lucius' control over Saden would be complete, and nothing Serrakus did could change that.

Lady Ilsa gave a curt nod. "I understand. Tell the ex-Drakon to come to me when he's ready."

Lucius closed the rift then walked to the liquor cabinet against the wall to his right. After pouring several fingers into a snifter, he took a long swig and let the smile he'd been holding in spread across his face. Never had his curiosity been so fortuitous, and this was just the beginning.

Allorha emerged from the shadows on the other side of the room. Her burnished skin glinted in the flickering light of the torches lining the walls as she sauntered over to him. The revealing silks she had changed into two days ago when she'd returned from the human realm flowed along her generous curves. Everything about her was provocative, and she was all too aware of the effect she had on Lucius.

He felt himself grow hard as she pressed her body seductively to his. "Not yet, my little minx. I still have a few things to take care of, then I'll give you your reward."

"Are you pleased?" she purred demurely.

He threaded his fingers through the braids at the back of her skull then crushed them in his hand to give a measure of erotic pain. "You know I am."

Her role in all of this had yielded far more gains than he ever could've hoped for. She had been a background witness to the events leading to this point. Everything from Saden's meeting with the Rakshasas to the night of Gabriel's murder, she had been there, walking through Saden's mind and experiencing what he did. The information she'd provided him with was invaluable.

She was definitely far greater an asset as a spy than a converted Drakon.

"I still don't understand," she said. "How can you be sure Saden will work with you?"

He took another drink then put down his glass with a smile. "I'm going to petition Tallos for Mckenzie's soul. After I tell him how Serrakus had set Saden up for failure from the beginning by indirectly informing Gabriel he was under investigation, he'll agree with me that taking away his rights to Mckenzie is a suitable punishment. Saden will be forever grateful to me for taking possession of the halfling, knowing as he does from personal experience how Serrakus will treat someone so young under his control. He'll do whatever I ask in exchange for my preferred treatment of the girl."

Allorha ran her tongue along the angle of his jaw up to his ear like a sultry feline. "Handsome and devious. How did I get so lucky to have a master like you?"

Despite the false flattery, his erection swelled in the confines of his pants, forcing him to adjust himself. "Stay here until I get back. I shouldn't be long."

He kissed her pouting lips then strode from the room. Outside, the stagnant atmosphere colored the outlying fields of his territory a flat maroon. He climbed up two flights of stairs to the platform at the top of his main building and cast out a mental summons to Tallos, the god and creator of Vampyres. Since Saden was a former Vampyre, he would fall under Tallos' area of command.

Several minutes passed, and just as Lucius was tempted to try again, a cool breeze where there should be none swept the loose hairs at his back. He turned to find the god standing behind him dressed in flowing black robes. For the most part, Tallos resembled a Drakonem. Approximately seven feet tall, finely-boned and long-limbed. His white hair was held back by a silk ribbon and his facial structure was nearly androgynous in its elegance.

The only remarkable differences were his ice-violet, glowing eyes and the seeming translucency of his skin that shone with inner radiance, bearing evidence to the power he held within.

As a god, Tallos could choose to appear in any form he wished. Although, unlike most of the others, he often chose the form of those he conversed with out of familiarity's sake.

Lucius had been hoping to catch the god in a good mood, but Tallos' expression was reserved and slightly annoyed. "Something bothers you, my lord?"

"I have a matter on my mind, yes," Tallos replied impatiently. "Why have you called on me?"

He decided to get straight to the point, not wanting to test the god's patience. "I would like to discuss a situation I think is worthy of your attention, if you'll indulge me."

When Tallos gave a slight nod, he went on to give an account of Saden's predicament, up to and including Mckenzie's crime of murder. How Lucius had used his slave to spy on Saden then set Saden free to complete his assignment and save the innocents. He left nothing out save for the close involvement of the Rakshasas. That had been an interesting development and one he wanted to continue keeping tabs on without interference from the gods.

"I'm sure you can agree," he concluded, "that giving ownership of the girl to me would be a suitable punishment for Serrakus. After all, she would not have committed the crime if Serrakus had let Saden finish his job in the first place."

Tallos narrowed his gaze. "And you want me to believe you freed this Drakon out of the goodness of your heart? To see justice done in an unjust realm?"

He was no fool to deceive a god. If Tallos wanted, he could tear apart Lucius' mind piece by piece to find the truth, leaving behind only an empty shell. Lucius had seen it done too many times to his brethren during the fall of his kind.

He chose his next words carefully. "Admittedly, my curiosity to see the outcome drove me to release Saden. Though I'm glad it got the best of me. Many of the Djinn were conspiring with this Gabriel Aikins to an end I can only assume would have brought about another war. As it is, the Djinn have tipped the scales with their acquisition of countless Vampyre offspring. We'll need to keep a close eye on them."

"You may be right," Tallos said grimly. "But what you've told me has made up my mind on another matter regarding the girl. I have already been petitioned on her behalf by a Drakon who wishes to accept her punishment and have her sentence added to his. I think I will grant his request in light of Serrakus' loss of Saden. It could have been years before the girl was ready to take on assignments and if what you say about the Djinn is true, we'll need all the trained Drakons we have in the field."

Lucius let his jaw drop in shock. This he had not been prepared for. It had to be the doing of Saden's friend, Blade. Allorha had spoken of their close relationship. How loyal they were to one another. Yet, he hadn't considered that either one might make such a sacrifice for the other.

He quickly tried to think of something, anything to sway the god's decision. "I urge you to reconsider. Mckenzie is already nine years of age. I could have her ready—"

"Desperation does not look good on you, Lucius," Tallos cut in. "Don't think I'm not aware that you have an ulterior motive to claiming the girl. Now, is there anything else you have to say before I confront Serrakus?"

With an inward curse, he shook his head and watched as the god's corporeal body faded from his sight. He shifted to his dragon form and sped through the skies toward Serrakus' territory. Once there, he changed back then hurried to Serrakus' office where he knew Saden was being held. Allorha had snuck in earlier to confirm it. There was a chance he could still convince the ex-Drakon to work with him, though it would be out of guilt rather than leverage.

After all, it was he who had given Saden a second opportunity to take down his target and rescue the human he'd fallen in love with. For a criminal with morals, that just might be enough.

As he hastened down the hidden stairwell from the top of the main building, he heard Serrakus shouting repeatedly. From the muffled words, it sounded as if he were interrogating Saden to find out who had released him from the dungeons.

The noise stopped by the time Lucius entered the room where he found Tallos already standing at its center. The god must have just materialized, for in front of the large fireplace, Serrakus was panting with exertion and covered in a fine sheen of sweat. A bald warder stood a few yards away and on the floor between them was Saden.

The ex-Drakon lay on his side, dressed in only a pair of jeans and showing several injuries that weren't all consistent with torture. Dark bands of dried blood covered his throat and abdomen, and his right arm was streaked with blood down to his hand. It appeared Serrakus had merely healed him enough after his battle with Gabriel to keep him conscious. The mass of bruises coloring one entire side of his chest and the smattering of cuts on his face were more recent. Still red and angry in contrast with his ashen pallor.

"My lord," Serrakus said in surprise. "What are you doing here?"

"Answer the question, Serrakus. Why are you punishing this man? He is no longer under your control. I felt the return of his treasure days ago."

Serrakus' eyes widened. Apparently, it had slipped his mind that the gods could sense when a Drakon's treasure was returned by another. In most cases, however, the gods didn't take it upon themselves to ensure the Drakon's freedom. This case was most definitely an exception.

"He doesn't deserve his freedom. He violated the laws by returning to the human realm without my permission and taking an innocent life. I felt it while I was on my vacation."

Tallos turned his glowing stare to Lucius. "Were you aware of this?"

"He has no place in this. I demand to know—"

"Shut up, Serrakus!" Tallos bellowed. "I will get the truth if I have to rip the two of you open to find it."

Serrakus fumed quietly, glaring at Lucius with deadly intent.

Lucius rapidly sifted through the information Allorha had given him, trying to recall who Saden was being accused of killing. There was someone. A man in league with Gabriel. One who had sought to avenge his leader's murder. Allorha's recounting of the scene played out in his memory.

"Rhys," he blurted out. Then more firmly, "Saden is responsible for the death of a leisonguarde associated with Gabriel. But it was after Mckenzie had given him back his treasure by killing Gabriel. At that moment, he was a free man who killed in defense of an innocent. He cannot be penalized for the crime. Lady Ilsa, the Rei'jin of the house of Avram, has already declared Gabriel guilty of his sins, along with those they know he was involved with. Rhys falls into that category. The Lady can confirm it."

"That is no excuse!" Serrakus roared with an edge of panic. "Saden must pay for his crime."

Tallos cast a glance at Saden who hadn't moved from his position on the floor. "I'm inclined to agree with Lucius on this matter, although I will be verifying the truth," he said in a warning tone more for Lucius' sake than Gabriel's.

Serrakus snarled menacingly at Lucius. "You released him, didn't you? And my slave. Whatever you're trying to gain from this, I will stop you."

Lucius spread his arms with a devious grin. It wasn't the first time he and Serrakus had come to odds, and it would doubtfully be the last. "I look forward to your challenge, brother."

As soon as the words crossed his lips, Serrakus charged him only to be hurled in the opposite direction by an invisible force. As if a large hand had picked him up and tossed him violently against the obsidian wall at his back.

"Enough!" Tallos roared. "I grow tired of listening to your petty squabbles. Withdraw your soul from this man. The decision has been made."

Reluctantly, Serrakus righted himself and moved to follow the order. When he reached down to touch the ex-Drakon's chest, however, Saden jerked back with a harsh growl. His eyes were feral and bloodied teeth bared like a caged animal. At that moment, he resembled nothing of the cool, collected man Lucius had spoken with earlier. In fact, from the maddened expression on his face, it was possible he had finally succumbed to insanity.

Just as Serrakus pulled away, Saden snatched the Drakonem's hand in a grip that turned his knuckles white. Skin to skin contact so that the transfer could be made.

Not insane after all, then.

Saden's eyes grew distant and when Serrakus wrenched his hand back seconds later, he nearly fell flat on his face.

"Lucius, take the Drakon and leave us," Tallos said. "I'll conclude my meeting with Serrakus in private."

Lucius didn't argue, wanting time of his own alone with Saden. The ex-Drakon stubbornly refused his help, though. Instead, climbing slowly to his feet and staggering out of the room. The bald warder was dismissed as well and took up his station outside of the office at the door.

Saden didn't stop until they rounded the corner at the end of the long corridor where he hunched over with one hand on his knee for support and the other clutched to his side. When Lucius moved to heal him, he stiffened and said in a low voice, "Don't touch me."

Lucius withdrew to put space between them.

Eventually, Saden unfurled to his full height with only a slight grimace. "What just happened?"

"You're free now. Your treasure was returned. Surely you felt it at Gabriel's facility immediately after he was taken down."

"How?"

Lucius frowned. "As I said earlier, Mckenzie's sacrifice of her innocence was made for you. Your sentence has been revoked."

"No," Saden whispered, then turned on his heel in the direction of Serrakus' office.

"Where are you going?"

"To accept her punishment."

Lucius grabbed his arm to stop him. "There's nothing you can do."

Faster than should've been possible, Saden whipped around and slammed Lucius against the wall. "I will not let Serrakus have her!"

"He won't. Your friend has already petitioned Tallos for her sentence to be added to his. Tallos has agreed to allow it."

"Blade?" Saden asked, staggering back.

Lucius readjusted his clothes. "The girl will remain with her mother. As for you, I have spoken to Lady Ilsa regarding your future. She's prepared to offer you a position as a korvaute to head the extraction team that will be needed to bring Gabriel's accomplices to justice."

"What do you stand to gain from it?"

He didn't bother to couch his words in guile. If he'd learned anything from the events Allorha had reported, it was that Saden was a man who acted on honesty. "Merely an understanding. I would like for you to use two of my best Drakons to assist you in apprehending the criminals. I want them to take credit for the captures, which will give me the authority to punish the criminals. In exchange, my Drakons will be at your disposal and under your command. This will be beneficial to you if you are fortuitous enough to catch some of the Djinn involved."

Saden immediately shook his head. "No deal. I'm not going to risk the safety of the men I work with just so you can fill your ranks."

Damn Blade, Lucius cursed silently. If not for that Drakon's interference, he could be using Mckenzie as leverage right now instead of having to resort to underhanded manipulation. "I think I'm entitled to some compensation for my efforts. You would still be in Serrakus' dungeon if it weren't for me, and your human lover would still be Gabriel's plaything."

When Saden's face hardened to a cold mask, he changed his approach. "All I ask is that you consider this an opportunity to rebuild your life. You've had a Drakonem, a god and a friend intervene on your behalf. Don't throw this chance away."

A tense silence filled the air as Saden studied him until finally saying, "I'll be in touch."

Lucius nodded, satisfied with that answer for now. He opened a rift and watched Saden pass through to the human realm where night reigned over the land. It was almost that time of year again, when he could vacation and indulge in the sins of mankind. But he would ensure Saden's cooperation first, even if he had to find another source of leverage to get it.

Then again, that little girl and her mother were still out there. The only question was, just how far would Saden go to protect them?

* * * *

Morning light broke the darkness of night outside, seeping into the still dawn and bringing with it a new day. A day for changes that were both daunting and necessary. Dim light spilled in from the open curtains on the window and slowly illuminated the face that peeked above the blankets on the bed. So young and fragile yet full of inner turmoil. The faint creases on Mckenzie's forehead and dark circles under her eyes belied the stress she held within.

Daneya watched her daughter toss fitfully from the doorway of the room. It had been three weeks since their ordeal at Gabriel's facility and Mckenzie still suffered greatly. She stayed awake until exhaustion took over, and despite her repeated claims that she was fine, the haunted veil over her eyes told differently.

Daneya had coaxed the events of that night from her. How Gabriel and Cherri had died and about Saden's false declaration of responsibility for Gabriel's death. She worried Mckenzie might never fully recover from what she'd done, even though the murder was more than justified.

How had Saden done it? Survived the death of his parents only to be betrayed by his uncle then abused for years afterwards.

As her thoughts drifted to him, she heard his voice in her mind. *Leisontee.* She remembered nothing after Gabriel had drugged her except that one strangled word and a look of worry of Saden's face. Not knowing what had happened to him was like a chain around her heart, squeezing unbearably at times. She couldn't believe how much she wanted to see him again. To thank him for all he'd done so they could both have closure.

At least that's what she told herself in a vain attempt to keep her emotions at bay. Almost impossible at times when she could see them reflected in Mckenzie's behavior. Her daughter hadn't spoken of Saden or Blade since the truth of that night had come out, but it was obvious she missed them in her frequent bouts of despondency.

After Marco had rescued her from the first facility, she'd always known Gabriel would come back to impact her life. Had spent what seemed like a lifetime preparing for that day. In the end, however, it hadn't been him who had irrevocably changed her again. It had been a man who'd been there all along, watching her from a distance.

She jumped when a hand touched her shoulder and turned to see Vincent standing behind her. "Sorry," she said quietly. Her nerves had been all over the place lately.

"Don't apologize." He glanced past her to where Mckenzie slept. "How is she doing?"

Daneya breathed a deep sigh and scraped a hand through her hair. "She has nightmares, but she won't talk to me about them. Dr. Addison prescribed her mild sleeping pills that are helping a little. I just wish there was something more I could do."

"Cherri was like a second mother to her. That kind of betrayal will take time to forgive and recover from. As for what happened to Gabriel Aikins, we can only assure her that what she did was necessary."

Small comfort in light of the circumstances. Still, there were other things to consider. Mainly, whether the authorities in charge of cleaning up Gabriel's mess held the same opinion.

She knew the Drakonem had little care for the reasons behind any murder that fell under their jurisdiction, as evidenced by Saden's past conviction. If they were to find out it had been Mckenzie and not Saden who had killed Gabriel, Mckenzie's life could be at stake. A concern that wouldn't even matter if Mckenzie were fully human and therefore subject only to human laws.

She kept this from Vincent, though. He had enough to deal with as it was. On the day Blade had anonymously contacted him to pick up her and Mckenzie three weeks ago, he'd put in his resignation as director of their DCM unit. He claimed the decision had been a long time coming. That he needed a break from the constant demands of his job. A sabbatical during which he would stay in Oregon on his horse ranch and reunite with his brother and sister whom he hadn't seen in years.

When he had extended another offer to take her and Mckenzie with him, Daneya had accepted. There was nothing keeping her here anymore. The threat of Gabriel was gone and staying in the same house that contained so many memories of Cherri was out of the question. As much as her anger over her friend's actions still held, her grief was stronger. In the end, Mckenzie had made it clear that Cherri had tried to save her. It was that act Daneya wanted to remember her by.

Then there was Saden…

She shook herself from her reverie, afraid to dwell on questions she would never get answers to. "How is your replacement adjusting to the unit?"

Vincent grimaced and pinched the bridge of his nose. "It's more a matter of how the unit is adjusting to her. She's old school. Trained by the best but completely devoid of any leniency or compassion. I've already had requests for transfers from a handful of the vigilantes. A few even mentioned quitting if she stayed."

"Wow. That bad?"

"Let's just say she could impersonate a functioning sociopath with a God complex without breaking a sweat. She's really done a hell of a job managing the intake and care of the second batch of survivors, though. Through her request, the superiors at DCM headquarters have provided funding for a private psychologist and medical doctor and a program to support the reintegration of the women into civilian society."

Daneya lifted her brows in pleasant surprise. A week after her rescue, Roshon had contacted Vincent to arrange the delivery of the women who'd been held at the same facility. Apparently, accounts of the events surrounding their captivity had been taken for each of the women by the Vampyres under Lady Ilsa's orders.

Roshon had informed Vincent that the Lady had originally planned to have their memories wiped for security purposes, but he'd overruled that option. According to him, Saden had put him in charge of the survivors and he wasn't about to let some 'old lady' jeopardize their welfare.

The decision to overrule Lady Ilsa's plan had been a smart one. There were several records of humans having their memories erased by Vampyres, and all too often, the process was done with blatant negligence. Which resulted in entire lifetimes of memories being removed.

"I think she'll come around eventually, though," Vincent continued. "Fortunately, that won't be our problem."

Daneya smiled and nodded. A part of her pitied her comrades for having to break in a new director, though not enough to make her stay and endure the aggravation with them.

He glanced at Mckenzie then said, "I've already put your bags in the car. Are you sure you packed everything you want to take for now?"

"Yeah. I'll wake up Kennie. We'll meet you outside in a minute." They were taking only the bare minimum for the trip to Oregon. Movers would come in later to load the rest of her belongings and drive them to the ranch.

She'd gone back to Saden's manor earlier to retrieve the weapons and clothes Saden had brought from her house to his. It was an empty shell now. The fire had destroyed nearly half of the front and rains had caused water damage to the exposed interior. It had been such a beautiful place, and was now no more than the abandoned remnants of lives cut short more than half a century ago.

Mckenzie stirred drowsily at her touch. Daneya waited as she got dressed then walked with her to the front door. "Go ahead and get in the car, baby. I'm going to do one last check."

After Mckenzie went outside, she turned around to survey the house she'd spent the past year in. It was no more significant than any of the other houses she'd lived in. Still, leaving it seemed to hold so much more meaning. It was the start of a new chapter in her life. Not the one she might have hoped for, but not the worst either.

A shout from Mckenzie had her running through the front door only to skid to a halt on the walkway, frozen in surprise. At first, she didn't trust her eyes. Then her heart kicked into gear and thrummed with a mixture of relief and excitement.

It was Blade, standing in her driveway looking every bit the surfer turned ruthless assassin as she remembered with his spiked, blond hair and black trench coat. He bent to sweep Mckenzie up in a hug as she launched herself into his arms. The simple joy on his face was mirrored by her bright laughter.

Daneya held back the rush of questions that crowded into her mind to watch the two of them. It amazed her to think that not so long ago, she would've tried to castrate the Drakon for going near her daughter. Now, she only wanted to thank him for protecting them.

"Put the girl down and show me your hands." Vincent's hard voice cut into the moment. He stood by his car along the curb and held a gun aimed at Blade's head.

Blade put Mckenzie behind him then drew a knife from his belt.

Daneya took a step toward Vincent with one hand raised. "Wait."

"I know you, don't I?" Vincent said with a frown. "At my house. You were the one who broke my arm."

"You shot me in mine!" Blade retorted.

Daneya rolled her eyes. "Both of you, calm down! Vincent, this is the Drakon I told you about. The one who watched over Kennie and I at Saden's house. He's no threat to you."

"Really?" he replied sarcastically. "I thought Drakons weren't allowed to harm innocents."

Blade flashed a quick grin. "Our laws forbid us from love and arbitrary murder. Anything in between is fair game."

Daneya let out a low groan. "Kennie, go show Blade to the fridge. I think there's still some beer in there."

"Daneya!" Vincent cried incredulously.

She waved her hand behind her as she followed the pair inside. "You can beat your chest like an overprotective caveman later. I want to know why he's here." Once in the house, she began pacing the living room until Blade came out of the kitchen with a beer in hand.

He sat on the couch next to Mckenzie and kept one eye on Vincent who hovered warily by the front door. "I thought you might want to know that Kennie's off the hook for killing Gabriel. Apparently, some other Drakon accepted her punishment. I haven't been able to find out who it was."

Daneya felt the blood drain from her face. "Saden—"

"No. Not him. Although it wasn't for lack of trying. I'd have accepted it myself if this other Drakon hadn't beaten me to it."

Mckenzie shifted restlessly, her gaze somewhere in the distance. "It isn't fair."

"It is what it is," Blade said.

"No. I mean, I'm the criminal. I should pay for what I've done."

He grasped Mckenzie's shoulders firmly and gave her a little shake. "Don't ever call yourself that again. What you did took a lot of courage, and no one can say it wasn't the right thing to do. The only ones to blame are the gods for permitting the Drakonem their twisted justice system. You were an innocent caught up in the mix and you fought like a warrior. I'm proud of you." After wiping the tears from her cheeks, he pulled her into a tight hug.

Daneya blinked away the moisture in her own eyes and wondered for the first time how Blade had become a Drakon. It was a good life wasted, in her opinion. He'd have made an excellent father. "Thank you for letting us know."

He nodded and released Mckenzie. "You should also know that Saden's out. By killing Gabriel in his defense, Kennie gave him back his treasure. He's a free man."

Everything within her stilled as her mind tried to comprehend the meaning of his words. She furrowed her brow in confusion. "I don't… I don't understand."

"A demon is essentially reborn a Drakon after committing a crime worthy of the punishment. The key to that crime then becomes the Drakon's treasure. When someone sacrifices that same treasure for the Drakon, they're responsible for setting the Drakon's soul free."

When she didn't respond, he shrugged a shoulder. "I don't get the whole thing myself. It's so rare, most Drakons aren't even aware of it. All I know is Saden's been acquitted of his crimes. The Lady Ilsa has appointed him leader of the leisonguardes chosen to capture those who were involved with Gabriel."

A slow elation bloomed in her chest, narrowing her world down to the implications of Blade's statement. Saden was free? No more harsh restrictions or penalties. No more living under the shroud of his uncle's sins. He could finally have the life he'd deserved all along. Not only that. He was pursuing an endeavor that would've made his parents proud. Carrying on their dedication to protect their race, even from the dangers within.

The wild beating of her heart faltered when she realized what else his freedom meant.

His promise to Marco was fulfilled. She and Mckenzie were safe. There was no longer anything tying Saden to them. He could choose his own fate now. Re-establish himself with his kind, fall in love and take a preyuna. That was obviously what he wanted, wasn't it? Otherwise, it would be him sitting on her couch and speaking of the future instead of Blade.

"I can take you to him if you want," Blade said quietly.

Daneya stared at him unseeingly for countless seconds. The idea was both tempting and ludicrous. In the short time she and Saden had spent together, not once had they considered this outcome. Their bittersweet memories had been made of fleeting moments.

Now, he had more than the desolate fate of a damned soul ahead of him. He had advantages and choices. A place among his people. Her presence would only hinder that. She could never feel comfortable among his kind and he would never be accepted with a member of the DCM at his side.

She took a steadying breath then said, "That won't be necessary. I'm sure you'll tell him how grateful I am for everything he's done."

Blade frowned as if he hadn't heard right. "Saden misses you. I may still be a Drakon, but I know that having a soul means nothing if you can't find happiness. He was only happy when he was with you."

A hard lump formed in her throat. *Damn* him for making this harder! Couldn't he see that what she was doing was for the best? Saden needed a fresh start, and she was going to let him have it. "Thank you for coming but we really need to get going."

"Mom—" Mckenzie started.

"Daneya, can I talk to you privately?" Vincent interrupted. He led the way outside then rounded on her as soon as he closed the door after them. "Go."

"Excuse me?"

"Go to him. It's what you want to do, isn't it?"

A sharp bark of disbelief broke from her lips. "This is hardly any of your business. And since when did you start giving a damn about Saden?"

"I don't. I care about you." He sighed heavily then gestured to the porch steps. "Take a seat."

"Vincent—"

"We haven't officially left the DCM yet and as your commanding officer, I'm ordering you to sit."

She nearly grinned at that and sat down grudgingly. He took up position beside her and fixed his gaze somewhere in the distance. "I know you love him." When she opened her mouth to protest, he held up a staying hand. "Trust me, I'm the last one who wants to point this out, but it has to be said. I've known you for almost a decade, and in all that time, I have never seen you give in to emotion the way you have when you talk about him. There's something in your eyes that wasn't there before. Passion, I guess you'd call it."

"I've always had passion," she argued.

"About your work and your daughter, yeah. Not about yourself. I kept hoping maybe…" He gave a cynical chuckle and shook his head. "It doesn't really matter anymore. What I'm trying to say is you're different now, and that's a good thing."

Daneya eyed him askance then had to look away as unshed tears burned the back of her throat. She thought she'd hid her feelings well in regards to Saden. "You must think I'm a fool."

His face crinkled in a sideways smile. "You are a lot of things, Daneya Perodee. None of them is a fool."

"You don't understand. I can't just 'go to him'. It would never work. He's a Vampyre and an ex-criminal. I'm a human who's dedicated my life to eradicating demons who have crossed the line. We're from two completely different worlds. You can't build a paper bridge between two cliffs and expect everything to be okay." She swallowed repeatedly, trying to keep the futility of the situation at bay. "Even if I did love him, it wouldn't be enough."

The quiet of dawn spanned out around them, then Vincent said slowly, "Before I joined the DCM, I was in love with a civilian. We were high school sweethearts and I thought my world revolved around her. Then I ran into my first demon, a Rakshasa turned Vanara. It gave me a new perspective and suddenly my priorities had changed. I left my girl to become a vigilante. Be part of something greater. It took me a long time to realize that there is nothing greater than sharing a life with someone you love."

She twisted her mouth in a wry grin. "Have you turned shrink on me now?"

"No, but I do think I've sunk to a new low and hit the friend zone with you."

Her short laugh echoed with a hint of sadness. "He deserves a chance at happiness in his new life. Just like you do."

"He deserves to know the truth about how you feel," Vincent shot back. "And no man could be better off without you." After a pause, he said, "I'll be fine on my own. I can live with my regrets and the mistakes I've made. Question is, if you don't at least talk to him, can you live with yours?"

The tears she'd been fighting spilled down her cheeks. *"No regrets."* That had been her promise to Saden. Yet, leaving without seeing him felt like a regret she would hold onto for the rest of her life. At the same time, did she have any right to open old wounds when it wouldn't change the outcome?

She leaned into Vincent as he wrapped an arm around her, grateful for his comfort.

Behind them, the door opened and Blade cleared his throat. "I have to get going. Have you made a decision?"

Daneya pulled away slightly to look at Vincent and the deep understanding in his eyes. Then she turned around to face Blade with a sigh. "Yeah. I think so."

Chapter Twenty-One

After reading the same sentence for the fourth time in the dim light of his lamp, Saden set the document aside on his desk and scrubbed his eyes. The rays of dawning sunlight outside were blocked by heavy drapes over the floor to ceiling windows on both sides of his office. Now that he was a Vampyre again, he could no longer withstand the touch of UV rays on his skin.

The room was located in the west wing of Council Hall, a massive building erected in the early eighteen hundreds. It belonged to the house of Avram for the purpose of conducting business and storing some of the historical artifacts of their race. Which was why the walls of his large office were lined with bookcases holding hundreds of texts, some dating back several centuries.

The morning was coming up on another seventy-two hours of sleep deprivation for him. Fatigue and hunger ate away at his concentration. Their effects were different than what he'd learned to deal with as a Drakon. Instead of being a minor annoyance, the gnawing ache in his belly and tension in his muscles couldn't be ignored. He was losing both strength and weight as a result of negligence.

After three days of freedom when his body had reached its limit, he'd found he knew nothing of cooking or even what foods he liked. Unlike Blade, he'd never indulged in the luxury of eating. His years as Serrakus' slave had taught him food was merely another method of control he had no power over.

It was still difficult to remind himself to eat, and sleep was just as hard to come by. Thoughts of Daneya plagued him constantly. Day and night, he couldn't stop thinking about her. Where she was and what she was doing. Whether or not she blamed him for the trauma Mckenzie might be suffering from the murder she committed on his behalf. Guilt rode him hard for failing in his oath to protect them from Gabriel.

His only consolation was the knowledge that they were safe now. And he would keep it that way even if he had to become a Drakon all over again.

There was also the matter of energy, his main source of sustenance now. Only problem was, he no longer had his parents to provide it for him and taking a sexual partner was still something he couldn't bring himself to do. He could feel his aethra beginning to wither inside him, going through the first stage of what his kind called Xhohor. A slow starvation worse than the pangs of hunger. The need to feed would soon become compulsory. Until then, however, he would deal with the pain as he always had. Alone.

"You're starting to glaze. Why don't we finish this up tomorrow?"

Saden blinked and stared over at Roshon sitting across the desk from him. They'd been working for days on end, going through Gabriel's files to find the Vampyres he'd been involved with and determine the extent of their crimes. Those who had been directly connected with the kidnapping and abuse of the human females were sentenced to become Drakons while the rest were given lesser punishments.

It was also Saden's duty to identify every half-breed Gabriel was responsible for and ensure they had no ties to the Djinn. Since there were so many, Lady Ilsa had agreed with his suggestion to allow the Vampyres masquerading as their parents to keep them and either pay a hefty fine or go into servitude for half a century per child. Penalties which were too low in his opinion.

They'd all been aware of how the offspring had been conceived and, as far as he was concerned, deserved a bullet to the head for their silence. As Roshon had pointed out, though, killing that many of his kind would only further the Djinns' ultimate goal of rising against them in war.

Roshon had proven to be an asset in more ways than one over the past month. Despite the Lady's righteous indignation over having to tolerate the presence of a Rakshasa, he'd kept his word and, along with his team, supervised the care of the human females during their interrogations. He'd taken personal responsibility for their safety and had insisted on escorting them to Vincent Condretti when korvaute Weiss had concluded his questioning.

During this time, he'd also watched out for Saden in a way that went far beyond their shared understanding of each other. Taught him how to cook and doctored his wounds. He'd insisted on being there when Saden had negotiated the terms of his collaboration with Lady Ilsa. Through Roshon's insight, Saden had been able to work out a deal that satisfied both the Lady and Lucius while leaving him as an independent contractor of his services. Which put him in control of how he got the job done and who he worked with.

Afterwards, Saden had managed to convince Roshon and his team to stay on with him and assist in the capturing of those found guilty of conspiracy. In exchange, he and a group of leisonguardes under his command would help with the recent increase of Vanaras however they could.

Neither of their ruling authorities had been pleased by the arrangement, but necessity had forced their cooperation. Lady Ilsa needed Gabriel's treachery swept under the rug as quickly as possible to save face and Roshon's leader, Brice, couldn't afford to turn down the additional help.

Since then, Roshon had become invaluable as a partner and a friend. He was the only one Saden trusted at his back while surrounded by a race that had turned its back on him.

Saden clawed a hand through his hair in aggravation. "Every trail we have leads to this Djinn called Forrest, and we can't find a gods-damned thing on him," he said with vexation, his voice raspy from the damage to his vocal cords that'd healed naturally. "He's like a boogeyman. Always one step ahead and laughing at us from behind his followers. Someone has to have more information on him."

Because of their limited resources, they'd only been able to shut down one of the other facilities instead of all three at once. The remaining two had been found empty shortly afterwards and the female prisoners moved to locations unknown.

Among the guards at the facility had been three Djinn they'd captured and handed over to Lucius. So far, those Djinn had said nothing other than the fact that their orders came from the one named Forrest.

According to Gabriel's files, he'd been a major player from the very beginning. Possibly the Djinn Gabriel had originally made his pact with.

Roshon scratched the stubble on his jaw and frowned. "Maybe he's just a figurehead. It's possible Gabriel worked directly with an entire group of Djinn who didn't want their own identities on record."

"No, the Djinn don't operate like that. They conform. This Forrest is the one in charge now. If we find him, we'll find the rest of the females."

"That reminds me, Weiss should be done questioning the second batch we found. I'll contact Whitmore later to arrange for them to be picked up by the DCM."

"Who's Whitmore?"

"The new director of the DCM unit," Roshon replied as he began filing the papers on his own desk into a cabinet behind him.

"What happened to Vincent?"

"He called me last week to let me know he was leaving. Something about taking a sabbatical and moving to Oregon. He gave me his forwarding address in case we need to meet with him in the future."

Saden bit back the question riding the tip of his tongue, though he couldn't stop his thoughts from going there. Had Daneya taken Mckenzie and gone with Vincent? Despite the fact that he had no right to interfere in her life again, or even watch over her from a distance as he had throughout her adult life, knowing she would be hundreds of miles away somehow made the separation worse.

She deserves happiness, he told himself with no small amount of self-loathing. Something she could never find with him. While his soul may have been set free, his persona and reputation would forever be frozen in the past. He was a stain on the pride of his people and no title Lady Ilsa gave him or anything he did would change that. It was the reason why he'd kept the name Saden instead of reverting back to his given name, Jeremy Aikins.

Black stares and gossip seething with hatred followed him everywhere he went. Even the Vampyres he worked with viewed him as a savage intruder who had conned his way into the Lady's graces.

None of it phased him, however. None except for the opinion of his sister who had sought him out after hearing of his return. She'd met with him in his office, a stunning replica of their mother with straight midnight hair and expressive, jade-colored eyes.

For ten minutes he had stood in silence as she berated him. Listened to her vivid expressions of humiliation and shame over having the misfortune of being related to filth like him. The blame for the stigma she'd dealt with all her life had cut him deeper than any blade or whip that had ever touched his skin. With each curse she had flung at him, he'd felt his hopes for a loving reunion dissolve like bitter ash in his mouth.

When she had finally left him alone with her red handprint burning his cheek, there had been nothing but a cold, dead weight inside him. The crushing burden of sins he could never escape. If his own blood could find no forgiveness for him, why should Daneya?

"Look, about Daneya—" Roshon started in a sympathetic tone.

"Don't," Saden said curtly, then took a calming breath. "Go on home to your mate. I know she gets upset when I keep you overnight like this. Besides, there's nothing more we can do right now." He'd called Roshon last night on a hunch that had turned out to be another dead end. At this point, sending out discreet search parties for Forrest and the missing women was going to be inevitable.

A knock on the door sounded, stealing their attention. "Come," Saden called.

The female Rakshasa that was part of Roshon's personal team entered with a furtive glance to Saden. She hurried over to Roshon and whispered something in his ear. The chief's eyes lit up as he whispered back. Whatever he said had the woman running from the room.

Alarm chased away the fog of Saden's exhaustion. "What's going on?"

"You're about to find out, my friend." Roshon took two tumblers and a bottle of whiskey from the bottom drawer of his desk and poured them each a glass. "Kindra will be back in five minutes. Meanwhile, have a drink with me. You're going to need it."

Saden accepted the proffered tumbler with a suspicious frown and took a sip. "Why do I get the feeling you've been keeping secrets from me?"

Roshon flashed him an unapologetic grin. "Probably because I have. Trust me, though. You'll like this one."

He kept his doubts to himself. Truth was, he did trust the chief almost as much as he trusted Blade.

Roshon refused to give him any more information while they waited. Five minutes later, Kindra opened the door to the office again and stood aside to let a small figure walk in hesitantly. The tumbler nearly fell from Saden's grip as he stared in shock at the newcomer.

Mckenzie's sweet face perked up when her eyes met his and she shot like a rocket across the room. Saden put his glass down then scooped her into his arms, laughing out loud in relief. It was illogical how much he'd missed her, yet it couldn't be denied. She'd been a part of his life for years. A part of the anchor that had kept his sanity afloat. In a way, they would always be connected.

When her thin body began trembling against his, he set her on her feet and met her doe-eyed gaze. "What's wrong, little one?" The stoic expression she wore was familiar. Brow slightly wrinkled and lips pressed tightly together with unshed moisture coating her lashes. It caused his gut to clench in fear. Where was Daneya?

"I thought you would be in trouble because of what I did. I thought—"

"Shh." He knelt to wrap her in a strong embrace, his chest swelling with emotion. No one had ever cared what happened to him, or whether he deserved it or not. "You saved me. I've never known anyone braver than you."

A spark of doubt clouded her features then melted under a radiant smile.

"Where's your mother?" he asked.

Before Mckenzie could respond, a female voice spoke up from the doorway. "Her mother is right here."

Saden rose and turned to see Daneya standing in the middle of the room, more beautiful than he remembered. Jeans and a V-neck T-shirt hugged the slim curves of her figure and her russet hair fell in unbound waves past her shoulders. The only thing that marred her appearance was the faint trepidation in her amber eyes, but he couldn't focus on that. All that mattered was her presence and the overwhelming urge he had to touch her, hold her, make sure she was real.

Before he could think twice, he moved to close the distance between them and cradled her face in his hands. Her skin was soft beneath his, her lips curved up in an inviting smile.

Then it hit him.

The danger she was putting herself in just by being there—a DCM vigilante in the heart of Vampyre territory. Not even he would be enough to protect her if Lady Ilsa or korvaute Weiss decided to view her as a threat.

"What are you doing here?" Without waiting for an answer, he rounded on Roshon angrily. "How could you let her risk herself by coming here?"

Roshon raised his hands defensively. "Easy. She's not in any danger. As far as anyone besides us and my men know, she's an abductee from one of the facilities with more information to give and therefore under our authority." When Saden furrowed his brow in confusion, Roshon's mouth twitched in a failed attempt to hold back a grin. "I figure you two have a few things to discuss. I'll be waiting outside if you need me."

After he was gone, Saden looked to Daneya. "How did you find me?"

"Blade came to my house a week ago. He told me what'd happened to you and the position you took to search for the rest of the women. When I said I wanted to see you, he arranged this meeting with Roshon."

From her faltering tone, he knew Blade had to have convinced her to come in some way, but he didn't care. He was just happy she was there, with him. Unable to stop himself, he threaded his fingers into her hair and leaned down to take full possession of her mouth.

Daneya stepped away from the kiss and gently pulled his hands from her. "I'm glad things are working out for you. That you're finally getting the respect you deserve. You must be happy to be among your kind again. To be able to build a life now that you're free."

His confusion doubled as he watched her gaze bounce nervously around the room, focusing on everything except him. She was obviously upset about something, though he had no clue what it was.

He chose his next words carefully. "This is only a temporary life, and I wouldn't call it happy or respectful. What I'm doing is…" *for you. For the promise I made.* He swallowed heavily, then said, "I'm doing this because I'm the only who has a chance of bringing down what remains of Gabriel's operation. The Lady Ilsa knows that. To her and everyone else here, I'm just a means to an end. I may have been born a Vampyre, but these people are no longer my kind. I could never fit in with them, and I don't want to."

Daneya slowly shook her head and the sorrow on her elegant features tore at his insides. "This, whatever this is between us, won't work. There are too many variables." She spun on her heel and started to pace several yards away. "We built a relationship based on need and survival, charged with pure"—her eyes flicked momentarily to Mckenzie staring pensively from the other side of the room—"energy. I can't take from you what you've just found and you can't expect me to give up my life to be with you. It's too crazy! Where would we even live?"

She flung her arms out in exasperation. "You're a Vampyre and I'm a human with more reasons to hate your kind than I can count. Neither one of us will be accepted wherever we go. We might as well try to make a home out of sand. Like you said before, what we had was all a mistake, right? That both of us will be better off if we just go our separate ways."

His thoughts tangled in a struggle to comprehend what she was trying to get at.

From the hallway outside, Roshon yelled, "That's your cue to tell her she's wrong, but very, very delicately."

Saden strode to the door and shut it as Daneya's face flushed a bright red. He recalled the conversation she spoke of as if it were yesterday. How he'd tried to convince her that their feelings for each other were irrelevant in the long run. If he had known then what he did now, he'd have slapped himself.

Is that what she was trying to do here, convince him that he'd been right all those weeks ago? He took a second to look closer at her. At the way her body vibrated and how her gaze seemed to bore into him as if searching for answers. It suddenly dawned on him that it wasn't anger or the need for closure that had driven her to come. While he didn't know how to read or understand women, that didn't matter.

This was Daneya, and he knew her better than he knew himself. It was fear that emanated from her, and that more than anything, he understood.

"Telling you that was a mistake," he said quietly. When she scowled, he ignored it and pushed on. "I love you, and the only thing I've realized since being set free is that I miss you. I would do anything to have you again. Give you what I couldn't before."

Her silence filled the air with tension. "Where would we live?" she repeated.

For the first time since seeing her again, his heart rate spiked with hope. Daneya didn't entertain hypotheticals, which meant her question held the chance for possibility despite the doubt in her voice. "At my manor. I was planning on having the damages repaired. Or we can buy a house together. Wherever you want to live."

"And what would we do? I can't continue at the DCM with an ex-Drakon by my side and I'm sure your kind would feel the same way about me."

"I don't give a *fuck* what they think about you!" he said angrily, then took a deep breath when a corner of her mouth lifted in amusement. Behind the uncertainty in her eyes was a daring look he was all too familiar with. She was testing him to see how far he would go to keep her, he was sure of it. Confidence rushed in, overriding his fear of losing her forever.

This time when he approached her and took her face in his hands, he let every ounce of his determination show. "We would do the same as we've always done. Take out the bad guys. We don't need the DCM or the house of Avram for that. I need you and Mckenzie. If you give me a chance, I'll make you both happy."

A single tear spilled down her cheek as she shook her head with a smile. "I love you, too."

The feel of her lips touching his, the heat of her body pressed against him, sent a burst of sensation through his being. It was joy, pure and simple. Beyond anything he'd been capable of experiencing as a Drakon. He wrapped her in his arms and crushed her slighter frame to his, drinking in the taste of her on his tongue.

This was freedom. Right here. This was his salvation.

Eventually, the sounds of gagging pulled them apart. They turned to see Mckenzie standing close and watching them with a derisive grin on her face. "Grown-ups are so gross. Does this mean we can stay at the manor? Can I have a dog, and my own computer? Oh, and another gun?"

"Kennie!" Daneya exclaimed.

"What? You told me he was loaded, and he loves me too, right? I could get used to this."

Saden laughed and kissed her forehead. "I'll give you anything your mom approves of."

She groaned and rolled her eyes, mumbling something under her breath.

Daneya took his hand and leaned into him. "So what do we do now?"

A thousand ideas came to mind, though it was his stomach that settled the decision for him. "I take you two out to dinner. Anywhere you want to go."

Her eyebrows shot up in surprise. "You eat?"

"It's a work in progress."

She tilted her head then pulled him down to breathe seductively in his ear. "How about we stay in and order pizza? I don't want to share you with the rest of the world just yet."

Saden felt himself grow hard in the tight confines of his jeans. He delved into the warm cavern of her mouth and knew he was where he belonged. With her, he was already home.

Chapter Twenty-Two

Phoenix floated in a sea of emptiness for several seconds. Or perhaps it was an eternity. Time didn't exist where he was—caught somewhere between life and the promising finality of death. It was peaceful here. Quiet and devoid of the constant struggle for sanity.

Then it was ripped away by the searing agony of healing fire. Blazing, white light burned his corneas as the neurons in his brain were forced to resume activity, stealing him from the sweet release of death. His autonomic nervous system kicked into gear, heart beating wildly in shock and lungs violently purging themselves of the water that had drowned him.

One would think the pain of dying would forever be trapped in the recesses of the subconscious, but the mind always remembered. It recalled every excruciating moment in detail and threw them back into conscious thought. For Drakons, it wasn't the process of the body dying that should be feared during torture. It was the knowledge that they were powerless to prevent it from happening again and again, leaving them with no choice except to endure until it was over.

In Phoenix's case, he was tethered to sanity by more than just his strength of will. Giving in to the relief of madness wasn't an option. To do so would render him useless and essentially forfeit both his life and Sasha's.

Awareness gradually crept back to him. Shooting pains traveled from his wrists and ankles as he instinctively tried to curl in on himself. The iron shackles binding him to the cold, metal slab in a spread eagle position had cut deep into his skin. Sweltering heat from the half-dozen torches lining the walls of the cell caused streams of sweat to trickle into the numerous wounds covering his naked body. The glow of a red hot poker appeared above him before coming down across his belly.

After weeks of being subjected to concentrated abuse and water boarding, his resistance had finally snapped, leaving him vulnerable. A scream was wrenched from his raw throat, followed by the stench of burning flesh clogging his nostrils. Consciousness ebbed as his mind desperately sought refuge.

Serrakus was having none of that, however. He backhanded Phoenix hard then yanked a fistful of his hair. "Say it! You were the one who released Saden from my dungeon, weren't you? Tell me!"

Phoenix took a ragged breath and finally decided to give the only answer he knew the Drakonem would accept. "I did it. I got him out." It was a lie, of course. But no matter how many times he claimed he didn't know who the culprit was, it wouldn't matter. Serrakus needed someone to blame and the chances that he might believe he'd been betrayed by Lucius were slim to none.

No, it was better this way. Phoenix just wanted the interrogations to stop and the torture to go back to what he was used to dealing with.

Serrakus sneered in contempt. "You disappoint me, Phoenix. I had thought you were above such petty emotions as sympathy. You've cost me two Drakons with your little rebellion. Be assured, the consequences will fit the crime." He gave the poker to Laurs who stood to the side. "Leave him here until I've decided what his punishment shall be."

Laurs snuffed the torches then followed his master out of the cell, locking the door behind him. Phoenix let his aching muscles relax and concentrated on taking even, shallow breaths. As much to ease the pain of his broken ribs as to tolerate the thick plumes of rancid smoke filling the air.

After a short period, he felt a wisp of enquiry across his senses. Sasha's gentle presence began to rise to the surface at the lull in his suffering. He quickly sent a response of warning, telling her it wasn't over yet, and felt her slowly withdraw again. In truth, he didn't want her to witness this. There was no need for her to be aware of how much his actions were costing him.

He was the one who'd agreed to her request, and he would bear the consequences alone.

Too soon, the door to the cell was opened and light spilled into the comforting darkness. He tensed and shut his eyes, waiting for whatever sadistic craving Laurs had chosen to indulge in now. It wouldn't be the first time the warder had secretly defied Serrakus just to seek out further pleasure in delivering pain.

When a wet towel was pressed to his forehead, he jerked and looked up to find Lucius peering down at him. The Drakonem's expression was unreadable, his sharp features eerily pronounced in the flames of a single torch that had been placed in a nearby sconce. Next to him was the Dresidien slave Phoenix recognized from before. She was holding a small bowl of what he assumed held water.

Lucius dabbed the towel lightly over Phoenix's fevered skin. "What a charming mystery you are, my fierce warrior. I've just been informed by my brother that you took responsibility for my part in Saden's success. I'm curious. Was this due to the noble nature you keep so hidden within?"

Phoenix wanted nothing more than to call the Drakonem out on his cowardice, but he was too afraid to move or say anything. Afraid that Lucius might take the soothing balm of the cool towel from his forehead. He hated himself for the weakness while at the same time, was too far gone to care.

"Don't bother denying it," Lucius went on to say. "You see, I know about your arrangement with Tallos to have that halfling girl's sentence added to yours. Quite chivalrous, I must admit. Though not your idea, was it? No. I think you did it at the request of your precious Djinn. How might Saden react, I wonder, if he knew Mckenzie's life had been saved by his enemy and a man he despises for no other reason than mere rumor?

"An interesting juxtaposition, really, that he chooses to hate you for a past you had no more control over than he had of his own. Do you think he would show gratitude or spit in your face as he condemned you?"

It was a rhetorical question, and still, the obvious answer made Phoenix avert his gaze in humiliation. He knew exactly what Saden would think if he were made aware of the truth. That it was all somehow part of an elaborate scheme that would only prove Phoenix's selfish and immoral nature in the end. It shouldn't have bothered him. All his life he'd been the scapegoat, the black stain on the history of his former clan and the Drakon who exemplified everything a criminal should be reviled for.

Saden's opinion shouldn't even touch him.

That would also be a lie, however. While it was true Sasha had urged him to contact Tallos on Mckenzie's behalf, that wasn't the only reason he'd requested to accept her punishment. Saden had done everything within his power to protect the little girl and Phoenix respected that above all else. Was it worth the punishment he would endure for the next year at least?

Probably not.

Lucius was right. It wouldn't change the way anyone viewed him. Though none of that mattered, right? He was the filth that deserved whatever came to him.

So long as Sasha remained safe and happy within him, he was all right with that.

Lucius dipped the cloth into the bowl his slave held then continued to wipe the sweat from Phoenix's face. "What about your brother, Roshon? Because of your interference, he and his clan, your clan, will benefit greatly from an alliance he's made with Saden and the house of Avram. Pity he's not accrediting you for the role you played. What I find most compelling, however, is the way you talked Mckenzie into taking that last step necessary to kill Gabriel."

Phoenix narrowed his gaze on Lucius. He recalled with perfect clarity the events of that night at the facility. How Mckenzie had clung to her innocence and sense of morality in the midst of a situation that challenged them. It had been clear she wanted to do what was right, and at the same time, couldn't bring herself to do it. As harsh as his words may have sounded, they'd been nothing more than a simple push to make her realize what she already knew. That she cared for Saden enough to make that sacrifice.

If someone had been there for him, urged him to do what was necessary, maybe his life would've turned out differently.

"How?" he croaked. Lucius shouldn't have known about what had happened unless Saden had told him.

The silver-haired Drakonem cast him a deprecating frown. "Did you really think I would force Saden to take you with him if I didn't have some way of observing the outcome? You've been around long enough to know me better than that. My beautiful Allorha here witnessed everything through Saden's mind. I must say, it was ingenious, the way you manipulated her emotions like that. It's almost a shame Saden was too blinded by his love for the halfling to see your purpose.

"I, myself, do not have such blinders. I see how your Djinn's request to take the place of the halfling is costing you. While your actions are admirable, they're also foolish and a waste of energy. No one will bother to find out the truth of what you've done, let alone thank you for it. And you're certainly no martyr.

"I have a better solution. Rescind your offer to carry Mckenzie's sentence. It's not too late. I can contact Tallos and convince him to place the girl under my control. You have my word I will treat her fairly and you can look in on her any time you like. I will also see what I can do to have you removed from Serrakus' service and assigned to mine. Give up this travesty of heroism and let me help you."

Phoenix stared at Lucius for countless seconds. Admittedly, a part of him wanted to abandon his promise to Sasha and accept the Drakonem's offer. He was so tired of it all. Sick of the hatred he warranted from a past he couldn't change. The bleakness of eternity was wearing him thin and this situation with Saden was only another crack in the well of his sanity.

But he knew he wouldn't go through with it. Sasha saw the memory of her own daughter in Mckenzie. A child that had been ripped from her arms and, along with her son, deemed as collateral damage and murdered by her own kind. In the long run, a year or more of torture was nothing compared to the solace he could give Sasha by taking Mckenzie's punishment.

"No one can blame you for being selfish in this matter," Lucius added with smooth persuasion. "How far are you willing to let that Djinn take advantage of you?"

"The same way you're taking advantage of me?" Phoenix let out a rough laugh. "Go fuck yourself."

Lucius' expression contorted with anger then settled into a mask of serene arrogance. "Have it your way. I look forward to the next time we meet. Hopefully under more…fortuitous circumstances."

After Lucius and his slave left, taking the light with them, Phoenix released the tension in his sore muscles and let his mind wander. He thought of his brother and the way Roshon's geis had greeted him. With trust and affection, like the panther used to when Phoenix and his brother were children. Since Trax was the physical manifestation of Roshon's desires, perhaps it was possible Roshon still cared beneath his logic and animosity.

Phoenix killed that thought instantly and shook his head. He was a fool to even consider it. Whatever ties they'd shared had long ago been severed. Roshon was a rightful chief now, and he the pariah that should've remained forgotten. He laughed bitterly into the darkness and for the first time in centuries, prayed for a death that would never come.

* * * *

One year later…

Daneya studied the reflection in the full-length mirror with a mixture of amazed apprehension. The stranger staring back at her wasn't a woman she recognized. Her long, burgundy tresses were swept up in an elegant roll at the back of her head with curled locks framing her angular face. Lipstick painted her lips rose-red and her eyes were lined with coal mascara, adding an element of exotic mystery to her features. A white, satin gown clung to her body and accentuated every curve, making her tan skin seem to glow in contrast.

The woman in front of her was absolutely stunning, and couldn't possibly be the same woman she'd woken up as that morning.

The door to the bedroom opened and Erin practically danced inside, beaming from ear to ear. She let out an ungodly squeal then began adjusting the jeweled net pinned to Daneya's hair. "You look gorgeous! Didn't I tell you it would be worth it?"

Daneya twisted her face in a frown. She still wasn't quite sure giving her friend free reign as bridesmaid and coordinator of her wedding had been such a great idea.

Erin had been a whirlwind of frenetic energy over the past month, taking it upon herself to arrange everything from the reception to the gown and makeup Daneya wore. What had started as a simple affair born of legal necessity had quickly turned into a monumental event. "Why did I let you talk me into this?"

Erin adjusted the silver necklace at Daneya's throat then stood back to admire her handiwork. "Because you love me. Because I'm married to a man whose idea of romance is trimming his nose hairs and refraining from disgusting bodily functions one day out of the year. And because I need my vicarious thrills! Don't ruin this for me."

Daneya smiled and hugged her friend. When she had turned in her resignation to the new director of the DCM, she'd had to cut all ties to that life, including her friendships with everyone except Vincent. It would have been too complicated to explain her relationship with an ex-Drakon and why she allowed her daughter near him. Erin, however, had stubbornly refused to say goodbye and had remained close despite the wild rumors still circulating over Daneya's departure. Even after being told of Saden's previous life and Mckenzie's father, she hadn't been deterred.

She was a true friend without fail.

"Do you know if Blade has arrived yet?" Daneya asked.

Erin shook her head grimly. "I don't think he's coming. I overheard Saden this morning talking with Roshon about the new assignment Blade was working."

The new assignment. Daneya had forgotten about that in all the fuss over the wedding. Blade had come to them a week ago to let them know he might not be there as Saden's best man due to the job he'd been given. Although he had said nothing more on the issue, his distress had been obvious. Whatever it was Serrakus had him doing must have bothered him greatly.

"I'm sure he's fine," Erin said soothingly.

"Yeah," she agreed, trying to dispel her worry for the cocky SOB she'd grown to care about. "You're right." He would've at least told Saden if the job were something he couldn't handle, wouldn't he? "Where's Kennie?"

As if on cue, Mckenzie raced through the doorway and skidded to a halt in front of Daneya. Her hair had also been intricately styled atop her head and a light dusting of makeup applied to her maturing features. She'd been appalled at first at the prospect of wearing a dress as the flower girl, until Saden had given her a credit card and told her to order anything she liked. The result was a remarkable, deep violet dress with lavender lace trim, subtle jewelry and black combat boots boasting silver spikes down the front. Saden had been so proud of the boots, he'd bought her an ivory switchblade to conceal in one of them.

Overall, she was radiant with her own touch of style. Daneya blinked back tears and grabbed her daughter in a tight embrace. It still amazed her that Saden had asked her to marry him almost solely for the purpose of making Mckenzie legally his. The human ceremony meant nothing to his kind who had their own, more permanent ritual of binding, and she had never laid much stock in a piece of paper.

When Saden had found out the law required him to be Mckenzie's stepfather before he could adopt her, though, he'd proposed immediately and announced his intentions to everyone.

The elaborate fanfare of the occasion was all due to Erin. Once she had discovered what was going on, she'd seized control and told Saden to just 'sit back and enjoy the ride'. That had been nearly a quarter-million dollars ago. Not even Daneya had been able to curb her enthusiasm.

Surprisingly, the leisonguardes Saden worked with had taken the news rather well. Only a handful of them had protested Saden's union to an ex-vigilante of the DCM. Their obnoxious disapproval had been silenced, however, when he'd threatened to leave the Lady's service and let them finish picking up after Gabriel on their own. After only a year in his position, he was already too valuable an asset to risk losing. And while none of them would admit it, Daneya had also proven invaluable at Saden's side.

Mckenzie had benefited most from their work with the house of Avram. Finally, she was able to make friends with other children like her. Saden had even enrolled her in the private school staffed and operated by his kind in their region. The kids she attended with were unaware of her connection to Gabriel and the staff had been sufficiently threatened to keep it that way.

Mckenzie squirmed out of her arms and bounced on the balls of her feet. "Are you ready? Roshon says the geis are going to start eating the food if no one else does."

Daneya rolled her eyes with an exaggerated sigh. "Yes. Go tell them to start the music."

Just as Mckenzie reached the door where her new best friend waited, a sweet little Vampyre named Michele, she turned around and smiled brilliantly. "I love you, Mom."

"Love you, too, baby." A single tear trickled down her cheek as she watched them leave. Her daughter looked so happy. More than she had in her entire life. It seemed ludicrous how close Daneya had come to letting that slip away, that chance at what was now a reality. If it hadn't been for Blade and Vincent...

"Don't start that," Erin admonished with tears in her own voice. She handed a tissue and the bridal bouquet to Daneya, made a few more last adjustments to their gowns, then ushered her from the room.

"Remember," she said in a hushed tone as they hurried down the main stairwell of the manor, careful not to disturb the white garlands draped over the banister, "You come in when the wedding march song begins. Try not to walk too fast and don't lose sight of your target. I wish you'd put on the veil I got for you. Are you sure you don't want anyone walking you down the aisle? Floyd could do it. He wouldn't mind, really."

When they came to an ached trellis placed in front of the doorway to the living room meant to close it off with hanging vines and irises, Daneya took Erin by the shoulders and gave her a little shake. "I'm fine! Shouldn't I be the nervous one here?"

Erin's high chuckle crackled with the tension and excitement she was emanating. "You're right. On the other hand, you're so damn calm, it's disgusting. I'd slap you but I don't want to ruin your makeup. All right, I'll see you in there." She pecked Daneya on the cheek then vanished on the other side of the hanging flowers.

Two minutes later, the wedding song filled the air and Daneya took a deep breath before entering the living room. Then instantly froze as she gazed out on the sight in front of her.

The whole scene could've been plucked directly from a bridal magazine showcasing a millionaire's wedding. Not only had the room been extended by several tens of feet to accommodate the guests, but it had also been excavated then filled with rows of chairs on either side. Colorful bouquets adorned the chairs lining the center aisle and more sat atop short, standing pillars placed at intervals against the side walls.

A pianist sat at a grand piano toward the front and played the music seamlessly while sunlight streamed in through the new skylights that had been installed. Although there was no color scheme to the multitude of decorations adorning the walls, everything flowed with a breathtaking grace that sent chills over her skin.

More impressive than all of this was the assortment of guests that sat waiting patiently with their eyes fixed on her. Much of Roshon's clan was gathered on one side of the room with half of their geis perched on chair backs or laying between the rows. The rest, she knew, were out exploring the expanse of Saden's land. On the other side of the room was a large cluster of Vampyres. Mostly those who owed a debt of gratitude to Saden for his mercy in their sentencing. There was even a handful of members of the DCM who had put aside their unease for her and Mckenzie's sake.

As one of them had put it, if they couldn't convince Daneya to change her mind, they may as well join in on the festivities.

A year ago, these people likely would've scoffed at the idea of such a diverse group gathering to celebrate the wedding of an ex-vigilante and ex-Drakon. Yet, here they all were, bearing smiles and gifts. It was all too incredible to take in at once.

She looked straight ahead and felt a shiver of electricity race up her spine when her gaze caught Saden's from across the room. He stood to the right of the dais wearing a black tux that molded to the contours of his tall, lean frame. His hair was slicked back to display the handsome lines of his face and green eyes lit with a familiar flare that always caused her skin to tingle. Behind him was Roshon with Erin standing opposite them, but it was only Saden she saw as she made her way slowly down the aisle.

Deep within, she could feel the spark of his aethra that was irrevocably entwined to her own soul. A faint, warm sensation that grew as she moved closer until it was a vibrant hum echoing with the beat of her heart. It pulled her toward him, giving her strength as surly as her energy gave him life. A perfect, reciprocating bond that would endure until death took one or both of them.

Which wouldn't be for at least the next six hundred years since his aging had been mostly suspended as a Drakon.

She recalled the night of their Sek'le Taunt. The sacred bonding of their souls that had changed her physiology as well as marked her as his preyuna. Unlike a human marriage, this was performed in private and more evident than a simple piece of paper. A part of her belonged to him now, and he to her. The memory of it sent a surge of heat coursing through her blood.

Saden took her hand as she stepped onto the dais then turned with her to face the human minister. The rest of the ceremony passed by in a blur. They repeated their vows and exchanged rings, though it wasn't until a thundering roar went up from the crowd that the significance of the event hit her. She was living the happily ever after she'd never have dreamed of before. Suddenly, she wished her parents were there. Especially her sister, Emily, and Marco. They had given their lives, their future, to protect her. She would give anything to let them know it hadn't been in vain.

Her next thoughts were banished when Saden captured her mouth in a drowning kiss that brought another deafening cheer from their audience. Seconds later, a small body collided into them and Daneya laughed as Saden picked up Mckenzie and twirled her around.

He faced the crowd and shouted above the din, "Let's eat!"

The following half hour was a barrage of cheerful energy and enough to make her long for a gun. Apparently, the custom of wishing the happy couple well and offering unsolicited advice on the future crossed the lines of all the species in attendance.

They bombarded her and Saden, one by one, with well-intentioned platitudes on the way to the back yard where the reception was being held. Freestanding torches and paper lanterns chased away the darkness of the night and lent an ambient feel to the festivities. Somewhere along the way, Erin relieved her of the bridal bouquet. They'd decided to forgo trying to explain that particular oddity of human tradition, as well as the tossing of the garter belt.

After a while, Roshon took pity on them and pulled them aside in a hurry as if he had a pressing matter to discuss. Eventually, the people around them caught on and dispersed across the lawn. The three of them picked their way through lavish picnic tables and open tents containing elaborate platters of food until they came to an outdoor wet bar. Roshon handed over two glasses of champagne then ordered a snifter of brandy for himself.

He held up his glass for a toast and puffed up his chest. "To the oddest couple I've ever had the good fortune of knowing. May your days be marked by joy and your nights filled with sinful pleasures."

Daneya lifted a brow as she tapped her glass to theirs. "Speaking from experience?" His wide-toothed grin told her more than she wanted to know.

"I've been mated for almost two centuries. Gotta keep the romance alive somehow." To Saden he said, "Congratulations on becoming an official father. A word of advice for the future, if you two plan on having another kid, try to make it a boy."

"Why?" Saden asked suspiciously.

"With a boy, you only have to worry about one penis. A girl…you have to worry about every penis in the world."

Daneya hid a smile behind a sip of champagne when Saden blanched considerably. She put her glass down then kissed Roshon's cheek. "Thank you for coming. If you'll excuse me, I'm just going to take a quick breather."

She left them at the bar and made her way toward the nearest line of trees. Gradually, the noise of the party faded to a distant buzz. In the cool shade of the foliage, she let her thoughts trail back to the issue that had been bothering her for weeks.

Where does she go from here?

It had been months since they'd rescued the latest batch of human survivors from Gabriel's operation. While they hadn't managed to discover where the females in the last facility had been taken, it was likely they never would after so long of an abeyance in new information. The Djinn had gone underground and there was even a lull in the activity of Vanaras.

Of late, the only actions that could be taken were the rebuilding of the leisonguarde force in the house of Avram and the continual search for halflings that had been sold to Vampyre buyers. Both tasks which fell to Saden as most others in authority refused to work with her.

She realized she missed the constant bustle of her old life. The feel of being essential to a cause greater than herself, and the rush of fulfillment that came with it.

"Something's bothering you."

She turned to find Saden standing behind her with a look of concern on his face. There was no point in lying. Their bond would tell him the truth whether she tried to hide it or not. Before she could answer, he stepped in close and curled a hand loosely around the column of her neck.

"You're wondering what to do next, aren't you?"

"How did you know?"

His lips curved in a small smile. "You never were one to settle for the simple life."

That was an understatement. Nothing about her life had been simple, except her love for her daughter and him. "I'm fine, really. I still have my degree in weapons design and engineering. I could open a shop in town."

He cocked his head to the side then took her by the hand and pulled her from the privacy of the trees. "Come on, I have something to show you. I wanted to wait until we got back from the honeymoon Erin set up for us, but I think you should see it now."

"Where are we going?"

His only response was a mischievous, backwards glance. They skirted the edge of the lawn to avoid the guests, eventually coming around to the front of the manor. He led her past the rows of cars to where his Maserati sat along the side of the driveway and gestured for her to get in.

"What about Kennie?" Daneya asked. It wasn't like Saden to leave guests unattended, let alone their daughter in the midst of virtual strangers.

Their daughter. The reality of those words sent a warm shiver over her skin.

Saden climbed into the driver's seat and started the engine. "She'll be fine. I asked Roshon and his mate to watch her while we're gone. We'll only be about thirty minutes."

She bit her lip to keep from asking more questions, her trust in him implicit. He turned onto the main road at the end of the drive then took an immediate right onto a dirt road she hadn't noticed before. It was somewhat set back and lined with trees on both sides that nearly obscured its entrance. Ten minutes later, it curved to the right and ended at a wide, open area where the evergreens and brush had been culled back.

Daneya stared in stark amazement as he brought the car to a stop. In front of them was a massive, two-story colonial-style house with cultivated hedges surrounding it. It was lit by security lampposts erected in the front and on both sides. The second story boasted at least twelve small balconies outside of tinted, sliding glass doors and its red brick exterior was softened by white, arched paneling framing each of the many windows. Two thick pillars stood on either side of the extended porch with a pair of solid oak doors between them.

She got out to get a better look then shook her head slowly as she realized the house's location. They were still on Saden's land, which meant he'd had this built in secret. It was too clean, the planted lawns too fresh to have been there for more than a year.

"It was Kennie's idea," Saden said next to her. "She told me she wished there was a place you could've gone after she was born that wasn't as harsh as the DCM. A safe house where you could've been protected without a price."

A sliver of pain stabbed Daneya's chest. "She thinks I paid a price?"

His expression became tender as he squeezed her hand. "We all know the DCM will only support civilians of their own kind and only for a short while. The women we've rescued were turned out after six months regardless of whether they were ready to live on their own or not. Unless they agreed to take a position at the DCM. You became a vigilante, but not everyone is a warrior like you.

"This refuge house can harbor both humans and demons who need a new start in life. We can offer them more alternatives and longer protection. Lady Ilsa has already conceded to let us take in any Vampyres who need time to heal for whatever reasons. They deserve shelter and security as much as humans do. Here, we can give others the kinds of choices you never had. Kennie wants to use her power to help those we take in. She wants to become a doctor."

Daneya continued to stare at the house in stunned disbelief. A wave of pride swelled within her and tightened her throat. Her daughter wanted to help others—humans and demons alike without prejudice or hatred—despite the chaotic upbringing Daneya had given her. All this time she'd been worried that the issue with Gabriel may have had lasting repercussions.

This put all of those fears to rest, and so much more.

"Erin and Floyd want in on it, too," Saden went on. "Erin says she wants to retire from the DCM and start a family of her own. When they heard of my plan, they insisted on being a part of it. Roshon also wants to include his Thorien clan and the Mirkshaws. They're tight-knit but even they have members who could use a place to recover from the recent activity of the Djinn. You'll be in charge, of course. Once the inside construction is complete, you can set up a system for the refugees and start taking them in. I'll provide as many leisonguardes as you'll need."

When she didn't answer for several seconds, he said, "Leisontee?"

Tears pricked her eyes when she finally turned to him. "You did this all for me?"

He framed her face with both hands and moved in close. "I want you to be happy. I would do anything for you."

She melted into the kiss he pressed to her lips. Breathed in his masculine scent as his tongue gently guided hers in a slow, passionate dance and his arms encircled her smaller body.

This was her happiness. Right here in his strong embrace where she knew she was safe. She wanted to throw time away, put the hours aside and stay with him in this moment. Forever and always, he would be her savior, as much as she was his.

About the Author

I absolutely love escaping into my own little world of words. Anything can happen in a book, but usually I find the book writes itself. It lets me know the pace and heat, and I simply go along for the ride. Of course, the inspiration of my family helps out a lot! They give me the humor, love and passion I pour into my characters, making them come to life on the pages. I always know it's going to be a good book when I find myself laughing and crying along with the characters.

Nikki McCoy loves to hear from readers. You can find her contact information, website and author biography at http://www.totallybound.com.